Michael Wood is a freelance journalist who, before living in Sheffield. As a journalist he has ██████████████ throughout Sheffield, gaining first █████████████ procedure. He also reviews books ████████████ dedicated to crime fiction.

Also by Michael Wood

SILENT VICTIM

MICHAEL WOOD

One More Chapter
a division of HarperCollins*Publishers*
1 London Bridge Street
London SE1 9GF
www.harpercollins.co.uk

HarperCollins*Publishers*
1st Floor, Watermarque Building, Ringsend Road
Dublin 4, Ireland

This paperback edition 2022
1
First published in Great Britain in ebook format
by HarperCollins*Publishers* 2022

A catalogue record of this book
is available from the British Library

ISBN: 978-0-00-853560-5

Printed and bound in the UK using 100% Renewable Electricity
by CPI Group (UK) Ltd

*To celebrate TEN books in the DCI Matilda Darke series I'm
dedicating this one to all the amazing editors who have helped make
each one a success.*

*Kate Stephenson, Lucy Dauman, Finn Cotton, Charlotte Ledger,
Bethan Morgan. There wouldn't be ten books without you.
Thank you.*

Chapter One

Tuesday 15th December 2020 – Brincliffe Edge Road, Sheffield

The van doors slammed shut, plunging Tilly Hall into darkness once again.

She was in pain.

She'd never known this much pain in her whole life. Her brain was struggling to comprehend what had just happened.

It seemed like merely minutes ago she had been walking along the street listening to the Radio 1 podcast, laughing along to Greg James, when … she had no understanding of what occurred next.

She tried to pull her skirt down below her knees, but it was torn. Her shirt had been torn open too. She'd heard the sound of the plastic buttons clanging off the sides of the metal bodywork of the van.

She was so cold.

She crawled into the furthermost corner of the van and pulled her knees up to her chest. She wanted to cry, but the tears wouldn't come. This was horror, pure and simple. She was living in a horror film, there was no other explanation for it.

She looked around her for a sign of a way out of this living hell, but everything was plunged into pitch darkness. There was a smell – petrol, stale body odour, cold, fear, dread, death.

The van began to move. Tilly tried to work out where she was, how many times they'd turned left and right, how long they'd been travelling for, but she had no idea. Were they even still in Sheffield? Was she being taken out of the country, sold into a paedophile ring or something? Wasn't she too old for that? She'd watched a documentary recently with her mum on Channel 4 about human trafficking. Was this what was happening to her? Were her organs about to be harvested for profit and the shell of her body dumped in the River Don?

'Mum,' she whimpered quietly. She felt her tears begin to flow down her face. She wanted her mum so much right now.

Tilly suddenly remembered about her school bag, her rucksack with all her books and folders in, and her mobile phone. She was alone in the van. Surely, she had time to make a quick call to her mum, tell her what had happened before the van came to a stop.

She fumbled around in the darkness, one hand running over the roughness of the floor in search of the rucksack while the other held her shirt and blazer in place across her exposed chest. The cold went right through her to her bones. She was shaking. But that could have been fear.

She found her bag. The relief was palpable. Once her mother knew what had happened, she'd find her. Their phones were linked so that her mum could locate her in an emergency. Tilly had always scoffed at that. What kind of emergency could there possibly be that her mother needed to track her down? Suddenly, it wasn't so funny.

She scrambled around in the bag, grabbed the phone and pulled it out. She unlocked the screen, and the brightness lit up the whole van and made her squint. The screen was cracked. It had probably broken when she'd been tossed inside. She was scrolling through the contacts when she heard the sound of the van doors being unlocked. They'd stopped. When had that happened? She quickly put the phone in the inside pocket of her blazer.

It was dark outside. The only light inside the van was from a nearby lamppost. Whoever had kidnapped her, slammed her head down on the floor of the van, torn her clothes open and raped her, was hidden in the shadows. She tried to make out his features. She knew it would be important when she was interviewed by police to tell them as much about the man as possible, but all she saw was a silhouette.

He climbed inside. Was he going to rape her again? She hoped not. She didn't think she could take any more pain. She crawled further into the corner of the van, but there was nowhere else for her to go. She was trapped.

He grabbed her. His meaty hands gripped the front of her blazer and dragged her towards him. She tried to resist, but it was no use.

'Please. No,' she cried. She fumbled around for something to hold onto, to keep her in the relative safety of the van, but there was nothing there.

She fell onto the cold concrete of the ground. A strong wind was blowing, and it was sleeting. She was pulled up off the pavement and swung around. The man had his left arm around her chest. She could feel his heart beating rapidly against her. She saw what he was holding in his raised right hand and her legs buckled beneath her. If he hadn't been holding her so tightly, she would have fallen.

It was a knife. The sodium yellow from the streetlamps glistened against the sharp stainless steel. It wasn't an ordinary knife. It was a horror film knife. She'd seen the whole of the *Scream* series; she knew the damage something like that could do.

Tilly thought of her mum again. There was only a week until Christmas. Her mother was so happy. They always had a wonderful time, just the two of them. Her mum tried to come across as a strong woman, but with the amount of grief she'd had to cope with over the years, she was close to losing it completely. Her daughter being raped and murdered would surely tip her over the edge. The thought of her mother suffering the aftermath of losing her only child to a violent rapist and killer made her cry. Her poor mum.

'Mum,' Tilly cried out loud. The word barely left her lips. 'Please, no, don't do this. Please. I'll do anything,' she pleaded through the tears. 'Let me go. Please. I haven't seen you. I swear. Please.'

She felt the knife slice across her neck. Strangely, it didn't feel as painful as when she was raped. Her body began to relax, as if it had already died, yet she could see what was going on around her. She felt the warmth of the blood flow from her neck down her exposed chest. It was the warmest she'd felt in hours.

She tried to speak, but when she opened her mouth, nothing came out. If this was what death was like, it wasn't as bad as she'd expected it to be.

She was lifted up, but Tilly had no idea who by or what was happening. Was this God lifting her up to heaven? No, that was ridiculous. She felt light, and the pain seemed to be drifting away.

Suddenly, the pain was back with a thud, and she was rolling. She closed her eyes tightly shut as rocks and branches hit her face and pulled at her skin. She hit something heavy and stopped.

Tilly didn't dare open her eyes. She didn't want to see where she'd ended up. Was it heaven or hell? Her breathing was ragged and short and she tried to calm herself. There was a sound. It was the engine of the van starting up. She braved herself to open her eyes, looked up and saw the bright lights of the van fade away.

It was going.

She'd been dumped.

And she was still alive.

Wasn't she?

She looked around in the darkness and could make out bare trees and an uneven ground.

She was in woods somewhere.

How close was she to home?

Could she walk it?

She put her hand to her throat. She could feel blood flowing. Jesus Christ, she was losing so much blood.

Tilly wasn't proficient in first aid, but she'd seen enough episodes of *Casualty* and *Grey's Anatomy* to know that you had to stem the flow of blood until help arrived. She struggled out of her blazer, balled it up, and pressed it firmly against her throat.

Her phone had fallen out of the pocket and landed beside her. She picked it up, unlocked it and cried at the smiling face of her boyfriend looking back at her.

She could feel herself weakening as death came for her. She was in a race against time.

With blood-soaked shaking fingers, she held down the side button and one of the volume buttons on the iPhone.

A countdown came up on the screen. Within ten seconds, an emergency SOS message would be sent to the police, and her mother.

She just hoped they'd get here in time.

Chapter Two

Emergency SOS

Tilly Hall has made an emergency call from this approximate location. You are receiving this message because Tilly has listed you as an emergency contact.

A my Hall had been home from work for over an hour. After a cup of tea and a chat with the dogs she decided to make a start on the tea. She squeezed past the Christmas tree and headed for the kitchen. The cupboards were stocked with food, but she couldn't think of anything to make. Everything she'd been buying for the past couple of weeks was for Christmas and it was too early to start eating it now. She knew Tilly wouldn't settle for a bowl of soup and a breadcake. As much as it pained her to do so, she'd have to get the salmon fillets out and replace them when she went to Tesco at the weekend.

Her mobile beeped. She looked around at the cluttered worktops for it. She remembered firing off a text to a colleague while waiting for the kettle to boil but couldn't think of where she'd set it down.

Amy wiped her hands on a tea towel and found her phone on the windowsill. She unlocked the screen and read the emergency SOS message. She stared at it for a long while, wondering what it meant. Was this a joke?

She dialled Tilly's number and paced the kitchen impatiently listening to the rings, willing her daughter to answer.

'Hello? Tilly?' Amy said when it was answered. She pressed it firmly against her ear. All she could hear was the sound of air rushing. 'Tilly. Tilly! Tilly, it's your mum. Are you there? Speak to me. Tilly!'

The call ended.

'*Fuck!*' Amy screamed. She dialled again. It went straight to voicemail.

'Hi, you've reached Tilly Hall. You can leave a message if you like but I never listen to them, so you'll be wasting your time. Drop me a text. Bye.'

'No, no, no, no, no,' Amy cried as she dialled once more. The dogs had run into the kitchen, worried by Amy's cries.

'Hi, you've reached Tilly Hall. You can …'

'Oh my God!'

Amy's eyes darted around the kitchen, searching for her car keys. They were on the table next to the apples and satsumas she'd bought on her way home. She grabbed them and ran out of the house, slamming the door behind her, not caring if it was locked or not.

In the car, she looked at the SOS message on her phone. Tilly's phone was somewhere in Brincliffe. Amy's mind went blank. She suddenly had no idea where Brincliffe was.

She fumbled to put the key in the ignition, started the car and reversed out of the driveway. She brought the screen on the dashboard to life and hit the voice recognition button.

'Brincliffe Edge Road,' she shouted as she struggled to put her seatbelt on.

'*I'm sorry. I did not recognise your location. Please try again,*' the computer said.

Amy turned left out of the road without slowing down or indicating. She heard the beep of a car but ignored it.

'Brincliffe. Edge. Road,' she said, slowly but not at all calmly.

'*Calculating.*'

'Shit,' Amy said to herself. She slammed her foot down on the accelerator. There was nobody else on the road but her. She was blind to her surroundings.

'*At the first opportunity, make a U-turn and head ...*'

'Fucking hell!' Amy screamed. Her eyes were blurred with tears. She was panicking. Her daughter, her only child, was in serious danger, and there was nothing she could do about it.

She slammed her hand on the sat nav, turning it off. She pulled over and screamed and yelled as loud as she could.

Tilly was leaning against a tree. She was squeezing the blazer to her throat as tightly as she could, but she was losing her grip. It was soaking with blood. She was losing too much, and her life was slowly ebbing away.

Her phone rang. She saw her mum's face lit up on the

screen. She started to cry and quickly swiped to answer. She heard her mum calling for her. She sounded frightened, scared, desperate. She tried to answer, tell her to help. She opened her mouth, but no words came out. She cried and screamed for her mum but made no sound. The screen went dark, and the phone died. She knew she had plenty of charge left as she'd used Kelly Green's charger in English. It must have been more damaged than she thought.

The woods around her were plunged into darkness, and the sleet turned to snow. She could see a blanket of white forming around her. She was freezing cold, and she was tired. Nobody was coming for her, or if they were, it was too late. She closed her eyes.

Amy Hall turned into Brincliffe Edge Road and slammed on the brakes. How she'd managed to get here, she had no idea. A mother's instinct perhaps. She got out of the car and shouted for her daughter. It echoed around the quiet street.

The road was lined on one side by woodland and on the other by old houses. They all had their curtains closed and a light on. Families had come home from work and school and were settling down for their tea. Normal life was taking place, and barely meters away, Amy Hall was living a nightmare, screaming for her daughter.

She looked at her phone. The flashing dot which was Tilly's location was directly next to her own dot. She was close. She was so close.

'*Tilly!*' she screamed.

She ran along the pavement, looking behind parked cars to see if her daughter was curled up or hiding. There was nobody there. She crossed over and looked into gardens. She crossed back and looked over the fence into the darkened woods.

'Tilly!' she shouted. 'Tilly, it's your mum, I'm here for you. Where are you?'

Going back to her phone, she dialled 999 and listened while the call connected, running along the edge of the woods, peering into the darkness.

'Emergency, which service do you require?'

'Police,' Amy spat.

The phone started ringing. Once, twice, three times.

Amy continued to run along the road, looking over the walls of people's gardens, under cars, behind bins.

'We are currently receiving a high volume of calls. Please stay on the line and you call will be answered as soon as possible.'

Amy looked up and around her. Tears were streaming down her face. Why couldn't there be a neighbour walking their dog right now or a random good Samaritan? She felt completely alone in the world.

'We are currently receiving a high volume of calls ...'

'Jesus Christ!' Amy cried. She leaned against a lamppost. This was too much. She couldn't lose Tilly, she couldn't. She needed her. She was all she had.

'South Yorkshire Police,' the call was answered.

'Thank God,' Amy said, wiping her eyes with her free hand and taking short, sharp breaths. 'Something's happened to my daughter. I don't know what. I've received an emergency SOS message from her phone. I'm ... I'm where it said she was but I can't find her. You need to send someone quickly.' Her words tripped over each other as she panicked.

'Okay. I need you to calm down and tell me what time ...'

'Oh my God. They're here. There's a police car here.'

Amy saw a marked police car heading towards her. Forgetting about her call, she stepped out into the road and flagged it down waving both hands. It stopped and two uniformed officers climbed out.

'Oh, thank you, God,' Amy said. 'Are you here for my daughter? Tilly Hall?'

'An emergency SOS call was received for this location,' one of the officers said. He was fresh-faced and his cheeks red with the cold.

'I'm her mum. Where is she?' Amy asked, pleading in her voice.

'Have you tried calling her?'

'I have. She's not replying. It's just going straight to voicemail.'

'Okay,' the officer said. 'We're going to call the DI on duty and have a search team sent out to help.'

Amy clung onto the constable's arm. Tears were streaming down her face. The reality of the situation was finally sinking in. 'Not my daughter,' she cried. 'Not my Tilly.'

'Mrs Hall, please, you need to remain calm. We will do everything we can to find your daughter. Is there anyone I can call for you?'

She shook her head. She was too distressed to speak.

'Okay, the best thing for you to do is stay calm. We don't know what's happened yet. Maybe her phone was stolen. Maybe it was cloned. We shouldn't jump to conclusions. Look, stay with my colleague. I'm going to have a look around.'

The PC went back to the car and got a torch out of the boot. He switched it on and walked along the edge of the woods. Amy followed. She couldn't just stand back and do nothing. Tilly was her life.

A few feet ahead, the PC stopped. The beam of the torch

was aimed at the ground. He bent down and dabbed his fingers into the tarmac.

'What is it? Have you found something?' Amy asked. She ran up to him and looked at what he was pointing the torch at. 'Oh, no. Is that what I think it is?' The PC didn't reply. 'Is that blood?'

The second constable put his hands on Amy's shoulders and tried to pull her away. She shook him off her.

'You need to find her. Please. I'm begging you. Please. Find my daughter,' she sobbed. '*Tilly!*' she screamed. 'Tilly! We're here. The police are here. Where are you?'

Lights started to go on in the surrounding houses and people came out of their front doors to see what all the commotion was about.

The PC went further into the woods and cast the light from his torch slowly around him.

'Tilly!' the PC called. 'TILLY!' His voice was much louder than Amy's and travelled further into the woods.

There was no reply, just the sound of scuttering wildlife on the woodland floor.

'Wait. What's that?' the second PC asked. He took the torch from the first and aimed it at a tree. 'There. What is that?'

They both frowned as they tried to make out a mound of … something.

'Okay. I need you to stay here while I go and have a look,' one of them said to Amy.

'No way. She's my daughter.'

'Please. Just let me take a look first,' he said, blocking Amy from charging down the embankment.

Amy saw the determined look in the officer's eyes. She could read the message on his face. Whatever was down there, he had to be the one to see it first. Reluctantly, she nodded.

'Liam, can you stay with …?'

'Amy,' she said.

'Stay with Amy while I take a look.'

'Will do. DI Brady's on his way.'

PC Corbett nodded, turned and carefully made his way down the embankment, not taking his eyes from the undistinguishable mound by a tree. He slipped and fell on his arse. He pulled himself up, wiped his muddy hands on his trousers and grabbed for the torch he'd dropped. When he pointed it at the tree again, he was close enough to make out the slumped figure of a semi-naked young woman.

'Jesus Christ,' he said quietly to himself.

He swallowed hard and went over to her.

'Tilly. Can you hear me?'

He bent down to his knees and studied her. Her head was slumped forward. She was muddy, covered in cuts and bruises. Her breasts were exposed and were caked in blood. With shaking fingers, he felt for a pulse on her neck. It took a while, but he found one, though it was incredibly faint. He placed his fingertips on her chin and carefully lifted her head up. Her eyes were closed. With his other hand, he shone the torch to see the extent of her injuries and had to swallow to prevent the vomit ruining the crime scene.

He'd never seen inside someone's throat before.

Chapter Three

It wasn't easy to erect a forensic tent over a crime scene on a steep embankment on soggy ground with a gale force wind blowing, but that was what DI Christian Brady had spent the last fifteen minutes watching from the warmth of his car. Still, at least it had stopped snowing.

Tilly Hall had been removed from the woods once she was stabilised by paramedics and sent to Sheffield Children's Hospital. Christian had stood back and watched as she was wheeled into the back of the ambulance, her mother holding her hand, and had no idea if she'd be waking up. Surely, she'd lost far too much blood to survive such an attack.

The front passenger door opened, making Christian jump. DS Scott Andrews climbed in and slammed the door closed.

'Bloody hell, it's cold out there,' he said, placing his hands in front of the heating vents. 'They're making a meal out of putting that tent up.'

'It'll be a waste of time anyway. It's been raining and snowing on and off all day and blowing a sodding gale. Any evidence will have been washed or blown away. Not to mention the paramedics and uniformed officers contaminating the scene. We'll be lucky to get so much as a cotton fibre.' His voice was flat, monotone, tired.

'Hopefully someone will have seen something. It's pretty built-up around here,' Scott said, looking out of the window. 'Finn and Tom are going door-to-door, and I've got CCTV and ANPR cameras being checked back at the station.'

'Good work, Scott,' Christian said, looking at his DS and giving him a weak smile.

'The problem is, we've got six DCs off now. Two have tested positive for Covid, four are self-isolating, and uniform is down by twenty percent.'

'You don't have to tell me, Scott, I know the numbers,' he said, running his hand over his buzzcut hair.

Scott looked back out of the window. The tent was now in position, but it didn't look too stable.

'PC Corbett described Tilly's injuries to me. They sound frighteningly similar to the previous three. It's got to be the same bloke, hasn't it?'

Christian didn't say anything.

'The time between each attack is getting closer. He's escalating.'

'I know.'

'And we don't have a single—'

'Scott, I'm aware of the situation,' Christian snapped. A gust of wind buffeted the car.

'What are we going to do?'

'You can start by rolling up your sleeves and giving Finn and Tom a hand with the door-to-door enquiries.'

'Is everything all right?' Scott asked, a concerned expression on his face.

'If you want the truth, Scott, no, everything is not all right,' Christian said, exasperated.

'Is there anything I can do?'

'Yes. You can start by doing the job you're paid to do.'

Christian's gaze was fixed dead ahead. He was under a great deal of pressure with a dwindling workforce and an absent DCI. He had no one to turn to, no one to talk to, and he could feel the weight of the world pushing him further and further into the ground. He felt a gust of cold wind on his face and guessed that Scott had got out of the car. When the door slammed closed, he leaned back in his seat and closed his eyes. He could feel emotion rising up inside him. This was too much. He couldn't cope.

South Yorkshire Police was going through a rocky patch at present. Earlier this year, following the brutal murder of businessman Richard Ashton, a Pandora's box of evil had been unleashed. Historical child sexual abuse had been uncovered involving several local politicians and police officers. The Police and Crime Commissioner had been a habitual abuser and the Chief Constable had been caught in the web of the cover-up that spanned almost thirty years. It was a case incredibly personal to Christian Brady and one that forced him to confront the horrors of his own childhood. In the aftermath, the force had been placed under special measures, which meant greater scrutiny from the Home Office until improvements were made.

Fortunately, this came at a time when violent crime was at an all-time low for South Yorkshire Police. The various lockdowns and restrictions placed on the public caused by the coronavirus pandemic meant CID had fewer murders to investigate. Domestic abuse incidents were on the rise, but in the majority of cases, the perpetrator was swiftly identified, caught and prosecuted. The number of cases solved was on the increase.

Unfortunately, police were not immune to Covid-19, and officers who caught it were off work for a long time. Anyone in close contact with an infected officer was forced to self-isolate, and morale at police headquarters was at an all-time low.

Many uniformed officers and plain-clothed detectives were suffering with depression caused by being overworked, understaffed and abused on a daily basis by an uncaring public who objected to restrictions on their lives enforced by the government. Many couldn't, or refused to, understand that wearing a mask or socially distancing yourself from others was in their own interest. When the police turned up, called for by worried and nervous shop managers, they were abused, sworn at, spat on, by a volatile public. This had been going on for nine months and there was no sign of an end to restrictions, or to the pandemic. In fact, infections and death numbers were rising once more and different areas of the country were placed in tiers representing the level of restrictions people faced. This Christmas was going to be as far away from normal as it was possible to get, and people didn't like that. Once more, it was left to the police to be on the receiving end, and they simply didn't have the resources.

The last thing any police force, but South Yorkshire Police in particular, needed right now was a serial rapist and murderer on the loose.

DI Christian Brady smoothed down his shirt, tightened the knot on his tie and knocked on the door of Chief Constable

Benjamin Ridley. He was called to enter and took a deep breath before he did so.

Benjamin Ridley was the only person who did well out of the abuse scandal. He was Assistant Chief Constable at the time and as he was relatively new to the force, he wasn't implicated in the cover-up scandal. Resignations from people high up happened on a daily basis and Ridley was promoted to Chief Constable to oversee a new chapter in the force and root out any corrupt officers that threatened to damage its reputation further.

Everyone always said it was possible to tell the time of day simply by looking at CC Ridley. First thing in the morning, he was clean and smart in his uniform. The jacket was buttoned up, his tie was centred and his hair neat. As the day progressed, the jacket was opened, then removed altogether, the tie was loosened, the hair ruffled, and by the end of the day he looked ready to hit the nearest bar and down a couple of double Jack Daniel's. No ice.

Since the scandal, he permanently had the grizzled look of a seasoned alcoholic. His brow was furrowed, his eyelids were heavy, his tie was crooked and each day there seemed to be more grey in his thick mound of hair.

'Christian, take a seat,' Ridley instructed.

Usually, Ridley liked to be out of the station by five o'clock at the latest. For the past three months, he'd been one of the last to leave and, although he lived only a ten-minute drive away, he rarely walked in the front door before ten o'clock.

'I hear you have another rape on your hands.'

'Yes, sir,' Christian said. He hitched up his trousers and plonked himself in the seat opposite Brady's desk.

'This one is still alive, I've been told.'

'So far. I'm not sure if she'll survive. The extent of her injuries looked massive.'

'Any news from the hospital?'

'Not yet. I'll give them a call … at some point.'

'Where are we in the investigation?'

Christian almost scoffed at the word 'we'. He certainly didn't feel part of a team at present. He felt like he was trying to keep South Yorkshire Police running single-handedly.

'We have no witnesses, no evidence, nothing to link the victims. I just hope this one survives so she can give us something to go on.'

'Door-to-door?'

'I've got a team out but I'm really short of officers at the moment, sir. It's not going to be long before the press is all over this and as soon as they get a sniff that we don't have the resources, we're screwed.'

Ridley nodded. 'I'm aware of the situation. I spoke to DCI French this morning and there is no sign that she's going to be ready to come back to work. As you know she was very ill with Covid in the summer and she's still struggling with fatigue. Long Covid, I believe they're calling it.'

Christian shook his head and looked down. He took another breath and looked back up into the eyes of his boss. 'I'm not exaggerating when I say we can't cope, sir. Whoever is out there raping and killing these women, he knows what he needs to do to evade capture, and we're putting women's lives at risk by not being able to hunt him down.'

'Christian, if I had the officers available, I'd hand them to you. There is nothing I can do at present.'

'Yes. There is.'

Ridley frowned.

'You can bring back DCI Darke.'

Chapter Four

Sheffield's Children's Hospital was the main paediatric trauma centre for the whole of South Yorkshire. Tilly Hall was whisked straight into A&E where she was assessed. Once her oxygen levels and heart rate were stabilised, she was sedated and sent straight to theatre to repair the damage to her throat. Several cuts from a serrated blade had ripped through the flesh, tearing veins, muscle, and tissue. The extent of the damage would not be known for several days – if Tilly survived the operation in the first place. She was given a fifty-fifty chance.

Amy Hall was alone in the relatives' room. She had done all the crying she could and there were no more tears left to fall. A plastic cup of tea brought to her by a kindly nurse had been left to go cold on the table.

She dug her phone out of her pocket and looked at the screen. The wallpaper showed her daughter smiling at her. The picture had been taken last winter when snow had been thick on the ground. She and Tilly had gone for a long walk in the countryside. They'd wrapped up against the elements and spent the day together, trekking the hills of Derbyshire, having snowball fights, warming up in a coffee shop, then back out into the snow. It had been a perfect day.

Amy scrolled through her contacts, but she had nobody to call. Everyone listed was a neighbour or a colleague – none of whom she would call an actual friend. She had no family left and, despite believing herself to be popular, she suddenly realised there wasn't a single person she could call whom she wanted to be with her during this time.

Amy took a deep breath and let it out slowly. She sat on the uncomfortable faux-leather chair with the stuffing coming out of a torn seam and put her head in her hands. It was just her and Tilly. It had been the two of them since her husband died ten years ago. She hadn't realised how much she depended on their relationship.

The sight of Tilly as the paramedics brought her up from the woods was indescribable. She didn't look like her daughter at all, more like a dummy used in a crime drama to depict a dead body. There was so much blood. How could someone possibly survive losing so much blood? She was asking a great deal of the doctors and nurses, and of Tilly herself.

She *needed* her to live. This couldn't be the end.

It wasn't fair.

The door opened and Amy looked up. She wiped her eyes with the sleeves of her sweater.

A shattered-looking woman with unruly hair entered, closing the door behind her. She was wearing hospital scrubs. Her face was free from make-up; her skin was dry and tired. She looked at Amy and proffered a weak smile.

'Mrs Hall, I'm Victoria Harman. I'm part of the surgical team that's been looking after Tilly.' She sat on the edge of the coffee table directly in front of Amy.

'How is she?' Amy asked. Her voice was quiet.

'She's in intensive care. The operation took longer than we anticipated. She lost a great deal of blood and had to have a blood transfusion. I won't blind you with a lot of medical jargon right now, but there were several cuts to Tilly's throat, some deeper than others. There has been a great deal of nerve damage, the extent of which we won't know until she wakes up. However, there is every likelihood the damage will be permanent,' Victoria Harman said in her best placatory tone.

'What does that mean?' Amy asked. 'What kind of permanent damage are we talking about?'

'The larynx has been severely damaged. The common name for that is the voice box. It is possible she may not be able to talk again.'

Amy froze in horror.

'What?'

'I'm only saying it's a possibility at the moment, but you do need to prepare for the worst. There's a long road ahead to Tilly's recovery, and she will need further surgery.'

'But if you're planning further operations, that means you can repair the damage to the voice box, right?' Amy asked.

'I'm afraid not.'

'I don't understand any of this.'

'It's a lot to take in, I know, but I will explain everything to you over the coming hours and days.' She gave the same mollifying smile.

Amy took a ragged breath. 'Was she ...?' She composed herself. 'Was she ...?' She needed to know the answer to this

question, but she couldn't bring herself to ask it. 'Is there …
you know … do you know if she was raped?'

There was a heavy beat of a silence before the doctor
answered. 'There is evidence of sexual activity having taken
place. Tests have been carried out and the police will keep you
informed.'

Amy bent her head and cried.

'I really am sorry, Mrs Hall. Is there anyone you'd like me
to call to be with you?'

She shook her head. 'I'm on my own. I've only got Tilly …
Can I see her?' Amy asked, wiping her eyes again.

'Not at the moment. What I suggest you do is go home and
try to get some rest and come back tomorrow. We'll have more
information once a consultant has seen her.'

'She will be all right, though, won't she? I mean,
eventually?'

'Mrs Hall, your daughter lost a great deal of blood and has
suffered a major trauma. The next twenty-four to forty-eight
hours are the most critical. If we can get through that, I believe
she will be able to adapt to her injuries. However, there is a
very long road ahead.'

'Is there anything I can do?'

'Not right now. Like I said, go home, get some rest and
come back tomorrow. Maybe bring her some pyjamas and a
few personal items you think she'd like around her.'

Amy nodded. 'She has a teddy bear she's had since she was
born. She's always slept with it. Shall I bring that?' She tried to
smile through the tears.

'I think she'd like that,' Victoria said. 'If there's any change
throughout the night, we'll give you a call. Honestly, she really
is in the best place.'

'What about this virus?' Amy asked.

'Every doctor and nurse take a test every day. We change PPE with every single patient, just like we've always done. There's no greater risk of Tilly catching Covid in here than there is in her everyday life.'

'Thank you.'

Victoria smiled and quickly left the room.

Amy watched the door as it closed and felt the warmth of silence envelop her. She tried to take in everything the doctor had told her but couldn't. Her daughter was still alive, that was the most important thing. But what did she say about her not being able to talk again? The larynx had been cut, was that what she'd said? Surely, if it had been cut, it could be put back together again. How can a person go through life without being able to talk?

Confusion danced across her face. None of this made sense.

She wanted to stay but knew that wouldn't be possible. The doctor had told her to go home and rest. As if she'd be able to go to bed and sleep. But the dogs would be wondering where she was, and they'd missed their tea. They'd be hungry. She needed to go home for them. They'd most likely be the first thing Tilly asked about when she woke up. Although, how would she be able to ask about them if she couldn't talk?

'I don't understand,' Amy said out loud.

Slowly, she stood up. Her car was still at Brincliffe and her purse was on the kitchen table. It was at times like this she wished she wasn't so alone in the world. Like any good mother, she'd put her daughter first, but right now, she needed a strong pair of arms around her to tell her everything was going to be all right.

Chapter Five

Former Detective Chief Inspector Matilda Darke wasn't a fan of having therapy. If she was truthful with herself, she hated it. However, she had to admit, it helped, and she had grudgingly come to respect the advice of the sickly sweet and cloyingly annoying Diana Cooper-bloody-sodding-smith over the years.

In January 2019, Matilda was shot in the head. Several months in hospital and a rehabilitation centre were followed by physical and psychological therapy and she was back to her fighting best.

That was a lie she told herself every day.

Physically, she was fine. Mentally, she was not. The nightmares were few and far between these days. She hadn't had a flashback in months and her panic attacks had eased. What she struggled with was survivor's guilt. How had she managed to survive a mass shooting when so many of her colleagues and friends hadn't? Why was she constantly checking the mastermind behind the attack, Steve Harrison, was still safely locked up and hadn't, somehow, managed to escape? It was these niggling annoyances she was trying to overcome. Since her unit at South Yorkshire Police had been closed down and she'd been made redundant, Matilda had more time to concentrate on her own wellbeing, and, since the summer, even she noticed a change in her attitude. She was more positive. The fractious relationship with her mother was much improved and she was beginning to enjoy life more. Work, as far as she was concerned, could piss right off.

Sitting in the consulting room opposite Diana Cooper-bloody-sodding-smith, Matilda was wearing black Levi jeans, black Doc Martens and a cream DKNY sweater. She had allowed her brown hair to grow back but kept it short in the neck and long and wavy on top. She enjoyed running her fingers through it again.

By contrast, Diana Cooper-bloody-sodding-smith was wearing a white shirt with a ridiculously huge bow at the neck and the cuff of the left sleeve frayed. Her navy corduroy skirt was floor-length and looked like it had been through the washer too many times. It was bobbly and faded and needed binning in Matilda's opinion. Her shoes were dated and scuffed. One hundred and ten pounds per hour she was charging for these sessions; surely, she could afford decent clothes.

'Are you still out of work?' Diana asked. Her voice was unnaturally soft and accentless. Though, occasionally, Matilda caught a hint of Brummie in some of her words.

'I'm not out of work. I simply no longer work,' Matilda said with a smile.

'You always said work was your life. It was your identity.'

'I did. It is. It was. But it was taken away from me. There was nothing I could do.'

'You could have looked to another force.'

'I like where I live.'

'You could have commuted.'

'I think I've needed this time off. You know, I've only had one holiday since my husband died in 2015. All I've done is work. Even when I was recovering from being shot, I was thinking about work, planning to go back to work, surrounding myself with work. It wasn't healthy. I see that now.'

'So, you're not out of work, but rather on a sabbatical?' Diana smiled.

Matilda thought about the question. She smiled back. 'Yes. I will go back to work. I doubt it will be with South Yorkshire Police, but I've worked hard to be a DCI. It's what I love doing.'

'But you fell out of love with it, towards the end, didn't you?'

'No. But I was beginning to. Things had changed since the shooting. I couldn't expect them not to.' Matilda paused and took a breath. 'When you're working on a case, something big, you still need to enjoy being with your colleagues and friends. I mean, we'd have a laugh and a joke, but there was an underlying sadness to everything. I've needed this time off to recharge, take stock, work out what's important to me.'

'And what is important to you?'

'I am,' Matilda answered straightaway. 'My life. My friends. My family. I need them around me.'

'Which is more important to you – your friends and family, or your work?'

'Friends and family,' she replied without thinking.

'So, if you went back to work, you wouldn't be working round the clock, sacrificing your personal life for the job?'

'Well, I don't really have a personal life as such, but no.'

'That's good.' Diana smiled. 'So, what's next for Matilda Darke?'

Matilda took a deep breath as she thought. 'I'm going to enjoy Christmas, as much as we're allowed to this year, and in the new year I'll think about what I want to do with the rest of my life. I'll see what's out there and available for an ex-DCI. Whether it's another force or something completely different, who knows?'

'You're feeling positive?'

'I am.'

Diana Cooper-bloody-sodding-smith adjusted herself on her chair. The smile fell from her lips. 'The phone calls. The cards being delivered. Are they still happening?'

So much for feeling positive.

'The phone calls seem to have stopped,' Matilda said. She closed her stance. She pressed her legs together and folded her arms. 'I received another card a couple of weeks back.'

'What did it say?'

'The usual. A repeat of the same taunting phone call I received before I was shot.'

'Have you told anyone yet about them?'

Matilda shook her head.

'Why not?'

'I don't want to worry anyone.'

'Are you worried yourself?'

'I'm not sure,' she said after a lengthy silence. 'I think if someone wanted to hurt me, they would have done it by now. They've had ample opportunity. I really do think it's someone connected to Steve Harrison. I know he's got plenty of fans.

There are lots of sick women out there who become fixated with a serial killer. I'm sure they'll move on eventually.'

'Do you genuinely believe that?'

'The phone calls have stopped. I'm sure the cards will stop, too.'

Diana frowned as she studied Matilda. 'Something tells me you don't quite believe that.'

Matilda shrugged.

No, I don't believe it.

———

Matilda took a taxi to the much-loathed Meadowhall where she elbowed a few of the more militant shoppers to buy a few extra gifts for her mum and sister, then took another taxi back home. The effects of the shooting meant she was no longer able to drive, though she lived in hope of being given her licence back one day. Not that she had a car to drive any more thanks to some bastard blowing it up earlier this year.

The bone-shaking track from Ringinglow Road to Matilda's old farmhouse had been levelled and tarmacked and was now smooth. Her best friend, Adele, had purchased a Porsche 911 in the summer and complained on an hourly basis that the rough driveway, potholes and gravel were killing her car. Matilda didn't like it. It weakened the effect of living off the beaten track and meant she could no longer hear anyone coming to her house until they were right outside her front door. When the taxi rounded the bend, she spotted a car she didn't recognise. She tried to see who was sitting behind the steering wheel but couldn't from this angle. She paid the taxi driver, picked up her bags and stepped out into the cool winter afternoon.

Matilda bent down to look through the window of the BMW. Her eyes widened at the slumbering Chief Constable Benjamin Ridley. She rapped hard on the glass, and he jumped awake. He looked around, wondering where he was, wiped his chin of drool and looked up at Matilda.

'I must have nodded off,' he said as he opened the door and stepped out. 'What time is it?'

'Half past one,' she said, looking at her watch.

'Bloody hell, I've been asleep for two hours.'

Matilda smirked. 'You obviously needed it.'

He dug his phone out of his pocket and looked at the screen. 'I've missed eight calls. I must have had it on silent.'

'Would you like a coffee?'

'Industrial strength, please.' He yawned, following her to the front door. 'Nice wreath.'

'Thanks,' she said, stepping back and looking at the elaborate Christmas wreath on the door. 'Don't you think it's a bit on the large side?'

'A tad.'

'I thought that, too. If I scratch myself once more, it's going in the bin.'

Matilda unlocked the front door and entered the warm house. She disabled the alarm and placed her shopping in the corner of the hallway.

It was the first time CC Ridley had visited Matilda's house and he looked around him as he followed her into the kitchen.

'This is a stunning house, Matilda. Eighteenth-century?'

'Oh.' It was the first time anyone had asked Matilda the age of her house. Her husband, an architect, would have been able to answer straightaway. 'Do you know, I'm not entirely sure.'

'That would be my guess. The stonework around the eaves

and the style of the chimneys make me think eighteenth-century.'

Matilda turned to look at her former boss. 'I had no idea you knew so much about architecture.'

'I watch a lot of documentaries. They help me relax.'

She made them both a coffee and took it into the conservatory where Ridley marvelled afresh, seeing Matilda's garden.

As she was out of work, she wanted to enjoy her home more, and during the summer months she wanted to sit outside with a good book and a glass of wine. She had no idea how to go about turning the wasteland of overgrown trees and weeds into something presentable, but thanks to the internet, she soon found someone who did. Now, it was a verdant space, with clean lines, trimmed-back trees, manicured evergreens, well-kept lawns and, at the very bottom, where the majority of the oak trees were, a wild-looking area expertly planted to encourage wildlife to thrive. Matilda had no idea what she wanted from a garden, but when it was finished, it was exactly how she'd imagined. There was even a newly planted oak tree outside the conservatory in memory of her husband.

'I'd kill for a garden like this,' Ridley said. 'It's so private.'

'Are you overlooked?'

'My wife likes new-builds. The problem with those is that the developers try to squeeze as many houses on the plot as possible. Privacy is the first casualty.'

He turned away from the view eventually, sat down and picked up his coffee mug. He inhaled and a took a lengthy sip. A smile spread over his face.

'I needed that.'

'So, why have you come all the way out here to see me? I'm guessing it wasn't simply to nod off on my driveway.'

'No. I'm sorry about that.'

'It's fine.' She smiled.

He took another drink and placed his mug carefully on the wooden table. He cleared his throat a few times.

'We have a case at work which is proving to be problematic. A fourteen-year-old girl was raped and left for dead yesterday evening. How she's managed to survive is beyond me. Her throat was practically torn open. It's the fourth attack in as many weeks.'

'Scott's mentioned it,' Matilda said. DS Scott Andrews lived in the flat above her garage.

'We have no forensics, no eyewitnesses, not a scrap of evidence to point us in the direction of the attacker.'

'Why are you telling me all this?'

'We need your help. *I* need your help. You are the best detective I've ever met, Matilda.'

'Okay. Cut the flannel. First of all, I'm no better than any other detective. I just happened to choose the right people to be on my team. Christian, Sian, Scott, Finn were all exceptional detectives. Together, we were a brilliant unit. And you closed us down.'

'That was not my decision.'

'You've been Chief Constable since the early summer. I've not heard any rumours of you reinstating the unit.'

Ridley sighed and sank in his seat. 'South Yorkshire Police is still under special measures. I simply cannot reopen the unit the way things stand. However, we've got many detectives off with Covid. DI Brady is doing the work of God knows how many and he's close to burnout. I cannot afford to lose any more officers.'

'Then reinstate the unit.'

'I can't do that either.'

'You really are in a pickle, aren't you?' Matilda stood up and returned to the kitchen. Ridley followed.

'Matilda, I know you were treated unfairly. But you also know it wasn't me who made you redundant and closed the HMCU. If you want me to get on my knees and beg you to come back, I will.'

She turned to look at him, took in the look of genuine pleading on his face. 'There's no need for that. I was in charge of an elite unit for years. We worked on some high-profile cases and had a very high success rate. If you were offering me my old unit back, I'd come back in a shot. But I am not heading up CID.'

Ridley pulled out a chair at the table and sat down. 'Can I offer you a deal?'

Reluctantly, Matilda sat down opposite him. 'Go on.'

'If we can solve this, it will look good for the force as a whole. It might even pull us out of special measures. The minute that happens, I'll reopen HMCU, and you can hand-pick your team. I'll even recommend you be awarded the Queen's Police Medal.'

Matilda laughed. 'You think I'd be tempted back by a medal?'

'No, but I'm getting desperate.'

She sighed.

'A fourteen-year-old girl, Matilda. If she does survive, she'll never speak again. She had her larynx cut. The nerves are severed. He's leaving no evidence of himself behind. He knows exactly what he's doing, and his attacks are getting closer together and more violent.'

'I can't say no, can I?'

Ridley smiled.

'I'm just working on this case, though. I'm not getting involved in any of your Covid violations crap.'

'That's fine.'

'I do have one more condition,' Matilda said, looking down, her expression grave.

'Go on.'

'I don't want to work with DI Christian Brady.'

Chapter Six

Amy Hall opened the front door to two detectives in suits. She invited them in and headed for the kitchen. The cupboard doors were open, and everything had been taken out and placed on the table and work surfaces. She was giving the kitchen a thorough clean.

'I've called the hospital God only knows how many times this morning and they've told me the same thing each time, that Tilly's still unconscious. I thought I'd do something productive to take my mind off things for a while. It's just … it's having the reverse effect.' She looked at the large clock on the back wall. 'I can't believe how slowly time's going. Have a seat, somewhere, if you can find the space.' She climbed back up the stepladder and began vigorously cleaning the shelves.

'Mrs Hall, we'd like to talk to you about Tilly,' Detective Sergeant Scott Andrews said as he picked up a grill pan off a chair and placed it on the floor so he could sit down.

Detective Constable Tom Simpson looked around him. There really was nowhere for him to sit. He leaned against the back wall, arms folded.

'Go ahead. Do you know, I can't remember the last time I cleaned these shelves. I found a bottle of soy sauce that went out of date in 2017.'

'Mrs Hall …'

'Call me Amy.'

'Amy, please, could you come and sit down for a few minutes?'

Amy stopped what she was doing and looked over her shoulder. She took in the grave faces of the detectives. She nodded and slowly descended the steps.

'I was looking on the news this morning,' she said, head down, playing with her fingers. 'There have been other attacks in Sheffield in the past couple of months, similar to what's happened to my Tilly. They were raped. They had their throats cut and were then just tossed away when he'd finished with them. That's what happened to my Tilly, isn't it? It's the same man.'

'It's too early to tell. That's why we'd like to talk to you about Tilly.'

Amy nodded. 'We can't sit in here with all this mess. Would you like to go into the living room? I'll bring in some tea.'

The two made to leave the room when Scott stopped in the doorway and turned back.

'Would you like me to make the tea?' he asked.

'No. I know where I've put everything. I think,' she said, looking around her. 'Go on through. I won't be long. Do you both take milk and sugar?'

'Milk and no sugar for both, thank you.' He smiled.

DS Scott Andrews entered the living room and was struck by the immense size of the Christmas tree. It took up almost a third of the room. It was tastefully decorated, but Scott guessed Amy misjudged the size of her room when purchasing.

An elderly Dachshund looked lost in an oversized bed in front of the fire, a larger dog of indeterminate breed snuggled next to it, and Tom was struggling under the fussy demands of an excitable black Labrador.

'Oh, my goodness, I don't think I've seen anything as cute in my life,' Tom said, happily sprawled out on the sofa with a large puppy on top of him, trying to lick his face.

'Tom, will you behave?' Scott chastised in a low voice.

'It's not me, it's him. He's so strong. I think he can smell the bacon butty I had for breakfast.'

'I'm not surprised. You did spill most of it down your shirt.'

'That was your fault for taking those speed bumps too fast.'

Amy pushed open the door with her foot. She was carrying a heavy tray. Scott immediately took it from her while she went to the aid of Tom Simpson, grabbed the dog by the collar and pulled him off.

'I'm sorry about him,' she said. 'We haven't had him long and he's still getting used to being around people. All you have to do is make eye contact with him and he jumps all over you.'

Amy sat on the armchair and began pouring the tea while Scott and Tom shared the sofa.

'He's lovely,' Tom said, smoothing down his clothes.

'He's Tilly's dog,' Amy said, sitting down on the sofa. The Labrador went over to her and placed her head on Amy's lap. She stroked him. 'She's animal mad. She wants to train to be a vet and work with wild animals in Africa. I don't suppose she'll be able to now.'

Scott and Tom exchanged awkward glances.

Amy handed them both a mug of tea each.

'The Dachshund is called Sausage. Can you believe that?' Amy chuckled. 'Tilly chose the name when she was young. I asked her what we should call him, and she just came out with Sausage. I started laughing and it stuck. It's not been fun in the park shouting "Sausage" over the years.'

Scott smiled. 'Amy, I just want to say how sorry I am for what's happened. We've got a team doing everything possible to find the man responsible.'

'The other one, well, we don't know what breed he is,' Amy said, ignoring Scott. 'Even the vet was stumped. We did one of those tests where they take a blood sample, and they match the DNA. He's got various breeds in him. He's a stray. He followed us home from the park one day about five or six years ago while we were walking Sausage and he just sat outside the house. Poor thing. Tilly sat at that window looking out at him, begging me to bring him in. I didn't have a choice once it started raining. Tilly called him Ted. He settled in straightaway, bless him.'

Amy took a sip of her tea and continued. 'The Labrador is an offspring of one of my neighbour's dogs. As soon as Tilly found out she was pregnant she wanted one. Actually, she wanted all of them, but I talked her down to just one. He's called Kit. After Kit Harington. She's got his pictures all over her wall.'

'Amy …' Scott began.

'I can't take any of this in,' Amy interrupted. 'It's like it's happening to someone else. Yesterday morning, we sat at the kitchen table and talked about Christmas lunch. She's gone vegetarian, but I was trying to talk her into having Christmas off and cooking the usual turkey and she was trying to convince me to do some kind of nut thing she'd found on the internet. It sounded revolting. I just … I can't get my head around any of this happening.' Amy was on the verge of tears. She kept running her fingers through her hair, adjusting her position on the armchair, stroking the dog, unable to settle.

'It's a lot to take in, I know. We do have people you can talk to, if you want,' Scott said.

'And here I am talking about dogs,' she half-laughed. 'As if you're interested.'

'That's okay,' Scott said with a smile.

'I love dogs,' Tom said. 'We had a Basset Hound when I was growing up. Charlie. We had to loosely tie his ears back using a scrunchie at mealtimes because they were always getting in the way of his food. Even the vet said he'd never known such long ears on a Basset Hound before.'

Amy turned to Tom and gave a genuine smile. 'They're great company, dogs, aren't they?'

'They really are. I'm in an upstairs flat at the moment so can't have one. But the minute I buy a house, I'm getting one.'

'Tilly's always said that one day—' Amy stopped herself. The sadness was back, not that it had been gone for very long. 'Sorry,' she said.

'That's okay,' Scott said. 'Is Tilly your only child?'

Amy nodded. 'I always said I'd like to have three children. No idea why. But from when I was young, I always wanted three. When Tilly was four, my husband, Shane, died at work.' She looked over to the mantelpiece where a silver-framed photo, of a man sitting on a beach with a small child on his lap, took centre stage. 'We didn't have time to have any other children.'

'I'm so sorry,' Scott said.

'You have plans, don't you? About how you want your life

to be. You don't expect things to go wrong. I thought me and Shane would grow old together. We were married six years. That's all. I try to remind Tilly about the things she and her dad did together, but she can't remember them. She's forgetting him already.'

The Labrador at Amy's feet sat up and looked at her. She placed her hand on his head and he snuggled against her.

The room fell silent. A clock was ticking in the kitchen. Outside, cars were crunching over the ice that had formed overnight.

'We'd like to try and pinpoint Tilly's movements in the run-up to the attack and if there's any possibility she might have known her attacker.' Scott flicked open his notebook, a biro poised.

She nodded. 'She left the house at the normal time yesterday to go to school. Eight o'clock. She met—' She stopped. 'Oh my God, I can't remember her name,' she cried. 'Oh, that's so bad of me. I've known her since she was a baby.'

'It's all right, Amy. It'll come to you,' Scott soothed her.

'Lucy,' Amy said. 'That's right. Lucy Armitage. She lives three doors along. They always walk to school together.'

Scott made a note of the name. 'Do they come back home together, too?'

'Not always. It depends. Lucy does all kinds of after-school things. She's in a few sports teams and I think she plays an instrument. Tilly just likes to come home straightaway.'

Scott nodded. 'I can understand that. I was the same. Does Tilly have a boyfriend?'

'No,' she quickly answered.

'Would you know about it if she had? I know I was very secretive at her age.'

'No. She's all about her dogs and studying conservation.'

'Has she mentioned any new names recently?'

'Not that I'm aware of,' she replied.

'Have you noticed anyone hanging around, anyone new in the area?'

Amy thought for a moment. 'I don't think so. No. I'm pretty sure I would have noticed.'

'Is Tilly street smart?'

'Yes. She is,' she said firmly. 'She wouldn't have gone off with someone she didn't know.'

Scott nodded. 'We have Tilly's mobile phone and we're going through it to see if she's received any text messages or emails from someone who wanted to meet her. Is she on any social media sites?'

'She's on them all,' Amy said, rolling her eyes.

'Does she have her own laptop or a tablet?'

'You think she was being groomed?' she asked, her voice shaking with emotion.

'At the moment, we don't know. But we need to check all possible options.'

'She's got a tablet and a laptop,' Amy said.

'Would it be possible for us to take them away to analyse them?'

'Of course.'

Scott cleared his throat. 'Where were you when you received the SOS message?'

'I was here,' Amy said. 'I'd been home about an hour, I think. I was about to start making the tea when the message came through. I grabbed my keys and went straight to Brincliffe.'

'Just one more question: Is there anyone you can think of who might have wanted to hurt Tilly, or anyone in your family?'

'You think it might be someone we know?' Amy asked.

'Like I said, we need to cover every angle.'

'I can't think of anyone who would want to hurt us. We keep ourselves to ourselves. We're just a normal family.'

———

Scott and Tom walked back to the car. It was a relief to get out of the house with its oppressive and heavy atmosphere.

It was a cold day and both detectives were wrapped up against the elements. A stiff breeze was blowing and there were light snowflakes in the air. Scott stopped at the driver's side of the car and looked back at the Halls' innocuous semi-detached house. He noticed a few curtains twitching at houses either side.

'Are you opening this car or not? I'm freezing my balls off, here,' Tom said.

Scott unlocked the car and they both climbed in.

'What are your first impressions?' Scott asked as he put his seatbelt on and tried to start the engine, which came into life on the third attempt.

'She's close to losing it,' Tom said, balancing the laptop and iPad on his lap. 'Cleaning the house from top to bottom. She's got no friends or family around. The phone didn't ring once. She's all on her own.'

'Any suspicions?'

Tom looked across sharply at him. 'You don't suspect her, surely?'

'I'm asking you. When I asked if Tilly had a boyfriend, she answered no very quickly.'

'You think she was lying?'

Scott shrugged.

'Why would she lie? Her daughter is her whole life. She's going to want to find the bloke who did this. She wouldn't hide anything from us. Would she?'

'When you've seen what I've seen over the years, nothing is off the table.' Scott pulled away from the kerb and slowly drove off.

Chapter Seven

Matilda Darke was sitting at the dining room table, laptop open, notepad beside her. Chief Constable Ridley had sent her an email within five minutes of leaving her house. He thanked her for returning to help and attached case notes on the three rapes so far.

Matilda had encountered more than enough depraved killers in her time on the force, but this man seemed to be attempting to claim the number one spot of Britain's Evilest Killer. She read the police report of the first victim, Daisy Clough, aged twenty-three, and had to stop twice as the level of violence inflicted upon the defenceless woman was too much to take in.

Daisy was a slight woman, five feet tall in heels, and less than seven stone in weight. She worked as a nurse in the Accident and Emergency department at Sheffield's Northern General Hospital. The statements given by her friends, family and colleagues all described how she was dedicated to the job, how she'd thrived during the coronavirus pandemic, working extra hours, sometimes sleeping in the staff room rather than going home. Despite what they'd all endured over the past year, Daisy was always there to comfort members of staff who'd lost patients during their shift, even when she'd lost patients of her own. They joked about how she looked like a little girl playing dress-up and how they'd had to order a special uniform size to fit her as she was so tiny. But her personality was huge in comparison. She was so full of life. Until she crossed paths with the man who sought to destroy it for his own sick pleasure.

On Thursday 29th October, she left work several hours after her shift was due to finish and headed home for two days' leave. She never made it. She was found the next morning in woodland close to the hospital. Her uniform had been savagely torn open, her body was a map of bruises and her face and head had suffered multiple blows, rendering her unrecognisable. She'd been raped and her throat cut so deep her trachea was almost completely severed.

The crime scene itself was difficult to process due to local wildlife having nibbled at her in the hours from the attack until daylight the next day when she was found by a dog walker.

The scene-of-crime photographs were upsetting to say the least, and Matilda had to leave the table on more than one occasion to compose herself before returning. She printed off a photo of Daisy in her uniform, happy and smiling, her eyes twinkling, the picture of happiness. She was doing a job she'd dreamed of doing since she was a little girl. She was helping people, and although she was working backbreaking hours and had very little time for a social life, she was genuinely happy. That was the Daisy Clough Matilda wanted to remember.

A few of the photographs from forensics were of Daisy's uniform laid out on a white table. It was covered in dried blood stains and mud from the woodland floor. There were several close-ups of the tears where it had been savagely ripped open. Matilda frowned as she zoomed in. It didn't look like scissors or a knife were used to cut the material, and some of the buttons were still done up. Strong hands, or someone with so much rage and venom burning inside them, had pulled the uniform apart.

The front door opened and slammed closed. Adele Kean, Matilda's best friend, was home from work. She called out a tired hello and dragged her feet along the hallway. She headed for the kitchen but stopped on the way when she saw Matilda in the dining room.

'Oh, there you are. I didn't think there was anyone in,' she said, pulling out a chair and falling into it. 'I'm dead on my feet.'

'Poor choice of words for a pathologist,' Matilda said.

'Have you been crying?' Adele asked.

Matilda wiped her eyes. Her fingers came away wet. 'I appear to have been recalled to life.'

'What does that mean?' Adele frowned.

'I had a visit from Benjamin Ridley earlier. He wants me back.'

Adele's face seemed to light up. 'Oh, that's wonderful news. So, are they tears of sadness or joy?'

Matilda turned her laptop to face Adele. 'Definitely sadness.'

'Ah. That's a post mortem I'm not going to forget in a hurry. I need a drink.' She pushed herself up and staggered to the kitchen.

Matilda and Adele had known each other for more than twenty years. Following the murder of Adele's son almost two years ago, the two women decided to live together so neither was alone and left to dwell on their own personal tragedies. Without Adele, Matilda knew she wouldn't be back to her fighting best, and now, living in the uncertain time of Covid, she needed someone strong and stable by her side. They buoyed each other up. It worked, and they were both relatively happy in their lives at the moment. As happy as a Home Office pathologist working eighteen-hour days and an out-of-work Detective Chief Inspector can be.

Adele opened the fridge and took out a bottle of white wine while Matilda grabbed a couple of glasses from the cupboard. They sat at the small round table in the kitchen and Adele poured them both very large measures.

'There's been another one,' Matilda said. 'A fourteen-year-old girl.'

'Within South Yorkshire? I haven't had anyone brought in.'

'She's still alive. For now.'

'Jesus Christ!' Adele exclaimed, swigging back the wine. 'Did he do the same to her as he did to Daisy and the others?'

'I don't know. I presume so.'

'How the hell has she survived?'

'I don't know that either.'

'So, Ridley just turned up on the doorstep and asked you to go back to work?'

'He was actually asleep on the doorstep.'

'What?'

'It doesn't matter,' she half-smiled. 'There are a lot of detectives off with Covid. DCI French, who's in charge of CID, is off with long Covid and there are all other reasons and illnesses why staffing levels are down. Ridley looked like he was about to burst into tears at one point.'

'Emotional blackmail?'

'No. I think it was genuine.'

'So, you're back in work?' She raised her glass in a toast.

'For now,' Matilda replied, wistfully.

'You're not going to leave me hanging here, are you?'

Matilda smiled and they clinked glasses.

'It's good news, surely?' Adele asked.

'Yes. I think so,' Matilda said.

'Do you plan on telling your face that?'

'It won't be the same though, will it? I won't have my old team back. Sian isn't there.'

'You'll have Scott and Finn. And Christian.'

'I've told Ridley I don't want to work with Christian.'

'What? Why?'

'I can't. Not after everything that happened at Magnolia House.'

'But you've been told what happened.'

'I haven't been told the truth. They're all lying to me. Even Sian.'

'Do you honestly know that for a fact?'

Matilda drained her glass. It was a while before she answered. 'I don't know what to believe.'

'Well, it's been nine months since Magnolia House. Things have settled. The inquiry is done and dusted. You could sit down with Christian, informally, and ask him to tell you exactly what happened. It doesn't have to go any further than the two of you.'

Matilda mused over what Adele had said. 'But what if I don't like what I hear?'

'Then you don't work with him. But you'll know. Your mind will be at rest.'

'But if he tells me what I think he's going to tell me, I'll be compelled to arrest him. Nobody is above the law, Adele.'

'Ah. I hadn't thought of that. There were extenuating circumstances though.'

'Oh, don't get me wrong, I can completely understand why he did it. But if he did, there's no way he should still be a serving police officer.'

Adele refilled their glasses. 'So, what are you going to do?'

Matilda took a deep breath. 'Well, it's taken me a very long time, but I'm starting to understand what Diana Cooper-bloody-sodding-smith has been saying all this time. If we keep things bottled up, they take root and spread and fester, and we become all knotted up and full of anger and resentment. I don't want to go back to those dark days. If I'm going to go back to work, then everything needs to be out in the open. I'm going to need to get the whole truth from Christian Brady.'

'And if you hear what you don't want to hear?'

'I will …' She paused while she thought. 'I'll cross that bridge when I come to it.'

———————

DI Christian Brady wasn't a great multi-tasker. He was currently trying to fill in an overtime report as well as work out which detectives were off work with Covid, and which ones were off due to the stress of overwork and dealing with Covid-related incidents. Why everything had to be separated, he had no idea. It would be much simpler if he gave one figure saying how many officers he was down. Unfortunately, a police force under special measures required greater scrutiny, and that meant more forms to fill in. This wasn't even his job. DCI French should be doing this, but it didn't look as if she would be returning to work any time soon, if at all, so it had fallen onto his shoulders, as had everything else in this sodding building.

He looked up and out into the open-plan CID suite. There were so many empty desks, it was frightening. Those that were occupied were filled with harassed-looking detectives, any one of them ready to drop. He missed being part of an elite team. He missed the rapport and camaraderie of the Homicide and Major Crime Unit. Those days were long gone. Policing had changed. Life had changed. And he didn't like it.

There was a tap on the glass door. He looked up to see DC Finn Cotton standing in the doorway.

'Come on in, Finn,' he said, tiredness evident in his voice.

'Is everything all right, sir?' Finn asked.

'Why does everyone ask me that?' Christian asked, an iciness to his tone.

'You just look, I don't know, tired, I suppose.'

'Of course I'm tired. We're all tired. I've been at this desk since before eight o'clock this morning. I haven't even had lunch yet and it's already going dark out there. I've done nothing but write reports and fill in forms all day and I know for a fact nobody's going to sodding read them.'

'Shall I come back?' Finn asked, edging towards the door.

Christian sighed. 'No. I'm sorry. I shouldn't be taking it out on you. What is it you want?'

'Well, it's not good news, I'm afraid. We've conducted house to house enquiries at Brincliffe and nobody saw anything. A few of the properties have CCTV but they haven't picked up anything either, though we haven't finished going through them all yet. ANPR hasn't been any use. Forensics didn't find much from the crime scene and Tilly's clothes are simply covered in mud and her own blood. Her mother consented to her being physically examined while she's unconscious in intensive care and we can confirm she was raped.'

Christian slumped forward. He ran his hands over his head. 'That's four in ... how long?'

'End of October. Less than two months.'

'How can we have no evidence whatsoever from four victims?'

'He leaves them out in the open. At this time of year, the weather isn't great, and it washes or blows away any trace evidence, or wildlife get to them before we do. Don't forget, there's always a large amount of blood, foxes can smell that from a long distance.'

'I don't understand how CCTV hasn't come up with something. I thought Sheffield was supposed to be covered with cameras.'

'It is. Supposedly.'

Christian sighed. 'I'll have a word with the Chief Constable. I think we're going to have to go public with this.'

'I didn't think you wanted to do that?'

'I don't. What this force doesn't need right now is more publicity. Leave it with me. I'll give it some thought.'

'Okay.' Finn stood up. He was about to leave the room when he stopped and turned back. 'Sir, is it true that DCI Darke is coming back?'

Christian's head snapped up. 'What? Who told you that?'

'Ah. Erm ... Scott may have mentioned it.'

'Oh. Well, I haven't been told anything. I guess we'll have to wait and see.' He smiled and Finn left the small office.

Christian turned his back on the suite and looked out of the window at the grey and depressing view of the steel city.

He took a deep breath. So, the Chief Constable had listened to him. It was good to know his words weren't falling on deaf ears for once. Although, suddenly, the prospect of Matilda Darke returning to work filled him with dread. Maybe he should have kept his mouth shut.

Chapter Eight

Thursday 17th December 2020

'Ooh, you look nice,' Adele Kean said, looking up when Matilda entered the kitchen.

'You make it sound like I always dress like a tramp,' she said, smoothing down her white shirt.

'It's just been so long since you've not been wearing jeans and jogging pants that it's a change to see you in something designer and decent. You're wearing make-up as well, I see.'

'I wasn't going to, but I woke up and found a bloody spot on my chin. Acne at my age.'

'Do you want some breakfast?'

'I'm not sure I could keep anything down. It's like first day at secondary school all over again.'

'My first day at secondary school was terrifying,' Adele said. 'I caught glandular fever over the summer holiday and by the time I was well enough for school, it was already two weeks into the new term. Everyone had met and made friends and little cliquey groups and then I arrived. A complete new girl.'

'That must have been scary,' Matilda said.

'It was. Talk about a dent in your confidence.'

'What did you do?'

'I brought sweets in and shared them around. I made friends very easily after that.'

'I might pop into the shops and buy a few bags of Haribo.' Matilda smiled nervously.

Adele stood up and placed two slices of granary bread into the toaster. 'You're blowing this out of all proportion. You're going back to work in the same office with the same people. Give it five minutes and it'll be like you've never been away.'

Matilda popped a coffee pod into the machine. The small cup was filled with an industrial-strength black liquid. She took a sip and felt the rush of caffeine begin to soothe her nerves.

'Why does everything get scary when you get older?'

'You're not old.'

'I didn't say I was old. I said older.'

'I don't know. I'd have thought life experience would give us more confidence, but it doesn't, does it?'

Matilda sat at the table. 'Am I making the right decision? Maybe I should have joined Sian in her dog walking business. She seems happy enough.'

'Sian is miserable. She might be smiling, but you look in her eyes. She misses being a detective,' Adele said, buttering two slices of toast and joining Matilda at the table. 'You'd be miserable, too, if you didn't go back to work.'

'I've enjoyed having these few months off.'

'Yes, because you've known it wasn't permanent. Ridley always said as soon as the force is out of special measures, he'll do everything he can to get your unit reinstated, and you knew he'd come calling. You've had that at the back of your mind while you've been reading in the garden.'

'I suppose.'

'There's no suppose about it. You're a born detective. You're only nervous because you've been asked back earlier than you expected. You've been caught off guard. Maybe that's a good thing.'

'Maybe.'

Adele pushed her plate across the table towards Matilda. 'So, Detective Chief Inspector, eat my breakfast, finish your coffee, then go to work with your head high, your shoulders back and your arse out. Be confident, be stylish, be determined and be sexy.' She smiled.

'What's being sexy got to do with me being a detective?'

'Absolutely nothing. But being sexy is a great confidence booster. Giving lectures scares the crap out of me; all those annoying students gawping at me. Before I go into that hall, I look at myself in the mirror in the toilets and say to myself , 'My God, Adele, you're hot.' It gives me a rush of adrenaline and makes me smile.'

Matilda laughed.

'Why are you laughing? Don't you think I'm hot?'

'Not while you're wearing Winnie the Pooh pyjamas, no.'

There was a knock on the front door.

Matilda's smile dropped. 'That'll be Scott.'

Adele ran out into the hallway. She opened the front door and told Scott Matilda would be right out and to get the engine running. She closed the door as Matilda came out of the kitchen putting her coat on.

'Come here.'

'Why?'

Adele grabbed Matilda by the shoulders and led her to the mirror in the hall.

'Say it?'

'Say what?'

'Say, "My God, Matilda, you're hot."'

Matilda laughed. 'I'm not saying that.'

'Why not?'

'Because it's ridiculous.'

'Does it matter?'

'Yes.'

'Why?'

'Because.'

'That's not an answer. Look, there's only you and me here. I'm not going to laugh. Come on. A boost of confidence. A rush of adrenaline. Look deep into your eyes. Say it. Believe it.'

Matilda looked at her reflection. Her hair was neatly styled. Her clothes were new and fitted perfectly. She was wearing just a touch of make-up and sprayed a small amount of expensive fragrance. She had to admit, she liked what she saw. She took a deep breath.

'My God, Matilda, you're hot,' she said, not believing a single word of it.

Adele slapped her on the back. 'Atta girl.' She opened the front door for her. 'Go out there and take no prisoners.'

Matilda walked out with her head high and her back straight. She immediately turned around and ran back into the house.

'What's wrong?' Adele asked.

'I need a pee.'

Chapter Nine

The last time the suite of offices that was home to the Homicide and Major Crime Unit had been used was nine months ago in March. Matilda Darke had told her team that the unit was being closed. The reason given was budget cuts caused by the coronavirus pandemic. The truth was that they were on the hunt of a serial child sex abuser who had friends in high places and didn't appreciate Matilda and her team asking questions. They'd won by having the unit closed, but Matilda continued in her task of seeking retribution for the victims. Eventually, she succeeded, but at a huge personal and professional loss.

She walked through the double glass doors and saw the desks set out as before but devoid of life. There was a fusty smell in the air, and it was cold. She went over to the windows and opened them all as far as they'd go to let in a blast of cold December air and rid the room of its staleness. She placed a hand on the radiator. It was freezing. So much for a warm welcome.

She headed for her old office and stood in the doorway. She

gave a hint of a smile. She'd worked in many offices in her career, but this had been the largest, and the one she felt most settled in. As she went over to the chair and sat down, she ran a finger over the top of the desk. It came away with a coating of dust.

There was a tap on her door. She looked up and saw DS Scott Andrews in the doorway.

'What's it like being back?' he asked with a smile.

'You'd have thought Ridley would have sent the cleaners in first.'

'I don't think he had time.'

'Maybe not,' she said, looking around her.

'I've brought up the relevant case files.'

'Thanks, Scott.'

'I also thought about doing a case review to get up to speed. But you need to choose who you want on your team.'

Matilda looked up at him and saw the hopeful smile spread across his smooth face. There was no doubt in her mind to accept Scott back.

'Sit down, Scott.'

He pulled out the chair opposite and sat on the edge, his eyes wide and eager.

'You're definitely back. That goes without saying. However, I have one proviso.'

'Go on?' A frown appeared on his face.

'I want you to go in for your inspector's exams.'

'What? I've only been a DS for a couple of years.'

'It's long enough. I want you as my DI.'

'What about DI Brady?'

Matilda hoped her inner baulking at the name wasn't evident. 'This is a new chapter, Scott. I want fresh blood.'

'I'm not fresh blood.'

'You will be if you're a DI.'

'What's happened between you and DI Brady?'

Matilda stood up and went over to the window. The view – the back of the custody suite and the industrial bins – was exactly the same as before and lacked inspiration. 'I'd like DC Cotton, too. How's he getting on with his Open University degree?'

'Very well. He's in his third year now.'

'Excellent. I'll have a word with him, though. He needs to think about moving up to Sergeant. Right.' She clapped her hands together. 'Your first task as acting DI is to find me a few DCs you think will fit in. I'll get this place warmed up and the murder board set up and we'll see what we've got to work with. What do you say?'

Scott smiled. 'I feel like I should be saluting you.'

'Try and contain yourself, Scott.'

'Will do.'

Scott stood up and left the room, leaving Matilda alone. She looked around her. A new chapter. A new team. A new-found confidence.

Her phone beeped an incoming text. She took it out of her coat and looked at the display. Adele had sent her a text.

My God, Matilda, you're hot.

Matilda burst out laughing. It was just what she needed.

———

The suite was aired, but was now bloody freezing, so Matilda went around the empty room pulling the windows to but leaving a gap for fresh air to circulate. The pandemic had made her paranoid about germs and she insisted on there always being a source of fresh air in every room she was in. Even in the midst of winter when the temperature struggled to reach more than four or five degrees above freezing, she had to have a window open.

Matilda had printed off the photographs of the four victims, three dead and one clinging to life, and stuck them onto the white board at the top end of the room. As she stood back and surveyed them, her heart sank. Usually, you could tell a lot about a killer from the kind of victim's he'd chosen. In this case, that would be almost impossible, which scared the life out of Matilda. This was a killer who knew exactly what to do in order to escape capture. She wondered how many more photographs she'd be sticking up on the board before she caught him.

The door to the suite opened. Matilda turned and saw a young face smiling up at her. Matilda smiled back.

'Zofia, it's lovely to see you,' she said, genuinely meaning it.

Last autumn, new recruit DC Zofia Nowak had gone undercover as a street prostitute to lure out a serial killer targeting sex workers. When the killer was revealed, Matilda went into a kind of shock. She knew him. She was friends with him. She liked him. As he tried to escape, Zofia put herself into the path of his car, believing he wouldn't run down a police officer. She was wrong, and she was pinned to a tree. Zofia would spend the rest of her life in a wheelchair, and Matilda blamed herself.

There was no doubt in Zofia's mind that she would return to South Yorkshire Police, and, during her recovery, Matilda had told her there would always be a place on her team. Unfortunately, a great deal had happened in the past year, and the team no longer existed. Or did it? Matilda still wasn't sure. However, seeing Zofia, looking happy and healthy as ever, wheel herself into the suite was more than enough to brighten Matilda's day.

'Thank you. I appreciate you having me back on your team.'

'I told you there was a place for you when you felt ready. Are you … ready?'

'I'm absolutely fine,' she beamed. 'I've been back for about six weeks now. I was knackered for the first couple, but I've settled back in. I spoke to DCI French about going on a cyber course seeing as I can't go out chasing killers any more, but she's off now with Covid. I was wondering if you could help me look into it?'

'Of course. I think that's an excellent idea.'

'Erm …' Zofia looked over her shoulder. The door to the suite had closed behind her. It was just the two of them here. 'Before anyone else gets here, I want to thank you for what you did.'

'Sorry?'

'Mum and Dad told me about the anonymous donation to the GoFundMe page they set up to help adapt the bungalow they'd bought for me. I knew straightaway it could only have come from you. I really am incredibly grateful.'

Matilda swallowed hard. She had been over and over the scene in the woods where she'd frozen while Zofia had leapt into action. She had failed her and would have to live with the consequences. The only thing she could do to atone was make Zofia's life as easy as possible.

Reluctantly, Matilda nodded. 'It's the least I could do.'

'While I was in hospital, I just kept thinking that I'd have to move back home with Mum and Dad. Don't get me wrong, I love them to bits, but my mum is a born worrier. She'd have smothered me. Dad found the bungalow and said he'd do everything to make it habitable for me. Mum was dead set against it, naturally, but we both talked her round.'

Matilda went over to a nearby desk and sat on the edge. 'Is the house fully equipped for you?'

If it was possible, Zofia's smile widened.

'I've got everything I need and more. Dad got someone round from the hospital telling him to point out what needed to be adapted for me. He had all the light switches lowered and the plug sockets raised. I've got an en suite wet room and a huge kitchen with everything on one level. It's perfect. You'll have to come round and see it one evening. I'll cook for you.'

Matilda smiled. 'I'd like that. Thank you.'

The doors opened and DS Scott Andrews entered with DC Finn Cotton following and a young DC Matilda had never seen before.

'Finn. Nice to see you again,' Matilda said. 'Scott tells me you've finally found a house you like.'

'Yes. We signed last week and should be moved in by early February, fingers firmly crossed.'

'Excellent. New year, new start.'

'Zofia, the desk by the window is the height-adjustable one,' Scott pointed out.

'Cheers, thank you.' She wheeled herself over and set about making herself comfortable and fiddling with the control to get the desk at the right height for her.

'Matilda, can I introduce you to DC Tom Simpson?' Scott asked.

'Sorry?' Matilda had been watching Zofia and how she seemed so at ease with the wheelchair, manoeuvring herself between the desks and setting up her own workstation like everything was normal. She supposed, to Zofia, it was normal, now. The new normal.

'You asked for a DC. Tom's been with CID for over a year. DCI French speaks very highly of him. He's done a family liaison and an advanced driver's course. He's also got a degree in psychology. He's a bit like Finn only …'

'Not as handsome,' Finn interrupted.

'I was going to say not as geeky.' Scott winked.

'It's nice to meet you, Tom,' Matilda said.

'Thank you. I'm looking forward to working on a dedicated unit, ma'am. I promise I won't let you down.'

'Don't call her ma'am,' Scott said out of the corner of her mouth.

'Sorry.'

Matilda smiled. 'That's fine. Shall we all get comfortable and settled and begin the briefing in about ten minutes? Scott, a word,' she said, heading for her office.

'Is something wrong?' Scott asked as he entered Matilda's office and closed the door behind him.

'No. Nothing's wrong at all. I want you to do me a favour, though. Keep an eye on Tom.'

He frowned. 'What are you talking about?'

'When Zofia first joined the team, she was eager to please, too, and look what happened to her. If you see any sign of Tom trying to be some kind of a maverick, I need you to stop him. I will not have detectives putting their lives in danger simply to make a good impression.'

He nodded. 'Understood.'

'I'll be out in a few minutes.'

Scott left, and Matilda looked out at her meagre team. Scott, she knew very well. He'd recently celebrated his thirtieth birthday and was now the oldest member, apart from Matilda, who suddenly felt ancient when she looked at the fresh faces of Finn, Zofia and Tom. Finn seemed older than his mid-twenties. His wife was a good deal older than him and some of her life experience seemed to have rubbed off, giving him a more serious outlook. Zofia had aged, too, in the past year. She had obviously adapted well to life in a wheelchair, and it was evident she wasn't going to allow it to stop her doing what she wanted to achieve. There was a determination in her gaze that wasn't there before.

Matilda looked over at the new recruit, Tom Simpson. He was chatting, animatedly, to Scott while they moved desks around. He was young, early twenties, Matilda guessed. He was tall, well over six foot, with short dark brown hair, smooth skin and brown eyes. He was slim but the tightness of his trousers revealed muscular legs. He'd come in handy if there was any chasing of killers to be done. He seemed to ooze confidence. He reminded her of DC Rory Fleming, who had been killed in the shooting almost two years ago. She wondered if that's why Scott had chosen him. Scott and Rory were best friends. Was Tom a replacement?

Matilda sat back and looked at them all as one team. She smiled as she heard her mother's voice in her head saying, 'You know you're getting old when policeman get younger.' She was right. Scott was a young thirty, Finn and Zofia were both mid-twenties and Tom looked like his chin was a stranger to a razor. She missed Sian. She missed Christian. Suddenly, coming back to work felt like the biggest mistake since Ben Affleck was cast as Batman.

Chapter Ten

'Okay, I'm assuming you've all worked on these cases at some point, while I only read through the files last night. However, before Scott takes us through the victims in detail, I want you to have a good look at these women,' Matilda said as she stood at the whiteboard in front of her new team. 'Daisy Clough, Joanna Fielding, Dawn Richardson and Tilly Hall. What does the victimology tell us about the killer?'

'They're all young women,' Scott answered.

'Yes. The first victim, Daisy Clough, is the oldest at twenty-three, while the most recent victim, Tilly Hall, is only fourteen. What else?'

Her question was met with silence.

'Nothing,' Finn eventually spoke up. 'Daisy is slim, pale, mousy hair. Joanna is mixed race, athletic build, short hair. Dawn is, erm... curvier, long hair, short. Tilly looks very young, slim. None of them look alike.'

'Exactly.' Matilda smiled slightly.

'Tilly was wearing her school uniform,' Tom pointed out.

'Daisy was wearing a nurse's uniform as she'd just left work. Could it be the uniform that's attracting the killer?'

'Joanna and Dawn weren't in uniform, though,' Scott added.

'Usually, to understand the killer, we look at the victimology,' Matilda said. 'Unfortunately, these four women can tell us nothing about the kind of man we're looking for. He's not going after one particular type of woman. What do we learn from that?'

'He's playing a game,' Tom said without looking up.

'Go on?' Matilda instructed.

'If he had some kind of perversion, like an unhealthy fascination with women in uniform or a fixation with obese women, then he'd target them solely. What he's doing here is picking women who are a complete contrast to each other. It's not about the victim, it's about getting away with a crime.'

Matilda smiled. 'Exactly.'

Tom sat up straight, pleased with his own answer.

'So, he's not getting some kind of thrill out of raping or killing them, it's simply about committing a crime and not being caught?' Zofia asked, pen poised over a notepad.

'Not necessarily. He's chosen this kind of crime for a reason. He could easily get a gun and shoot these women or strangle them, but he's chosen to rape them, cut their throats, and throw them away when he's finished. He wants to put them through unimaginable hell and then discard them.'

'He hates women?' Finn asked.

'I think so. But not one type of woman. If he hated his wife or his mother, he'd go after women who looked like the person he really hated, but he's changing the type of victim with each one. He hates all women,' Matilda said.

'So, how do we catch him?' Scott asked.

Matilda turned her back on the team and looked at the four women. They were all smiling, the photographs of them taken during happier times in their lives when they had everything to look forward to, their whole lives stretching ahead of them, until one man decided to destroy them.

She turned back to her team. She had no idea how to answer Scott's question. Yet. 'Scott, come and give us chapter and verse on the victims. I know you'll all know about them, and I read through them all last night, but, together, something may click into place.'

Scott grabbed his iPad and went to the top of the room while Matilda perched on the edge of a nearby desk.

'Okay. Victim number one is Daisy Clough, aged twenty-three,' he began. 'On Thursday, the twenty-ninth of October, she left work at the Northern General Hospital. She was a nurse in A&E. I don't need to tell you how busy they've been with the pandemic. Her shift ran over, and it was dark and late by the time she left. Usually, she caught the bus at Herries Road. That night, she didn't. We've looked at the time she left work and the length of time it would take her to get to the bus stop. We've checked with the bus company, and she would only have been waiting at the stop for six minutes maximum before her bus came. Why she didn't get on it, we don't know. Did someone pass in a car she knew or was she grabbed? The next morning, she was found by our good friend the dog walker in woodland in Roewood Allotments, not far from the bus stop. She'd been beaten, raped and her throat cut several times.'

'Her file is thick. I'm surmising it's been a thorough investigation,' Matilda said.

'We've interviewed every doctor and nurse who worked with her in A&E, her family, friends and neighbours. They all, more or less, said the same thing: she was a dedicated professional. She was wise and street smart. She would never have accepted a lift from a stranger,' Finn said, reading from his notes.

'So, she either knew her killer or she was snatched,' Matilda said.

'Before the pandemic, she took several fitness classes and she and a few colleagues went on a self-defence course. The Herries Road area isn't the nicest area in the city. They wanted to be able to defend themselves if ever approached as there have been several attacks there in the past,' Finn said.

'She'd have put up a fight if she'd been grabbed then,' Matilda mused.

'So it had to be someone she knew,' Zofia added.

'We've interviewed all the men in her life,' Scott said. 'They all have alibis that have stood up.'

Matilda turned to look at Daisy's picture. She looked so happy, so proud to be wearing a nurse's uniform. She would have worked tirelessly during the pandemic, and this was how her life had ended. It was incredibly cruel and unfair.

'She either knew him, which is looking unlikely, or he is so clever that he was able to manipulate her into going with him.'

'How?' Tom asked.

'He could work at the hospital. Maybe she only vaguely knew him and not well enough to come onto our radar. Maybe he was wearing a doctor's uniform as a disguise, or some other kind of uniform. I think she was duped into going with him. She would not have willingly gone off with a complete stranger. This man, whoever he is, is cunning and devious, and incredibly dangerous.'

The room fell silent.

'Scott, what's happened to our kettle? I could do with a cuppa right now.'

'That was the first thing to be pilfered from this room. I think it's now in the custody suite.'

'Bastards. I bought that with my own money,' Matilda said.

'Do you want me to do a Costa run?' Tom asked.

'No. I'll be fine. Who's sitting at Sian's old desk?'

'I am,' Finn said.

'There are no stray bars of chocolate in her drawer, are there?'

'No. She took everything with her when she left.'

'Tight arse,' Matilda said with a smile. 'I'll be having words with her when I see her next. Right, next victim, Scott.'

'Joanna Fielding, aged twenty. On Wednesday the eighteenth of November she met a friend for a coffee, and they had a walk around Weston Park. When it started to rain, they went their separate ways. The friend, Sally Musgrove, said she turned back when she reached the exit of the park and saw Joanna walking very slowly past the bandstand with her head down. She didn't think anything of it and headed for home. It was around seven o'clock. Joanna was found the next morning in woodland just off Mushroom Lane. She'd been raped, severely beaten and her throat cut wide open. During the night it seemed that wildlife had got to her. She was identified by a tattoo on her left thigh and a metal plate she had in her left leg from a car accident when she was five years old. The crime scene photos are not something you should see if you don't have to,' Scott said, looking up at the team.

'Did she have a boyfriend?' Matilda asked.

'No. She'd recently split up with a bloke on her course. We interviewed him extensively and his alibi checked out,' Finn said.

'Anything in her phone to suggest she was meeting someone else?'

'No,' Tom said. 'She had a lot of contacts in her phone and was very popular on social media. We've interviewed them all and everyone on her psychology course at the university including her lecturers and staff she came into contact with.'

'Who did she live with?' Matilda asked.

'She lived in shared accommodation on Kingfield Road. Six women in total. They were all home on the night she was killed. A couple of them knew she was planning to meet Sally and assumed she was coming straight home afterwards.'

'Didn't any of them report her missing?'

'I don't think any of them noticed,' Finn said. 'They all had their own plans for the evening.'

'Fair enough. Who is this Sally she was meeting?'

'Hang on,' Finn said, scrolling through his iPad. 'I interviewed her. Where is it? Here we are. Sally Musgrove had to go home to Birmingham for a funeral in October. She then tested positive for Covid and had to isolate. By the time she returned to Sheffield she'd missed a lot of work. She met up with Joanna for her to catch up. They were good friends, by all accounts.'

'So, when Sally turned back and saw Joanna by the bandstand, did she see anyone else in the vicinity?' Matilda asked.

'Nobody stood out. That part of the park is often used as a cut through.'

'CCTV from the museum?'

'It picked up Joanna and Sally walking through the gates with a takeaway coffee in their hands. About fifty minutes later, Sally is seen going back out on her own. She does turn back and look over her shoulder,' Tom said.

'Why does she do that?' Matilda frowned. 'What made her look back?'

'She didn't say,' Finn said.

'We've been through her phone, laptop, all her contacts. There's no evidence of a conversation to meet someone else after Sally,' Zofia said.

'I'm guessing her phone was on her person when she was found,' Matilda said, looking through the file.

'Yes, it was,' Zofia said.

'And it was dusted for prints?'

'Yes. None were found.'

Matilda looked up. 'Not even her own?'

Zofia's eyes widened. She quickly turned to her computer and began hammering away on the keyboard. She found the relevant file. 'No. It was clean.'

'Unusual, don't you think?' Matilda asked. 'Every phone is touchscreen these days. We always manage to get good fingerprints from them.'

'She was wearing gloves. Maybe she wiped it clean while looking at the time or something,' Tom suggested.

'It's possible,' Matilda mused. 'How did she get on with her housemates?'

'Very well. Me and Tom went round there,' Scott said. 'They were shocked by Joanna's death but said they all got on incredibly well. They were like sisters.'

'Sisters tend to fall out from time to time,' Zofia said.

'I said that,' Tom smiled. 'They said they never had a cross word between them.'

'Liars,' Zofia hissed.

'I agree,' Matilda added. 'Put a group of women in a house together and the claws are going to come out at one point or another.'

'It's not a woman doing this, though, is it?' Tom asked. 'Does it matter if they had a falling out or anything?'

'It's not unusual for a couple to be working together. Maybe the female of the couple befriends a victim, lures them somewhere for the male to attack,' Matilda said.

'Do you honestly think that's what's happening here?' Finn asked, a look of horror on his face.

'I don't know, Finn. There's nothing to suggest anything so far. Victim number three, when you're ready, Scott.'

Scott cleared his throat. 'Victim number three is Dawn Richardson, aged nineteen. She worked for a hairdresser on Devonshire Green and lived in a flat with her sister on the Park Hill estate. She didn't drive and there's no direct bus route, so she always walked home. On Saturday the fifth of December, she worked later than normal as she had appointments booked up until seven o'clock. She sent her sister Louisa a text as she was leaving, asking if she wanted anything picking up from the shops on her way home. Louisa replied asking her to pick up a bottle of wine. Dawn replied with a smiling emoji. An hour later, Dawn hasn't returned home and she's not answering her phone. An hour after that, Louisa and her boyfriend Greg go out to look for her. They found her dead, slumped up against the Cholera Monument not far from where she lived. She'd been raped, beaten and her throat cut so deep her head was almost severed.'

'Bloody hell,' Matilda said softly. 'Now, she will have had to walk through the city centre. You're not telling me CCTV didn't pick her up.'

'We've tracked her movements completely from leaving the hairdresser, popping into Sainsbury's, buying the wine, leaving the store and walking home. On a normal route home, she would have cut through the train station. On this particular night, she didn't. CCTV from the train station picked her up walking past. She took the long route round as she went to post a birthday card to a colleague who was self-isolating. We even picked her up on someone's doorbell camera as she passed. After that, we lose her,' Zofia said, reading from her own iPad.

'Same questions: boyfriends?'

'No. She's been single for about a year. Her ex is in Exeter at university,' Scott said.

'Friends? Family members? Social media contacts?'

'She has a professional page on Facebook to do with her hairstyling. That's it. She's not a fan of social media. We went through her phone and spoke to everyone she knew. They all say she was likeable, friendly and approachable. She'd help anyone if they needed it,' Zofia said.

'The sister's boyfriend, Greg. Does he fit into this at all?'

'He was at the flat with Louisa the whole time. They're both devastated.'

'So.' Matilda stood up and went over to the board, looked at the four smiling faces then turned back to her team. 'We have an opportunistic killer. There is someone out there prowling around looking for the perfect time to strike. It doesn't matter what these women look like, skin colour, hair colour, height and weight, none of that bothers him. He sees a lone female and grabs her. Nobody is safe.'

'Shouldn't we warn women to be careful when out on their own?' Zofia asked.

'Absolutely,' Matilda replied quickly. 'I'll have a word with the Chief Constable. We need to put out a statement. Moving onto our fourth victim, Tilly Hall. Where are we in the investigation?'

Scott scrolled through his iPad. 'We have statements from

all the occupants of the houses on Brincliffe Edge Road and nobody saw anything at the time of the attack. We've been through her phone and social media pages and are currently interviewing anyone she interacted with on a regular basis. We've also got uniformed officers at the school talking to her classmates, friends and teachers.'

'CCTV?'

'Nothing.'

'Forensics?'

'They're still at the site, but they're not hopeful. The ground was soaking, and it was very windy.'

'Anything from Tilly's clothes or under her fingernails?'

'Not yet.'

'I didn't ask for the other three, but in the internal examinations … was semen found?' Matilda asked.

'Erm … give me a few seconds,' Scott said as he scrolled through his iPad. 'Yes. A trace sample was found on Joanna Fielding, but a better sample was taken from Daisy Clough, Dawn Richardson and Tilly Hall. We're waiting on the test results.'

'Fingers crossed,' Matilda said. 'What we need to ask ourselves is how and why Tilly survived. He successfully managed to kill his first three victims without detection, but his fourth, he didn't. Technically, he failed. Why?'

'Maybe he was interrupted?' Zofia offered.

'That was my first thought, too. If he was interrupted, then we need to discover who interrupted him. I want Brincliffe Edge Road blanketed with uniformed officers. I want people out and about stopped and questioned. Dog walkers, joggers, people coming to and from their homes. Someone saw something. Also, Tilly activated the emergency SOS message on her iPhone at –' she looked down at her notes '– 4:57. We have an exact time of the attack taking place, or at least an exact time of her having her throat cut and being thrown into the woods. We can use that to track all vehicles using CCTV and ANPR in the area around that time.'

'I'll see to that,' Zofia volunteered.

Tom raised his hand.

'You don't need to do that, Tom,' Matilda said.

'Sorry. When me and Scott went to talk to Amy Hall, we asked if Tilly had a boyfriend. She said no, but she answered a bit too quickly for our liking. In interviewing her friends, one name has come up a few times – Ryan Cook. Apparently, they were seeing each other until the summer then it just fizzled out.'

'Has Ryan been interviewed?'

'No. He's isolating as his mother has Covid.'

'Okay. We obviously can't talk to him without an adult present. Tom, give his mother a ring and see if we can put them on a conference call or something. Just have a general chat with him, find out why they broke up.'

'Will do.'

'Finn, I want you to check the sex offenders register and have everyone questioned. I want alibis for where they were at the time of Tilly's attack and the other three, too. Have them checked and double checked.'

'I get all the glamorous jobs,' Finn said to Tom.

'What do you want me to do?' Scott asked.

Matilda proffered a hint of a smile. 'The job of an acting DI,' she said, heading for her office.

Scott turned to Finn. 'I have no idea what that is.'

Chapter Eleven

Tilly Hall opened her eyes. She felt numb and for a few long seconds she had no idea where she was. Then, her memory returned. She remembered being grabbed and thrown into the back of a van. She remembered holding onto the sides as she was driven away at speed to God knows where. Then the van stopped. The doors opened and a man crawled in. He came towards her. He looked her in the eye as his hands went down to his jeans and he unzipped them. She saw …

She screamed, but no sound came out. She put a hand to her throat, but all she could feel was a thick bandage. Her right arm was in a plaster cast. What the hell had happened to her?

The room was dark and far too hot. There was a window with a half-closed Venetian blind. Through the narrow slats, she could see people walking quickly back and forth. They were all wearing uniforms, so she guessed she was in a hospital. She turned to look at the bedside cabinet, full of items she didn't recognise. She started crying and let the tears flow down her face.

There was a button attached to a wire dangling off the metal barriers that would stop her falling out of bed. With shaking fingers, she grabbed and pressed it. In less than a minute, the door was opened, and two nurses stood in the doorway. She looked at them and burst into tears.

Chapter Twelve

Matilda ordered a taxi through an app on her phone and decided to wait outside for it to arrive. It was a freezing cold morning, but after the intensity of the briefing, looking at crime scene photos of young women being tortured and simply thrown away, she needed some fresh air, and it didn't come fresher than a bitter easterly wind in the midst of winter.

As she reached the pavement, she saw a figure coming towards her, a large takeaway coffee in hand. She recognised DI Christian Brady straightaway and her heart sank. She wasn't ready for this. She hadn't prepared for what to say.

'Good morning, Matilda,' he said. He was wrapped up against the cold in a thick padded coat and scarf, a beanie hat pulled down low over his head.

She gave him a weak smile. 'Christian. How are you?'

'I'm fine.'

She saw through the lie immediately. He had dark circles beneath his eyes. His skin was dry, and he seemed to have aged a decade in the past year. The struggles of a dwindling police force during a pandemic were etched on his face.

'I heard you were back today.'

'Only temporary,' she said, looking at her phone, willing the taxi to appear suddenly like a TARDIS.

'Oh.'

'Ridley is worried there's a serial killer operating in Sheffield. He wants it cleared up quickly.'

'So you're reopening the old team?'

'Sort of,' she said, looking at the ground, kicking at a few loose stones.

'Who's your DI?'

She looked to him. 'Christian, it's not a full team. I don't know if I'm coming back yet and with the force in special measures, there's no chance of the unit being opened.'

'You need a DI.'

'Scott is acting DI.'

'Oh.' He looked hurt.

She looked at her phone again. 'Fuck!'

'Something wrong?'

'I'd ordered a cab. I was tracking it and it's just … disappeared. Either it's been cancelled, or it's blown up.' She half-laughed.

'Where are you going?'

'Watery Street.'

'I'll give you a lift,' he said, fishing his keys out of his pocket.

'There's no need. I'll order another one.'

'And stand out here freezing for twenty minutes?'

'I'll ask a uniformed officer to drive me.'

'They're all out.'

'Really?'

'The force has changed a great deal since you've been away. Twenty-three percent of uniformed officers are off and Covid isn't the main reason. The rest are all out there splitting up illegal gatherings. Sheffield is suddenly like 1920s America at the height of prohibition,' he scoffed. 'I'll drive you.'

Matilda remained rooted to the spot while Christian headed for his car. Her phone pinged. She looked at it and saw an email from the taxi company saying her booking had been cancelled due to a lack of available vehicles.

'Bollocks,' she muttered as she grudgingly followed Christian.

The atmosphere in the pool car was heavy. Matilda glared out of the window and watched life in Sheffield pass her by. There were fewer than ten days until Christmas, and the streets should have been bustling with shoppers and festive cheer, but that was seriously lacking on the few faces she saw. She hadn't been in Sheffield City Centre for a while but had heard a large number of shops had closed down due to the pandemic and more people were turning to internet shopping for fear of contracting Covid. The future of the High Street was in doubt. The world was changing by the day. Matilda wondered if it was a permanent shift or if there would be a return to the good old days. Somehow, she doubted it.

'How is the latest victim?' Christian asked. 'Tilly … what is it?'

'Hall. She's still in intensive care as far as I know,' Matilda said, still looking out of the window.

'Four victims in less than two months. He's not wasting any time, is he?'

'No.'

'Have—'

'Did you hear on the news about a new variant of coronavirus being detected?' Matilda interrupted, changing the subject. She didn't want to discuss work with Christian. 'Apparently, it's spreading faster than the first one. Not surprisingly really. Viruses tend to mutate, don't they?'

'Matilda …'

'I wonder if this is what will finish the humans off. We certainly seem to be in a rush to destroy the planet. Mind you, the lockdowns have helped with putting back the Earth Overshoot Day by a couple of weeks. I was reading on the news the other week about how—'

'Matilda!' Christian called out. 'Is that really what you want to talk about?'

'And what would you like to talk about?'

'I want to talk about why you didn't tell me you were coming back to work, why you've chosen Scott as an acting DI rather than have me back, why you won't even look me in the eye when you're talking to me.'

'For a start, I didn't know I was coming back until yesterday. Secondly, I'm only back temporarily until I've solved this case, as I've already explained. Thirdly, I can't look you in the eye while you're driving and we're sitting side by side.'

'Don't be facetious. You didn't look at me once outside the station. What have I done?'

Matilda let out a heavy sigh. It was a while before she answered. 'I can't get over what happened at Magnolia House,' she said, her voice low.

'I've explained all that. More than once,' he said. 'There's been an inquiry, for crying out loud. The facts are all there for you.' He pulled up outside the mortuary.

'Then why do I feel like I'm being lied to?' she said, turning to him for the first time.

'Who's lying to you?'

'I've no idea. You. Sian. Everyone. I don't believe Jamie Cobb pulled the trigger, which leaves just you and Guy Grayston.'

'Jamie Cobb fired that gun,' Christian said, firmly.

'Why do I get the feeling you're trying to convince yourself more than me?'

'It's not my problem if you have trust issues.'

'It's not a trust issue, Christian, it's a truth issue. When you're ready to sit down and give me the full story of exactly what happened at Magnolia House, I'll listen. Until then, I can't work with you.' She opened the door and shivered as a blast of cold air blew in. 'I'll make my own way back to the station.' She climbed out and slammed the door behind her.

Matilda washed her hands using sanitiser from the dispenser just inside the reception of the Medico-Legal Centre and masked up. She made her way to the mortuary where Adele was waiting for her in her impossibly tiny office.

Life in the mortuary suite had changed dramatically since the beginning of the pandemic. They were much busier, and the storage facilities were at maximum levels, and had been for months. A temporary storage unit was erected in the car park and even that was running at full capacity.

'Morning, Matilda.'

She turned and saw Adele's technical assistant, Donal

Youngblood, heading towards her, fully scrubbed up. He was tall, young and slim. He had a shock of hair so black it was almost blue and cheekbones she'd kill for. He also had a look of worry on his face.

'Any chance of a quick word?' he asked in his soft Irish accent.

'Of course.' Matilda lifted two fingers up to Adele and mouthed, 'Two minutes.' Adele gave her the V-sign back and laughed. 'What's wrong?' Matilda asked as they stepped over to a quiet side of the large room.

'Has Scott said anything to you about me lately?' he asked. He looked hurt, as if he was about to burst into tears.

'No. Why? Has something happened?'

Scott and Donal were partners and had been since the early days of the pandemic. Matilda often joked about finding love in the time of Covid.

'We haven't seen each other much in the past few weeks. It's ages before he replies to texts and he's cancelling dates all the time. I've tried asking if there's anything wrong, but he clams up.'

Matilda frowned. 'I thought you two were getting on fine.'

'So did I.'

Matilda looked into Donal's sad eyes. 'Leave it with me, Donal, I'll have a word.'

'Thanks, Matilda. I hope you don't mind me asking.'

'Of course not. I'll let you know.' She turned away and headed for Adele's office.

'What was all that about?' Adele asked.

'It seems like Scott and Donal are having a few problems,' Matilda said, looking worried.

'I thought he'd been quiet lately.'

'And you didn't question him?'

'It's difficult to talk about anything when you're elbow-deep in dead bodies and taking fluid samples from people's eyeballs.'

Matilda pulled a face. 'The first time I saw you do that, I genuinely thought I was going to faint.'

'*I* did. So, are you going to speak to Scott?'

'Definitely. He's obviously keeping things bottled up. That's not good.'

'Hmm, I wonder who that reminds me of,' Adele said, sardonically.

'Cheeky sod. Come on, then, you say you're always busy, but every time I come in here, you're sat staring into space.'

'I'm contemplating.'

'Well, contemplate with my victims, please.'

'With pleasure. It'll be nice to talk about something other than coronavirus for a change. Covid deaths are on the increase again. I've literally run out of space to work in. I've got three members of staff off. And I received an email today from my publisher wanting the revisions back by the New Year. He's got no chance.'

Adele turned in her swivel chair and picked up a couple of files from the messy pile behind her.

'Right then, I performed the post mortems on your three victims and was able to assume they were all killed by the same person judging by the similarity in the extent of the injuries to the neck. I've had the report into Tilly Hall's injuries sent over to me for a comparison and I'm surmising she was attacked by the same person as the other three. How she's managed to survive is beyond me.'

Adele made space on her worktop and spread out a few photographs taken during the autopsy. 'This is your first victim … erm …'

'Daisy Clough,' Matilda said.

'That's right. Now, the blade of the knife cut through the great vessels of the neck, the carotid arteries and the internal jugular veins.'

'Would there have been a lot of blood?' Matilda asked.

'Absolutely. The killer is standing behind his victim and he's slicing from left to right, making him right-handed. Blood would have spurted out, but none will land on him, apart from on his cutting hand, obviously. Death is caused, in part, by exsanguination and airway haemorrhage. Basically, blood flooded the airways and she effectively drowned in her own blood. Now, I've said in my report the weapon you're looking for is something like a hunter's knife. The reason I've said that is because of the wounds to the neck. If you look at this photo here,' she said, pointing to an incredibly detailed close-up of Daisy's throat, 'you can see tearing of the skin. I think he slit her throat with the smooth side of the blade, turned it around, and used the serrated edge to cut away at the veins and tissue beneath the skin.'

'Why would he do that?'

'I can only assume he believed he'd need something to tear away at the muscle and veins beneath, and he wanted to make sure his victim died. He would have achieved that anyway with the smooth edge of the blade. It was certainly sharp enough.'

'So, he cuts open the neck, turns the blade around, and with the teeth of the blade he begins hacking away at what's underneath?' Matilda asked.

'Precisely. Several times, too. He's making sure she'll die from her injuries.'

'And you said Tilly Hall's injuries were the same?'

'Similar. But I'll come back to her in a while. The second

victim, Joanna Fielding, has almost identical injuries to Daisy Clough. However, victim number three, Dawn Richardson, is different.'

'In what way?'

Adele took out photographs from another file and spread them on the desk. They were pictures from the scene of crime where Dawn was found at the Cholera Monument, and close-ups taken during the post mortem.

'We can see a similar attack took place. She was killed from behind. The smooth edge of the blade was used to slice her throat open, then the serrated edge tore away at the muscle, tissue and veins beneath. However, the level of frenzied tearing is taken up a notch. He was close to decapitating her.'

'Bloody hell,' Matilda said.

'There are high blood markings on the monument itself which shows the killer is really hacking away at her neck and flicking up huge sprays.'

'Why would he do that with his third victim?' Matilda asked.

'I'm not a detective. I can't answer that question,' Adele said.

'Do you know what? I think he's angry,' Matilda said. 'His level of intensity is growing. He's managed to kill twice without appearing on our radar and his confidence and excitement are growing. The power coursing through his veins with his third victim is off the scale. He feels like he can do anything he wants, and nothing will happen to him. But then, why did he stop?' She frowned. 'If he was close to decapitating her, he will have known he was, why not continue? Why not take off her head completely?' She was asking herself the question more than Adele.

'I think he was tired,' Adele said.

88 MICHAEL WOOD

'Sorry?'

'He's kidnapped her. He's raped her. He's cut her throat and he's hacking away at her neck. He's running on adrenaline and it's only going to last so far. I can't tell for certain, obviously, but I wouldn't be surprised if he stopped simply because he didn't have the energy.'

'Bloody hell! I've got an actual monster on my hands, haven't I?'

'Moving on to Tilly Hall,' Adele continued. 'I think the killer was interrupted. He sliced across her throat, a cut, I might add, which was nowhere as deep as the other three victims. He then turned the blade around and cut once with the serrated blade. That's it. On the previous victims, we're looking at six, seven, sometimes eight cuts. He only cut Tilly twice.'

'It was on the edge of some woods with houses opposite,' Matilda said. 'Maybe a light was turned on or something. His confidence will have grown with the previous three and he's taken a risk by killing so close to houses. However, it's a risk too far and he's realised he's not as confident as he thought. He's made his first mistake.'

'I'm no psychologist, obviously,' Adele said. 'But might I add my own hypothesis?'

'Go on,' Matilda said.

'He was gaining in confidence with his first three victims, as you've said, and he took a huge risk with Tilly, which didn't pay off. His next victim will not be so lucky. I think he'll try again, very soon, and this time, he'll make her suffer in ways we haven't seen before.'

Matilda nodded. 'I think you're right. Jesus Christ. Let's hope we find him before he kills again. Adele, is there anything you can tell us about who we're looking for? Please tell me you've found skin samples under their fingernails or something.'

'I'm afraid not.'

'What? Nothing?' Matilda asked, incredulously.

'What one thing do all four victims have in common?' Adele asked. 'They're all going home after a day at work, university or school. It's dark. It's the middle of winter, so it's cold. All four victims are wrapped up against the elements in coats, scarves and gloves. Even if they did scratch at their attacker, they wouldn't have been able to get skin samples because they were all wearing gloves.'

'Jesus!' Matilda spat. 'What about semen samples?'

'Semen was found in two of the victims – Daisy Clough and Dawn Richardson. We may as well throw the sample found in Joanna Fielding away as there wasn't enough to get any results from. As for Daisy, I'm afraid her own DNA won the battle and we've only found partial foreign DNA. I've sent a sample off for Y-STR testing, but that'll take a while to come back. I've put in a similar request for Tilly Hall, too.'

'You're blinding me with science,' Matilda said.

'Y-STR looks specifically for the Y chromosome in a sample. If one is found, then there's evidence that the DNA most likely belongs to a man. If you get DNA from a suspect, we should, fingers firmly crossed, be able to match the two chromosomes.'

'Have you got anything from Tilly Hall?' Matilda asked, pleadingly.

Adele rifled through the loose pages in a file. 'Nothing under her fingernails or in her mouth. She was swabbed anally and vaginally. We've detected a small amount of semen which has been sent off for testing. There is no evidence of foreign saliva anywhere on her.'

'What about hairs? He's raped these women. Surely, his pubic hairs would have attached onto the hairs of his victims.'

'They were all thoroughly combed and nothing.'

'I'm sorry, but I find that incredibly hard to believe. You're telling me he didn't lose a single pubic hair while raping these women?'

'Normally, we'd get some, and I'd be telling you to find me a suspect and we'll match his DNA with the root of the hair, but I'm sorry, Matilda, there's nothing here.'

Matilda thought for a while. 'Maybe he's shaved himself. He's obviously a very clever bloke. He's thought about this and put a lot of time into planning how he's going to attack, kill and get away with it. I think he will have realised his pubic hair might become attached to theirs, so he's shaved his off.'

'You've got a point there. Leaving hairs at a crime scene is forensics one-oh-one,' Adele said.

'So, we're not going to find him through forensics, then?'

'Not at the moment.'

Matilda unbuttoned her coat. She was suddenly very warm. 'I haven't got a clue how I'm going to catch this man. I've got nothing to work on.' She looked worried.

'I wish I could give you something more.'

'It's not your fault. Thanks for all this. I'll see you later.'

Matilda left the room with her head down. The first thought that popped into her head was that maybe the killer would make a mistake with his next victim, but she wanted him caught before he had a chance to strike again. She couldn't let another woman go through such horror.

Chapter Thirteen

'South Yorkshire Police has released a statement urging all women not to venture out alone in the wake of four violent attacks in Sheffield which have left three women dead. We can now go live to our Sheffield studio and talk to Chief Constable Benjamin Ridley.'

The camera in the BBC studio panned out from the perfectly made-up woman behind the desk and showed Ridley on a large screen in his pristine uniform. His tie was straight, his buttons were polished and his hair was neat, an unusual look for him so late in the day.

'Chief Constable, what details can you give us about the ferocity of these attacks?'

Ridley cleared his throat. 'First of all, I'd like to point out that at South Yorkshire Police we have a dedicated unit working around the clock on finding the man responsible for these attacks. However, the investigation is a delicate one and sifting through all the evidence and talking to witnesses takes time. This is why we're advising women not to walk around Sheffield alone after dark. To answer your question, there have been four attacks which have left three women dead and one with life-changing injuries.'

'What measures are you putting in place to make the women of Sheffield feel safe until the perpetrator is caught?'

'We're increasing patrols of uniform and plain-clothed officers throughout the city. However, due to the increase of Covid cases, and pubs and restaurants remaining closed, I'm hoping people, women especially, will be staying home and keeping safe. With Christmas around the corner, I'm aware some people will be popping over to visit friends and family and exchange gifts. I don't want to put any extra pressure on people's lives at this already difficult time, but I want everyone within South Yorkshire to be safe. Women should be free to come and go as they please, but until we catch this man, they need to be hyper-vigilant, and not go out on their own, for their own safety.'

'What can you tell us about the man you're looking for?'

'The man we're seeking is local and has an incredible knowledge of the city. He's intelligent and has done his research in how to evade capture so far. He's dangerous and he will use every trick in the book to lure women into his trap. I cannot stress this enough, but the women of Sheffield need to be on their guard and question everything and everyone.'

'South Yorkshire Police is still under special measures following the exposure of a historical child sex abuse scandal uncovered earlier this year. How can the women of Sheffield put so much faith into the police force following such a shocking revelation?'

'I'm fully aware of public feeling towards the police at this time, towards South Yorkshire Police in particular. In the last few months, every single officer employed by this force has been thoroughly investigated. Any hint of scandal, corruption or deviation from the code of contact and they've been removed. I have one hundred percent *confidence in every single officer working within South Yorkshire Police.'*

'But a force in special measures …'

'Turn it off,' Matilda said.

Adele leaned forward on the sofa, picked up the remote and silenced the television. 'I bet you're glad you're not the one giving the interview.'

'Ridley did suggest it, but I told him I was still only back on a temporary basis. I knew they'd bring up the special measures bit. The media only care when there are juicy murder scenes to show. An appeal for safety isn't interesting. They want scandal, blood and guts. Bastards. Maybe I should have done the interview.'

'Why? You can't answer questions about operational information within the force.'

'Precisely. I would have stopped her dead in her tracks and stuck to the subject about the killer. All that has been buried by politics. It's not gone far enough. We need a more in-depth interview, focusing solely on our victims.'

'So, apart from that, how was your first day back at work?'

Matilda looked over at the opposite sofa where Adele was sitting with her legs curled up beneath her. She smiled. 'It was good being back. It was lovely seeing Finn again, and Zofia's doing better than I could have expected. I've told Scott to keep an eye on the new bloke, Tom. I don't want him doing something silly and putting himself in danger like Zofia did.'

'Did you speak to Christian?'

'I did. I told him when he's ready to tell me the truth, I'll listen.'

'And will you?'

'Of course I will.'

'Good. And the hunt for this killer. Do you think you'll catch him?'

'There is no doubt in my mind I'll catch him,' she said firmly.

Adele's smiled dropped as she studied her friend.

'What?' Matilda asked.

'You've just said that you've asked Scott to keep an eye on this new bloke to stop him doing anything silly, anything risky. Who is going to keep an eye on you to stop you doing the same?'

'What do you mean?'

'In the past you've always had Christian and Sian as the voice of reason. Somehow, they've always managed to rein you in. Who's going to do that now?'

Matilda swallowed hard. Her mobile started vibrating on the coffee table. She looked at the display and saw it was the Chief Constable calling. She grabbed it, swiped to answer and left the room, thankful she wouldn't have to answer Adele's question.

Amy Hall was alone in her house in Greystones. It seemed strange there was no Tilly bounding about the house or the sound of music thumping from her bedroom. She watched the interview with the Chief Constable of South Yorkshire Police on the BBC News channel in silence curled up on the sofa. There was a full glass of wine on the coffee table in front of her, and an empty bottle next to it. Tears were streaming down her face as she watched the news. There was a vile, evil, depraved subhuman out there, and he'd got his talons into her only child.

She looked down at the three dogs, curled up on their beds. They were looking at her with large eyes. They knew something was wrong. They all missed Tilly and when Amy had come home earlier, she'd found all three of them on Tilly's bed.

Kit stood up, walked slowly over to the sofa and climbed on it, resting his head on Amy's lap.

'You miss her, don't you?' she asked, her words slightly slurred. 'She'll be home soon. I promise.'

She leaned back on the sofa, her hand on the dog, closed her eyes and cried.

***

Former Detective Sergeant Sian Robinson knew today was Matilda's first day back at work. She'd tried ringing her on three occasions, but each time, the line was engaged. She'd left a voicemail and sent a couple of text messages but guessed Matilda would be busy.

Since leaving the police force earlier this year, she'd taken to watching more news programmes, eager to keep up with what was happening. It was usually all about Covid or the fallout from leaving the EU. Her ears were pricked by the mention of South Yorkshire Police and three women being killed and a fourth with life-changing injuries. This must be the case Matilda was being brought back for.

She watched the interview with Chief Constable Ridley, and thought it went rather well, despite him getting flustered towards the end when the newsreader wouldn't drop the subject of the force being under special measures. Cow. She turned off the television and sat back. For the first time since leaving, she wished she was back among her colleagues investigating this obviously complex case.

The living room door opened and her only daughter, Belinda, came in, bringing with her a wave of strong perfume. She sat in the armchair opposite and began putting her shoes on.

'What are you doing?' Sian asked.

'I'm going out?'

'Who with?'

'Jen. I told you earlier I was going round tonight.'

'Have you not seen the news?'

'I've got a face mask for when I'm in the taxi and plenty of hand sanitiser.' She rolled her eyes.

'I'm not talking about that. There's a killer in Sheffield. He's killed three young women and left a fourth with life-changing injuries. Chief Constable Ridley's just been on the news telling women not to go out on their own.'

'I'm not going out. I'm going to Jen's.'

'You've got to get there, though. And come back.'

'I'm sending for an Uber,' she said, getting her phone out of her pocket and waving it at her mother.

'You're bloody not.'

'Mum. You can't stop me from going out.'

'I'll take you,' Sian said, standing up.

'I don't think so,' Belinda protested. 'I'm eighteen. I can take myself.'

'Three women have been murdered, Belinda. If you insist on going out, then I will take you. And I'll bring you back home, too.'

'This is stupid. It's five minutes in a taxi. Nothing's going to happen to me.'

'I bet all four of those women said exactly the same, too. I'll go and get my keys,' she said, leaving the room.

'You know something, Mum, you need to go back to being a detective. You weren't half as uptight as you are now,' Belinda sulked.

'I've got my own business, Bel. I'm a dog walker,' Sian called out.

'Yes. That'll get us out of this shithole and into a new house, won't it?' Belinda said under her breath.

'I heard that.'

The killer also watched the interview on the news in which the Chief Constable of South Yorkshire Police warned all women not to go out alone at night after dark. He almost laughed. There were warnings all over the country thanks to the Covid pandemic, telling people to stay apart, wear masks in shops and on public transport and not mix with anyone outside of their household, and nobody was taking a blind bit of notice. The Pitsmoor Hotel and The Staffordshire Arms had both lost their licence due to remaining open during the lockdown. People didn't seem to care, and that's why he was able to kill three women.

He was surprised his last victim had survived. He was convinced he'd done enough to kill her, but that jogger coming around the corner like that scared him. He'd taken a risk dumping her so close to some houses, but thought he'd be fine. He'd not make that mistake again.

He wondered if she'd be able to identify him. He never covered his face because his plan was always to kill his victims.

Fortunately, he was a very plain-looking man. There was nothing that stood out about his appearance. He doubted she'd be able to give the police much when she spoke to them. He wondered what life-changing injuries she'd suffered. Had she landed funny when he'd thrown her over the fence into the woods, and broken her spine? Maybe that was better than killing. His handiwork would be known for years to come, even when he was jailed or dead and buried. The mark of his crimes would be evident to the victim and their friends and family.

He lay back on his bed and closed his eyes and imagined a funeral in seventy years' time when his latest victim finally died of old age, peacefully in her bed. Friends at her wake would say how she'd lived a happy and full life, despite being violently raped and left paralysed when she was a schoolgirl. He'd be long dead by then, but his legend would be known. Wow. He could feel himself getting hard at that thought.

So, the women of Sheffield now knew there was a killer on the loose, targeting them as they walked alone in the dark. They'd be on the lookout for him now. They'd be second-guessing everything they saw and heard. But he was confident he would succeed. He was Mr Invisible, after all.

Chapter Fourteen

Friday 18th December 2020

On the journey into work, Matilda tried to broach the subject with Scott of his relationship with Donal, but Scott was talking about the Chief Constable's appearance on BBC News last night. He'd already phoned the station and asked for a progress report. They'd had many calls come in overnight and they were currently being sifted through. By the time Matilda found a gap in the conversation, they were turning into the car park. It would have to wait.

DC Tom Simpson was the last to arrive for the morning briefing. As soon as he'd parked his bike in the car park, he received a text message from Scott asking him to pop to Costa and get everyone a drink. He entered the Homicide and Major Crime Unit carrying a cardboard tray in each hand. He was dressed in a full leather biker suit and heavy boots. He said his good mornings, placed the drinks on the nearest table and said he was just popping to the changing rooms to get out of his leathers. As he turned, Matilda almost blushed. The leather suit was incredibly tight and snug around certain parts of Tom's anatomy.

'Sticky bun?' Zofia asked.

'I'm sorry?' Matilda asked, wide-eyed. She turned around to see Zofia behind her with a Tupperware tub on her lap.

'I made some sticky buns last night in the absence of Sian's snack drawer. They've got a toffee glaze.'

'Oh. I see. I thought you meant… Thank you,' she said, taking one. She could feel herself reddening with embarrassment. 'Shall we get started?' she said to the room.

She glanced over to Scott whose eyes were on the door as Tom left the room. Scott had a twinkle in his eye and a sweet smile on his lips. Was Tom the reason he was suddenly so distant in his relationship with Donal?

———

'I've been through all the initial forensic reports on the first three victims,' Scott began. 'And the reason there's little evidence is due to the fact they were left exposed to the elements. Even with the third victim, Dawn Richardson, she was found relatively quickly after she was killed, but it was pissing it down and blowing a gale. Our best bet is to concentrate on Tilly Hall.'

Matilda nodded. 'I agree.' She was sitting at the top of the room by the murder board, nursing her half-drunk Americano. 'However, I was talking to Adele yesterday and there are no hair samples left on Tilly or any of the bodies. With four women being raped, I'd expect at least one to have a foreign public hair. I'm wondering if the killer is shaving himself.'

'Maybe he has alopecia,' Tom said.

'Maybe. But I think it's more likely he's shaving himself. He knows what he has to do to evade capture through forensics, and he's doing it.'

'He's not that clever, though, as he's left semen samples for us to trace,' Zofia added.

'Yes. But until we can match them, they're not much use. He'll make sure he'll stay off our radar.' Matilda said. 'We don't even know if the semen samples will be any good yet until we get the results back.'

'I'm still going through ANPR and CCTV,' Zofia said. 'All attacks took place around evening rush hour so there's a lot of traffic about. I'm hoping I can find the same vehicle at least twice so we have a starting point, but it's not going to be a quick result.'

'That's fine. Thank you, Zofia.'

'I was also thinking maybe we should issue a press release asking if anyone in the vicinity had dashcams recording. They could send us the footage and we can sift through it.'

'Good thinking. I'll get onto Ridley. He's handling everything press-related,' Matilda said, making a note.

'I'm about eighty percent done with all known sex offenders. So far, their alibis check out,' Finn said. 'I think we might be dealing with a new kid on the block.'

'But why has he started now and why so intensively so quickly?' Scott asked. 'Four attacks in less than two months. That's a huge change in someone's personality.'

'I was thinking about this last night,' Finn said. He took a swig from his cardboard cup of tea. 'If this bloke isn't on our radar, and he's just suddenly taken it upon himself to become this prolific rapist, then something huge has happened in his life to make him begin. What that is, we don't know, but someone else will, and hopefully they'll come forward now this story is out in the public domain.'

'What kind of huge thing, though?' Zofia asked, pen poised over her notebook as always.

Finn took a deep breath as he thought. 'I don't know. Maybe a trauma of some kind. Maybe he was publicly dumped or humiliated by his wife or partner. Maybe his boss is female, or a female colleague rejected his advances and it spread through the company and he feels spurned. Something has happened, recently, that's made him suddenly hate women.'

'I'm sorry, but people get dumped all the time,' Zofia said. 'They don't suddenly decide to take revenge on all womankind and go on a killing spree. I don't think there's any deep psychological reasoning behind it at all. The bloke is sick. End of.' She was clearly upset by the investigation.

'Finn isn't making an excuse for him, Zofia,' Matilda said. 'He's trying to see it from his point of view'

'No. I know that. It's just … that's exactly what he'll do when we catch him and interview him. He'll try to rationalise it.'

'Yes, he will. Be we don't let him.'

'You're right. I'm sorry. Sorry, Finn.'

Finn smiled at her. 'I think he will have always had some kind of a strange relationship with women, whether it's a fixation, or an obsession with a particular woman, someone unobtainable. I wouldn't be surprised if he hasn't been cautioned at some point in the past for stalking or pestering a woman. But something has been triggered that's tipped him over the edge into this violent person he's become.'

'We need to make an appeal directly to the public to get them to come forward and identify anyone who has changed recently,' Scott said. 'Like Finn said, if there has been a big trauma in this bloke's life, someone else will know about it. You don't kill three women in the space of two months and not be affected by it. Someone will have seen a change.'

Matilda nodded. 'I'll be having a chat with the Chief Constable in a while. I'll see how he wants to play it.'

'Could I mention something?' Tom asked, half-raising his hand.

Matilda smiled. His naïveté at being the new boy was endearing. There was something about his boyish charm she was drawn to. 'Go ahead.'

'I spoke to Ryan Cook's mother over the phone late yesterday evening. She'd tested positive for Covid but doesn't feel particularly unwell. She put the phone on speaker, and I was able to ask Ryan a few questions about his relationship with Tilly. He said they dated for about six months, but he was warned off. However, they still kept seeing each other, but in secret.'

'Who warned him off?'

'He was very reluctant to say but I managed to worm it out of him. It was Tilly's mum.'

'Amy?' Matilda asked, incredulously.

'Yes. She objected because of the age difference.'

'What is the age difference?'

'About two and a half years.'

'It's hardly a huge gap.'

'Ryan will be seventeen at Easter and Tilly will still be fourteen then. According to Ryan, Amy said some harsh things to Tilly.'

'Right. What's Ryan's alibi for the night Tilly was attacked? Was he isolating then?'

'No. He was at school that day. When he got home, his mum was there and said she'd tested positive.'

'I think I'd better introduce myself to Amy and find out what's happened,' Matilda said. 'Is there any news from the hospital? Is Tilly conscious, do we know?'

'She is, but according to her doctor, her vocal cords are damaged beyond repair. She'll never talk again,' Scott said.

'Ah. Poor girl. Unfortunately, she's going to have to answer our questions somehow. I'll pop along and see her after the weekend; give her a few days to come round. In the meantime, we need to concentrate our efforts on witnesses, and tracing a vehicle. We need to be fast, yet methodical. I will not allow him to claim another victim.'

Chapter Fifteen

'Did you see the interview last night?' Ridley said as Matilda entered his office.

'I did. She certainly questioned you about the special measures.'

'I know. I tried to keep getting the topic back onto the murders, but she wouldn't let it go.'

'Sir,' Matilda began, sitting down in the overly comfortable leather chair. 'As valuable as I'm sure the interview was last night, I don't believe it went far enough. This killer is highly intelligent and he's doing everything in his power to stay off our radar, and he's succeeding. It's my belief he'll kill again, and very soon. Tilly Hall was a failure because she survived. He's going to want to make up for his mistake. His next victim is going to suffer before he kills her. We haven't a clue who he is, but someone out there does. They'll have seen a change in his demeanour over the past couple of months, and they need to come forward and tell us.'

Ridley sat back in his chair. He thought for a moment. 'Maybe we could put something in the national papers.'

Matilda bit the inside of her mouth. She could taste blood. 'I was thinking … what if … what if *I* were to be interviewed?'

'You? You hate the media. Look at how that Danny Hanson has treated you over the years.'

'I'm aware. But I'm not doing this for me. I'm doing this to stop some other poor young woman suffering. If I, as a detective, sit down with a journalist, and talk solely about the killings and the type of killer we're looking for, that should result in a detailed feature we can use to alert the public on what to look for.'

Ridley leaned forward on his desk, interlocking his fingers. 'No offence, Matilda, but I know the media. They're looking for something punchy and visual to grab their audience.'

'Then that's what we'll give them. We line up photos of all four victims. We show them how happy their lives were. We describe, in detail, how they've been destroyed.'

'The timing is all wrong. The media do not want to be filling their pages with horror in the run-up to Christmas in the middle of a pandemic.'

'Oh, I'm so sorry,' Matilda said, sarcasm in her voice. 'Maybe we can ask the killer to hang on until the spring before he kills again. Or maybe next October and his next victim can tie-in with the next *Halloween* film that's due to come out.'

'There's no need for flippancy.'

'I don't care about the timing,' Matilda said, raising her voice. 'This man has attacked four times in less than two months. He's killed three times. He's going to do it again. You've asked me back to help solve this and this is the direction I want to take.'

Ridley closed his eyes and let out a sigh. 'South Yorkshire Police cannot afford any more media scrutiny.'

'In that case, we'll forget all about it and let the bodies pile up,' she said, getting up and headed for the door. 'Four in two months, sir,' she reminded him harshly. 'He'll kill again before the new year, and he'll grow in confidence, too. Soon, it won't be long before killing isn't enough and he'll start flaunting his success. If we don't get the media involved, he will. Then you'll have the newspapers and TV crews from all over the world camped outside this building asking why you have more than a dozen dead women and not a single suspect.' She pulled open the door. 'Why ask me back if you won't allow me to do this my way?' She left the office and slammed the door hard behind her.

Chapter Sixteen

Saturday 19th December 2020

Matilda didn't sleep well last night. When she woke, her duvet was half hanging off the bed, one pillow was on the floor and the fitted sheet had come away from the mattress on two corners. She could never remember what her dreams were about, which was a good thing. They were frequently dark and disturbing. She was always glad when she woke with an empty mind.

She trundled down the stairs, tying her dressing gown tightly around her waist. She took in the tall Christmas tree in the corner of the hallway and glared at it blankly. There was less than a week until the big day and she didn't feel at all Christmassy yet.

In the kitchen, she flicked on the coffee machine and inserted the strongest pod she had left. While it was brewing, she pulled back the curtains and looked out at the expanse of back garden. It was lifeless, as Sheffield was in the midst of a harsh winter.

The temperature had been hovering around zero degrees for the past week and night-time temperatures plunged well below freezing. The ground was covered in a harsh frost. It looked so cold out there. Matilda shivered beneath her dressing gown.

'Do you think there'll be a white Christmas this year?' Adele asked.

Matilda jumped. She was in a world of her own, looking out at the barren landscape, and hadn't heard Adele coming into the kitchen.

'I don't know. It would be nice if it were.'

'And by a white Christmas, I mean a proper one with deep snow and blizzards, not just a few flakes on the roof of the Met Office. Is that coffee for me?'

'No, it bloody isn't. It's the last number thirteen left. It's mine.'

Matilda went over to the coffee machine and took the cup from the tray. She inhaled the dark liquid and could almost feel it working its magic and waking her up, body and mind.

'Speaking of Christmas,' Adele began. 'Have you made up your mind what we're doing yet?'

Matilda rolled her eyes. 'It all depends on what that buffoon who's running the country allows us to do. Is it two or three families who are allowed to mix? If it's two, we're buggered. If it's three … well, we're still buggered.'

'Well, it's me and you. Harriet and the boys. Your mum. That's three households.'

'I really want Pat Campbell to come,' Matilda said. 'Her son's in Manchester and will be working over Christmas. Her daughter's in Scotland. It's her first Christmas without Anton. She shouldn't be alone.'

'But that's four houses mixing. If you weren't back at the

police, I'd say screw it, but you don't want the press getting a whiff of you breaking any Covid rules.'

'I know,' Matilda sighed. 'Although my mum is at Harriet's almost every day. They're practically one household.'

'You're not thinking of breaking the rules, are you, DCI Darke?' Adele teased.

'Maybe just bending them slightly.' Matilda smiled.

'Are you working today?' Adele asked.

'No. There's not much I can do at the moment until Zofia has tracked down all the vehicles from ANPR and CCTV. And Tilly isn't up to being interviewed yet. What about you?'

'I'm afraid so. ' Adele glimpsed the time on the microwave. 'I'd better make a move, actually.' She swigged back what was left of her coffee. 'Quick shower then I'll be off. Do you want me to give you a lift anywhere?'

'No, thanks.'

Adele left Matilda alone in the kitchen. She turned to look back out at the cold landscape. It was the perfect weather to light the fire and curl up on the sofa with a coffee and a good book, but Matilda knew her mind would wander, and it wouldn't be long before she thought back to the silent phone calls and the taunting cards she'd had delivered. It had been several weeks since the last one. They'd stopped as suddenly as they'd started, and that worried her more than actually receiving them.

'Screw it,' she said to herself. She threw her cup into the dishwasher then ran upstairs two at a time to get ready. She knew just where to go and who to visit to take her mind off things.

Dressed in layers, scarf, gloves, two pairs of socks and a bobble hat pulled down around her ears, Matilda entered Millhouses Park. She passed the grey Vauxhall Vivaro with Donnie Barko written on the side. There were very few people around, not surprising considering it was so bloody cold, just a few hardy joggers and dog walkers. She walked slowly along the River Sheaf towards the Sensory Garden and then saw the exact person she expected to see. She smiled.

Sian Robinson was being walked by four dogs on leads – a Yorkshire Terrier, a spaniel of some variety, an excitable German Shepherd puppy and another of indeterminate breed. All of varying age and size and all wanting to go in their own direction. Sian had lost all control of them.

Matilda stood with her arms folded and a grin on her face.

'Are you laughing at me?' Sian asked as she came closer.

'Would I?'

'Yes, you bloody would.'

'Sorry.' Matilda laughed. 'Would you like me to take one off you?'

'You can take two. Here.' She handed her the leads of the Yorkshire Terrier and the German Shepherd. 'Meet Rolo and Charlie. Now, Charlie may look like a German Shepherd, but I actually think he's part Velociraptor.'

'Can't you just put the Yorkshire Terrier on the back of Charlie and let him carry it?'

'It's not it, he's a boy. And, no, you can't.'

They set off walking. The Yorkie was no trouble. He only had tiny legs which were almost blurred as he tried to keep up with Matilda. Charlie, on the other hand, seemed to be on full alert. Anything that caught his eye, he wanted to dart off in that direction. Matilda struggled to keep him under control.

'So, how's the dog walking business doing?'

'Not good, actually,' Sian said. 'Cases of Covid are on the increase so people are working from home again. They're taking their own dogs out. This is my only shift today. Usually, I'm back and forth all day.'

'What are you going to do?'

'I've no idea. I've had to let that house I was going to buy go, as mine didn't sell for as much as I hoped. You'd think with all those true-crime dramas and podcasts being so popular, people would be queuing up to buy the house where a serial killer lived.'

Matilda half-smiled. 'Aren't there any others you like?'

'There are plenty I like, if I was buying just for me. But I've got four kids that need a room, too. Do you have any idea how much a five-bedroom house costs in Sheffield? It's so bloody expensive here. God knows why. Have you been into town lately? It's virtually empty.'

'Sian, will you—'

'No,' Sian interrupted. 'I appreciate the offer, but no. I'm not going to let you buy me a house.'

'I wasn't going to say that.'

'Oh. Sorry.'

'No. I was going to say I'll lend you however much you're short by. Call it a loan or an investment. When you come to sell in however many years' time, you can give it me back then.'

Sian seemed to think for a moment. 'No. Thank you, Matilda, but I wouldn't feel right borrowing money from a friend.'

'It's not like I won't be getting it back. I'm guessing once all your kids have left home, you'll downsize. You can return the money then.'

She frowned as the thought. 'Thank you. Let me think about it.'

'Okay.'

'So, how does it feel being back at work?'

'Like I've never left.'

'Is that good?'

'It is, actually.' She smiled.

'I saw the interview with Ridley on the news. He's aged in the last few months.'

Matilda laughed. 'I don't think he's enjoying all the meetings and scrutiny with the Home Office.'

'How's the case going? Three murders in less than two months. That's certainly a committed killer.'

'I know. He knows his stuff, too. He's leaving nothing at the crime scenes. There's no forensics at all. No eyewitnesses, nothing.'

'What about this fourth victim? Can't she tell you anything?'

'She's had her vocal cords cut. She won't be talking ever again.'

'Bloody hell.'

'It's going to be a long process getting information out of her.'

'You've got a good team around you, you'll be fine,' Sian said, looking at Matilda out of the corner of her eye. 'Speaking of which, I had a call from Christian last night.'

'Oh.' Charlie the German Shepherd squatted. 'You can pick that up.' Matilda smiled.

'Do you want to know what he said?' Sian asked while she scooped Charlie's poop.

'Who?'

'Christian.'

'I can guess.'

'You honestly think he's capable of shooting someone?'

'He was angry. The case brought back memories he thought were long since buried.'

'Christian is a dedicated detective. He wouldn't jeopardise everything he's worked for like that.'

Matilda stopped in her tracks. 'Sian, from where you were standing, you could see who was holding the gun.'

'Yes. And I told you, it was Jamie.'

'But he killed himself in the remand centre at the earliest possibility. He could easily have turned the gun on himself right there at Magnolia House, but he didn't. Why? Because he wasn't holding the gun in the first place.'

'I'm not lying to you, Matilda.'

'I'm not saying you are. Look, here, take these, I need to go,' she said, handing Sian back the dog leads.

'Oh. I was going to treat us to a coffee.'

'I've got some Christmas shopping to do.'

'Matilda …'

'I'll call you in the week.'

Matilda turned and walked away, her hands plunged into her pockets and her head down. She'd known Sian for more than twenty years and assumed they were close, that there was nothing secret between them, but Sian was keeping the truth from her about what really happened back in March at Magnolia House. She couldn't blame her. Sian and Christian had been through a great deal together. During the shooting in January 2019, when so many of their colleagues had died, they'd helped each other in the investigation and immediate aftermath. They'd grown closer. It's only right Sian would stand by him at any cost. It left Matilda in an awkward position where she didn't know who she could trust to be close to any more.

Chapter Seventeen

Adele Kean arrived at work all set to make decent headway with the reports she had to file and those sodding chapters her publishers was hounding her for, when she was waylaid by a telephone call that knocked her sideways. When it was finished, she closed her office door, slumped in her seat and cried.

'Adele, is everything all right?'

She looked up to find pathologist Simon Browes standing in the doorway. She hadn't even heard him come in.

'Simon. What are you doing here?' she asked, quickly wiping her eyes.

'I'm covering this weekend. It's in the book.'

'Is it? I thought I was.' She looked at the rota in the open diary beneath a mound of unorganised paperwork. 'Oh, yes, it is.'

'Is everything all right?'

'Yes. Fine. I'll get out of your way.' She grabbed a folder and stood up to leave. Simon stood in the way.

'What's wrong?'

'Nothing.'

'You're crying.'

She let out a heavy sigh. 'I've just had a phone call from Ben Maltravers.'

'Who's he?'

'Lucy Dauman's fiancé. It's been a year since she went missing,' Adele said, pushing past Simon and out into the main autopsy suite.

Lucy Dauman had been Adele's technical assistant. She spent the majority of 2019 preparing for her dream wedding and three weeks before the big day, she disappeared. Her car was found abandoned less than a week later, but there was no sign of Lucy. Her phone was turned off not long after she left work on the last day she was seen, and her bank account and credit cards hadn't been used. A year later, and there was still no news of her whereabouts.

Simon followed Adele out into the suite. 'I can't believe it's been a whole year.'

'No. I have to admit, I haven't thought about her much, lately. I've been so busy. I feel awful.'

'You can't blame yourself, Adele.' He reached out to place a comforting hand on her shoulder and thought better of it.

'I should be doing more. I know people in the police. I should be pressuring them to keep looking for her.'

'I'm sure they are.'

The double doors crashed open, and a gurney was wheeled in by two assistants. Another one instantly followed. Two more victims of the Covid pandemic, Adele presumed. She turned away and went back into her office. Simon followed. He was a tall man in his late forties with receding sandy hair and light blue eyes. He was permanently stubbled, and the gossip mill was in full flow following the disappearance of his wedding ring since the early summer.

'Adele, I know I'm not the most approachable of blokes, but if you ever want to talk, I'm always here for you.'

'Thanks,' she said over her shoulder.

'Things are really busy right now, aren't they? I can always come and do a few extra shifts if you want to take some time off over Christmas.'

She turned to look at him. 'Won't you be with your family at Christmas?'

He held up his left hand. 'Me and the wife split up in June.'

'Oh. I'm sorry,' she said, though she wasn't totally surprised.

'My fault. I'm never at home.'

'This job tends to put a dampener on the personal life, doesn't it?'

'Only if you allow it to. And I'm afraid I did. Why don't you take a few extra days off over Christmas? I can cover the fort here.'

'Are you sure?'

'I wouldn't have offered otherwise. You can catch up on the revisions for the book, too.'

'Don't remind me. I haven't even started them yet. How are you getting on with yours?'

'All done and back with the publisher.'

'I should dislike you,' she said, punching him lightly on the arm.

'Oh, I hope you don't mind, but I was looking on the database this morning at those three rapes and murders South Yorkshire Police are investigating. You've sent some samples off for Y-STR testing.'

'That's right.'

'I'm sure you're aware, but I doubt DCI Darke is, Y-STR cannot be used with familial DNA and you can't search Y-STR profiles on the National DNA Database.'

'Can't you?'

'No. It's also a very expensive test to run. We're talking nearly three grand per sample. And you're planning on sending four off and you won't be able to do anything with the results. I've held them back in case you want to run it by DCI Darke first.'

Adele's eyes darted left to right as she thought. 'I hadn't realised we couldn't run the profiles through the database.'

'They'll only be useful once the police have a suspect in custody and they've taken his DNA for testing. Even then, with other evidence, they may not need the Y-STR profile.'

'I see,' she said, uncertainly. She should have known all this herself. She frowned. It wasn't the first lapse of concentration she'd noticed. She was taking on far too much work. 'Thanks, Simon.'

At six foot tall, he loomed over Adele. He looked down at her and tilted his head to one side. 'Is everything all right with you, Adele?'

'Yes. Fine. Just busy.' She turned to look at her office. She couldn't even see the wood of the desk under the number of files and textbooks.

'I'll help you in any way I can,' he said, softly.

She grabbed the file of her notes for the book she and Simon were working on and picked up her bag. She made to leave the office, but Simon was in the way.

'Thank you,' she said again.

He placed his right hand on Adele's left shoulder. 'I think a lot about you, Adele.'

'Really?' she asked, wide-eyed.

'Yes.'

She swallowed hard. 'I really should be going. I need to pick Matilda up and I'm already running late.' She avoided eye contact with him, squeezed past him and ran out of the suite.

Chapter Eighteen

The shortest day of the year was only a couple of days away and by four o'clock it was already dark. It was the final weekend before Christmas and people were in a world of their own as they hurried to get the last of the presents they needed. They didn't take any notice of the people next to them in the queue at the counter or walking past them as they left and entered shops. Everyone was wrapped up against the freezing cold and wearing face masks. Suddenly, everyone was anonymous.

The killer was in the main car park at Meadowhall, parked at the back, watching as a sea of shoppers came out of the vast shopping centre. He never went here to shop. He hated the place. It was too busy, too noisy. He felt claustrophobic just looking at the building. But here, in the safety of his van, in the darkness, sunk down low in the driver's seat, he watched and waited for a lone female to stand out among the rest.

He'd know her straightaway.

When he'd found Tilly, she was among almost a dozen girls as they left school and headed for home. He'd watched as she walked with her friends to the end of the pavement, laughed and joked, crossed the zebra crossing, then they split up. Tilly put her earbuds in, selected something to listen to on her phone, then, with her head down, she aimed for home. She was alone. The timing was perfect.

He watched as women came and went. The majority were on their own, carrying armfuls of bags. They looked harassed, troubled by the approaching festivities and the long list of things to get ready, as well as the worry of the pandemic and if they'd be able to have the family Christmas they were used to. He could have snatched any number of them, but he didn't even consider leaving his van. None of them were suitable.

That was the problem. He didn't know what type of woman he was looking for until his eyes landed on her. Then, something seemed to switch on in his mind and he had to have her.

A woman came towards his van, struggling under the weight of her shopping. She had a large M&S bag in one hand and, in the other, two bulging bags from Waterstones and HMV. She had dyed blonde hair, though the roots were in urgent need of touching up. She wore a long padded coat, buttoned up to the neck, and a thick knitted scarf wrapped around her. He couldn't tell if she was thin or fat beneath the layers, not that it mattered.

She stopped at the car parked next to his van and struggled to rummage in her pockets for her car keys while holding the heavy bags.

The car park was ill lit. There was nobody around. He could easily grab her, put a hand over her mouth, drag her into his van, drive off to nearby wasteland and slice her throat open. He loved to see the blood flow, especially at night, in the dark, when the thick liquid ran almost black.

He watched her closely. She opened the boot of the car and placed the bags inside. She had to move other things around to make them all fit. It was a very untidy boot. She had pale skin and thin lips. She loosened the scarf around her neck, and he saw she was actually quite slim beneath the layers of clothing. Her neck was slim, anyway. It was long and he could see her windpipe. A sharp blade would slice through that like a hot knife through butter. The warm blood, the fear emanating from the victim, the screams in his ear. It was orgasmic just thinking about it.

He couldn't take his eyes off the woman. She had wrinkles around her eyes, so he guessed she was in her forties. That made her older than all the others, but it didn't matter. It would certainly fox the police. And that was something else he needed to keep in mind when choosing his next victim.

He took off his seatbelt. She was perfect. He wanted to kill her while screwing her. He wanted to feel her warm blood spurt out and hit him in the face. He wanted to taste her blood, lick it up like a cat.

He opened the van door.

The woman's mobile rang. She fished for it in her coat pocket and swiped to answer.

'Hello, you,' she said, a hint of a smile in her voice. 'Yes, I got it. No. I'm in the car park now.' She slammed the boot closed and went around to the driver's door. 'I'll be home in about twenty minutes. Do you want me to pick something up on the way?' She opened the door, climbed in and slammed it behind her.

A lost opportunity. Oh, well, never mind.

He closed his van door and watched as the woman reversed out of the parking space, chatting away to whoever was on the other end of the phone. She had no idea, but she was the luckiest person alive right now as she'd been within seconds of being murdered.

He didn't have long to wait for his next possible victim. Her heard her before he actually saw her. A young woman, tight short skirt, black leather jacket, long black hair, heavily made-up eyes, impossibly high-heeled shoes and bare legs, trotted out of Meadowhall and walked with purpose, talking loudly on her phone. He lowered the window of his van a crack.

'...really, how convenient,' she said. She sounded angry, annoyed. 'Twenty minutes I've been sat waiting for you looking like a complete tit ... Well, maybe I just might forget I've got a boyfriend when I'm at work and Dieter asks me out again ... Do you know something, I can hear your excuses before they even come out of your mouth. Let me know when you're ready to act like an adult.' She ended the call and stuffed the mobile back in her pocket.

She slowed down as she reached the rows of cars and rummaged in her handbag, presumably for her keys. There was nobody else around. It was now or never.

The killer opened his van and jumped out, closing the door soundlessly behind him. He headed for her with determined strides. He was excited, almost salivating at the prospect of seeing the horror etched on her face when he grabbed her, spun her around and she saw her gaze reflected back at her through the steel of the knife. It was so quiet, he wondered if he could kill her right here in the car park, in the full view of hundreds of unsuspecting shoppers.

He drew closer, close enough to smell her scent. It was sweet, delicate, unobtrusive. He pictured her spraying it on her neck, the mist from the bottle lightly dusting the perfect skin. He wanted to lick it, to lick her. He wanted to taste that fragrance, to bite her, to draw blood, to listen to her cry, beg, plead, scream as he sank his teeth into her.

She stopped at a blue Ford Ka and deactivated the alarm on the car. He gained speed.

'Excuse me, love.'

The killer hadn't realised there was someone else nearby. He'd taken the odd glance but had been too preoccupied with his fantasy.

She turned to see who was calling her.

'You left your hat and scarf in the coffee shop,' the man said, holding them out for the woman.

'Oh,' she said. 'I didn't realise.'

'You did seem to leave in a hurry.'

'Yes. I had … I had an urgent phone call. Thank you so much. I really appreciate it.'

'You're welcome.'

Sheltered from view by a Land Rover, he listened as she started the engine and drove away. Another one he'd let slip through his fingers.

That was a close call. He needed to be more vigilant about his surroundings and not let his fantasies intrude until he'd successfully claimed a victim. He must always be alert.

'It's obviously not my night, tonight,' he said to himself as he went back to his van, head down, hands plunged into his pockets.

Chapter Nineteen

Sunday 20th December 2020

The Homicide and Major Crime Unit suite was empty apart from DC Zofia Nowak at her desk. She wasn't scheduled to work today, but the task she was undertaking was so vast she decided to come in to get on top of it.

She had two computer screens in front of her, both of them on and showing grainy CCTV footage of various crime scenes. She leaned forward, studying them intently, noting down car registration numbers. Occasionally, she sat back and looked out of the window to give her eyes something else to focus on. It was an important yet laborious task.

After an hour, she decided to have a break and wheeled herself over to the drinks station. She flicked the new kettle on and waited for it to boil. She looked around and smiled. It was good to be back working in an elite unit once again. There was a time, during her recovery, she doubted she would return to work at all. Zofia knew she was in a fortunate position and had many people to thank – her parents for constantly pushing her when she felt like giving up, her few friends, and Matilda, for giving such a sizeable donation to enable her to live in an adapted bungalow and regain her independence. She had no idea how she'd be ever able to thank her but would make sure her presence on the team was a valuable one.

That's partly why she had decided to come in on a Sunday. She wanted to show her appreciation to Matilda and would work round the clock if it was necessary. Being at work also stopped her mother from constantly phoning, calling round and checking she was all right. Despite the many times Zofia had told her she could do everything she could do before apart from walk, her mother insisted on trying to take over her life. She even offered to buy the bungalow next door, but thankfully her father managed to dissuade her. Her heart was in the right place, but Zofia often felt suffocated out of work, which is why she liked to spend as much time at the station as possible. She wasn't given preferential treatment (apart from a height-adjustable desk) and as far as Scott, Finn and everyone else was concerned, she was the same old Zofia, but now she came with wheels.

She took her tea back to her desk and had almost exhausted all the footage from the roads surrounding the Cholera Monument when the doors to the suite opened and DC Tom Simpson entered wearing tight jeans and a hooded sweater and carrying a takeaway coffee.

'What are you doing here?' Zofia asked.

'I could ask you the same thing,' he said.

'There are more of these registration numbers to check up than I originally thought. I spent all day yesterday worrying about them so thought I'd come in today and try to catch up. What's your reason for earning extra Brownie points?'

'Same thing as you really. I saw how much footage you had

to go through yesterday, so I thought I'd pop in and see if I could make some headway.' He sat at his desk and booted up his computer.

Zofia watched as Tom began to work, his fingers flying over the keys of the keyboard, leaning forward to read the screen, then back to the keyboard.

'Have you come on your bike this morning?'

'No. It's being serviced. I borrowed my brother's van.'

'Oh,' she continued, watching him. 'What's it like, riding a bike?' Zofia asked.

Tom turned to look at her. 'Exhilarating,' he said with a smile.

'Really?'

'Absolutely. There's nothing else like it in the world. You feel so free on a bike rather than in a car. You can zip in and out of traffic, and when you leave the city and you're in open countryside, well, you just let rip and away you go.'

'Sounds amazing,' she said. There was a hint of sadness in her voice, and she quickly turned back to her computer.

An hour later, Zofia looked up.

'I think I've found something. Tom, come and have a look at this, let me run it by you and you can tell me my imagination isn't working overtime.'

Tom scooched over to Zofia's desk on his chair.

'We had a phone call yesterday from a woman who lives around the corner from Brincliffe Edge Road where Tilly was found, and who has a doorbell camera. She offered to send us the footage and it was emailed to me. Now, at 4:55pm, a jogger passes the house on Brincliffe Edge Close. Look.'

The footage was in black and white, but crisp and clear. A slim male jogger, dressed in all the right gear with a weighted backpack over his shoulders, ran past the house. Less than two minutes later, he came back, but running much faster.

'Now, that's the same man, isn't it?' Zofia asked.

'I'd say so.'

'So, why turn around and come back less than two minutes after passing?'

'Maybe he'd reached the end of his route and was turning back.' Tom shrugged.

'I thought that at first, but it makes no sense. This house with the doorbell camera is right on the turning with Brincliffe Edge Road. He'll have turned into the road, run a few metres or so, then turned back. Why would the end of his route be the middle of the road?'

'Well, it wouldn't, would it?'

'Exactly. I think, he turned into Brincliffe Edge Road, saw the killer with Tilly, panicked, and ran back.'

'You think?'

'As he's going back past the house on the Close, he's running much faster. He's scared by what he's seen.'

Tom thought for a moment. 'Have we received any calls from members of the public saying they saw something?'

'No.'

'So, how do we identify him then?'

'I've followed him,' Zofia said with a smile. She brought up a map of the area. 'Using CCTV footage and a couple of ANPR cameras in the area I've been able to pick up our mystery jogger. Fortunately, Brincliffe Edge Close is a cul-de-sac so he has to cross a narrow track onto Brentwood Road. He's picked up here by camera from Brentwood Tennis Club.' Zofia played the footage of the jogger hurtling along the dark road. 'He then turns left into Union Road, right into Chelsea Road and this camera here picks him up going into a house. We have to zoom in on a camera on Adelaide Road to pick him up, and it's very grainy, but I'm pretty sure we'll be able to figure out which house it is.'

Tom leaned back in his chair. There was a smile on his face. 'Wow. I'm impressed.'

'Thank you,' Zofia said, beaming.

'I would never have thought of doing that.'

'Once I realised my days of chasing criminals on foot were over, I began to look more into how to use technology and camera footage. I've got a map somewhere that points out every single CCTV camera in Sheffield.'

'This is amazing. You've got us our first witness.'

'Potentially.'

'Definitely, I'd say. Shall I go along to Chelsea Road and try and find him?'

'No. We need to run all this by DCI Darke first.'

'You're right. Well, I think you deserve a break. How about I go out and get us a couple of bacon butties?'

'Erm … do you mind if I ask you a really big favour?'

'No.'

'You can say no if you want to, I won't take offence.'

'What's the favour?'

'When you get your bike back, will you take me for a ride on it?'

He looked at her and smiled. 'I'll have it back by this afternoon. What are you doing this evening?'

'Seriously?' she asked, her eyes wide with excitement.

'I'll take you out into Derbyshire. You'll love it.'

He grabbed his keys and left the suite leaving Zofia behind on her own. She couldn't stop smiling. She was so happy.

Chapter Twenty

Monday 21st December 2020

'Mrs Hall?' Matilda asked. Amy was sitting in the family room all on her own. She looked lost, deep in thought, fear and uncertainty etched on her pale face.

Amy looked up at her name being called. She quickly dried her tears then ran her fingers through her dry hair.

'I'm Detective Chief Inspector Matilda Darke from South Yorkshire Police. Is everything all right?' Matilda asked, entering the room fully and closing the door behind her.

Amy sniffled, wiped her nose and stood up, moving over to the window. 'I just can't stop crying. Just when I think I'm managing to hold it all together, I start crying again.'

'That's perfectly understandable.'

'I'm trying to be brave in front of Tilly, but it's so hard. She looks so …' Her words were lost as she wiped her eyes and blew her nose.

'Are you here on your own?'

Amy nodded. 'I don't have any brothers and sisters. My parents are both dead. It's just me and Tilly.'

'Aren't there any friends you'd like to have with you?'

'Nobody close.' She gave a sad smile. 'A couple from work have offered to sit with me, but I prefer to be on my own for now.'

'What do you do?'

'I'm a deputy head teacher,' she said, wiping her eyes hard with a tissue and composing herself. 'Not at Tilly's school. It's a primary school. Tilly would have hated us being at the same school,' she said with a hint of a chuckle in her throat.

Matilda sat down opposite her. 'Is Tilly's dad not around?'

'No. He died when Tilly was four. It was an accident at work.'

'I'm so sorry.'

'Thank you. It was a long time ago. You learn to adapt.'

Matilda smiled. 'How is Tilly doing?'

There was a hint of brightness in Amy's eyes, momentarily. 'She's awake. She's off the ventilator and breathing for herself.' The tears returned. 'She's … so withdrawn. She won't even look at me.'

'I'd like to see her; ask her a few questions.'

'She can't talk. The doctor said her vocal cords …'

'I know,' Matilda interrupted, seeing the reality of Tilly's injuries was too much for Amy to comprehend. 'We can work around it. Amy, I'm not going to lie to you. There is a man out there raping and murdering young women. He's killed three and very nearly killed Tilly. The problem is, he's incredibly clever and we have no forensic information to go on. Your daughter is my only hope in trying to catch him.'

Amy looked at Matilda, took a deep breath and swallowed hard. She nodded. 'I'll take you through.'

Matilda wanted to bring up Ryan Cook, but now was not the time. Amy needed to be more lucid and right now she looked like she could shatter into a thousand pieces.

———

The single room where Tilly Hall was recovering was small and dark, lit only by a lamp on the bedside locker. Tilly was sitting up, a hardback book on the slanted table in front of her. Her right arm was in a cast, her throat heavily bandaged. She had a black eye and a few grazes and cuts to her face. At the sound of the door opening, Tilly turned to see her visitors. The movement seemed to cause her pain as she winced. Her face was pale. There was no emotion upon seeing her mum.

'Tilly,' Amy began. She sat beside her and took her daughter's hand. 'This woman is with the police. She needs to ask you some questions. Are you up to it?'

Reluctantly, Tilly nodded.

Matilda entered the room and closed the door behind her. She looked around at the cards and teddy bears she'd been sent. Tilly was obviously a very popular girl.

'Hello, Tilly. I'm Detective Chief Inspector Matilda Darke,' she said in her best soft voice. She went over to a chair at the bottom of the bed and sat down. 'I used to get called Tilly a lot as a child, too. It was my dad's nickname for me for years.' She smiled.

'Tilly's name is short for Clothilde,' Amy said. 'It was my mother's name. Tilly doesn't like it though. That's why we shortened it.'

'Oh. I like it.' She turned to Tilly. 'I know the extent of your injuries and that you're unable to talk. I really am so sorry. I promise you that I'll do everything I can to find the man who did this.'

Tilly began to cry. She reached for a tissue from the locker, but the box was empty. Amy rummaged around in her bag again and pulled out a small packet for her.

Matilda's eyes flitted around the room. They landed on the book. 'What are you reading?' She asked. She didn't want to go straight into the attack. She could see how distressed and fragile Tilly was and wanted to get her onside, win over her trust.

'*Planet Earth*,' Amy said.

Tilly held up two fingers.

'*Planet Earth II*,' Amy corrected herself. 'She loves those David Attenborough documentaries.'

'So do I,' Matilda said with a smile. 'Is *Planet Earth II* the one where those snakes ran after those tiny lizards?'

Tilly nodded. There was a hint of a smile on her lips.

'That scared the living daylights out of me. I had to watch it behind a cushion. Those poor lizards. And – where was it –I think it was Australia where those little sea turtles hatched and went the wrong way from the ocean because they were distracted by the bright lights of the nearby town. Am I remembering that right?'

Tilly nodded. Her face had lit up.

'Poor things. I do enjoy those nature documentaries, though. It's interesting seeing different parts of the world, how different cultures and animals interact. I like the ones in the Arctic best. I love polar bears.'

Tilly nodded.

'It's Tilly's ambition to go to the North Pole someday. She'd love to see the Northern Lights, too.'

'That's definitely a trip on my bucket list, as well. It looks so magical, almost alien.'

Tilly leaned forward in her bed. By the expression on her face, she was enjoying the conversation, even though she couldn't actively take part.

'It looks far too cold for me. Give me a beach any day,' Amy said.

'I'm not a beach person,' Matilda said. 'Don't get me wrong, I love sitting by the ocean with the sun on my face, but I couldn't do it all day like some do. I like an adventure holiday.'

'She sounds like you, doesn't she, Tilly?' Amy said with a smile. 'Whenever we've gone on holiday, Tilly's always wanted to go off exploring. I'm shattered by the pool and she's full of energy wanting to trek up a mountain or something.'

'Not long after I was married, me and my husband went for a week away. We drove from Sheffield to the Highlands of Scotland and spent the week walking in the Cairngorms. It's my favourite holiday ever,' Matilda said, smiling at the memory. 'It was so quiet. The air was so pure. At times it seemed like it was just the two of us in the whole world.'

Tilly winced, obviously in some pain.

Amy jumped forward, fussing around her daughter, asking if she should call for a nurse. Tilly pushed her away, adjusted her position in the bed and seemed fine.

'How are you feeling?' Matilda asked.

Tilly shook her head.

'Almost two years ago now, January 2019,' Matilda began, 'I was shot. A man arranged it so the fire alarm went off at the police station. We all filed out into the car park, and he opened fire on us—'

'I remember that,' Amy interrupted. 'Our school was placed in lockdown.'

'I lost quite a few of my colleagues that day,' Matilda continued. 'I was shot once in the shoulder and another bullet grazed along the side of my head. I was lucky to survive. I was in a coma for about three weeks, I think it was. When I woke up, and I was told who'd died, I ... well, I struggled to come to terms with it. I couldn't understand why or how I'd managed to survive. It was so hard to get my head around it all.'

Tilly nodded. She understood every word of what Matilda was saying.

'When I was well enough to leave hospital, I had to move into a rehabilitation centre. My speech was slurred, and I had to learn how to walk again. Looking back, those first few weeks and months seemed like they went on forever. I thought the physical and mental pain would never go away. It was too much for me to cope with. There were times when I wished I'd died.'

Tilly wiped a tear away. So did Matilda.

'Within nine months I was back at work,' Matilda said with a nervous smile. 'I've no idea how I managed it, but I did. I'm guessing, right now, you're wondering how you're going to be able to cope.'

Tilly nodded.

'That's perfectly understandable. I'm also guessing that you've got doctors and nurses coming in with silly grins on their faces saying how you'll be up and about in no time.' Again, Tilly nodded. 'And, let me guess, you'd like to give them a good slap.' She grinned and almost laughed. 'I was exactly the same. People kept coming in and saying how well I looked, how they thought I'd look much worse, and making jokes about being in bed all day and getting back to work. It's annoying, isn't it?'

Tilly nodded.

'You take as long as you need, Tilly. Also, you're in a better position than me because you can use your inner voice and tell the patronising doctors to piss off. I used my outer voice and was told off by the matron.'

Tilly laughed. Her face momentarily lit up with happiness. It was what she needed, for someone to treat her like the fourteen-year-old she was and not an antique vase that would break if not handled with extreme care.

'Tilly.' Matilda leaned forward. Her voice took on a more serious tone. 'Will you help me in catching the man who did this to you?'

It was a while before Tilly replied, but she did with a simple nod of the head.

Matilda smiled. 'Thank you. Can you remember what happened?'

She nodded and tears filled her eyes.

'Would you be able to write it all down?'

She held up her right arm, which had the plaster cast on.

'Ah. I'm guessing you're right-handed. I'll bring you in an iPad or something to type on. I know things will feel incredibly dark and frightening for you right now, Tilly, but I promise you, they will get better. And I will help in any way I can.'

Matilda stood up. Tilly held out a hand. Matilda grasped it and Tilly squeezed it tightly. They made eye contact and an understanding was passed between them. They were both victims of very different attacks, but the suffering and the aftermath and the mental torment were the same.

'I'll come back and visit you tomorrow. Is there anything you'd like me to bring you?'

Tilly thought for a moment before shaking her head.

Matilda dug around in her pocket and brought out a dog-eared business card. She handed it to Tilly. 'My contact details are on there. Email, text, whatever. My phone is practically glued to my hand these days.'

She couldn't take her eyes from Tilly. She genuinely felt like she was looking at herself recovering from the shooting. It was eerie. Eventually, she tore herself away and left the room.

Amy followed Matilda out into the corridor. 'Thank you so much for what you said in there,' she said once the door was closed. 'I was beginning to doubt I'd ever see her smile again.'

'Can I give you some advice?'

'Of course.'

'Don't treat her any differently to how she was before the attack. People were doing that to me, and it drove me mad. She's still the same Tilly who enjoys David Attenborough documentaries and wants to visit the North Pole. None of that has changed. Make jokes, take the Mickey out of each other. That's the only way you'll all survive this.'

Amy wrapped her arms around Matilda and pulled her into a tight embrace. 'Thank you,' she said. When she stepped back, her eyes were wet with tears. 'Thank you so much,' she said again, before turning and going back into Tilly's room.

Matilda remained in the corridor. She felt emotionally drained herself, but she also felt buoyed. Now she'd met Tilly, she knew what she had to do, and she would move heaven and earth to catch this evil, misogynistic, psychopathic wanker if it was the last thing she did.

Chapter Twenty-One

Matilda entered the HMCU suite with a plastic carton of salad in hand for her lunch. With Christmas just around the corner and her cupboards at home stocked with more calories than a Cadbury factory, she thought it best to eat sensibly now so she could pigout over the festive season. Tom and Zofia were sharing Zofia's desk, laughing animatedly as they worked.

'They seem very close,' Matilda said to Scott as she made her way to her office.

He jumped up from his desk and followed her. 'They both came in yesterday to work.'

'Why?'

'To get ahead of checking CCTV footage. Tom even gave Zofia a ride on his motorbike.'

'Is that a euphemism?' she asked, smiling to herself.

Matilda sat down, lifted the lid on her salad and pulled a face. It didn't look appetising. She looked at Scott. 'Not jealous, are you?'

'What of?'

'Sit down.' She motioned for Scott to close the door and take a seat. 'I think we both know you find Tom attractive. I've seen your face light up when he enters the room.'

Scott looked uncomfortable. 'I'm going out with Donal,' he said, looking down.

'Yes. It doesn't stop you fancying other people. But I think you're in danger of allowing your attraction to get in the way of what you have with Donal.'

'I like Donal. I really do. It's just … we don't have that much in common. When I was with Chris, we did everything together. We went running together and to the gym. Donal isn't into any of that. And Tom is.'

'Scott, you can't replace Chris. So don't even try. Look at when I went out with Daniel. He was an architect, just like my James. They were even mates. Of course he was a substitute for my husband. It would never have worked. My feelings for him were based solely on the fact he reminded me of James. If you want things to work out with Donal—'

'I do,' he interrupted.

'Then make it work. It's fine you don't have the same interests. You can go to the gym or running while he's …'

'Collecting fossils,' he said with a hint of bitterness.

'Really? Oh. Well, that can be fun.'

'Can it?'

'I don't know anything about fossils, sorry. Ask Adele, she's six months older than me.' She laughed.

'I just don't feel the same way about Donal as I did about Chris.'

'Did you expect to?'

'Yes.'

'Well, I'm sorry to go tough love on you here but it's not

going to happen. You can't replace Chris. Don't try. But you can be happy with Donal if you allow yourself.'

'I know.'

'You're pushing him away, aren't you?'

Scott nodded.

'We shouldn't be having this conversation here, but you need to share all of this with Donal. He will understand. He cares for you a great deal. If you tell him what you've just told me, he'll help you.'

'Has he said anything to you?'

She nodded. 'He knows you're confused about something.'

'I'm scared of liking him too much and something bad happening again,' he said, tears in his voice.

'You were robbed of happiness in the cruellest way possible, Scott, but you've been given a second chance. You need to grab it with both hands and do everything you can to make it a success.'

He looked up at her. 'You're right.'

'Of course I'm right, I'm a DCI. We're never wrong.' She smiled.

'Moving on, before your head gets so big it can't fit through the door, I need to fill you in on what Zofia and Tom uncovered.'

_____

Matilda was delighted with Zofia's stellar work and had to stop herself telling her to treat herself to something illicitly stolen from Sian's snack drawer. It still felt strange with Sian no longer being a part of the team. She told Scott and Finn to head out and track down the mystery jogger.

'It's nice being back on the old team, isn't it?' Finn said from the front passenger seat as Scott drove to Chelsea Road.

'Hmm,' Scott agreed.

'You don't seem so convinced.'

'Don't get me wrong, I'm thrilled to be working on something other than coronavirus restrictions and breaking up illegal parties, but I don't know, something doesn't feel right.'

'I think it's Sian not being here. She was a huge character. She held us all together.'

'Probably.'

'Do you think DI Brady should be back on the team, too?' Finn asked after a short silence.

'I do.' Scott replied firmly.

'So do I. Has something happened between him and Matilda?'

'I think so but trying to get one of them to tell me isn't easy.'

'Maybe we should stage an intervention. Get them both in a lift at the same time and have it break down so they have to sort out their differences.'

'I think that kind of thing only happens in cheesy sitcoms. Here we go, Chelsea Road.'

While Scott pulled up, Finn pulled out the photographs Zofia had printed off for him. One was a close-up of the jogger so they could easily identify him, another showed the house he went in, though it was zoomed in so closely it was just a blur of pixels. Other pictures showed the jogger running past the doorbell camera on Brincliffe Edge Close in both directions. Both photos were time stamped.

They climbed out of the car and shivered in the coolness of the afternoon. Chelsea Road was in an affluent part of Sheffield. Detached houses lined either side with tall trees in most front gardens giving the occupiers privacy. It was quiet and the further down the road the detectives walked, the closer they came to Chelsea Park. The trees were tall, the houses fewer and further apart.

'Which one do you think it is?' Finn asked, looking at the over-pixelated photo and then up at the houses.

'I've no idea. I reckon we just knock on a door and show the photo of the jogger and hope they recognise him.

'Good idea.'

They walked down the driveway of a beautiful stone-built building with leaded bay windows and Tudor style frontage. The garden, despite it being in the depths of winter and devoid of life, was still well kept and as tidy as it could be at this time of year.

Scott rang the doorbell and stood back from the front door. 'Lovely area.'

'Way above our pay grades.'

The oak door was pulled open to reveal an elderly woman in navy trousers and matching cardigan. A wave of warmth came with her. She was tiny but had soft features and a welcoming smile.

Scott held up his warrant card. 'Good afternoon. I'm DS Scott Andrews from South Yorkshire Police. This is DC Finn Cotton. We're trying to trace the whereabouts of this man.' He held out the best image he had of the jogger. 'We believe he lives on this road. There's nothing to worry about,' he added, noticing the smile drop and replaced by a worried frown. 'He's helping us with our enquiries, and we didn't get an address for him.'

'Oh.' The smile returned. She fished a pair of oversized glasses out of her cardigan pocket and put them on. She took the photo from Scott and studied it. 'Yes. I know him. What's his name?' She asked herself. 'He lives down the road, number seventy-eight, I think. No, I don't know his name. I know his wife, though, Suzanne. She works for the same company as my daughter. I think she's a buyer or something. It's a medical company. They supply things to the NHS. I don't know what he does.'

'What's Suzanne's surname?'

'Now, there's a question,' she mused. 'Is it Barker or Baker? I think it's Barker.'

'Thank you.' Scott smiled, taking the photograph from her. 'You've been very helpful.'

'They're not in any trouble, are they? They're a lovely family. They've got twins.'

'No. No trouble at all. Thank you for your help.'

They left the elderly lady's property and were walking along Chelsea Road when Finn glanced over his shoulder.

'She's still on the doorstep watching us,' he said.

'I get the feeling this is one of those streets where people have nothing to do with each other, yet they know everything that's going on.' Scott said with a smile.

Number seventy-eight was a different house entirely from the elderly woman's. It was still detached, and stone-built, but there were no Tudor style beams on the front or lead at the windows. It was more modern, and the garden had a wild, unkempt look about it.

Scott had to knock three times before a man answered. He was tall and slim and bore an uncanny resemblance to the man in the photographs they were looking for.

'Mr Barker?' Scott asked.

'That's right.'

He introduced himself and Finn. They both showed their warrant cards.

'We'd like to ask you a few questions about an incident that took place a couple of nights ago on Brincliffe Edge Road.'

The man's eyes widened.

'An incident? What kind of incident?'

'A young girl was attacked. We were wondering if you saw anything.'

'Why are you asking me?' He had one hand on the door, getting ready to close it.

'We believe you were in the area at the time and want to know if you saw anything that may help us.'

'What time was this?'

'Just before five o'clock in the evening.'

'No,' he said with a painful-looking smile. 'I wasn't on Brincliffe Edge Road at that time. You're mistaken. Sorry.' He began to close the door.

'Mr Barker, we have photographic evidence of you passing a house on Brincliffe Edge Close and turning into Brincliffe Edge Road just before five o'clock,' Scott took the file from Finn and pulled out the photo. 'Could we come inside for a quiet word? We won't take up much of your time, I promise.'

The man looked over Scott and Finn and out into the road, obviously checking for nosy neighbours.

He looked back at the detectives and found they'd already masked up, waiting to be invited in.

'As long as you're not long,' he said, reluctantly stepping back and allowing them inside.

He led them down a wide hallway and into a brilliant white kitchen that had been extended. Bi-folding doors gave the room extra light and opened onto a huge garden. Finn was impressed and marvelled at the high-end kitchen.

'I'd offer you a drink, but with the pandemic, I don't suppose that's wise,' the man said.

'That's fine.' Scott waved him away. 'Can I take your full name please, sir?'

'Malcolm Barker.'

'What do you do for a living, Mr Barker?'

'I'm an illustrator.'

'Really?' Finn asked. 'I bet that's an interesting job.'

'It can be.'

'Do you work from home?' Scott asked.

'Yes. I have a studio upstairs. Look, I don't mean to sound rude, but if we could get on with it, I am very busy.'

Malcolm Barker stood by the white island, his arms firmly crossed against his chest. He was tall and slim, unshaven, and his dark brown hair was cut short. He was wearing tight tracksuit bottoms and a polo shirt. Scott doubted if there was an ounce of fat on him.

'You go jogging?' Scott asked.

'I do. Every day.'

'At the same time?'

'Usually, yes. Any time between half past four and five o'clock.'

'And you always take the same route?'

'Yes.'

'Can you talk us through these pictures?' Scott asked, laying them out on the island. 'As you can see, you're captured on this doorbell camera on Brincliffe Edge Close at 4:55pm and less than two minutes later, you're coming back, running much faster. Why is that?'

Malcolm swallowed hard. His prominent Adam's apple bobbed up and down. He couldn't take his eyes off the photos.

The silence grew.

'At that time,' Scott continued, 'on Brincliffe Edge Road, a fourteen-year-old girl, Tilly Hall, had her throat cut and was thrown into Brincliffe Edge Woods. It's the fourth incident in less than two months. The three previous victims all died. We believe it was you turning into the road that spooked the killer and he fled. Unbeknown to you, you saved Tilly Hall's life.'

Malcolm looked up. A glimmer of a smile flashed across his face.

'Will she be all right?'

'I don't know. Her vocal cords are damaged. She'll never talk again. She's suffered a severe trauma. It'll be a long road to recovery. Mr Barker, what did you see?'

He shook his head.

'You saw something that made you turn back and run home.'

'I didn't see anything,' he said, quietly.

'Then why turn round and go straight back home?'

'I … I … I'm sorry. I can't help you.'

'Can't or won't?' Scott asked, an icy edge to his tone.

Conflicting emotions played out on Malcolm's face. He was struggling with something internally. He chewed his bottom lip.

'I'm sorry,' he said, pushing the photos back to Scott. 'I don't want to get involved.'

'Malcolm, a fourteen-year-old girl will never speak again. She was violently raped and had her throat sliced open. The man who's doing this has killed three times before. He cut one woman's throat so deep, she was almost decapitated.'

Malcolm was rapidly shaking his head.

'Tell us what you saw.'

'No. I'm sorry. I'm not getting involved. I hope you catch him, I really do, but I can't. I'm sorry. I'd like you to leave, please.'

'Mr Barker …'

'Please. Leave my house right now,' he said, finding the strength from somewhere to conjure up a shout.

'Well, that didn't go entirely to plan, did it?' Finn asked, as they stood in the driveway of Malcolm Barker's home.

'No. If he's got a wife and kids like that old woman said, why won't he help us? He's potentially putting his own wife's life at risk.'

'Maybe he's thinking of his family. By not getting involved, he's keeping them safe.'

'That's bullshit,' Scott said, storming off. 'If there is another victim, then he'll have their blood on his hands.'

Chapter Twenty-Two

Matilda had thought they were finally getting somewhere after Zofia's excellent trawling of the CCTV footage, but Malcolm Barker's refusal to get involved was a major setback. On the way home in the car, she looked out of the window, taking in the view of the sprawling steel city. She was still seeing women walking on their own and wanted to wind down her window and tell them all to go home.

The investigation into the murders was a slow burner. There was no physical evidence and interviewing Tilly Hall was going to take time. They needed to act fast to stop any more women being killed, and all hope rested on what Tilly would tell them tomorrow during the first interview.

Matilda asked Scott if he wanted to come in for a drink when he dropped her off, but he declined. He was having a night on his own so he could think about his future with Donal.

'All you need to do, Scott, is ask yourself one question,' Matilda said.

'What's that?'

'Do you love him? If the answer is yes, then you make the relationship work. Comparing him, or anyone, to Chris is not healthy, and no one can win against a dead man. I know that more than most. But if you genuinely love Donal, don't turn your back on him.'

'It's not just that.'

'What else?'

He looked to the flat above the garage, then back to Matilda. 'When Donal stays over, I wake up in the morning and I think I've got Chris in bed next to me. I can't get that out of my head. I've tried.'

'Maybe you should move.'

'On my salary? Have you seen what places cost in Sheffield these days? I wouldn't mind if it was a city to shout about.'

'You sound like Sian.' She smiled. 'Look, why don't you come in for a drink, we can have a good chat.'

'No. I'm going to have an early night, I think.'

Matilda watched from the doorstep as Scott made his way to the garage. His head was down, and he was dragging his feet. She turned back to the door, rolled her eyes at the ridiculously large wreath Adele had bought and entered the warmth of her home.

She stopped in her tracks as she saw two suitcases at the bottom of the stairs. Adele came into the hall from the kitchen.

'I've been trying to call you all afternoon.'

'Sorry. I've been so busy. I haven't looked at my phone once. Are you leaving me for someone else, you hussy?' Matilda smiled.

'No. I've sort of taken it upon myself to solve the Christmas situation.'

'Why do I get the feeling I'm not going to like this?'

'Come with me. There's someone in the kitchen who wants to say hello.'

Gingerly, Matilda walked slowly into the kitchen and visibly relaxed when she saw retired detective Pat Campbell sitting at the table nursing a mug of tea.

'Hello, Pat. What brings you here?'

'Adele's Porsche.'

'Sit down, Mat, let me explain,' Adele said, forcibly sitting Matilda into a chair opposite Pat.

'Now, our useless leader states that no more than three households can get together at Christmas. And it doesn't matter how we add them up, your mum, your sister and nephews, us and Pat, does not make three. So, Pat has decided to move in with us. Unfortunately, we'll have a blazing row just after New Year and she'll decide it's not working and move back home.'

'That is incredibly sneaky and underhand. I love it,' Matilda said.

'You don't mind?' Pat asked.

'Of course not. I should have thought of it myself.'

'You're certainly devious enough,' Adele added.

'Thank you. This will be so much fun. I'm definitely looking forward to Christmas now.' She reached across the table and held Pat's hands. 'I didn't want you spending your first Christmas without Anton all on your own.'

Pat gave a painful smile. 'I know I moaned about him a lot, but when you've been married as long as we had, you can take the piss out of each other. It doesn't mean I didn't love him.'

'I know you did.'

'I told him one day playing bowls would kill him. Fool.'

Matilda frowned. 'He died from Covid.'

'I know he did. But if he hadn't gone to that bowls meeting, he wouldn't have caught it. I told him to embrace the power of Zoom, but he wouldn't listen.'

Matilda gave her a sympathetic smile. She could see the sadness in her eyes. Her words were simply bluster. She loved Anton and missed him so much that it was causing physical pain.

Pat had lost weight since Anton had died. It suited her but losing more would make her look ill. She was a tiny woman, not much taller than five feet, and had short grey hair and a friendly, worn, face with light brown eyes and a sweet smile. Lately, there hadn't been much for her to smile about and as Christmas approached, she seemed sadder. Adele's scheme would work wonders for Pat and give her something to look forward to.

'So, which room would you like?' Matilda asked. 'We've got one with an en suite or one without. The one without has better views of the countryside.'

'I'll take the one with, please. I've always wanted an en suite.'

'Excellent. I'll show you to your room, madam,' Matilda said, standing up. 'Adele can make a start on the tea. We've got gammon steaks.'

'I love gammon.'

Adele rolled her eyes.

'Actually, Pat, it's good you're moving in for a few weeks.' Matilda linked arms with Pat, and they walked out of the kitchen together. 'How do you fancy casting your eyes over a triple murder?'

'Oh, Mat,' Pat said, a smile on her face. 'And I didn't get you anything.'

It was a little after midnight. Adele had long since gone to bed and Matilda and Pat were on opposite sofas in the living room, the coffee table in front of them littered with statements and crime scene photographs from the three murders. The log fire was blazing, the room was lit by a couple of standard lamps and a third bottle of wine had recently been opened.

Pat finished reading the final crime scene report, picked up her full glass of wine and leaned back on the sofa. In the dim, warm lighting of the room, the wrinkles on her face showed up more. She looked tired. The death of her husband had aged her terribly. Matilda knew she was somewhere in her seventies but wasn't brave enough to ask the exact number. Even when Pat's birthday came around, it was never revealed how many she'd had.

'You're going to tell me he hates women, aren't you?' Matilda asked.

'You don't need a detective to tell you that, retired or otherwise,' Pat replied. Her voice was slightly slurred through drink and tiredness.

'Where should I be looking?'

'He's intelligent. He knows all about crime scenes, what's gleaned from them, and how not to leave a trace of himself behind. In my day we'd say he was obviously a detective or a SOCO, but nowadays, you can get all that information from *Silent Witless*, or whatever it's called. Terrible programme. However, I do think he's a clever bloke, and he'll have had a job where he needed to use his brain.'

'Had?'

'Oh, yes. He's not working now.'

'How do you know that?'

'I don't. The first three women were all killed outside of regular office hours and Tilly Hall was attacked on her way home from school, during working hours. However, he's followed these women. He's watched them and waited for the perfect time to strike. That takes time. He hasn't simply clocked off work at five o'clock and found a victim on his way home.'

'You think he's unemployed?'

'I think he's lost his job for some reason. Maybe he's been made redundant. Maybe he's had a new boss and there's been a clash of personalities. I think there was a woman involved in why he's no longer working, and that's what's tipped him over the edge.'

'But if there was one woman who he thinks has ruined things for him, wouldn't he go after someone in her likeness? All four victims look completely different.'

'No,' Pat said, taking another sip of wine. 'I think women have been a problem with him all his life. His mother will have been domineering and I don't think he'll have ever been married or had any long-lasting relationships. Women will see him as a friend, not a lover, and he's hated that.'

'What age range am I looking at?'

'That's a tricky one. Definitely older than his victims. He wants to be seen as being in complete control, dominant almost. He'll be thirty plus, but he could be in his forties, fifties, or sixties. Although I doubt he really will be that old. I'd put money on him being in his thirties or forties.'

'He's attacked four women in two months, three of whom are dead. Why hasn't anyone noticed a change in his behaviour and come forward? He will have changed, won't he?'

'Absolutely. But I think he has very few people in his life to notice in the first place. And those who do know him won't give him a second glance. He'll be one of those men you only think about when you need to, or when you see him in the street. But when you do catch him, everyone will say how it's obvious he was a killer.'

'We can all say that after the event,' Matilda said. 'So, the million-pound question: how do I catch him?'

Pat screwed up her face as she thought. 'Well, keep your fingers crossed that Tilly Hall is able to give you something substantial to work on when you start talking to her, because on what you've got here, it's going to be bloody difficult.'

'And what if Tilly can't give me anything? Where do I find my killer?'

'I really don't know, Matilda. But I'll tell you one thing; this man is dangerous, and your next victim is only a few days away, if that.'

Chapter Twenty-Three

The killer climbed out of his van and went around to the back. It was dark, cold, windy, and snow was falling heavily. He opened the rear doors and had to use the torch on his phone to find his latest victim. She was curled up in the furthest corner of the van. She looked so scared. Her brown eyes were wide, tears were streaming down her face. Her make-up had run. She was shaking with cold and fear. He was so turned on.

He climbed in and grabbed her. She screamed and cried and tried to hold onto something so he couldn't pull her out of the van, but she was no match for him. When he felt like this, he could move mountains.

He yanked her out of the van, and she fell onto the cold, hard ground. She screamed again, and he let her. He'd purposely driven into the middle of nowhere so nobody could hear her scream but him. He wanted to listen to her beg for her life.

He stood back and watched as she scrambled to her feet in the slippery, wet snow. She ran and he followed her, grabbing her, rugby tackling her to the ground. He turned her over, tore off her impossibly tiny skirt and yanked her underpants down with a single movement.

From his back pocket, he pulled out his best friend, his trusted hunter's knife, and showed it to her. The look on her face, the horror, the fear, the torment, was almost orgasmic.

She fought to free herself from beneath him. She scratched and clawed at him with her sharp nails. She drew blood on his face. It hurt, and he smiled at the pain.

'Come on,' he spat through gritted teeth. 'Fight back. Hit me. Come on. *HIT ME!*' he screamed, his voice echoing around him.

She froze in fear. Nothing she could say or do would stop this man from attacking her, from killing her. Whatever she did just turned him on all the more.

The killer leaned down over her and kissed her hard on the mouth, pushing his tongue between her lips. He heard her whine and squirm.

'You are my favourite,' he said with a smile.

He unzipped his jeans then clamped his hand firmly over her mouth. Her cries were muffled. He could feel her warm breath against his palm. He could smell her scent, it was sweet and reminded him of summer, but there was a hint of fear she was radiating that drove him to plough harder and harder into her. Her screams and terror were turning him on. As he reached a climax, he held the hunter's knife to her throat, pressing it hard against the flesh, watching blood trickle down her neck. He began to cut and slice. Blood shot out of the torn veins and arteries. He could feel the warm sprays hitting him. It was bliss. Her body began to go limp beneath him, but he continued to cut, deeper and deeper. He was still inside her when she died.

He woke up with a jolt and looked around him. He was in bed, alone, as always. The curtains were wide open, and the room lit up by the brilliant light from the full moon. He always slept with the curtains open. He hated being plunged into total darkness.

He was hard. His violent dreams always gave him an erection. He was also wet. Nocturnal emissions – he'd looked it up online. The dreams were getting more vivid, darker, and even he was scared by them. But the release they gave him was enormous. During every single waking minute, he was tense and angry, annoyed and screaming inside. The dreams were a sign of what he needed to do in order to feel better about this pathetic existence he was forced to endure on this godforsaken planet.

He needed to kill again. Tomorrow night, he would go out, find someone, anyone, and inhale their screams, feel the warmth of their blood on his cold skin, listen as their heart beat one last time and savour the presence of death.

Chapter Twenty-Four

Tuesday 22nd December 2020

Matilda entered the stifling hospital room. Tilly was sitting up in bed, reading, once again, from *Planet Earth II*, while next to her Amy looked as if she wanted to be anywhere else in the world but here. She wasn't doing anything. She wasn't reading, doing a puzzle, scrolling through her phone or knitting, she was simply sitting there, tears in her eyes, giving the oppressive room its air of sadness and depression.

'Good morning,' Matilda said. 'How are we both today?'

Tilly looked up and a genuine smile appeared on her face. She seemed pleased to see Matilda. Amy's smile didn't reach her eyes and her bottom lip wobbled.

This room needed levity, and while Matilda wasn't the happiest person in the world, she was able to detach herself from her own issues and provide Tilly with the support she actually needed to aid in her recovery rather than that of an anxious parent.

'I asked my boss for an iPad and he gave me several forms to fill in and asked me to do a risk assessment, so I filed them in the bin and just nicked this when no one was looking,' Matilda said to Tilly as she handed her the white Apple box.

Tilly smiled as she gratefully took it.

'If I'd known how easy it was to nick supplies from work, I'd have done all my Christmas shopping there.' She grinned. 'How are you feeling today on a scale of one to ten?'

Tilly held up four fingers.

'Ah. That's not good. We need to get that above five at least, don't we? I'm guessing Covid rules mean we can't decorate the room for Christmas,' Matilda asked Amy.

She wiped her nose with a tissue. 'I don't know. I haven't asked.'

'Do you have an advent calendar at home?' Tilly nodded. 'I'm sure you'd be allowed to bring that in at least,' Matilda said to Amy. 'Why don't you go and have a word with the nurses while we set up the iPad? We'll be ready to go by the time you get back.'

'Oh,' Amy said, reluctant to get up from her chair.

'We'll be all right for a few minutes, won't we?' Matilda smiled at Tilly, who nodded and smiled at her mother.

'Oh. Okay. I'll only be a few minutes, mind.'

Matilda waited until Amy had left the room and the door had fully closed behind her. 'She's a worrier, your mum, isn't she?' Tilly rolled her eyes. Matilda perched herself on the edge of the bed. 'Let me guess, she's treating you as if you're made of glass.' She nodded. 'My mum did the same after I was shot and I'm in my forties. The thing is, we only see things from our own point of view. I was shot and I kept thinking how it was going to affect my life from that point onwards. I never thought about how my mum and sister and friends were going to deal with it. I'm ashamed to say that I snapped at my mum a few times. I upset her. That was the last thing I wanted to do. But look at what your mum is facing right now; her only child has suffered a great trauma. A mum's job is to protect her children and she'll be feeling terrible that she wasn't there when you needed her the most. Don't be too hard on her if she's struggling to think of something to say.'

Tilly nodded and wiped the tears from her eyes.

'You can keep that iPad, by the way. Nobody knows it's missing, so download anything you want to it.' Matilda smiled.

Amy returned to her daughter's room with a smile on her face and a bounce in her step. The nurses said Tilly's room could be decorated, as long as it wasn't too much and didn't get in the way of doctors doing their rounds or the medical equipment.

Matilda sat at the bottom of the bed, notepad open on her lap. Amy was by her daughter. They were holding hands.

'Tilly, we'll take this as slowly as you like. There's absolutely no rush at all,' Matilda said. It was a lie as she still had Pat Campbell's words from last night racing around her mind. The killer would strike again soon, and she wanted him caught before he had the chance. 'If you get tired, or distressed, or simply want to stop, just let me know and I'll come back another day. Okay?'

Tilly nodded. She'd closed the book she was engrossed in, and the iPad was on the table in front of her.

'Tell me what happened when you left school.'

Like most teenagers, Tilly was adept at typing quickly on a tablet and despite being right-handed and it being wrapped in a thick plaster cast, her fingers were still nimble over the keyboard and her less-dominant left hand soon picked up the slack from her right.

I was walking with Chloe, Martha and Jas when we left school as far as the traffic lights. They turned left and I went right. As soon as we split up, I put in my earbuds and listened to the Radio 1 podcast. I was listening to highlights from Greg James. I didn't hear anyone around me. I just felt someone grab me. It was strange. Before I realised what had happened, I was halfway in the back of a van. It was too late to do anything.

Tilly turned the iPad around for Matilda to read while she pointed to the box of tissues on the locker for her mum to pass her one. She wiped her eyes.

'Where did this happen?'

Tilly looked at her mum. Her face was fully of worry.

'Tilly, nobody is going to think anything bad about you. Are we, Amy?'

'Of course not, sweetheart,' Amy said, squeezing her daughter's hand firmer.

It was a long few minutes before Tilly began typing.

I usually walk down Highcliffe Road and then turn onto Greystones Road but that night I went down the track just before Highcliffe Road.

'What?' Amy asked, aghast, reading while Tilly was typing. 'It was dark. It's very poorly lit down there. You know not to do anything like that when you're out on your own.'

'Amy,' Matilda interrupted.

Tilly pushed the table away and pulled her hand out of her mother's grasp. She leaned back on the bed and turned to look out of the window.

'Tilly, did you arrange to meet someone?' Matilda asked in

her best soothing tone. 'You're not going to get into trouble, but I need to know everything that happened.'

'I'm sorry I shouted, Tilly,' Amy said. 'I'm really struggling right now, sweetheart. You're so much like me when I was your age. My dad kept wanting to pick me up from school, but I refused. I was far too independent for my age, and you're exactly the same. We worry as parents. It's the number one job description. I promise, whatever you tell us, I'm not going to get angry.'

Tilly returned to the iPad.

I was supposed to meet Ryan Cook.

'I thought you two had split up?' Amy asked.

I just said that because I knew you'd kick off again.

Amy turned to Matilda and filled in the gaps. 'Ryan is a lovely lad. He's sixteen and he doesn't live far from us. There's almost three years between them. When he turns seventeen, Tilly will still only be fourteen. I know what seventeen-year-old boys are like. He'll want to … I was worried he'd pressure Tilly into having sex before she's ready.'

Tilly banged on the table to get Matilda's attention. She'd typed something on the tablet. She looked angry.

Mum threatened Ryan. She took my phone. Text him and pretended to be me. She arranged to meet him and was really vile. She grabbed Ryan. He showed me the bruises on his arms.

Matilda looked up at Tilly, who was crying.

'Is this true?' Matilda asked Amy.

Amy was looking down at her feet. When she looked up, tears were running down her face. 'I didn't mean to. I like Ryan, I really do. He's a lovely lad. But he's done his GCSEs. He can relax. The next couple of years are important to you, Tilly. They will define your whole future. I just wanted you to concentrate on your schoolwork and not get distracted.'

'You assaulted him?' Matilda asked.

'I didn't assault him. I tried to reason with him, but I could see my words were just going over his head. If I'd been a man, he'd have listened to me, no worries. But the thing is, I have to be mum and dad to Tilly. When I saw he wasn't listening, I raised my voice, I got … I got a bit angry, and, yes, I did grab him. I didn't think I'd grabbed him hard enough to leave bruises.' She turned to Tilly. 'I'm really sorry, Tilly. I thought I was doing what was best for you. I was just thinking of you. If you feel so strongly about him then we'll sit down and discuss how to continue with you seeing him, so it doesn't interfere with your schoolwork. I got it wrong. I'm sorry,' she cried.

Matilda watched as mother and daughter cried. Amy was gripping Tilly's hand in hers. Tilly looked on. There were tears rolling down her cheeks, but her face was impassive. The emotion wasn't there. Matilda wondered who Tilly was crying for.

It's too late. Ryan's not going to want anything to do with me now, is he? Look at me. I'm a freak.

'Sweetheart, you are not a freak,' Amy sobbed.

'Have you been in touch with Ryan since you've been in here?' Matilda asked.

Tilly shook her head.

'Her phone has been vibrating all the time from friends asking how she is, but she won't even read the texts.'

'She will. In time. You need to get everything sorted out in your own head first, don't you?' Matilda asked Tilly.

Tilly nodded and gave a hint of a smile through her tears.

'So, you arranged to meet Ryan,' Matilda said, clearing her throat and getting back to topic. 'What happened after you'd left?'

Tilly wiped her eyes and picked up the iPad again.

We never met. I was halfway down the track when I got a text from Ryan saying he'd been kept behind at school and we'd meet tomorrow night instead. I just carried on walking towards Greystones Road.

'And you didn't see anyone around? No people or vehicles?'

No.

'Do you know what type of van it was you were in?'

It was silver. Not a huge one like the Amazon vans.

Matilda smiled. 'That's good. That's helpful. Thank you. The man who grabbed you; was he on his own, or was there more than one of them?'

He was on his own.

'Did you get a good look at him? Is there anything you can tell me about him? Hair colour, eye colour, his build, smell?'

Tilly turned to look back out of the window. She was crying and visibly distressed.

'You're doing so well, Tilly. We can take a break at any time,' Matilda said.

Tilly composed herself. She took several deep breaths which seemed to cause her physical pain and grabbed the iPad. She was typing for a long time. When she finished, she handed it to Matilda and fully turned over in bed, her back to them both.

I don't know how to describe him. He wasn't tall and he wasn't short. He was slim but he was strong. His grip was so tight. He was clean shaven, and I think he had light-ish hair, but it was dark so I'm not sure. I can't tell you what colour eyes he had. He was wearing dark jeans and a dark jumper with the sleeves rolled up. His arms were thin. I was in the corner of the van. I was trying not to look at him. I couldn't speak. I was just so scared of what was going to happen. I heard his belt buckle, and I knew he was going to rape me. He grabbed my legs and pulled me towards him. I felt so weak. I closed my eyes as tight as I could. It's like I was in shock or something. I didn't know what to do. I felt his breath on me. It smelled minty like he'd been sucking mints. It hurt. The rape. I've never known pain like it. He had his hand over my mouth. It was pressing down hard. It seemed to go on for ages. I can still hear him grunting. When he finished, I turned away and crawled back into the corner of the van. I heard him doing up his jeans and he got out of the van. Then we were moving.

Matilda finished reading. She looked up. Tilly was curled up in bed, her knees drawn up to her chest, her arms wrapped tightly around them. She imagined that's how she lay in the back of the van after the rape.

'I think we should leave it there for today,' Matilda said.

Chapter Twenty-Five

Matilda emailed everything from the tablet to herself, printed it off at the station and read through it several times in the silence of her office. Scott entered with a mug of tea and a dark chocolate KitKat and placed it on her desk.

'How did it go?'

Matilda shook her head. 'She's being incredibly brave. Amy has told her all about the dangers of talking to strangers and walking where there is good lighting, and Tilly is a level-headed girl. But all that goes out of the window when you're attacked, doesn't it? The shock and horror of it all render you numb. By the time Tilly knew what was happening it was too late for her to fight back.'

'Did she manage to give you a description?'

'A vague one. I'll go back tomorrow for the rest of the statement. She may have remembered something else. If only that sodding jogger would give us a statement. With what he saw and what Tilly remembers, we could put together a decent image.'

Scott pulled out a chair and sat down. 'I've noticed this

happening a lot lately. People just don't want to get involved in things any more. A shop on Burngreave was fire-bombed at the beginning of August. We were able to track down plenty of witnesses through CCTV but not one of them wanted to give a statement. If things don't directly affect their own lives, they're simply not interested.'

Matilda sat back and folded her arms. 'I find that incredibly sad.'

'It is.'

'It's also bloody inconvenient, too.'

'We can't make Malcolm Barker give a statement.'

'No. So, our only hope is Tilly. Let's hope she remembers something useful.'

Finn knocked on the glass door and walked in. 'Sorry to interrupt, but we've got a missing sex offender.'

Matilda's eyes widened. 'Go on.'

Finn looked down at his iPad. 'Andrew Lee Hawkesley, aged forty-three. He's originally from Barnsley but he's been living in Sheffield since March 2019. He's missed the last two meetings with his parole officer, and he hasn't reported into the police station. His last known address was a flat in Lowedges. I sent a team of uniforms round to pick him up and the flat is empty. The neighbours haven't seen him for months. I got onto the council and his rent hasn't been paid for five months.'

'Didn't they think to get onto him?'

'You know what the council are like,' Finn said.

'What's his original offence?' Scott asked.

'In 2010 he was sentenced to twelve years for raping two women he met through dating apps. He spiked their drinks, raped them and simply dumped them when he'd finished.'

'Bloody hell,' Scott said.

Matilda frowned as she thought. It was a while before she said anything. 'Under normal circumstances I'd say to get onto the press office and get them to have something put on local media, but the fact his parole officer should have flagged it up with us and didn't will not put South Yorkshire in a very good light, and the last thing we need right now is any more negative publicity.'

'You're starting to sound like a Chief Constable,' Scott said, a twinkle in his eye.

'Policing in the twenty-first century is all about politics and budgets. If it wasn't for people's lives being at stake, it would be laughable the way things are now. Finn, find out everything you can about this Andrew, what was it?'

'Andrew Lee Hawkesley.'

'Contact his family and any known associates. Get access to his flat, get a forensic team in there and see if there's anything that can give us a clue to where he might be. Everything must be followed up.'

'Will do.'

'Get onto his parole officer and extract as much information about Andrew as you can. When you're finished, skewer them to a spit and roast them. Useless bastard.'

Finn smiled and left the room, closing the door behind him.

'What do you think?' Scott asked.

'It's a possibility. Scott, dig out his case file. Let's see if his victimology matches ours. And get a photo of him, too. I'll see if Tilly is up to seeing a picture of him.'

When she was alone in her office, Matilda turned to look out of her window at the bland view. It was starting to go dark. Another day was over, and she was no closer to finding out who was destroying the lives of these women.

'The older I get,' she said to herself, 'the more I realise this world would be a much better place if it wasn't for all the men in it.'

Chapter Twenty-Six

DCs Finn Cotton and Tom Simpson were sitting in an unmarked pool car at the top of Gresley Road in Lowedges waiting for clearance to enter Andrew Lee Hawkesley's flat.

A team of uniformed officers had gone charging up the staircase to smash open the front door and check he wasn't hiding in there armed to the teeth and waiting to strike.

'According to his record he's a very clever bloke,' Finn said, reading the email sent to him by Hawkesley's parole officer. 'He's got a degree in electrical engineering and had a very good job before he decided to become a rapist.'

'Does it say anything about his motive for raping those women?' Tom asked, looking at his sad surroundings of run-down shops and people defeated by life standing at a bus stop.

'Ah,' Finn said. 'He said he was no good with women.'

'What's that supposed to mean?'

'Hang on,' Finn said as he was skim-reading. 'Apparently, he'd asked a few women out and they'd knocked him back. A couple of former girlfriends had dumped him for other men, more successful and better-looking men, according to Andrew. He said that women were all selfish bitches, and he was fed up with them thinking they were better than him.'

'Well, doesn't he sound lovely?' Tom said with sarcasm.

There was a tap on the passenger side window. Finn lowered it and a gust of icy wind blew in.

'The flat's cleared if you want to have a look inside,' a uniformed officer told him. 'He's not house proud, mind.'

'Smells?'

'Just a bit.'

'Thanks for that.'

The wind had picked up and whipped up the decaying leaves on the ground. Finn and Tom made their way to the row of maisonettes and the communal staircase leading to the flats. Their footfalls resounded around the walls, which were in urgent need of decorating. The stairs were grey concrete and there was an underlying smell of damp and urine. There was a heavy depressive atmosphere about the whole building.

The flat, according to Sheffield City Council, was a studio apartment, which was twenty-first-century-speak for a bedsit. The front door opened onto a square of hallway with three doors leading off it. One to a tiny kitchen; if two people could comfortably fit in there, it would be a miracle. A second led to a similar-sized bathroom and a third to a large living room cum dining room cum bedroom.

The same brown carpet was laid throughout. It was threadbare and covered in all manner of stains. Finn and Tom headed straight for the living room, took in the double bed with the duvet pushed back, the faux-leather reclining chair in the corner and the flatscreen TV on the wall.

'He lives here?' Tom asked, a look of disgust on his face.

'It would appear so,' Finn replied.

'It's horrible.'

'It's cheap.'

'What's that smell?'

'Probably best we don't know,' Finn said as he fished out a pair of latex gloves from his back pocket and struggled to put them on. 'Come on, it's not a huge place, it shouldn't take us long to search for something to help us find out where he is.'

'I'll have a look in the kitchen,' Tom said, leaving the room.

Finn pulled out the drawers of the divan bed and rifled through the folded clothes and sheets. He checked the pockets of the jackets and jeans. They were all empty. There was a bedside table, the top of which was covered in stains from coffee mugs. There was a well-thumbed paperback copy of a Lee Child novel and two further books by the same author in the drawers. He flicked through them; nothing was tucked inside.

Tom came back into the room and went over to a chipboard coffee table that leaned against a cold radiator. There were folded-up newspapers and magazines strewn on top. Tom picked one up.

'Finn,' he said. He turned around and showed him what he'd found. It was an edition of the local newspaper, *The Star*, dating back to October. The front-page story told of the rape and murder of Daisy Clough.

'Check the others. See if he's saving papers that mention the other murders.'

'They're all older than this. To be fair, it looks like he hasn't been here since October. There's food in the fridge that's mutating into biological weapons.' He pulled a face. 'It looks like he left in a hurry.'

'Maybe he saw the front page and decided to get out of Sheffield while he had the chance.'

'But where has he been staying if he's the one who killed all the others? He's got to be living somewhere in Sheffield still.'

'True,' Finn mused.

'Maybe he's leading a double life.'

'That's a frightening possibility.'

Chapter Twenty-Seven

When it came to Amy Hall leaving her daughter for the evening, her emotions built up and she struggled to hold back the tears. If it were possible, she'd bring in a sleeping bag and try to get comfortable on the hard floor in the corner of the room. Unfortunately, once eight o'clock came, it was time for her to go. She looked at her watch. It was ten to eight.

'Oh, I meant to tell you, Mr Burkett across the road has been walking the dogs during the day so I can come here. When I told him you named Kit after Kit Harington, he thought that was his name, so he'd been in the park shouting "Kit Harington" at the top of his voice,' she said, laughing.

Tilly smiled.

'I didn't have the heart to tell him it was just Kit, bless him.'

It wasn't easy having a one-sided conversation when all the other person could do was smile or shrug. She looked at her watch again. She should be packing up her things and making a move.

'Leslie, opposite, has said when you're feeling up to it, she'll come in and do your hair and nails for you. Everyone says she should do it professionally, she's really good, isn't she?'

Tilly nodded with a smile.

'I've said I'll let her know. Oh, and Mrs Goodrum from the school has been in touch and they're all thinking of you and you're not to worry about missing any work or anything; they're going to give you their full support when you're ready to go back.'

Tears pricked Tilly's eyes.

There were less than five minutes left of visiting time.

'I should be going,' Amy said, not making an attempt to move. Her bottom lip wobbled. 'I know Mr Burkett is taking the dogs out, but you know what Kit Harington's like. Blimey.' She laughed. 'He's got me calling him by his full name, too.'

She stood up and took a deep breath. She couldn't take her eyes away from her daughter.

She asked Tilly if there was anything else she wanted brought from home – more books, her dressing gown, another teddy bear, a thicker blanket than the ones the hospital provided, an extra pillow, her novelty slippers, her favourite sweater. Tilly shook her head.

Then there was twenty minutes of Amy kissing her daughter, hugging her, making sure her mobile was fully charged and within easy reach and telling her to text her any time if she needed anything or just wanted to chat.

'I love you so much,' Amy said softly as she smoothed Tilly's hair. 'We'll get through this. I promise you.'

Tilly gave her a pained smile. Tears filled her eyes.

'I'll be back first thing in the morning. Make sure you get some sleep.'

Tilly nodded.

Amy put on her coat, buttoned it up and picked up her bag. At the doorway, she stopped and turned back.

'I'm so proud of you, and the way you're handling all this.' She bit her bottom lip to stop it from wobbling, and she quickly wiped away a tear. She left, closing the door carefully behind her.

Amy managed to hold onto her emotions as she smiled an awkward goodbye to the nurses she passed in the corridors. In the lift to the ground floor, she maintained her stiff-upper-lip demeanour and made a play of buttoning up her coat and rummaging for her car keys. She left the overheated building, headed for her car, climbed in behind the wheel and the floodgates opened.

She cried.

Huge sobs and wails. She struggled to breathe and fished in her handbag for a tissue. She wiped her eyes, blew her nose and took huge breaths to calm herself down.

She hated herself for what she'd done. If she'd accepted Tilly and Ryan's relationship, maybe issued a few ground rules about them dating when it was time for Tilly to be revising for exams, they wouldn't have felt the need to hide and Tilly wouldn't have sneaked off the main road and into the clutches of a violent, evil, sick, twisted, perverted bastard.

He'd raped her. Tilly's first sexual experience had been one of violence and horror. It shouldn't have been like that. How was she going to approach intimacy in the future? She'd be scarred, psychologically, for life. How do you possibly get over something like this?

Amy wiped her eyes again and looked up. An elderly couple were passing her car, looking back at her. She'd obviously been crying louder than she thought. She started the engine and reversed out of the space. She needed to go home.

She needed the security of familiar surroundings to get her mind sorted.

Tilly was her only child, her only surviving relative. Her selfish actions had led her daughter to be violated and savaged in the most evil way. She made a promise to herself as she was stuck in traffic on Northumberland Road. She would do everything in her power to make Tilly's life as comfortable and as happy as she could. The next few weeks, months, maybe even years, were going to be hard, but they would survive this together.

She'd contact Ryan and his mother, apologise for her actions, and tell him he was welcome round at her house any time he wanted. But first, there was a rapist out there who needed destroying and as soon as Matilda Darke found him, she'd tear him apart with her bare hands.

Amy arrived home to an empty house. The dogs were impatiently waiting to be taken out for their evening walk. She changed into her walking shoes, put on their leads and collars and went back out. Her mind was all over the place. She couldn't get the ferocity of the attack on her baby girl out of her head. Why would someone do something so violent, cruel and hurtful? What could they possibly get out of it? There was obviously something seriously lacking in their lives if they took great pleasure in seeing others suffer so much. But why her Tilly? It wasn't fair. She was a good girl. She'd never done anything wrong, and the rest of her life was changed forever because one sick bastard had seen her and decided he wanted to destroy her.

Amy had no idea where she'd walked the dogs to, but she

soon found herself back on the front doorstep and digging around in her pocket for her keys. How long had she been out? She didn't remember stooping to pick up the dog poop. Her mind wasn't on anything. All she wanted to do was go back to the hospital, hold her daughter tight and never let go. If only that were possible.

She fed the dogs on autopilot. She should think about making herself something to eat, but she wasn't interested. She couldn't stomach anything right now.

She dragged herself through the living room on heavy legs, her feet barely leaving the floor. She trundled up the stairs and the dogs followed her. She didn't like the dogs sleeping upstairs. They had their own beds in the living room, but she didn't give it a second thought when all three jumped up onto her double bed. Well, Sausage needed a boost.

Amy stripped off her clothes, put on her nightie, pulled back the duvet and slumped into bed. She was shattered, physically drained. She wanted to sleep. Her body was so heavy, but her mind was racing at a hundred miles per hour. She kept seeing Tilly being dragged off the streets by a huge hulking man, thrown into the back of a van and savagely attacked.

Amy's mobile rang. The screen lit up the whole room. She looked at the display. Janet, her boss, and the head teacher of the primary school where she worked, was calling. She rolled her eyes. She couldn't face this right now, but she'd received so many voicemails, emails and text messages from concerned parents and teachers, both at Tilly's school and her own, asking how they both were. She swiped to answer.

'Hello,' she said in a tired voice.

'Amy, it's Janet,' she said in her best sympathetic tone. 'I just want to call to see how … well, how you and Tilly are doing really.'

Amy had no idea how to answer. 'She's, well, it's going to be a slow process, but she'll get there.' She tried to smile to make her voice sound more cheerful, but her lips were quivering.

'We're all thinking about her. And you. How are you doing, Amy?'

Amy was crying. She opened her mouth, and no words came out. She swallowed hard a couple of times.

'Amy, are you still there?' Janet asked.

'Yes. Still here,' she managed to say.

'Is … are you … are you all right?' Janet asked reluctantly.

'Am I all right?' she asked. She was audibly sobbing. 'No. No, I'm not. I'm as far away from all right as it's possible to be.' She cried through the tears. 'I've lost my baby girl.'

She ended the call and threw her mobile onto the floor. She curled up, pulling her legs up to her chest and screamed so loud, the dogs jumped off the bed.

Chapter Twenty-Eight

Tilly lay back in bed and wiped her own tears away. The physical pain she was feeling was immense. Every time she swallowed, breathed, yawned, hiccoughed, coughed or simply turned her head, she was in agony. The doctors told her it would heal, in time, but there was a long road ahead. If one more doctor mentioned that sodding long road once more, she'd scream. If she could scream, that was. Matilda was right about using her inner voice. She smiled at all the doctors but told them to piss off in her head on more than one occasion.

She knew her mother cared and what she was doing was for Tilly's own good, but it was too much. She was suffocating her. And the constant crying was getting on her nerves. As far as Tilly was concerned, her future was bleak. Her life was over. The last thing she needed was to look across at her mum and see her bawling her eyes out. It wasn't helping in the slightest.

She liked Matilda. She'd been through a trauma recently. She'd looked her up online while her mother was out chatting to one of the nurses. She was shot in the shoulder and in the head. Who the hell survives a bullet to the head? But she had.

And she was back to normal, back at work, walking and talking, and to look at her, you wouldn't think there had been anything wrong with her in the first place.

Tilly wondered what she was like on the inside. She'd heard about post-traumatic stress disorder and the way the mind can play bizarre tricks on you after a tragic event. She was already having nightmares. Would they be with her forever? And was it normal to see the man who attacked her every time she closed her eyes? She'd like to talk to Matilda more about her own recovery, but she didn't want her mother around earwigging.

Her mobile vibrated on the locker. She picked it up and saw it was a text from Ryan. He'd been texting constantly, asking how she was, telling her how much he loved her, and asking if he could visit. She replaced the phone back on top of the locker, message unread. Ryan should move on and find someone else. He wouldn't want her. She was scarred, emotionally and physically. Her whole life was changed. Everything she and Ryan had talked about doing in the new year, once exams were over, and long into the future, was redundant. This was day zero. She was starting afresh. She couldn't go to Meadowhall, hand in hand with Ryan, sit in the cinema with his arm around her, or in his parents' conservatory together on the sofa kissing and cuddling. All that was over. That had happened to a different girl, and she was no longer the fun, relaxed, smiling Tilly Hall, and she never would be again.

She'd been raped. She felt sick every time she thought of what he did to her. That was worse than having her throat slit. The image of him looming over her, grunting noisily as he was inside her, made her feel sick. She didn't want another man anywhere near her ever again. Not even Ryan.

Carefully, Tilly turned onto her side, facing the wall, and pulled the blanket up around her. It was only early, but she was tired, and there wasn't anything else for her to do in this bloody hospital other than sleep. She closed her eyes. Her body tensed.

The van door opened.

Darkness became light.

She inched her way further into the corner of the van, turning away from the man. She didn't want to look at him. She could feel his movements. He grabbed her legs and pulled at them. He didn't look it, but he was so strong. Or maybe she was so weak.

He pulled her out of the corner of the van so she was flat on her back. Her eyes were screwed tightly shut. She didn't want to see him. She felt his smooth hands on her legs, working their way up beneath her skirt.

Tilly opened her eyes and sat up in bed. She was struggling to breathe. Each intake of breath hurt and made her gasp harder, which caused more pain. She reached for the button and summoned help. She kicked away the blankets and looked down at her pale legs. She could still feel him on her.

The door opened and a concerned-looking nurse came in. Seeing Tilly in distress, she grabbed an oxygen mask and placed it over Tilly's nose and mouth.

'It's okay, Tilly, take slow breaths, nice and calm,' she said, sitting next to her on the bed. 'You're all right. You're perfectly safe. Slow, deep breaths. That's it. Good girl. Nightmare?'

Tilly shook her head.

'Panic attack?'

Tilly nodded.

'I know it's frightening, Tilly, but these things are going to keep happening to you. They will ease, but it's going to take a long time. We're all here for you. Any time you need us, just press the button. All right?'

Tilly nodded and smiled appreciatively beneath the mask.

'Would you like me to stay with you for a while?'

She nodded again.

'Okay. You need a distraction, something to take your mind off things for a while. I've got a sister, we're complete opposites. I was always academic and wanted to do nursing while she was always creative. Anyway, she did some work as a runner after college for a music company. Six months later she part of the backstage crew travelling around the country with Harry Styles. Do you like him?'

Tilly's breathing was back under control. She looked up at the kindly nurse and smiled.

'Shall I tell you what she saw in his dressing room?' the nurse asked her with a cheeky smile.

Chapter Twenty-Nine

Matilda was all settled for a night in front of the television with Adele and Pat when her phone rang. She looked at the screen, saw it was Chief Constable Ridley calling and rolled her eyes. So much for scrolling through the channels to see what festive shite was being offered up this year. It was forty minutes before she came back into the living room. Adele and Pat had opened a second bottle of wine and had found a saccharine made-for-TV Christmas film on some obscure cable channel.

Matilda sat on the sofa and released a heavy sigh.

'I'm guessing he wasn't calling to see what you wanted for Christmas,' Adele said.

'He literally wanted a minute-by-minute account of my day. I know he's under scrutiny from the Home Office, but he's made me feel like it's me personally who is being monitored.'

'What did you tell him?'

'Well, I blinded him with science with the Y-STR testing. That shut him up for a few minutes,' she said, reaching for the bottle of wine and pouring herself a glass. 'I told him that interviewing Tilly is going to be a long process, and about the witness who doesn't want to get involved.'

'I can't believe that,' Adele said. 'Surely, if you've seen something, and you're told a teenage girl has been raped, you'd want to help.'

'You'd think so, wouldn't you? I'm afraid things like community spirit and helping our fellow man are things of the past.' She turned to Pat. 'When you were on the force, did you have any tricks up your sleeve to get a reluctant witness to talk?'

'You could always send the biggest uniformed officer you've got around to beat the shit out of him.'

Matilda and Adele exchanged wide-eyed glances.

'I'm joking,' Pat said. 'Unfortunately, there really is nothing you can do if he won't give a statement. You could try appealing to his better nature or go to see him when you know his wife's there. Maybe she'll force him to talk.'

'Maybe,' Matilda said.

'What's on your mind?' Pat asked, studying Matilda's perplexed expression.

'I don't like a case that I can't get a handle on. Usually, there's some kind of motive involved, but this bloke, he's raping and killing these women because he's enjoying it. And that scares the living crap out of me.'

Pat placed her empty wine glass on the coffee table. She cleared her throat. 'A killer who is murdering for pure enjoyment is doing so because there is something missing in their lives.'

'I get all that. But how do I find someone like that? How do I even get a grip on who he is?'

'Shall I tell you what I'd do if I was leading this investigation?'

'Yes, please,' Matilda said, almost pleadingly, muting the television.

'I was watching that,' Adele moaned.

'Oh please. The man who doesn't believe in love meets the woman of his dreams and it snows on Christmas Day. The end.'

Pat smiled. 'You work out what kind of a killer you're looking for, then blanket news coverage to get someone to come forward and hopefully point you in the right direction.'

'Ridley doesn't want to draw much attention to South Yorkshire right now.'

'He's not going to have much of a choice. The killer is definitely going to be keeping an eye on the news, now more than ever, since his last victim survived. He's going to want to know your every move. Unless you tell the killer you're onto him, the bodies are simply going to pile up.'

Matilda took a shaky deep breath. 'So, you're suggesting I go on the news and say I'm looking for a hedonistic serial killer?'

'There's a lovely story to pull in the viewers in the run-up to Christmas,' Adele commented.

'You're looking for a process-focused killer,' Pat continued, 'who is hooked on the power and control he derives from the killings. He's highly organised. He'll enjoy torturing them, either physically or psychologically, and that will be sexually arousing for him. But it's always about the power and control he has over his victims. That's his driving force. Also, look at how he's managed to gain access to his victims. Yes, he kidnapped Tilly, and you have evidence of that, you don't with the other three. The first one, the nurse, she was lured, somehow. He's charming, charismatic, he appears non-threatening. He's highly intelligent and scheming.'

'He sounds like a complete psychopath,' Adele said, giving an exaggerated shiver.

'He's more than that,' Pat said. 'He's a stone-cold psychopath.'

'But if he's as manipulating and intelligent as you say he is, even if I went on the news and said this was the type of person I'm looking for, those around him are going to have been so won over by his lies and double-life-like behaviour that they won't for a second consider him being a killer.'

'Like Sian and her family were with Stuart,' Adele said, sipping her wine.

'No. But you give them the times and the dates of the killings. Let's say, for example, Adele is happily married.'

'There's an oxymoron if ever I heard one,' Adele interrupted.

Pat smiled. 'So, Adele's married to the man of her dreams. They're both hard working, it's coming up to Christmas, they're both busy, blah blah blah, the usual crap, then one day, she sits down to watch the news and a Detective Chief Inspector with split ends comes on and says they're hunting for a serial killer …'

'I had my hair trimmed last week, cheeky mare,' Matilda said.

'You say, for example, the first victim was killed on December the first, the second on December the fifth, the third on December the tenth. Something in Adele's head clicks. My husband was away on the first, and on the fifth, and now I think about it, he was late home on the tenth. She'll then start thinking about her husband more closely, and, fingers crossed, she'll give you a call and state her concerns.'

'Or Adele decides to mention it to her husband, and she becomes his latest victim,' Matilda said.

'Have you just killed me off? Thanks for that,' Adele said, picking up a cushion and throwing it at Matilda.

'Seriously,' Pat said, adopting a severe tone. 'By all means track down your missing sex offender. I don't know his original crimes, so I don't know how he operated. But you need to put together a detailed description of the kind of man you're looking for and tell everyone in South Yorkshire who *they* should be looking for. It's your only way of tracking down the killer. Because, based on his first four victims, he's left nothing of himself behind. Yes, he made a mistake with Tilly, but he'll make damn sure he won't make the same mistake again.'

The room fell into a heavy silence as the horror of the situation shrouded them all. The only noise came from the cracking wood in the fire.

'Well, I think on that note I might go on up to bed,' Adele said, standing up. 'Though I very much doubt I'll be getting much sleep tonight after that conversation.'

'I think I'll go up, too,' Pat said.

Matilda remained on the sofa.

'Mat, are you going to lock up?' Adele asked.

'Yes. Sure. You both go on up. I'll see you in the morning.'

Before she left the room, Pat leaned in to Matilda. 'The killer is operating well below the radar. You need to place him in the dead centre, and the only way to do that is to let everyone be on the lookout for him.'

'I know,' she said, a pained expression on her face. 'This is exactly what Ridley doesn't want, though.'

'To a Chief Constable, policing is all about politics. To a detective, it's all about catching the criminal. You're a detective.'

'I don't think Ridley will go for it. He's certainly not said anything about me doing an interview since I mentioned it the other day.'

'He doesn't have a choice. Matilda, your next victim is days away, and she's going to suffer terribly. You know it.'

'I know.'

'Convince Ridley it's the only way to go to catch this man. Goodnight,' Pat said, kissing her on the top of her head.

Matilda remained in the living room. She leaned forward and picked up her mobile from the coffee table. She selected Ridley's number. She knew she wouldn't be able to sleep until she'd spoken to him.

'Matilda, something wrong?' he answered. There was concern in his voice.

'I think I know how I can catch the killer.'

'That's good.'

'I just don't think you're going to like it.'

Chapter Thirty

Wednesday 23rd December 2020

'Good morning, Matilda. Have a seat.' Chief Constable Ridley's tone was anything but welcoming.

When Matilda knocked and entered his office, she found her boss pacing behind his desk in front of the window. He turned to greet her, looking as if he'd not slept a single minute last night. His uniform was pristine, as always.

'Would you like a bottle of water?' he offered, turning to the mini fridge next to his desk which contained nothing but tiny bottles of water.

'Oh. I'd rather have a coffee,' she said, taking a seat.

'I've been told to avoid caffeine. My blood pressure is through the roof. My GP has told me to cut out coffee, alcohol, cheese and fatty foods. Not the sort of thing you want to hear with Christmas fast approaching.' He pulled out his chair and sat down.

'Is everything all right?'

'Are you asking out of politeness or do you genuinely want to know? Because if you really do what to know, I'll tell you.'

'That bad?'

He released a heavy sigh. 'I spent the whole of last night thinking about our phone call. I've looked at your suggestion from every angle and the end result is always the same.'

'A positive one?' Matilda asked, hopefully.

'The complete opposite. My remit, right now, is to get South Yorkshire Police out of special measures, to get the Home Office off our back and allow us to get on with what we do best. To do that, I have to jump through hoops and play every kind of game the bastard politicians want me to play. Unfortunately, not one of those games is catching criminals. They really don't care about that. However, your remit *is* to catch the criminals. To say I'm stuck between a rock and a hard place is the understatement of the decade.'

Matilda looked at him and felt sympathy. She had been tempted, a couple of years ago, to apply for promotion and become an Assistant Chief Constable. The hours would be regular, she wouldn't have to place herself in danger hunting killers, and she'd get a plush office with a view of the city. It didn't take her long to realise she'd be bored within the first ten minutes. Placating politicians made Matilda's skin crawl just thinking about it.

'I did something last night that I've never done before in my whole career,' Ridley continued. 'I consulted my wife. We've always had this rule that we don't bring our work home, especially mine, but she could see I was tormenting myself, so we sat down, and she helped me to come to a conclusion of sorts.'

'What does your wife do?' Matilda asked.

'She's in PR for the English Institute of Sport.'

'Oh, wow. I had no idea.'

'You've never met my wife, have you?'

'No.'

'You'd like her. She refuses to take no for an answer, too. Basically, going on the news two days before Christmas to tell the people of Sheffield there's a serial killer butchering women is a PR nightmare. Surely, even you can see that.' Matilda nodded. 'So, my plan is to step up our campaign to keep the women of Sheffield safe over the Christmas period. In the run-up to New Year, I'll arrange for you to be interviewed by BBC News where you will state the kind of person you're seeking for these crimes.'

'That's another week away. We could have another victim on our hands by then.'

Ridley closed his eyes, contemplating his response. 'I know how bad it looks, Matilda.'

'We have nothing to go on, sir,' she said, stressing the 'sir'. 'There is not one shred of evidence and not a single witness willing to help us find him. Interviewing Tilly is a slow process, and she may not even be able to tell us anything at all. Waiting a week could be disastrous.'

'Matilda, we're in the middle of a pandemic. There are severe restrictions in place to stop people mixing over Christmas. That will help us. The pubs, restaurants and nightclubs are all closed. There are fewer people out on the streets. If we add an increase of patrols, it will seriously hamper the killer from claiming another victim.'

'I need to plant into people's minds the kind of person we're looking for. I need them to be looking at their husbands, fathers, brothers, uncles, boyfriends, best friends and neighbours and wondering if they're a killer. He made a mistake with Tilly Hall. His next victim is going to suffer in ways we can't even begin to imagine. I cannot sit back for another week and allow that to happen.'

'It's my decision to make, and I've made it. Get everything prepared for next Wednesday and I'll arrange for you to be interviewed.'

Matilda stood up. 'I think you're making a big mistake here.'

Ridley felt at his collar, loosening his tie. 'So do I.'

———————————

'How did it go?' Scott asked as Matilda entered the HMCU suite. She didn't stop and headed for her office.

'As I expected. Close the door behind you,' she instructed. 'Ridley has agreed for me to go on the news but not until next Wednesday. Basically, for the next week, we have to sit back and wait for the next victim to turn up.'

'That may not happen. Don't forget, it's Christmas. If this bloke has a family, he's going to have responsibilities. He can't pop out in the middle of Christmas lunch to go and kill someone. That will definitely give him away.'

'True. Let's hope he is a family man, then.' She looked at her watch. 'I need to get to the hospital to see Tilly again. Did you get me a photo of Andrew Hawkesley?'

'Yes. I've emailed one to you.'

'How's the search for him going?'

'We've interviewed his father, who says he hasn't seen him since he was arrested more than ten years ago. He washed his hands of him.'

'Can't say I blame him.'

'There are many foreign sets of fingerprints at his flat in Lowedges, but only Andrew's are identifiable. We're interviewing all the neighbours to see who visited him. We're also tracking down the victims and their families. You never know, they may have killed him in a revenge attack.'

'Keep me informed,' she said, grabbing her coat.

'Can I have a word?' Finn asked, knocking on the door and entering.

'Sure.'

He pushed his rimless glasses up his nose. 'It's about what you said this morning about doing an interview on the news to let people know the kind of killer we're looking for.'

'Okay,' Matilda said.

'It's not like you to volunteer to give an interview. You've always left it to someone higher up in the past. Are you setting yourself up as bait for the killer to come for you?'

'What?' Scott asked, looking, wide-eyed at Matilda.

'Of course I'm not.' Matilda didn't look at either of them.

'I think this goes much further than us thinking the killer is a misogynist,' Finn went one. 'We've already established he has a problem with women, either stemming from his childhood with his mother, or a domineering wife, maybe, but look at the level of violence he's put into his crimes. We're entering into torture porn territory. He stabs and attacks and destroys until he's literally no energy left and only stops when he's that knackered he can't lift the knife up any more. Given the chance, he'd obliterate his victims. This man is pure evil,' Finn stated.

The silence in the room was heavy.

Finn continued. 'The last thing he's going to want is a female detective leading the hunt for him. The moment he sees you on the news, he'll have found his next victim. He'll come for you.'

'Oh my God, he's right,' Scott said.

'But you'd already worked that out, hadn't you?' Finn asked. 'That's your plan, isn't it?'

Matilda concentrated on buttoning up her coat, checking her pockets for her mobile phone and wrapping her scarf snugly around her neck.

'Can you think of a better plan?' she asked, her voice quiet.

'Yes!' Scott exclaimed. 'You let Ridley do the interview and the same information will be planted in people's minds and we wait for the phone to ring.'

'Do you have any idea how many calls we're going to get after the interview has gone out?' she asked. 'They won't be from people concerned about the sudden change in behaviour of a relative, it'll be people telling us about people they don't like. The bloke across the road who won't trim his hedge and it's blocking out their light. The man next door who doesn't take his bins in straightaway when they've been emptied. That man down the road who parks anywhere he likes and not outside his own house. We've seen it before. We have four crime scenes from this man, and we haven't a single scrap of evidence. The only way to catch him is to get him to come to us. To me.'

'And what happens when he does come after you?'

'Scott, I'll have so many police officers hiding in my house it'll look like some kind of convention. I've no intention of putting myself in harm's way. I just need him to come into the light. Then we arrest him. Now, I'm late for interviewing Tilly, and you two have got plenty to be getting on with.'

She pushed past them both and left the suite, calling for an Uber on her mobile.

'We can't allow her to do this, Scott,' Finn said.

'I know. But she's got that determined look in her eye. Do you have any other suggestions?'

'Not right now. But we've got a week to find the killer before Matilda offers herself up as a sacrifice.'

'No pressure then,' Scott said.

Chapter Thirty-One

It didn't feel like Christmas to Matilda. It was cold, admittedly, and down every corridor of the Sheffield Children's Hospital, she was presented with huge drawings of Father Christmas and snowmen and tired-looking decorations, but she simply didn't have that excited anticipation that Christmas was only two days away.

Matilda assumed many people would be feeling the same this year with the coronavirus pandemic maintaining its grip. Case numbers were rising, and the death toll was at almost seventy thousand. That was a huge figure. A vaccine had been created and the rollout around the country was escalating by the day. Fingers crossed, by the spring, the world would have turned a corner. She was beginning to wish the government had the power to cancel Christmas completely this year. It would certainly solve a lot of problems.

Standing outside of Tilly's room, Matilda composed herself. The last thing she wanted was to go in with an angry expression on her face. She unbuttoned her coat and relaxed her body, not realising her shoulders had been almost up to her ears. She took a few slow, deep breaths, painted on a smile, knocked and entered the room.

'Good morning, Tilly. How are you feeling?' Matilda asked in a cheery voice and with a smile that usually could only be maintained by a handful of Prozac.

Tilly held up six fingers.

'We're improving.'

'The nurses came in this morning to change her dressing,' Amy said. 'It's healing up nicely.'

Matilda noticed there was less padding around Tilly's neck. 'That's wonderful news.'

'A second procedure has been booked in for the twenty-seventh, and they're talking about doing a skin graft as well, but that won't be until January at the earliest, once the wound is fully healed.'

Matilda looked over to Tilly. Her eyes were wider and brighter. She'd obviously had her pain medication reduced and was maybe more lucid this morning.

'How are you?' Matilda asked Amy.

Amy looked surprised by the question and smiled. 'I'm … okay.' It was an obvious lie.

'Tilly,' Matilda began, getting her phone out. 'I have a photo I'd like you to look at. There's a man who's appeared on our radar who we think might be the person who attacked you.'

Tilly became visibly frightened. She pulled the bed covers closer to her. Her face had paled, and her breathing quickened.

'I know it's scary, Tilly. But this is just a photograph. All I want you to do is nod or shake your head when you see him to let me know if it's him. Is that all right?'

Tilly gripped her mum's hand firmer. Amy stood up and went to sit on the bed next to her, wrapping her arm around her shoulders, holding her tight.

Matilda turned the phone slowly to Tilly. 'Is this the man who attacked you?'

Tilly shook her head firmly straightaway.

'Are you sure?'

She nodded.

'Thank you.' Matilda smiled. 'I really appreciate you looking.'

'Who is he?' Amy asked.

'He's someone known to the police who's gone missing. He has a history of violence towards women, so we needed to confirm if it was him or not. Tilly, thank you so much.'

Tilly smiled. She picked up the iPad from the bedside locker, opened the notes app and handed it to Matilda.

I've been thinking long and hard about the kind of van the man was driving. I didn't see the number plate but I pretty sure of the make of van. I googled it and saved a photo. It's in the photos app.

Matilda opened the app and looked at the picture of a silver Vauxhall Vivaro. 'Are you sure this is the van?'

Tilly nodded. She typed on the iPad and handed it to Matilda.

Ryan's dad has a Vauxhall Vivaro in blue. He took us for a drive in it to the coast when he first bought it.

'And the one you saw was definitely silver?'

She nodded.

'Could it have been another colour like grey or an off-white?'

It was a while before Tilly replied. She shook her head.

'It was definitely silver then. That's good. Was there any writing on the side of the van?'

I didn't see the side. I only saw the back of it. I remember seeing the VW logo and the word Viv. That's how I know it was a Vivaro.

'Thank you so much, Tilly. That really is very helpful,' Matilda said with a smile, knowing praise was important. 'Is there anything else you can remember about the man? Anything at all?'

She shook her head and took the iPad back from Matilda and began typing again.

I don't know if I've purposely blocked it out or if I didn't see him, but I can't see his face in my mind at all. I know he wasn't tall or big. He was quite thin, and I could smell his deodorant, but I didn't like it. That really is all I can remember about him.

'That's fine,' Matilda said after reading. 'I don't want you troubling yourself over remembering him. Don't get worked up about it. It's fine you don't remember.' *Except that it isn't.*

'It's probably for the best,' Amy added, squeezing her daughter's shoulders and smiling. She returned to her seat.

'Going back to the van, did you see what was inside it? Is there anything at all you can tell me about the inside of the van?'

Tilly took back the iPad and frowned as she thought.

It was very cold, and it smelled damp. There was a blanket laid out. It was thin and I think there was wood beneath it. The blanket was red tartan. The same type as Sausage's bed. There was a hi-vis jacket hung up in the corner. It was dirty but I couldn't see if it had any writing or logos on it.

Matilda read it and showed it to Amy.

'Sausage sleeps on a red tartan bed. It's just a red checked thing. I can send you a photo of it if you like?'

'That would be helpful, thank you.' She turned back to Tilly. 'I know you might not think you're giving us much information, Tilly, but you really are. This is all building up a huge picture for us to work on.'

Tilly gave her a warm smile.

'What's the plan for Christmas Day?' Matilda asked, changing the subject to something lighter.

'I'm going to bring her presents in the morning and stay for a few hours. We can't have the big meal we always like to have, but, well, it's just a fancy Sunday lunch, isn't it?' Amy gave a pained smile. 'We can have one of those any time.'

'I'll come and see you before Christmas,' Matilda said. 'You've got my mobile number and email address so if you think of anything, you can message me anytime. Or if you just want to have a chat. I'll be working most of Christmas so a distraction will be very welcome from all the paperwork.'

Matilda stood up, grabbed her coat and scarf and said her goodbyes. She was halfway down the corridor when Amy shouted after her.

'I didn't want to ask in front of Tilly, but are you close to catching who did this?'

Matilda couldn't lie to her. 'At the moment, no, but Tilly recognising the van is a great help. I will personally knock on the door of every silver Vauxhall Vivaro van owner in the county if I have to. I promise you, Amy, I'm not going to stop until I have the man who did this behind bars.'

'Thank you.' She smiled, but didn't turn to go back to Tilly's room.

'Is there anything else?' Matilda asked.

'About Ryan. Am I going to get into trouble for what I did?'

'There have been no reports of the assault, so no. I don't have children but even I can understand why you did what you did. It's only natural you want to protect Tilly.'

She gave an awkward smile. 'When Shane died, I really

struggled. I had no idea how to bring up a child on my own. I had to be tough and strong for Tilly and that's not me at all.'

'I think you're doing an amazing job. Shane will be proud.'

A tear rolled down Amy's cheek. 'I'm not sure about that. I think he'd have handled the Ryan Cook incident differently. If I hadn't have stuck my nose in, they wouldn't have had to be sneaking around and Tilly wouldn't have gone down that dirt track.'

Matilda shrugged. 'We all make thousands of decisions every day. Some of them end up having huge consequences. If we go through life analysing back and forth everything we do, we'll be nervous wrecks. I've been over the day I was shot countless times and looked at it from every angle. Would it have happened if I'd phoned in sick or if I'd been late or if my meeting with my boss had overrun? You were looking out for Tilly. Don't blame yourself for what happened.'

Amy sniffed back her tears. 'I need to blame someone,' she struggled to say, wiping her eyes with her sleeve.

'There is someone to blame. The man who did this. We don't have a name for him yet, but you can point all your angry energy towards him.'

Amy nodded. 'I honestly don't know how you do your job. When you meet killers like this, or child abusers, how do you stop yourself from wanting to kill them yourself?'

Matilda immediately thought of Christian Brady and the standoff at Magnolia House earlier in the year. Had he pulled the trigger and killed the man who'd been sexually abusing young boys for more than twenty years? It suddenly clicked into place that if he did, she fully understood why.

'It's all in the training,' she said with a hint of a smile. She turned on her heel and headed for the lifts. *Training my arse.*

Chapter Thirty-Two

'What are you doing here?' Matilda asked Scott when she saw him sitting in the waiting area of the Children's Hospital.

'I thought I'd come and pick you up.'

'Hmm. Your furrowed brow tells a different story.'

'I do have some information for you, but I also need to talk to you, too.'

'That sounds ominous.'

'I'm parked on a double yellow,' he said, heading for the doors. Matilda followed feeling like she was about to told off for staying out late.

It wasn't until they were both in the car, doors closed, seatbelts on, and they'd driven around the corner that Scott pulled up, turned the engine off and started talking.

'I know the Chief Constable asked you back specifically to help get the force out of special measures, but did he actually ask you to be a human sacrifice for a serial killer?'

Matilda half-laughed. 'Scott, that's not what I'm doing.'

'You told me, not two days ago, to keep an eye on Tom so

he wouldn't do anything stupid that could end up with him being injured, or worse, like Zofia did last year, and you're doing exactly that.'

'Scott, I understand you're concerned. I'm concerned myself. But you've seen the state of the investigation. Four victims and not a single piece of evidence. Can you think of a better way to lure him out?'

Scott didn't answer. He gave a heavy sigh and turned away.

'As soon as the interview goes out next Wednesday, I'll surround myself with protection. I can't let him claim another victim, Scott. If you saw how Tilly's coping, what this is doing to her mum, you'd understand.'

'I do understand. It's just … Why does it have to be you?' he asked, turning to her, tears glistening in his eyes.

'There is nobody else,' she said. 'Trust me, if you looked good in a skirt, I'd gladly let you step in for me.' She smiled.

Scott didn't respond. It was clear he was upset. 'I don't want anything to happen to you.'

'It won't. Besides, maybe it won't come to that. We've got a week. We could have a breakthrough.'

'That's the other reason why I came to meet you,' Scott said, fishing around in his pocket for his phone. 'Zofia has finally come through with the CCTV and ANPR. She's picked up a van close to two of the crime scenes, within the timeframe of the attacks taking place, with the same registration number.'

'I don't suppose there's any chance it's a silver Vauxhall Vivaro, is it?'

He looked at her. 'How did you know that?'

'What? Is it?' she asked, wide-eyed.

'Yes. How did you know?'

'Tilly remembered the make of the van she was dragged

into. Who does it belong to?' She leaned in to have a look at the screenshots on Scott's phone.

'Laurence Dodds. He lives on Ballifield Road in Handsworth.'

'Does he have a record?'

'No.'

'Ah. I don't know why, but I'm always nervous when someone's first criminal act is murder. When someone works up to it, you can see the criminal process from his record. A serial killer with no prior record means he's a very intelligent man who will have certainly done his homework.'

'Shall we go and pay him a visit?'

'Absolutely.'

Scott started the pool car and pulled out into traffic.

'This can't be a coincidence, can it?' Matilda asked. 'I mean, I'm guessing Vauxhall made more than one silver Vivaro, but Tilly was adamant it was the right colour and model.'

Scott slammed on the brakes, sending Matilda shooting forward in her seat. She didn't have time to get her hands up and almost knocked her head on the dashboard.

'Are you all right?' Scott asked.

'Yes. Fine,' she said, rubbing her neck where the seatbelt had dug into her. She looked up, out of the windscreen, and into the frightened eyes of a young woman driving a deep red Fiat Punto who had pulled out of a side road in front of them.

'She didn't even slow down,' Scott said. 'She just shot straight out at us.'

'No harm done. Wave her on.'

'She looks shaken up.'

'She's not the only one.'

Slowly, the Punto edged out into the road. She didn't wave thanks at them or apologise, and drove on her way.

'And a merry Christmas to you, too,' Matilda said flippantly.

'See what I said about people not caring about others any more? I'm definitely going to need a change of underwear when I get back to the station,' Scott said.

Ballifield Road was a long road with semi-detached houses on either side. They looked to have been built around the 1950s and most front gardens had been turned into driveways to accommodate an extra car or a caravan. Some were obviously bought and looked after, with neatly trimmed privet hedges and well-tended lawns, whereas others were either council or housing association rented and had been allowed to descend into disrepair. It was a neighbourhood which gave out mixed vibes. Some homes looked inviting and welcoming, others you wouldn't want to knock on their doors after dark for fear of what lurked inside.

'Wow, look at that one,' Scott pointed out. 'They've really gone to town with their Christmas decorations.'

The house in question was covered in flashing lights from chimney to doorstep. A huge Father Christmas in his sleigh with a couple of reindeer was balanced precariously on the roof. Each window had something twinkling in it and the door was wrapped as if it was a giant present with a bow around the centre.

'I'd hate to get their electricity bill in January,' Scott smiled.

'Will you be seeing Donal over Christmas?' Matilda asked.

'Yes. I'm spending the day with my mum and dad and going round to Donal's in the evening.'

'Is everything all right between you two?'

'I think so.' He gave a weak smile. 'I spoke to him on the phone for a couple of hours last night. I told him about how I felt when he stays over.'

'What did he say?'

'He understood. He said I can always stay at his whenever I want to.'

'There's no need to rush, Scott. Take things as slowly as you want. I know the way you lost Chris was a huge shock and it came out of the blue, but it doesn't mean the same thing will happen with Donal. You don't need to declare your love on the first date and get married on the second.'

'I know. It's …' He stopped.

'What is it?'

'A silver Vivaro.'

The van passed their car and pulled up on the driveway of a house a few doors down. A man got out of the driver's side and came around to the other side, pulling the door open and taking out a few heavy bags of shopping.

He was of average height, maybe five foot eight, and wore a black and grey bobble hat and a padded winter coat. He had sensible shoes with a good grip on and navy combat trousers.

The front door of the house opened and an elderly woman stepped out. She was wearing a red coat, black trousers and a beanie hat pulled down low.

'Thank you so much, Mrs Rosen. How is she?' he asked.

Neither Matilda nor Scott could hear Mrs Rosen's reply. She spoke softly.

'That's lovely. Thank you. I really do appreciate it. I've got more of that salt in the van if you want me to do your path so you don't slip on the ice.'

Again, they couldn't hear her reply.

The man placed his shopping on the doorstep and went to

help the elderly Mrs Rosen, taking her by the elbow and leading her to her own front door opposite. They were chatting and their voices were low. The man returned to his own house, picked up his bags and entered, closing the door firmly behind him.

'Is it definitely the same number plate?' Matilda asked Scott.

He looked down at his phone. 'YY67 MTC. Same number, same make and model, same colour. You think he's our killer?'

'It's either him or someone he lends his van to. Come on.' She opened the car door and shivered in the cold afternoon air.

———

The temperature had dropped, or maybe Matilda had been in the warmth of the hospital so long she'd grown used to the heat, but she shivered as she walked up the short path to the front door, pressed the bell and stood back.

'They said on the news earlier that we might be in for a white Christmas,' Scott said.

'They say that every year,' Matilda replied.

The door opened and Matilda faced the glow of the yellow light beaming out at her. The man who answered was slight in build, somewhere in his early fifties, Matilda guessed, with short, thinning, mousy hair. He wore black trousers and a navy sweater that looked a size too big for him. His sleeves were rolled up, his arms thin and bony.

'Laurence Dodds?' Matilda asked.

'That's right,' he said with a nod and a slight smile.

'DCI Matilda Darke, South Yorkshire Police,' she said, flashing her warrant card. 'This is Detective Sergeant Scott Andrews. Any chance of a word?'

The smile dropped.

'Oh. What's it about?'

'Is this your van?' She asked.

'Yes.'

'Your registration number has come up in our investigation and we'd like to ask about your whereabouts.'

'Oh. Of course. Go ahead. Oh, I'm sorry, come on in.' He immediately stepped to one side and let Matilda and Scott inside. 'I'm so sorry. You don't expect police to turn up on your doorstep, do you? My manners went completely out of the window there for a second.'

They stood in the small hallway while Laurence closed the door. The heat from the radiator was intense.

'If I could ask you to keep your voice low,' he said in a voice barely above a whisper. 'My mother is asleep in the sitting room. Go straight ahead to the kitchen.'

Matilda smiled. She looked around her. 'I like your painting,' she said, looking at a framed picture of the Arts Tower which was situated just outside Sheffield City Centre.

'Thank you. I painted it myself.'

'Really?' Matilda asked, impressed. 'It's very good.'

'Thank you. I used to work there, many years ago. I've always found it a fascinating building.'

'You're very talented,' Matilda said, looking closely at it. 'The way you've got the shadow and the sunlight on all the windows. It's stunning. Are you a professional artist?'

Laurence scoffed. 'No. It's just a hobby. I did sell a couple a few years back to raise money for charity, but I just enjoy painting. It's relaxing.'

Laurence led the way into the large but chaotic kitchen. Every work surface was covered with something, whether it was the preparation of a meal or medication boxes or bags of shopping. The round dining table was obviously where Laurence painted. There was an easel on it surrounded by various pots of paint.

'Please, take a seat,' he instructed. 'They are clean, I promise, just very old.' He laughed, nervously.

'Is this what you're working on at the moment?' Matilda asked, leaning over the easel.

'Yes. I'm painting Park Hill flats. I can't say I'm too keen on how they look now with all those brightly coloured blocks, but it makes for an interesting subject.'

Matilda looked at the painting. The sketch was outlined perfectly, and Laurence was barely a third of the way in with the watercolours.

'I think they should have knocked them down when they fell into disrepair,' Laurence went on. 'Brutalist urban architecture, apparently. I'm assuming that's twenty-first-century-speak for eyesore.'

Matilda smiled at him. 'I'm not a fan either. This is very good, though. You have a very creative eye.'

'Thank you. Sorry, I'm forgetting my manners again. Would you like a cup of tea? I've just made one for my mother, so it won't take long for the kettle to boil.'

'That would be lovely, thank you,' Matilda said.

'Right,' he said, heading for the kettle. He seemed edgy as he rapidly darted to a cupboard to get the mugs out, to the fridge for the milk and back to the cupboard for the tea bags.

Matilda looked to Scott and nodded for him to take the lead in the questioning.

'Mr Dodds,' he began.

'Laurence, please,' he interrupted.

'Laurence. I'm not sure if you've seen the news about the

attacks on four women in Sheffield over the past couple of months.'

'I'm afraid I haven't,' he said, concentrating on pouring boiling water into two mugs. 'Every time I turn the news on it's all about the pandemic or news briefings with that public-school buffoon. I'm sorry, but you'd think someone on his PR team would tell him to brush his hair before he went on television. Do either of you take milk and sugar?'

'Milk, no sugar, thanks,' Matilda said.

'The same for me,' Scott added. 'Well, four women have been severely attacked since the end of October. Three of whom were murdered.'

'Oh dear. That's tragic,' Laurence said, carefully bringing the full mugs over to the table. 'Just move my painting things to one side,' he said to Matilda so he could make room for the mugs.

'At the moment, we don't have much to go on so we're trawling CCTV footage and your van has appeared twice at two different crime scenes.'

'You mean I was nearby when the murders happened?' he asked, a hand to his throat. He played with a St Christopher on a thin chain around his neck.

'Yes.'

'Good grief. I might have seen something.'

'That's what we're hoping,' Matilda said, blowing on her tea.

'When was it?'

Scott got out his notebook. 'The first occasion was the eighteenth of November. It was a Wednesday. Your van was spotted at 18:58 on Mushroom Lane.'

Laurence frowned as he thought. 'The eighteenth of

November. I'm going to have to get my diary. Bear with me one moment, please.' He dashed out into the hallway.

'What do you think?' Matilda whispered.

'He looks a bit weedy, a bit pathetic.'

She smiled and nodded.

Laurence came back in, flicking through a slim-line diary. 'I don't get out much, I'm afraid. I'm a full-time carer for my mother. I'm afraid I rather … well, you don't want to hear all the ins and outs, but it was recommended that I do some voluntary work to get me out of the house from time to time. I deliver groceries for the food bank the church runs, and I volunteer to help out the elderly too with their shopping. I can claim back my petrol expenses, so I have to keep a regular note of all my journeys. I don't have anything written in for the eighteenth of November. I obviously didn't go out at all that day,' he said, handing the diary to Scott with it open on that week.

'Do you mind if I show you the CCTV footage in question?'

'No, of course not.' He leaned across the table and picked up his glasses. The lenses were smudged, and he rubbed them on his jumper. He leaned in close to Scott to get a good look at his phone. 'Oh, yes. That is my van. And this is Mushroom Road, you said?'

'Mushroom Lane,' Scott said, leaning further away from Laurence.

'Where is that?' he asked, looking up at Matilda.

'It's near the Children's Hospital. It's behind Weston Park Museum.'

'Oh, I know the area. I've been to the museum many times. Not for a while, obviously, with the pandemic. I certainly wasn't there on the eighteenth of November.'

'Have you lent your van to anyone?' Matilda asked.

'No. I wouldn't,' he said as if it was an abomination to lend someone his vehicle. 'Actually, no, I'm telling a lie. I've let the vicar borrow it once or twice. I don't know the exact dates. He might know, though. I can give you his contact details.'

'Thank you.' Matilda smiled.

'The second occasion was more recent,' Scott said, selecting another photo on his phone. 'December the fifteenth. It was a Tuesday. Your van was spotted here at 17:51 on the junction of Brincliffe Edge Road and Ecclesall Road South.' Scott looked up at Matilda and pointed to Laurence with his eyes widened in horror at how close he was to him.

Matilda struggled to stifle a smile. She turned away and began flicking through a pad of drawings. Laurence seemed to enjoy drawing buildings dotted around Sheffield. There was a rough sketch of Weston Park Museum, the Hallamshire Hospital, a couple more of the Arts Tower, Meadowhall, Orchard Square, the Clock Tower at the Northern General Hospital. There was no denying the man had talent.

Laurence was flicking through his diary. 'The optician came round to give my mother an eye test in the afternoon at one o'clock, but apart from that, I don't have anything at all for that day.' He handed the diary back to Scott to check. 'I don't understand it. It definitely looks like my van in the photos. And it's certainly my number plate.'

'Does anyone else have the keys?'

'No.'

'Have you had a break-in recently or misplaced your keys?'

'No.'

'Mr Dodds. Laurence,' Matilda said. 'Is there anyone who can account for your whereabouts on either of these two dates?'

'Only my mother. She had a stroke about, ooh, let me think,

it's more than ten years ago. I don't think she's left the house since. She's had a few more minor strokes since then. Her speech has almost gone, and she sleeps a lot. Not much of an alibi, is it?'

Matilda gave an awkward smile.

'It's strange, isn't it? I mean, I'm a law-abiding person. I've never so much as had a parking ticket, but if you can't prove it, you're as guilty as everyone else. I never realised that before now,' he said, placing a hand on Scott's shoulder.

Matilda and Scott exchanged glances again. Scott was clearly uncomfortable with Laurence's close proximity.

'Hang on a minute,' Laurence said. His face lit up. 'We have CCTV. That will show you my van on the driveway. I'll just go and get my iPad.' He darted out of the room.

'Can we go, please?' Scott asked.

'I think he's taken a shine to you.'

'He's making my flesh crawl.'

'I have warned you about wearing those tight trousers and fitted shirts.'

'Here we are,' Laurence said, a look of excitement on his face. He handed the iPad to Scott. 'I'm not sure how to look up the history of what's been recorded. I've never needed to before, but I'm sure you'll find that my van was parked on the drive all day on the fifteenth. And here are the contact details for the vicar. This is his card.' He handed it to Matilda.

Scott worked his way through the app.

'If you don't mind me asking, why do you have CCTV?' Matilda asked.

'I had it installed about, let me think, three, maybe four years ago now. There was a spate of burglaries in the street. Mrs Price, opposite, she was burgled twice, bless her. We weren't, thankfully, but some uniformed officers came round to tell us about improving our home security. I had new locks put on the doors and all the windows and had the CCTV installed, too. Not that I go out much, but the way the camera is angled, it takes in a few of the neighbours' houses, too, which is helpful.'

Matilda gave him an awkward smile. She could understand him talking so much if his only company was an elderly mother who slept a great deal. Maybe he didn't get many visitors and enjoyed two strangers coming into his home.

'Would either of you like more tea?' Laurence asked, more cheerful now his alibi seemed to have been confirmed.

'No. I'm fine. Thank you,' Matilda said, looking down at her half-drunk mug. It wasn't the best cup of tea she'd had. In fact, it was bloody awful.

'It's right here,' Scott said. 'December the fifteenth. You can scroll through at speed. Your van doesn't move all day.'

'Phew,' Laurence said in exaggeration. 'That's a relief. For a moment there, I was beginning to doubt my own innocence.' He laughed. 'Maybe we should all have a chip inside us that can let the police know exactly where everyone is.'

'I'd love to see the government try to get that act through Parliament,' Matilda said. She smiled and stood up. 'Well, we won't take up any more of your time. Thank you for the tea and I apologise for the misunderstanding. It would appear someone has cloned your number plate.'

'Cloned? How do they do that?'

'They obviously have the same kind of van and have driven around to find another one that's identical, taken down your number plate and had replicas made.'

'These people. They've no morals, have they?'

'I'm afraid not.'

Scott was already out of the kitchen and by the front door.

'It was lovely to meet you both. Merry Christmas.'

Matilda turned to look at Laurence. 'Merry Christmas. And to your mother, too.'

'Thank you.'

'I need a shower, then a bottle of brandy, then a bath, then another shower, followed by a third shower,' Scott said as he climbed into the car and put on his seatbelt.

The light had started to fade while they were in Laurence Dodds's house, and it was almost dark. Other houses in the street had turned on their lights and Christmas trees were lit up in the living room windows. Only Laurence's house was without any festive decorations.

'I sort of felt sorry for him,' Matilda said.

'Why?'

'If his mother had a stroke ten years ago and he's been her full-time carer ever since, he's not had much of a life, has he? Did you hear what he said before he told us about his volunteering work?'

'No.'

'Well, he sort of stopped himself. He mentioned that he was told to do something to get himself out of the house from time to time. I bet there was a time when all he was doing was caring for his mother. I bet he sank into a depression, and it was a doctor who told him to seek help, get support for his mum while he went out and had some kind of a life.'

'Oh. I didn't pick up on that.'

'I did,' Matilda said, looking up at the house.

'Can I drive away now, please? I can still feel his breath on my neck.'

'Go on.'

'Are we crossing him off our list?' Scott asked.

'For now. Although I want the vicar interviewing.' She looked back ahead once they were away from the house. 'Someone has been driving around looking for a silver Vivaro they can clone the number plate from. The more we learn about this killer the more intelligent he's appearing to be. He's thought of everything. Now do you see why I'm so keen to lure him out into the open?'

'I still don't like it,' Scott said. 'If, like you say, he's thought of everything from forensic evidence to cloning a registration plate, then that just makes him even more dangerous. If he does come after you following the news interview, you're going to be in serious trouble.'

Matilda took a deep breath.

Suddenly, she felt very nervous.

Chapter Thirty-Three

Tilly yawned. She finished reading the page, popped in a bookmark and placed it carefully on top of the locker. She looked at her mobile. Another four more messages from Ryan. She wanted to text him back, tell him how much she missed him, but she knew he'd ask to visit her, and she didn't want that. She didn't want him seeing her like this. He should move on, find another girlfriend. He wouldn't want to go out with someone who couldn't speak, who had an ugly scar on her neck and who never wanted to have sex or be touched ever again. The very thought of a man touching her, of Ryan touching her, made her feel sick.

She turned over and pulled the blankets up over her head. She was crying and the tears made her pillow wet.

She cried herself to sleep.

The door opened.

Tilly was on her back. Her right arm was above the covers

across her chest. She'd kicked the covers off and both legs were exposed. A sheen of sweat covered her forehead. Her eyes were darting rapidly beneath her closed eyelids and her lips were moving slightly. Whatever she was dreaming about, it was intense.

The room was dark, lit only by the yellow sodium of the streetlights outside filtering through the half-opened slats of the vertical blinds at the windows. The heat was oppressive.

He stepped into the room and closed the door carefully behind him. He was wearing latex gloves and placed a surgical mask over his nose and mouth. He wore a hooded sweater and pulled the hood up and tugged on the drawstrings, tightening it over his head. Only his eyes were visible. He watched as Tilly slept.

It would be so easy to finish her off right now. It wouldn't take long to pick up one of those pillows, place it over her face and press down hard until she stopped breathing. Or maybe he could remove the bandaging around her throat, yank out the stitches with his bare hands and attack the exposed wound, pull out the veins and muscles while she was still alive.

As much as he knew he'd enjoy that, there was something perverse about keeping her alive he'd enjoy more. He wanted to keep tabs on Tilly Hall. He wanted to friend her on Facebook, watch as she detailed her recovery, read the comments from friends, family and total strangers as they championed her survival and virtually held her hands through the setbacks. He could follow her, watch her, stalk her, frighten her, torment her, call her names, say how ugly and frightful she looked. That would set her back years and cause all kinds of mental problems. Killing people was so easy, and once it was over with, that was it. The greatest fun came from the psychological games that could follow such a life-changing attack. He smiled to himself and stepped closer to Tilly.

He placed a hand over her mouth and her eyes snapped open. They were wide and staring. He felt her entire body shaking. She'd recognised him instantly.

'Hello, Tilly,' he said. 'Remember me?'

She kicked out and tried to scramble out from beneath his hold, but she was no match for him.

'I'm guessing the police are asking you all kinds of questions about me. You can't answer them, obviously, but you'll be writing things down for them. I know I've been very careful, and there's not a scrap of evidence left for them at the scenes, and you're their only hope. You tell them anything about me, anything at all, and I swear to God I'll not only come for you, but I'll come for your mum as well and I'll hurt you both so fucking much.'

Tilly was choking, struggling for breath. Tears were streaming down her face onto the pillow.

'I like to play the long game, Tilly. I'll wait until you're recovered and back home, and I'll make you watch as I cut your mum up in front of you. Do you understand?'

She blinked hard and nodded.

'Good girl.'

He removed his hand, stepped back and smiled at her beneath his mask.

'You're a very beautiful girl, Tilly.' He turned and went to the door. With one hand on the handle, he turned back. 'Just one thing. I'm not sure if they've mentioned all the tests they've done on you, but have you found out if you're pregnant or not yet?' He winked, then left, closing the door silently behind him.

Tilly cried. She opened her mouth to scream but nothing

came out. She was struggling to breath and took huge gasps in horror. She scrabbled on the locker in the dark for the button to summon help but couldn't find it. She knocked her book onto the floor, the noise resounding around the silent room. She could feel the get-well cards toppling over. She eventually found the wire and the button, and pressed it over and over until the door opened, she was bathed in light, and a tired-looking nurse was standing in the doorway.

Chapter Thirty-Four

Adele struggled into the kitchen under the weight of her shopping.

'Right then,' she said, slamming the bags down on the table. 'That's all the veg. I've got sprouts, carrots, potatoes, parsnips and peas. I've got a dozen eggs and I remembered the flour even though it wasn't on my list. Your mum is doing the Yorkshire puddings, apparently.'

'Mum does amazing Yorkshires,' Matilda said to Pat. They were both in the kitchen with a glass of wine each.

'Harriet's bringing the dessert and me and Pat will be doing all the veg,' Adele added, grabbing a clean glass from the cupboard and holding it out for Matilda to fill. 'When are you picking up the turkey?'

Matilda stopped as if she was frozen in time. Slowly, she turned around. There was a look of pure horror etched on her face.

'You've forgotten the turkey, haven't you?' Adele asked.

'No.'

'And the truth?'

'Yes.'

'Matilda!'

'I know! I meant to order it, then Ridley came round and asked me back to work, and it went clean out of my head. I'll get a frozen one tomorrow from the supermarket.'

'The size we need, it won't be defrosted in time for Christmas Day.'

'Of course it will.'

'I don't want to be a downer or anything,' Pat said. 'But on the news, they were talking about a supply shortage of things like turkey and sprouts. It's something to do with Brexit and foreign drivers being stuck at the Channel Tunnel. I warned Anton this would happen if he voted to leave the EU, but he wouldn't listen to me.'

'I didn't have your Anton down as a Brexiteer,' Matilda said.

'Oh, my goodness, he loathed the EU with a passion. I think it started with the single currency. He kept saying that—'

'Interesting as this is,' Adele interrupted, 'what are we going to do about the turkey situation?'

'Well, until their economy is stable enough, I don't think they should be allowed to join,' Pat said.

'I meant the meat, not the country.'

Pat laughed. 'I know you did, I'm just … ah, not a joking matter, I see.'

Matilda was laughing. 'Adele, don't worry about it. If we can't get one, then we'll just have a vegetarian version of a Christmas lunch.'

'Leave it to me. Pat to the rescue, as usual. There's a bloke who belonged to the same bowling club as Anton who has a farm out towards Leicester. He always delivered us a fresh turkey every Christmas Eve. Obviously, I said I didn't need one this year, but I'll give him a call and see if he has any left.'

'And if he doesn't?'

'He will. I'll start crying until he goes and slaughters one especially for us.' She took her mobile out of her back pocket and left the room as she scrolled through her contacts.

'I can't believe you forgot the turkey,' Adele said, punching Matilda playfully on the arm.

'Yes, well, I have other things on my mind.' She rubbed at her shoulder and winced.

'Are you all right?'

'No. Scott had to brake hard earlier, and the seatbelt cut into me. Some silly bitch in a Punto didn't think you had to stop when joining from a side road.'

'Let's have a look.'

Matilda unbuttoned a couple of buttons on her shirt. Adele checked the wound. 'The skin isn't broken, but it's very red. You're going to have an amazing bruise there tomorrow.'

'Bloody women drivers,' Matilda said.

'Tough day at the office, dear?' Adele asked.

'You could say that.'

'Do you want to talk about it?'

'That depends. Do you want to listen?'

'I will gladly listen, obviously, but it would be nice to have an evening where our conversations don't centre on crime scenes and autopsies for a change.'

'Excellent news,' Pat said entering the kitchen. 'Geoff is going to slaughter a big fat bird for us.'

Matilda and Adele laughed.

'Oh, grow up, you two.'

'What do you think?' Matilda asked Pat as she finished relaying the day's events for her.

Adele had gone to bed with an Agatha Christie, leaving the two of them to discuss the hunt for a serial killer.

'I'd be very surprised if your killer turns out to be this Andrew Lee Hawkesley,' Pat said, wrapping her hands around a mug of hot chocolate. 'He's been quiet for the best part of ten years then all of a sudden he attacks four women in two months.'

'I don't think it's him either.'

'And you say Laurence Dodds's alibi checks out?'

'Well, his van was in his driveway at the day and time of Tilly's attack. He rarely goes out as he's a carer for his mother. Besides, he was more interested in Scott than anything else.'

'He's gay?'

'He didn't say, obviously, but he certainly wasn't hiding his attraction.'

'Any other suspects on the radar?'

'There's a vicar,' she said unconvincingly. She sighed. 'Ridley won't let me give an interview for another week. I'm just worried there's going to be another victim in that time.' There was a look of deep worry on Matilda's face.

'Some cases can't be solved overnight, Mat. I know you want to solve this quickly to help get the force out of special measures, but you may have to prepare for a long fight, here.'

'And let the victims pile up?'

'He's very clever. He's doing everything right when it comes to evading capture.'

'There's got to be something I can do,' she said, almost pleadingly.

'There are a few options, but I don't think you're going to like any of them.'

Hesitantly, Matilda said, 'Go on.'

Pat sat up and cleared her throat. 'One, you push Tilly harder, hoping she's got something lodged in her mind somewhere that you can force out.'

'I'm not doing that. I need to take my time with her. She's going through so much right now.'

'Two, you wait for the killer to strike again and hope he makes a mistake and leaves something of himself at the scene, or the body can tell you something.'

'I really don't want that to happen.'

'Finally, you step back. Take a couple of days off and relax. Hopefully, you'll look at the whole investigation with fresh eyes and something will jump out at you.'

'I was hoping you were going to be my fresh eyes.'

'There's nothing fresh about me at my age,' she said with a sly smile.

Matilda slumped back in her seat.

'I'm going to head off for bed,' Pat said, getting up. At the door, she stopped and turned to Matilda. 'I'll tell you one thing, though.'

'Go on.'

'When you do your interview next Wednesday, you won't need to worry about him making a mistake because he's the kind of killer who is going to make himself known to you. You'll be getting a phone call from him very soon after the interview goes out.'

Matilda gave her a weak smile.

'I'll see you in the morning,' Pat said, leaving the room and closing the door behind her.

'I'm hoping for more than a phone call,' she said to herself.

Chapter Thirty-Five

Thursday 24th December 2020

Scott dropped Matilda off at South Yorkshire Police HQ before eight o'clock and then headed off to run an errand.

It was still dark as she made her way across the car park. There wasn't a cloud in the sky, and it was lit up with an infinite number of stars. She stopped and looked up. It took her back to the early days of her recovery from the shooting. Matilda had always suffered with insomnia and the shooting made things much worse. The nightmares made her terrified of falling asleep. Some nights, she'd sit out in the back garden, wrapped up in layers if it was cold, and look up at the night sky. It emptied her mind of the dark thoughts and helped her to relax. A sudden gust of wind caused her to shiver. She lifted up the collar on her coat and headed for the warmth of the building.

There was a skeleton staff and civilian and uniformed members alike were already getting into the Christmas spirit by wearing Santa hats or draping tinsel around their necks. A sprig of mistletoe was hanging above the door to reception. Matilda smiled at the jollity of it all and tried to remember the last time she'd kissed anyone.

She placed the large bag she'd brought with her onto a desk in the HMCU suite and looked at the murder board. It contained all the information on the man they were hunting, the potential suspects and the four victims. She hoped the answer would scream out at her, but all she heard was silence.

The doors yawned open, and Zofia wheeled herself in. She was wearing a green Christmas jumper with a picture of a smiling Father Christmas on the front. Matilda turned and saw the young DC with a smile on her face.

'I've just been kissed by that gorgeous young PC Marshall. I've never thought of the police uniform as being sexy before, but he genuinely looks like he's on his way to perform at a hen party.'

Matilda laughed. 'You're looking very festive.'

'I thought I'd make the effort. There's not much to smile about at the moment, is there?'

'Not really,' Matilda said, turning back to the murder board. 'Are these really our only two suspects: a missing sex offender and a gay amateur artist?'

'I'm afraid so. Would you like a cup of tea?'

'Please.'

'You know, I was seriously thinking of getting an electric wheelchair, but I'm so glad I didn't. Have you seen my arms?' Zofia said, taking off her sweater. 'I've never been so muscular.'

'You'll be entering the London Marathon next.'

'Absolutely not. Though I have signed up for wheelchair tennis at my local club. Pandemic depending, obviously.'

'Zofia, did you suffer with any PTSD after your injury?'

She thought for a moment as she filled the mugs. 'I don't think so. I went to see a therapist for a few sessions. I never saw being in a wheelchair as my life coming to an end, but as the beginning of something new. I knew I could still be a detective, I'd just be on wheels.' She smiled. 'I think my mum had the PTSD for me,' she added with a laugh.

Matilda found herself smiling. When Zofia joined the team, she was eager to please, too eager, but she lacked confidence. Since returning to work she seemed like a different person and her confidence was through the roof. She was determined not to allow her disability to define her. Matilda hoped Tilly Hall would feel the same.

Scott and Finn pulled up at the Sheffield Community Evangelical Church in Greystones. A five-minute drive away from where Laurence Dodds lived.

Finn climbed out of the front passenger seat and looked up at the blue sky. He shivered in the cold. 'I was hoping for some snow today.'

'I checked the forecast over breakfast. There's none at all for tomorrow, now,' Scott said, rolling his eyes.

'Typical. Mind you, that means Stephanie's parents won't have an excuse to stay overnight and they can go home around teatime.'

'Not a fan of your in-laws?' Scott asked as they made their way up the uneven stone steps to the church.

'Oh, they're great, don't get me wrong. It's just, after a couple of a hours, I'm ready for them to go home.' He smiled.

Finn pushed open the green door and they were confronted by a wall of warmth. It was very welcome.

The Sheffield Community Church looked small from the outside, but once one was inside it was huge, with a high ceiling and brilliant white walls. Chairs were arranged in rows with an aisle down the middle, and at the top of the room was a long table covered in a white cloth with cardboard boxes covering every inch of surface.

'Hello,' Scott called out, his voice echoing around the room.

'I won't be a moment, Mr Fisher. I'm having a little problem with the keys,' a voice called out from somewhere behind the scenes.

'My name is Detective Sergeant Scott Andrews. I'm with South Yorkshire Police,' Scott said.

A door at the side of the room opened and a tall man somewhere in his mid-forties stepped out. He was dressed in the typical vicar costume of black shirt and white collar. The shirt wasn't tucked into his black trousers and the sleeves were rolled up.

'Oh. Sorry. I thought you were Mr Fisher. Erm … what can I do for you?' As he stepped forward, Scott noticed the sheen of sweat on the vicar's forehead. He was clearly doing several jobs at once. He approached and looked at Scott's ID he had held aloft.

'I believe you know a man by the name of Laurence Dodds.'

'Laurence? Yes. He's one of my best volunteers.' His smile dropped. 'Nothing's happened to him, has it? Or his mother?'

'No. Nothing like that. I'm sorry to bother you at this time, erm …'

'Jeremy. Jeremy Keats,' he said, angling his elbow for Scott to bump, the post-pandemic greeting that seemed to have replaced handshaking.

'Laurence's van has been caught on CCTV in the vicinity of

two violent crimes being committed. We don't believe he was responsible. We think his number plate may have been cloned. However, he's told us you have used his van on a couple of occasions and we'd like to know your whereabouts on the dates in question.'

'Oh, of course. Yes, Laurence has been kind enough to lend me his van whenever I've needed it. I only have a Skoda and, occasionally, I've needed something bigger. I set up a food bank a couple of years ago and the number of people requiring its services has escalated somewhat. What are the dates?'

Finn dug out his notebook. 'The first is October the twenty-ninth. It was a Thursday.'

'Ah …' He smiled. 'I can tell you that one straightaway. I was in Cardiff. My sister's birthday is the twenty-eighth. It was her fiftieth, so we had a socially distanced party in the back garden. Bloody freezing it was, too.'

Finn smiled. 'Wednesday the eighteenth of November.'

He thought for a moment. 'I'm stumped there. I'll just pop and get my diary.'

He walked quickly through the door and returned within moments with an iPad in his hands. He began scrolling through. 'I was at a funeral in Derby in the morning and I was with BD in the afternoon.' He frowned. 'What's BD?' he asked himself. 'Oh, BD is builder Derek. He's extending the old vestry for me. Well, I'm assuming he is. I haven't heard back from him yet. We spent the whole of the afternoon going over the plans.'

'Saturday, December the sixth?' Finn asked.

Jeremy scrolled through his tablet. 'Ah, that's blank. I'm afraid I've no idea what I was doing then. Most likely, I was here boxing up groceries. That's what I usually do on the weekends.'

'And on the fifteenth?'

He looked back down at the tablet. 'Two committee meetings from ten o'clock in the morning and nothing until the after-school club at four o'clock. What's this about?'

'Four women have been attacked, three of them murdered,' Scott said.

'Yes. I saw the news the other night. You think Laurence may be involved somehow?' He asked, an incredulous look on his face.

'What do you know about Mr Dodds?'

'He's a very generous man. Generous with his time, I mean. He doesn't get much, obviously, as he's looking after his mother round the clock, but any time he gets he's here helping with the food bank and helping the community in general. He's a kind man.'

'Do you know anything about his personal life?' Scott asked.

Jeremy looked from Finn to Scott and back again. 'I don't think he has a personal life. He—Look, take a seat.' Jeremy directed them both to sit down. He took a seat nearby. 'I probably shouldn't be telling you this as it was a private conversation, but it may help in your investigations. About a year or so ago, Laurence came to me and asked if I minded if he was gay. I said I didn't. He told me he'd never told his mother as he didn't think she'd understand and that it was weighing him down, having a secret from her. I sympathised and told him I'd be with him when he had the conversation if he wished, but he said the numerous strokes she's had over the year made the conversation redundant. She hardly recognises him at times. I think he was feeling guilty at a missed opportunity to tell her while she was still lucid.'

Scott folded his arms. 'So, he is definitely gay?'

'Yes.'

'Does he have a partner?'

'Not that I'm aware of. His mother really does take up a great deal of his time. I did ask Laurence if he wanted to settle down with someone at some point. He told me that he doubted it would ever happen for him. I said that we all have needs. He told me he sees someone, casually. He wouldn't elaborate.'

'Right. Well, thank you for your time,' Scott said, standing up.

'You're welcome. Merry Christmas to you both.'

———————

Finn buttoned up his jacket once they were outside and headed back for the car. 'A waste of time then?'

'Not really. We now know what we suspected: that Laurence Dodds is gay. We can definitely cross him off our minuscule list of suspects.'

'But can we?' Finn frowned. He was waiting for Scott to unlock the car.

'How do you mean?'

'Well, the vicar said Laurence asked him his opinion on being gay. He regrets not being able to have the conversation with his mum. He's in his, what, late forties, something like that? He's taken a very long time to come to terms with his own sexuality. What if he's struggling so much he's taking out his agony on women?'

'Is that possible? I mean, he's raping them,' Scott said.

They both climbed into the car and closed the doors. Scott turned the heating on.

'Hypothesis: He's struggled with his sexuality for years,

wanted to tell his mother but was unable to for whatever reason. The first person he turns to is a vicar. He trusts him. Maybe there's religion in the family. Maybe that's why he didn't think his mother would understand. Maybe he's been led to believe being gay is a sin. However, he can't ignore the feelings he has for other men. Yet, to try to prove to himself that he's not gay, he's forcing himself on women.'

'That's a lot of maybes,' Scott said. 'Besides, he's not forcing himself on other women, is he? He's torturing them.'

'I'm just trying to think outside the box.'

'Besides, the vicar said he's got a casual thing going on with someone. Would you really enter into a gay relationship simply to cover up being a killer?'

'We've only got the vicar's word on him having a casual acquaintance,' Finn said. 'This person might not even exist. Has the vicar seen him? I'm guessing not.'

'My goodness, it's like sharing a car with Sherlock Holmes,' Scott said, starting the engine.

'Personally, I think we should keep Laurence Dodds on the list. And add the vicar, too.'

'The vicar?'

'He was very quick when he went to fetch his iPad and give us his alibis. It's almost as if he was waiting for our visit.'

'Even for a detective you're far too suspicious of people,' Scott said with a smile as he pulled out into traffic.

'By the way, I've put in a request for my sergeant's exams.'

'That was quick.'

'My ten-year plan is to be where DCI Darke is right now.'

'Widowed, paranoid and on the cusp of redundancy? Nice goal.'

Chapter Thirty-Six

Scott found Matilda in her office, squinting as she read something from her computer screen. He filled her in on the interview with Jeremy Keats and Finn's theory.

'Finn has a point. We have nothing else to go on. I think we should give it some serious thought. We're only taking Laurence's word for it that he's gay. We know the killer is intelligent. Maybe that's his cover,' Matilda said.

'Another maybe.'

'Sorry?'

'Nothing. By the way, Donal told me to give you this,' Scott said, fishing in his coat pocket and bringing out a small white box. He placed it on the desk. He gave her an envelope, too. 'He didn't trust me to remember everything, so he's written it all down.'

'Thank you.'

'So, have I missed anything?'

'No. An email from Ridley asking for a progress report.'

'What did you reply?'

'I didn't. I can't tell him anything different from what I told him yesterday. Scott, why can't I get a handle on this killer? What am I missing?'

Scott pulled out a chair and sat down. 'I don't think you're missing anything. We're not doing anything different to what we've done before. Everyone has been interviewed, the crime scenes have been minutely picked at. We're just up against an incredibly clever murderer.'

'Pat was saying last night we may have to wait for him to kill again and hope he makes a mistake.'

'She has a point but the thought of sitting around waiting for the phone to ring saying we've got another body ...' He shuddered. 'It's like we're hoping for him to kill again.'

'I know.' She stood up. 'I think I might go and have another chat with Tilly. You never know, maybe the bloke had written his name on the label in his jumper or something.' She half-smiled.

'Do you want me to come with you?'

'No. You keep an eye on things here. If we don't get anything, send everyone home around lunchtime. Huh,' she said, looking out into the main suite.

'What?'

'I didn't expect Tom to have tattoo sleeves,' she said. Tom was at his desk wearing a Christmas T-shirt, arms exposed.

'Yes. He's covered in them.'

'I won't ask how you know that.'

'I've seen him in the changing rooms, like everyone else.'

Matilda grabbed for her coat. 'Years ago, you saw a bloke covered in tattoos and he was classed as being hard, someone you wouldn't dare approach. Nowadays, everyone's got them. Suddenly, a man covered in tattoos could simply be a mild-mannered barista in Costa.' She remained by her door, looking out at her team.

'What are you thinking?' Scott asked.

'Look at the three of them, Finn, Zofia and Tom. You wouldn't think they were detectives, would you? I mean, if we go on appearances and what we expect certain people to look like. Finn looks like an academic with his rimless glasses and his sensible haircut. It won't be long before he's coming to work with elbow patches on his jacket. And you don't expect to see a detective in a wheelchair, so Zofia certainly doesn't fit the image. As for Tom, well, he looks like he should still be at college.'

'What are you getting at?'

Matilda's frown intensified. 'Appearances. We've got someone who has attacked four women, killed three of them, and we expect him to be this big brute of an ogre. Look at those sex workers killed last year. When we uncovered the killer as being Sian's husband, he fitted the description of what we assumed he'd look like – tall, broad, strong. What if, in this case, the killer isn't like that at all? What if he's so unassuming that people look at him and don't see him as any kind of a threat? He's so insignificant, he's invisible. His disguise is his invisibility.'

'But who fits into that category?'

Matilda thought for a long moment. 'I don't know. Who do you look at, then immediately forget you've seen?'

Now it was Scott's turn to frown. 'People you see all the time,' he eventually said. 'The postman, the bin man, the Amazon delivery driver, the barista in Costa. The people we don't see are the ones who are hiding in plain sight.'

'And that's why we have no witnesses. People will have seen him, but he doesn't fit the image of a killer of women.'

'Am I alone in finding that incredibly frightening?' Scott asked.

'No, you're not. I really need to do that interview.'

'Next Wednesday can't come soon enough, can it?'

'Nope.' Matilda opened the door and stepped out into the suite. 'Look, everyone, we're all just wasting our time here, this morning. Turn off your computers, go home, be with your families and have a very merry Christmas.'

'Are you sure?' Finn asked.

'We need some time off to let our minds empty. Come back bright and early on the twenty-seventh, and be ready to kick some serious arse.' She smiled, picked up the bag from the table and began handing out presents. 'It's not much, just a little something to make you smile over Christmas. Now, go home, enjoy yourselves, eat too much, drink too much, forget about misogynistic killers and watch festive shite on TV.'

'Don't I get a present?' Scott asked.

Matilda turned to him and lowered her voice. 'Tell me, you and Donal, is it serious?'

He swallowed hard then nodded, his cheeks brightening slightly.

'You no longer need to pay me rent for your flat. Put that money in a savings account and put it towards a deposit for a flat or a house for when you and Donal want to move in together.'

Scott's mouth dropped open in amazement.

Matilda kissed him on the forehead. 'Merry Christmas, Scott.'

Chapter Thirty-Seven

The Sheffield Children's Hospital was full of festive cheer. All the medical and administrative staff were trying to make the best of a bad situation for all the children who would be spending Christmas away from home and their families. Seeing nurses wearing Santa hats and elf outfits and the odd doctor in a long flowing red coat even put a smile on Matilda's face as she walked down the corridor towards Tilly's room.

'Matilda!'

She turned as her name was called and saw Amy Hall trotting towards her.

'Can I have a word before you go in to see Tilly?'

'Of course.'

They went over to a corner next to the drinks machine. Matilda fished into her pocket for some loose change. The heat in the hospital was already drying her throat. Why did hospitals have to be so humid? She was sure the NHS could save themselves a few million each year simply by turning the heating down by a couple of degrees in every hospital.

'Is Tilly all right?' Matilda asked.

'Not really. She had a very uncomfortable night. She pressed the emergency button and one of the nurses ran in and found her in a lot of distress. She was sweating, hyperventilating, and she'd ...' Amy looked around to make sure they weren't being overheard. 'She'd wet the bed.'

'Oh, no,' Matilda sympathised.

'Apparently, it happened the night before, too. Well, she didn't wet the bed then, but she had a panic attack. The doctors think she might have post-traumatic ... what is it?'

'Post-traumatic stress disorder,' Matilda said. 'It's understandable given what she's been through. How is she this morning?'

'Fine. A little subdued. I just think maybe if you could not question her today. Let her have a couple of days' rest.'

It wasn't what Matilda wanted to hear, but Tilly's health and recuperation were paramount. Reluctantly, she nodded. 'Sure. Amy, I suffered with PTSD myself after being shot. Would you like me to have a word with her?'

'Would you?' Amy asked, her eyes brightening up.

'Of course. Maybe I should go in on my own though. One survivor to another.' She smiled.

'Yes. I think that might help. I'll pop and get something to eat. I haven't had breakfast yet.'

'How are things with you? Are you looking after yourself?'

Amy took a deep breath. 'I'm just operating on autopilot at the moment.'

'You need to take care of yourself, Amy. Tilly needs you to be strong.'

'I am. I will. I phoned Ryan Cook's mum last night. We had a long chat. We're going to meet up in the New Year. All of us,' she said with a warm smile.

'That's good.'

'I … I …' She wanted to say something but couldn't find the words. 'I'll go and get myself something to eat.'

Matilda watched her go then headed for Tilly's room. She knocked slightly, then opened the door. Tilly was sitting up in bed, watching something on the iPad. When she looked up and saw Matilda, she balked, and the tears came.

Matilda rushed in, sat on the bed next to Tilly and put her arm around her. She held her close and allowed her to sob, to let out all the emotions she was storing inside her.

'It's all right, Tilly. Everything is going to be fine. It'll just take time, that's all,' Matilda said. She grabbed a few tissues from the box on the locker and handed them to Tilly. 'Actually, I don't know why I said any of that. I bet that's what everyone's been saying to you, isn't it? That everything's going to be fine?'

Tilly wiped her eyes and nodded.

'It's not, though, is it? Everything isn't fine at all. I'd be lying if I said that when you're discharged and back home everything will be better. It won't. I still have nightmares about the shooting, even now, almost two years later. They're not as frequent, and they don't scare me as much, but they're still there. You've been through a huge, life changing experience that no one else can understand. They'll say they do, but they don't. And the advice they give, like telling you to take one day at a time, will seem trite and ridiculous, but, actually, it's true. The only way you can get through this is by taking it one day at a time, and at the end of every day, if you can look back and see that today has been a good day, then you're a step closer to recovery. Does that make sense?'

Tilly nodded.

'I'm not going to ask you any questions today. We'll have a couple of days off. I've actually got you a present,' she said, digging around in her pocket. 'A friend of mine is a fossil hunter in his spare time, and I told him all about you being a fan of *Planet Earth* and David Attenborough and how you're interested in evolution and conservation, and he gave me this to give to you.' Matilda handed Tilly a small white cardboard box.

She opened it and took out what looked like a piece of grey stone. She looked up at Matilda.

'It's a tool. It was found somewhere in the south of England a few years ago. You hold it in your hand, like this.' She showed her. 'The edge has been purposely sharpened so it could cut the fur from something like a mammoth, and they could also cut into the meat of the animal for food. It's thought … damn, I knew I'd forget, hang on.' She fished in her pocket for the envelope Scott had given her from Donal. She took the single page out of the envelope. 'Here we are. When things have been found in the past, they were thought to have been around ten thousand years old, but when they looked at soil samples and other bones and fossils nearby, they aged this particular tool at more than one hundred and twenty thousand years old, which means there were people in England earlier than originally thought.'

Tilly looked up at her. Her smile was genuine. Her eyes were wide in amazement.

'Unbelievable, isn't it?' Matilda said. 'That little piece of stone has survived all this time. It's survived countless battles and two World Wars and even Brexit.' She smiled. 'It was all the early people needed to be able to get fur and food. And it's yours to keep.'

Tilly mouthed, 'Thank you.'

'You're very welcome. Look, I know I'm not a trained professional or anything, and I know I've said this before, but if you ever want to talk about how you're feeling or anything at all, you've got my email address and my mobile number. Message me anytime. Okay?'

Tilly nodded.

Matilda stood up and went to the door. She stopped and turned back to Tilly. 'I know you don't think it right now, but you will recover, I can promise you that. You're a remarkable young woman and you're going to go on to do amazing things. Things look bleak right now, that's understandable, but hold onto the thought that life is going to be so great for you. I can feel it.'

A tear fell from Tilly's left eye, but she was smiling.

Matilda could feel the emotion rising up inside her so felt it was best to leave now before she embarrassed herself.

'Merry Christmas, Tilly.'

Chapter Thirty-Eight

'What are you still doing here?' Simon Browes asked as he entered Adele's cluttered office.

She jumped and turned around. 'Simon, you gave me a fright. I was just updating the system.'

'I thought you wanted to have left by one o'clock.'

'I did.'

'It's half past three.'

'I know. Time seems to have got away from me. Now, all the reports have been submitted and I've updated the emergency call list. Rebecca and Josh are working tomorrow, and Josh said he'll come in on Boxing Day, too. He's very anti-Christmas. Don't ask him why, you'll never hear the end of it.'

Simon smiled. 'Adele, I've worked with these people before. Turn off your computer, put your coat on and go home.'

Hesitantly, she obeyed his order. 'Promise me, if anything urgent comes up, you'll call me. I can be here within half an hour. Sooner, in fact.'

'I promise I'll call you.' He placed his hand over his heart.

'Thank you, Simon,' she said as she squeezed past him.

'Adele,' he called after her. 'I … Well, I was planning on giving you this next March when our book is published as a kind of happy publication day present, but after seeing how upset you've been lately with the anniversary of Lucy's disappearance, I thought I'd give it you now as a sort of Christmas gift but not, if you know what I mean.' He handed her a small, perfectly wrapped box with a red bow on top.

'Oh, Simon, you didn't need to buy me anything,' she said, genuinely touched. 'I haven't …' He waved her sentence away. 'I mean, I've got something in mind to get you for publication day. I've found a bottle of gorgeous vintage champagne, but I haven't ordered it yet or I'd give it you now.'

'Adele, don't worry about it. Just, please, take this.'

'I don't know what to say.' She took the box and glared at it.

'You're supposed to undo the wrapping in order to see what's inside,' he said with a laugh.

Adele tore off the paper like an excited child. She opened the box and gasped. Inside was a silver necklace with an oval pendant, in the centre of which was a single diamond. It was simple in its design but elegant, and screamed expense.

'Oh, Simon, this is beautiful,' she said, taking it out.

'Do you like it? Really?'

'I love it. It must have cost a fortune.'

'Here, let me put it on.'

Adele handed it to him, turned around and swept her hair out of place. As he fumbled with the clasp, Adele could feel his cold fingers shaking as he brushed her neck. He turned her around and held her by the shoulders.

'It looks beautiful on you,' he said softly.

'Thank you so much, Simon. I really appreciate it.'

'It's not been an easy year. You deserve it.' He leaned down and kissed her on the lips.

Adele looked up at him after the kiss. Their eyes met. She smiled, and they kissed again.

'I should be going,' Adele said. She edged away towards the door. 'Thank you, again, for my present.' She smiled and could feel herself blushing.

'Merry Christmas, Adele.'

'Merry Christmas.'

She turned and went through the doors, stopping when she saw Donal Youngblood standing just outside with a huge grin on his face.

'How much of that did you see?'

'Enough to say that you can never criticise me for kissing Scott in the workplace again.'

'Bugger!' she said, head down, heading for the doors.

'Adele and Simon sitting in a tree, K-I-S-S-I-N-G,' he sang.

'Give it a rest, Donal.'

'If you get married you could cut the cake with a bone saw,' he said as he followed her into the car park. 'No, I've got a better idea, as you walk out of the church all us technicians can stand either side holding up scalpels and you could walk underneath them.'

'Donal,' Adele said as she reached her Porsche. 'I live with a Detective Chief Inspector. I'm a Home Office Pathologist. Between us, we can make sure no trace of your body is ever found. One more snide comment and all that will remain of you is a symbolic gravestone in a Dublin cemetery. Understand?'

'Wow,' he said, the smile suddenly dropping from his face.

'Goodbye. Merry Christmas, and I'll see you the day after Boxing Day.'

Adele lowered herself into the Porsche and closed the door behind her. She looked down at the pendant and smiled.

Chapter Thirty-Nine

Matilda held the pendant on the tips of her fingers while it was still around Adele's neck, once Adele had finished telling her what had happened at the mortuary.

'That is a beautiful piece of jewellery.'

'I think so.'

'And you never realised he had feelings for you?'

'No. The thing about Simon is that he's always been a bit aloof and distant. I've been able to have a conversation with him, but never anything personal. To be fair,' she said, going into the kitchen and flicking on the kettle, 'I've never given him a second thought. Does that make me a bad person?'

'No, of course it doesn't.'

'When he kissed me and I looked up at him, it was like I was seeing him for the first time. I've known him for more than ten years, but I've never seen him as anything other than a fellow pathologist. That makes me sound really self-centred, doesn't it?'

'No.'

'It does. I mean, he could have been flirting and giving me

signals all this time and I've never picked them up. I call him aloof and distant, but maybe I'm the one who's aloof.'

'You're not aloof. Maybe Simon just has an understated personality.'

'Yes,' Adele agreed. 'That's it. He's like Mr Reliable. You know he's always going to be there, just in the background.'

'Nothing wrong with that.'

'No. Not at all.'

'And now he's making himself known to you.'

'It would appear so.'

'How do you feel about that?' Matilda asked, taking a mug of tea from Adele.

'I'm not sure. Maybe we'll see how things go. I mean, we work together, maybe that's all it should be. Are you in pain?' Adele asked as she saw Matilda rub her shoulder and wince.

'A little. I've got a massive bruise from that sodding seatbelt.'

The front door opened and slammed closed.

'Are you both in?'

'In the kitchen, Pat.'

Pat entered, wrapped up against the elements, carrying a large cardboard box. She placed it carefully on the table. 'One Christmas turkey, fresh from the farm.' She smiled and began taking off her coat and hat.

'That's wonderful, Pat, thank you,' Matilda said.

'Is it big enough?' Adele asked.

'It's certainly heavy enough.'

Adele peeled back the flaps of the box and she and Matilda looked inside.

'Ah,' Adele said. 'I'm so glad I'm on vegetable duty tomorrow.'

'What am I supposed to do with this?' Matilda asked.

'What's the problem?' Pat asked, coming back into the kitchen from hanging her coat up. She looked inside the box. 'Oh.'

'He hasn't plucked it. It's still got its head and feet on,' Matilda said, a look of horror on her face.

'He was in a bit of a hurry,' Pat said.

'How am I supposed to cook that? I wouldn't know where to start plucking a turkey.'

'I think I've seen it done on *River Cottage*,' Pat said. 'You know, that Hugh Fearnley-Withery-doo-dah. I think you just pull them out.'

'And the head?'

'I don't know about that. Maybe there's a YouTube video on how to pluck and prepare a turkey.'

'When did he kill it? Don't you have to let it rest or drain the blood or something before you can cook it?' Adele asked.

'Drain the blood? Oh my God!' Matilda exclaimed.

'I think it's been a few days. He didn't grab a live one and throttle it in front of me. It's not even warm.'

'Why does it have a little tag on its foot saying Gwyneth?' Adele asked, lifting it up.

'That's her name,' Pat said. 'All the turkeys are labelled so he knows when they're born, and he can keep an eye on their weight.'

'She's called Gwyneth?' Matilda asked, aghast. 'Well, there's no way I can eat it now I know her bloody name. Oh God, I can't believe I've got a dead animal on my kitchen table.'

'You've got a freezer full of dead animals,' Adele said.

'Yes, but they've all had their heads removed. I'm sorry, I'm not cooking that. You'll have to do it, Adele.'

'Why me?'

'You're a pathologist.'

Adele peered into the box. 'It's dead. There you go. My job is finished.'

'It's easy for you, you cut people open all the time.'

'Yes. I also sew them back together again afterwards. I don't pluck out their body hair and cut their heads off.'

'Pat?' Matilda asked, looking hopefully at the retired detective.

She pulled a face. 'You know, I've never really been a fan of turkey.'

'If we don't eat it, it's a waste,' Adele said. 'We either cook it and eat it, or dress in black and give it a burial in the back garden.'

'Oh, bloody hell,' Matilda moaned.

'I tell you what, if we're going to do this, we do it together. Agreed?' Pat asked.

Matilda and Adele nodded.

'Right,' Pat began. 'I'll get my iPad and see if there's something on YouTube. Adele, lay down plenty of newspaper. Matilda, get a few very sharp knives.'

Matilda grabbed a few knives from the drawer, went over to the table and looked tentatively into the box. 'Merry Christmas, Gwyneth,' she said, sadly.

Chapter Forty

Friday 25th December 2020

Matilda woke early and remained in bed for a while before getting up. She could hear the sound of movement downstairs so guessed Pat was already getting the day started. She had said she was an early riser when she moved in, and spent the time pottering about the house doing chores Matilda said she really didn't need to do.

There were certain times of the year that were difficult for Matilda, and Christmas Day was one of them. She never needed a special reason to remember her husband, James, but there were occasions she missed him more than ever. She remembered their last Christmas together and smiled, though her bottom lip wobbled. She wasn't sure if she was remembering it with rose-tinted glasses or whether it was an actual perfect day, but she was woken with a kiss, a huge smile and a bottle of champagne.

'Champagne. Really? At 8am?' she'd asked.

James squeezed out the cork. 'On Christmas Day, all the rules are thrown out of the window.'

He poured two glasses and handed her one. They both took a sip.

'This is so decadent,' Matilda said.

'It's supposed to be.' He took the glass from her and handed her a small, perfectly wrapped box from his dressing gown pocket. 'Present number one.'

Matilda's eyes lit up. 'Oh, my goodness,' she said excitedly. She pulled off the ribbon and tore the paper. It was a velvet box which she opened to reveal a pair of diamond stud earrings. 'Oh, James, they're stunning,' she marvelled. She couldn't take her eyes off them.

'They should be. Do you have any idea how many litres of petrol I had to buy to get them?' he joked. 'It was either the earrings or a set of wine glasses.'

'I think you made the right choice.'

She leaned over and kissed him. She could taste the champagne on his lips.

It was only on very special occasions that Matilda now wore those diamond earrings. One of those occasions was Christmas Day. She sat up in bed, took them out of the top drawer of her bedside cabinet and went over to the mirror to put them on. She wanted to smile, but they reminded her of what she'd lost, what she missed more than anything in the world.

She padded downstairs and went into the kitchen, where the smell of coffee grew stronger. She could hear quiet chatter and guessed Adele was up too. She opened the door to find them both sitting at the table.

Wishes of merry Christmas and hugs were swapped and Pat gushed over Matilda's earrings.

'The most romantic present my Anton ever bought me was a sandwich toaster when I had shingles,' she said. 'He didn't have a romantic bone in his body. Do you know what we did on our wedding night?'

'I don't think I want to know this,' Adele said.

'We had a fish and chip supper, watched a Hitchcock double bill at the local pictures and were in bed and fast asleep by eleven. Mind you, just before he nodded off, he did tell me he loved me. And that was the first of only two times he ever told me that,' she said with a wistful smile.

'When was the second time?' Matilda asked.

She swallowed hard and tears pricked her eyes. She reached into her pocket for her mobile, opened a text and handed the phone to Matilda.

I've enjoyed every minute we've spent together. I know I've not been the most exciting of husbands, but you've made my life so much better by being in it. I love you so much, Pat. I couldn't love you more if I tried. Look after yourself. Xxx

'I couldn't be with him at the end. The nurse typed that out for him, but he told her exactly what he wanted to say. He said to make sure she put three kisses on the end of it, too. He died less than half an hour after sending that message.'

'Oh, Pat,' Matilda said, emotion in her voice.

Adele wiped away a tear before it had chance to fall.

'I think I'll go and give our Cheryl a ring,' she said, taking the phone from Matilda and dashing out of the room.

'She puts on this tough exterior, but the first Christmas and birthday on your own are the hardest,' Matilda said. 'What have you got her as a present?'

'I bought her a blouse from John Lewis. You?'

'I've got her a new Kindle and an Amazon gift card. We've got to give her more than that.'

Adele thought. 'Oh, I know. I've got that antique gold necklace of my gran's.'

'Don't you want it?'

'It doesn't really go with anything I've got. And it's not like I've anyone to leave it to. She could hand it down to her Cheryl or any of her grandkids.'

'Are you sure?'

'Yes. It's only sitting in a box and has been for the best part of thirty years. I'll run upstairs and wrap it. You keep her busy.'

'I'll make us all a Bucks Fizz and we can swap presents.'

Adele ran out of the room while Matilda dug out the glasses.

Matilda and Adele were crying with laughter. They'd handed each other their gifts, unwrapped them, then looked at each other with bemused expressions. They'd bought each other the exact same watch.

'What are the odds of that happening?' Pat asked. She sipped her drink and reached for the jug for a refill.

'When I bought it, I actually said to the woman in the shop that I wouldn't mind one for myself,' Adele said.

'Your wish has been granted,' Matilda said with a smile.

'I also wished I'd find Idris Elba under the tree this morning. I see that one hasn't bloody come true.'

'Here you go, Pat,' Matilda said, handing Pat the small parcel. 'This one is from me and Adele.'

'More presents? You've bought me enough,' she said,

looking slightly embarrassed. She took the box, opened it and her eyes widened at the necklace. 'Oh, no, I can't accept this. It's far too expensive.' She looked up at them both. There were tears in her eyes.

'Let me put it on for you,' Matilda said, taking it from her.

Pat stood up, went over to the mirror above the fireplace, stood on tiptoe and looked at her reflection in the mirror. 'Oh, it's gorgeous. I love it. Thank you so much. I'll never take it off.' She turned back to them. 'I honestly thought I'd be on my own today. I wasn't looking forward to Christmas at all, but you've made it so special. Thank you.'

In all the years Matilda had known Pat, she'd never seen her with such a genuinely warm smile on her face before.

———

At midday, Harriet pulled up in her Citroen with her two sons, and her and Matilda's mother, Penny, following in her Mini Cooper. As usual, Penny had gone all out in her appearance. She wore far too much make-up and had sprayed more than enough perfume on her. Her dyed red hair was flowing around her like a lion's mane. She wore a tight white shirt, too many buttons open at the neck for a woman of her age, and black trousers. Harriet, by contrast, was understated in smart but casual clothes and a touch of lipstick, and if she had sprayed any perfume, Matilda couldn't smell it. Her mother's fragrance had killed off every other scent. The two boys, Joseph and Nathan, were at the age when they didn't really want to spend Christmas Day with adults but weren't old enough to be on their own. They wanted gifts but didn't want to look excited by them. Teenagers and Christmas were an odd mix.

Presents and greetings were exchanged, drinks were

handed out and an hour later they were all sitting at the beautifully laid table in the dining room.

'You've gone all out with this table, Matilda,' Penny said. 'Matching cloth and napkins. Candlesticks. It's not like you at all. I'm impressed.'

'You have Pat to thank for that. She spent several hours yesterday afternoon getting everything set up. If it had been left to me, we'd have all been eating on our laps in the living room,' Matilda replied with a smile.

Matilda and Adele brought in the plates of food and everyone tucked in.

'Hang on, why aren't you three having turkey?' Harriet asked.

Matilda, Adele and Pat shared furtive glances.

'That's my fault,' Pat said. 'I was in charge of buying the turkey, and I'm no good for catering for so many people. I bought the wrong size.' She smiled. 'There wasn't enough for us all.'

'I'm sure there's enough to go round if we all give up a slice or two,' Harriet said.

'No!' Matilda almost snapped. 'I mean, no. It's fine. We don't mind, do we?'

'Of course not.'

'But the turkey is the best part of Christmas lunch,' Penny added. 'Come on, I've got far too much on my plate.'

'Mum, it's fine.'

'I'm vegetarian anyway,' Pat said, lying.

'Matilda, you put a vegetarian in charge of buying the turkey?' Penny chastised. 'No wonder she didn't know what size to buy for seven of us. I'm so sorry, Pat. She can be incredibly insensitive at times.

'That's fine.' Pat waved her apology away.

Matilda turned to Pat and raised an eyebrow. 'I wasn't aware you've gone vegetarian, Pat.'

'It's a recent thing.'

'But I made that gravy from the turkey juices. You can't eat your meal now. It's ruined.'

'Oh, I'm not totally committed. I'm sure a bit of gravy won't hurt.'

'Are you sure? I can always rustle up a cheese sandwich or something,' Matilda said, a sarcastic glint dancing in her eye.

'No. I'm fine. Thank you. So, Harriet, how's the new job going?' Pat asked quickly to change the subject.

'Very well, thanks. I never thought of being an estate agent before, but it was buying the new house that made me look more into it. I'm enjoying it.'

'And you're off to university next year, aren't you, Joseph?'

Joseph looked up from his plate and nodded. 'Yes. If I get the results I need.'

'He will,' Harriet said. Joseph shrugged.

'What are you studying?'

'Psychology. Hopefully.'

'Interesting subject.'

'If you need anyone to chat to, Joe, talk to Pat,' Matilda said. 'She has an amazing insight into the human mind.'

'Twenty-something years on the police force. I've certainly met a wide variety of people in my time.'

'You retired early, didn't you?' Penny asked, forking more turkey into her mouth.

'Yes.'

'How come?'

Pat and Matilda exchanged a glance. 'I felt like I'd done enough. My husband had retired, and we decided to spend more time together,' she said, her eyes looking everywhere but at the people around the table staring at her.

'Does anyone want more sprouts?' Matilda asked. She was the only person who knew the real reason for Pat taking early retirement. 'Here you go, Mum,' Matilda said, dishing more onto her plate. 'Go mad, it's Christmas.'

'So, Nathan, what did you get for Christmas?' Adele asked Harriet's youngest son.

'Football boots,' he said, almost glumly.

'He's a bit down at the moment,' Harriet said quietly. 'He split up with his first girlfriend last week.'

'She was not my girlfriend,' Nathan protested.

'Okay. I'm sorry. She was just a friend who happened to be a girl.'

'I don't know, teenagers today,' Penny said. 'They think they've got all the worries of the world on their shoulders. Like they're the first generation to have feelings. You'll get over it, Nathan. When I think of the number of boys I went out with when I was—'

'Mum, please, we don't want to know,' Matilda interrupted.

'Mat, are you sure you don't want any of this turkey?' Harriet said.

'I'm sure.'

'You should at least try some. It's so moist.'

'That's the gravy. It makes everything moist.'

'If you can't finish it, Harriet, leave it and I'll make Matilda a turkey sandwich later,' Adele said with a malicious smile.

Matilda shot her a daggered look. 'Did I say that Adele's seeing a new man?'

'Really? Who?' Penny asked.

'Simon Browes.'

'I don't have a new man,' Adele said, blushing slightly.

'That's wonderful news, Adele. You're still a very attractive woman. So, what's he like?'

'I'm not seeing him. We're writing a book together and he bought me this necklace for Christmas. That's all.'

'You should think about getting yourself back out there, too, Matilda,' Penny said. 'It's been a couple of years since Danny,' she said, sweeping her hair away with the back of her hand.

'I'm fine on my own, Mum.'

'You say that now, but before you know it, you'll be retiring and drawing your pension. It's harder to meet someone in your sixties than it is in your forties.'

'Don't worry. Me and Adele have a pact. If we're both still single when we're fifty, we're going to marry each other.'

Everyone around the table fell silent.

'Remind me again whose idea it was to have my family round for Christmas,' Matilda said.

She, Adele and Pat were in the kitchen stacking the dishwasher while the others were in the living room attacking the chocolates.

'I forgot how difficult my mum can be sometimes,' Matilda added. 'She can't have a simple conversation. She always has to be asking questions and digging into people's lives.'

'She's harmless,' Pat said. 'She just wants everyone to be happy. I'm sure I'm the same with my kids.'

'I'm pretty sure you're not.'

'Matilda, are you expecting any more guests?' Penny called out loudly from the living room.

'Bloody hell, her voice grates through me sometimes,' Matilda said to herself. 'No, I'm not,' she called. 'Why?'

'There's a woman walking down your driveway.'

Matilda frowned and went into the living room. 'Where?'

'She's gone now,' Penny said. She was by the window, an empty wine glass in her hand.

'What did she look like?'

'I don't know. I only briefly saw her. Small. She had brown hair, shoulder length, I think. Is there any more wine left in that bottle?'

'Maybe it's a neighbour posting a card through,' Harriet guessed.

'I don't have any neighbours.'

Matilda went out into the hallway. There was nothing on the mat. She unlocked the door and pulled it open. There was nothing outside. She stood on the doorstep and looked out. A gust of wind blew, and she shivered. As she turned to go back into the house, she stopped dead in her tracks. Her mouth fell open and the blood drained from her face.

'Mat, what is it?' Adele asked.

Matilda couldn't speak. She stood still, her eyes glued to the front door.

'What is it?' Adele repeated, approaching the door.

The Christmas wreath had been removed from the door and replaced by a hangman's noose.

Chapter Forty-One

The day was starting to go dark by the time Amy packed the Christmas gifts away, getting ready to leave and return to an empty house.

Tilly quickly typed something on the iPad and handed it to her mother.

Do you have to leave?

'I can't stay, sweetheart. I've already been here longer than I should have done. I've got the dogs to feed, too. I'll come back tomorrow.'

Tilly looked at her mother with wide, tear-filled eyes. She really wanted her to stay.

She'd been there since early morning and brought Tilly a huge mound of presents. She'd been given books, Blu-rays, jewellery, clothes, perfumes, all manner of gifts, and she'd smiled and marvelled at them all. For a while, she could forget the discomfort she was in and what had happened to her and simply enjoy the day for what it was. But now, as her mum was leaving, and taking everything with her, she would be left alone in her small room, with the door unlocked so that anyone could come and go whenever they wanted to.

She squeezed her eyes closed and turned to look out of the window at the darkening sky.

Amy sat on the edge of the bed and put her arm around her daughter. 'Tilly, I know this hasn't been the Christmas we wanted, but it won't be much longer until you're back at home in your own bed. I promise you, things will get better. It's just going to take time, that's all.'

The silence was palpable while Amy tried to think of something else to say. Everything she thought of sounded so trite in her head.

'Would you like me to have a word with one of the nurses and see if they can give you anything to help you relax and have a good night's sleep?' Amy asked. 'You're looking very tired.' She'd mentioned the dark circles beneath Tilly's eyes more than once today.

Tilly shook her head.

'I really do need to go, Tilly,' Amy said, standing up and reaching for her coat. She hated leaving her, especially when she was so obviously distressed, but there was nothing else she could do. 'Your mobile is fully charged. You can text me any time. Why don't you message some of your friends, too? They've been texting all day.'

Tilly's mobile had been pinging and vibrating on the top of the bedside locker most of the day, but she'd ignored it every time, as if it didn't exist.

Amy leaned down and kissed Tilly on the forehead. 'I love you so much, sweetheart. We'll get through this together. I know we will.' She was struggling to fight back her own tears, but she needed to be strong for Tilly.

Reluctantly, Amy left. She paused in the open doorway for

a lingering moment, looking back at her only child, her only surviving relative, and watched her with tear-filled eyes. She felt so helpless. She opened her mouth but didn't know what to say. There were only so many times she could wish her a merry Christmas or say she loved her before it sounded like noise to fill a silence. In the end, she turned and pulled the door closed behind her.

———————

Tilly watched as the door closed. She heard her mother's footsteps fade as she walked away. She didn't take her eyes from the door. She wasn't safe here. She wasn't in the best place she could be. There was no lock on the door, no guard outside, nobody to stop someone simply walking in and … It didn't bear thinking about what else could happen to her.

She heard footsteps getting louder. They sounded heavy. They probably belonged to a man. Tilly pulled the blanket up and held onto it tightly. Her eyes were fixed on the door handle, watching, waiting for it to be pushed down, the door to open and the man who attacked her, raped her, cut open her throat and wanted her dead to come into the room to finish the job.

She could feel tears rolling down her face. She wanted to scream and cry for help, but she couldn't. There was nothing she could do if the killer came back. She was exposed. Vulnerable. The footsteps faded away, but there would be more, and next time, maybe they'd stop right outside her door.

Tilly reached for the iPad and started typing out a text message to Matilda:

The killer knows where I am. He came into my room and

warned me against talking to you. I know what he looks like but you need to protect me …

She paused. She squeezed her eyes tightly shut. She might only be fourteen, but she wasn't a stupid kid. She knew about South Yorkshire Police and the mess they were in right now and the corruption and cover-up they'd been involved in lately. Matilda might have sounded convincing, but even if she was one of the good ones, she was still only one person, and she wouldn't be able to protect her from a man who'd already killed three women. She deleted the message and threw the iPad onto the top of the locker. She turned onto her side, facing the door, and held the emergency call button in her one good hand. The moment that door opened, she'd press it, and just hoped a nurse would get to her in time.

Chapter Forty-Two

Matilda was alone in the middle of one of the Chesterfield sofas in the living room. The fire was raging, and she could feel the sweat prickling her underarms.

The festive atmosphere had been destroyed by whoever had come to the house, removed the wreath and replaced it with a noose. Matilda fired questions at her mother to try to get a clear description of the woman whom she saw walking away from the house. In the end, it was Harriet who suggested they should leave and come back tomorrow. Maybe when everyone had calmed down and slept on it, they could have a more reasoned conversation.

Pat came into the living room with a mug of tea and placed it on the coffee table in front of Matilda.

'How are you feeling?'

'I've ruined Christmas.'

'No, you haven't. The BBC did that by taking *Doctor Who* off.'

Matilda gave a painful smile. 'It was supposed to be a good day today.'

'It has been. We have a very funny turkey story to tell.'

'Who's doing this, Pat? I haven't had a phone call or a card in months, and today of all days, they start again. Why?'

'I honestly don't know. I've never understood why some people become fixated with a killer. You look at Steve Harrison and what he did and what he planned and schemed, and you can see that he's pure evil. Yet someone is drawn to that and, I don't know, thinks they can tame him, change him, continue what he started? It beggars belief.'

The living room door opened, and Adele came in, mobile phone in hand. 'Okay. I've just had Christian on the phone. I called and told him what had happened. He's been onto Wakefield Prison to check on Steve Harrison. He's still in the Supermax wing. Nothing has changed. He's had no visitors since before the shooting. All his mail is checked before he receives it and before any letters are sent out. Christian said he'll come over if you want him to.'

'No. There's no point in ruining anyone else's Christmas, is there?' She looked up at Adele and Pat. 'I'm really sorry.'

'It's not your fault,' Pat said.

'I know. I'm sorry you're dragged into this, though.'

'I hate to say this,' Pat began. 'But I think this is something you're going to have to get used to. People like Steve, they're going to have their fans. There was another book out about him a couple of months back. It went straight to the top of the charts. He was mentioned in that true-crime documentary series on Netflix, too. There was a whole episode on him. This will keep coming up and people with nothing in their lives will be attracted to him and blame you for locking him away. The fact he's a serial killer has nothing to do with it.'

'Pat's right,' Adele agreed.

Matilda took a deep breath. 'So what do I do? I can't ignore it. This person has been to my home, for crying out loud.'

'There's nothing you can do. Just keep your security upgraded. Learn a few self-defence moves and try not to let it intrude on your life.'

'That's easier said than done.'

'I know it is, but you can't let him win.'

'Let's change the subject,' Adele said. 'I suggest we flop in front of the TV and get drunk.'

'Good idea,' Pat said. 'Is there anything worth watching?'

'Of course there isn't, it's Christmas Day. How about a Marvel film and a bottle of champagne each?'

A smile began to spread on Matilda's lips.

'See,' Adele said. 'She's picturing the Winter Soldier and getting excited already.'

'I don't think I've ever seen a Marvel film,' Pat said.

'Oh, my God, Mat, did you hear that? We need to educate this woman. I'll get the box set; you get the champagne and snacks.'

Matilda watched as her two friends dashed off. She needed people around her to stop herself from falling into a pit of depression. Pat was right. There are always people out there who are drawn to serial killers for whatever reason. But Steve Harrison is on the never-never list and will be in Wakefield Prison until he's carried out in a pathetic pine box and good riddance to him. First thing in the new year, she'll organise for CCTV cameras to be installed around the perimeter of the house and maybe carry an unobtrusive weapon around with her, just in case. However, until then, it was time to get drunk and ogle Sebastian Stan.

Chapter Forty-Three

'I HATE CHRISTMAS. I FUCKING HATE CHRISTMAS. I FUCKING HATE FUCKING CHRISTMAS!'

He was screaming but nobody could hear him. He was using his inner voice that only he could hear, the voice that was desperate to get out and shatter windows and tell everyone around him how he really felt. If only he had the courage to do that. He'd only ever told one person how he truly felt, and she'd been asleep at the time. He often wondered if his words had ever been understood, if her dreams had absorbed them. She certainly looked at him more cautiously at times.

The clock on the wall said it was five o'clock. It seemed to have been Christmas Day for weeks. Surely, it should be over with by now.

Why did he hate Christmas so much? The answer was a simple one. Throughout the year, people are busy with their own lives, work, children, marriage, family ties and work-related issues, bills, holidays, childcare, pets and, this year in particular, a pandemic. However, at Christmas, you remembered those you might have neglected over the past twelve months, even if you didn't mean to, so you send them a lovely card, maybe a little gift simply to say you're thinking about them at this special time of year. But not this year. Not last year, either. In fact, he couldn't remember the last time he'd had anything to unwrap on Christmas Day.

He felt the walls closing in on him, squeezing him, keeping him prisoner in his own home. He had to get out. He grabbed his keys from the coffee table, his jacket from the cupboard under the stairs, kicked off his slippers and put on his walking boots. He needed a release, something to silence the screams within.

The streets of Sheffield were dark and quiet. In most houses he past he saw lights on in every room and silhouettes behind every curtain. Christmas was being enjoyed throughout the steel city. Money worries were forgotten for today. The pandemic was on hold. Today was all about overeating, drinking too much, spending time with loved ones and having a laugh.

'*FUCK!*' he screamed as loud as he could, hitting the steering wheel hard with the palms of his hands.

He drove above the speeding limit, aimlessly around the city. He had no idea where he was going. There was no plan. He just needed to get away, as far away as he could. It wasn't only Christmas he hated. It was the city as well. Sheffield was a horrible place to live with its fucking ugly buildings and its never-ending regeneration programme that was going nowhere. It was a dead city. And he was trapped here. He couldn't leave, even if he wanted to.

He slammed on the brakes as he noticed the traffic lights ahead were red. Not that it mattered. He hadn't seen a pedestrian or another vehicle since he set out. It felt like the end of the world had happened and nobody had told him. Christmas Day was the only day in the year where everything was silent and empty.

As he waited for the lights to change, his eyes wandered, and they fell on his Christmas present. A woman was dragging her feet, sleeping bag over one shoulder, bulging rucksack over the other. She sat on the steps of the Arundel Gate Bus Interchange and tried to get comfortable on the concrete. He couldn't make out her features from here, but judging by her movements and slight build, she didn't seem too old. He indicated right, turned into Norfolk Street and pulled up.

'Hello. Is everything all right?' he asked in his best soothing voice as he stood over the homeless woman. The light wasn't great here, but he could make out the dirty blonde hair, the smooth forehead, the hopeful eyes. She couldn't be more than twenty-five.

'Not really,' she replied, still struggling to find comfort on concrete.

'Are you planning on sleeping here?'

'Yes. Why? Are you going to move me on?'

'No. I don't have the authority to do that.' He smiled. 'It's Christmas Day, though. Don't you have someone to be with?'

'I have a nan in a nursing home who doesn't recognise me any more, a brother in Doncaster nick, a mother who won't talk to me and a stepdad who tries to fuck me. No offence, but I'm better off here.'

He looked around him. The coast was clear.

'I help run a charity for people who've fallen on hard times. We've had more than one hundred and fifty people today for

Christmas lunch. Some, who don't have anywhere else to go, can stay for a couple of nights in the community hall. You're more than welcome to sleep there. It's run by the church, but we're not going to ram religion down your throat. We just want you to have a hot meal, a warm place to sleep and access to hot water.'

She looked up at him. There was a hint of a smile on her dry lips and tears forming in her eyes.

He squatted to his knees and placed a comforting hand on her shoulder. 'Nobody should be on their own on Christmas Day.' He smiled. 'Would you like me to drive you over there?'

She swallowed hard. She tried to speak but a tear fell. She nodded.

'Good. Let me help you with your things.'

He picked up her rucksack. It was heavy. He threw it over one shoulder, and helped her up off the steps.

'What's your name?'

'Tracey.'

'Nice to meet you, Tracey. I'm Jeremy. Merry Christmas.'

She laughed and her face lit up. 'Thank you. Merry Christmas to you, too.'

Chapter Forty-Four

Saturday 26th December 2020

Matilda had barely slept. Along with Adele and Pat, the three of them sat through the *Captain America* trilogy, drinking champagne and eating whatever junk they could get their hands on. Adele explained the story and the characters throughout to Pat, though she said she preferred Chris Evans to Sebastian Stan, which led to them both going off on a tangent to discuss who was the better looking of the two.

Matilda wasn't taking any of it in. She'd seen the films many times before and, despite the efforts of Pat and Adele to take her mind off things, she couldn't stop picturing the noose on her front door and wondering who had delivered it. Her mother said it was a woman, so she surmised it was one of Steve Harrison's fans. Had he put her up to it or did she have a motive of her own? Steve didn't have any visitors in prison and his mail was vigorously checked. If anything had been flagged as worrying, she would have been informed of it. Wouldn't she?

When all three films were finished, they dragged themselves off to bed. Matilda walked around the house double and triple checking the locks on the doors and windows, but when she eventually climbed into bed and pulled the duvet up around her, she knew she wouldn't be able to sleep. More than an hour passed before her eyelids became too heavy to stay open and she drifted off.

'You're a survivor, aren't you, Matilda? But what's the point of surviving when everyone around you is dead?'

'Steve's brother was the gunman. Steve's been planning this since he was sent down. Your dad … he didn't make it. We tried to stop him, but … I'm so sorry.'

'Valerie, Rory, Ranjeet – they're all dead.'

'Sometimes, the best form of justice is what you dish out with your own hand.'

Matilda's eyes shot open, and she sat up in bed. She was wet with sweat. What had she been dreaming about? She had no idea, but she knew it wasn't good. The nightmares were back, and they were frightening.

It was a little after four o'clock, so she'd had a couple of hours' sleep at least. Any attempt to try to sleep now would be futile. Matilda got out of bed, put her dressing gown on and headed downstairs.

She was taken back in time to the early days of her recovery when she returned home from the rehabilitation centre. She couldn't sleep and would pace the house in the early hours, in total darkness, trying to make sense of what had happened. She never could.

Kettle boiled, Matilda sat at the kitchen table, her hands wrapped around the mug. There was something niggling at the back of her brain, but she couldn't pinpoint what it was.

Steve Harrison was back in her life, though he'd never

really left it. But there was something else, too. Something else had disturbed her sleep.

'Sometimes, the best form of justice is what you dish out with your own hand.'

Where had she heard that before?

———————————

A knock on the front door broke her reverie. She looked at her new watch. It was just after six o'clock and it was still pitch-dark outside. Matilda's heart sank. Who would be knocking on her door at this time of the morning?

'You're a survivor, aren't you, Matilda?'

'Shit,' she said to herself. She thought she'd heard the last of Jake Harrison taunting her. 'I am a survivor, you bastard.'

Not letting him win this time, Matilda walked confidently to the front door, prepared to confront whoever had arrived to destroy her. She undid the bolts, took off the security chair and unlocked the Yale and the Chubb. She pulled open the door and shivered as an icy cold wind hit her.

'Scott. What's wrong?' she asked. She stepped back to allow him to enter, quickly closing the door behind him.

'You were right,' he said. His face was grave and pale.

'Right about what?'

'He's killed again. And it really is as bad as we can imagine.'

———————————

Matilda ran back into her room. She picked up yesterday's discarded clothes, tore off her pyjamas and was still buttoning up her shirt when she ran downstairs. Scott was already in the car, engine warming. The snow forecast for yesterday hadn't materialised, but the temperature had plummeted well below freezing. Everywhere was covered with a thick layer of frost.

'Where are we going?' Matilda asked as she climbed into the front passenger seat.

'The Steel Steps,' he said, setting off down the driveway before Matilda had even closed the door.

'Where the hell are they?'

'Behind the train station. It's the Sheffield Amphitheatre, just off Granville Lane.'

Matilda frowned. 'I know it. It's close to the Cholera Monument where Dawn Richardson was found. Have you got any mints or anything in here? My mouth feels furry.'

'Glove box.'

She looked inside, found half a packet of Polos and threw three into her mouth. 'Have you already been at the scene?' she asked, looking at him dressed smartly in work clothes, minus a tie.

'No. Christian's on call. He's there waiting for us. He gave me a ring and asked me to wake you up. He's tried calling you several times, apparently.'

'I had a few drinks last night,' she said by way of an explanation.

'The thing is, you know how the previous victims seemed like they were thrown away, just dumped, well, this one's different.'

She looked over to Scott. 'Different? How?'

'She's been posed.'

'Oh my God!'

'I'm guessing you're reading something into that.'

'Yes. Posing her is a message. He knows we're onto him and this is his way of saying that he's aware of us looking for him but we're never going to catch him. He's being clever. Bastard.'

'I've called Zofia in and she's getting straight onto CCTV.'

Scott turned into Granville Lane and pulled up on the grass. Ahead, Matilda could make out the blue and white police tape. Several marked police cars were dotted about. A uniform constable was sitting on the bonnet of one, his face pale, vomit down the front of his jacket. A colleague was standing by with his arm around him. A white forensic tent had been erected and Christian was by the entrance wearing a white all-in-one suit.

Matilda stepped out of the car. The bitter wind tore through her. She had a massive headache and could feel it getting much worse in the next few minutes.

The amphitheatre gave a beautiful view over Sheffield. People spent hours in warmer weather sitting on the stone seats and spotting the hundreds of identifiable buildings that dotted the city. It was a glorious site to breathe in, though not on a sub-zero Boxing Day morning with a hangover.

Matilda was handed a forensic suit which she struggled to put on. Then she headed for the tent.

'Good morning, Matilda,' DI Christian Brady said to her.

'Morning. How are you?'

'Glad I didn't have breakfast before I came out.'

'You're pale. That's not like you.'

'I've never seen anything like this before in my life.'

Matilda's mouth fell open. She turned to look at the tent, flapping in the strong breeze, then looked back to Christian.

'I'm feeling a little delicate this morning,' she said, quietly.

He stepped towards her. 'There is nothing I can say to prepare you for this. I'm sorry.'

She nodded. Christian pulled back the opening to the tent.

Matilda and Scott headed inside. The first thing they noticed was the amount of blood on the ground. There was so much. Too much. It seemed brighter against the harshness of the frost. Slowly, Matilda looked up. The body of a young female was sitting upright on the stone seats of the amphitheatre. She was fully clothed and had a large backpack on her shoulders. She'd been decapitated. Her head was in her hands, on her lap, looking out at the sprawling view of the city.

Matilda held out a hand and placed it on Scott's arm for stability. She couldn't take her eyes from the disturbing tableau in front of her.

'This isn't real. Surely,' Matilda said, her voice barely above a whisper.

'I'm afraid it is,' Simon Browes said. He was wearing a blue forensic suit and standing over the body. His gloved fingers were covered in blood. 'The decapitation wasn't a single, clean cut. You can see the tears in the edges of the—'

'Not now, Simon,' Matilda interrupted.

'Sorry.'

Matilda was overcome with a wave of emotion. She felt a great sadness for this poor woman, horror at what she was looking at, anger at the sadistic bastard who felt he could do this and get away with it and a huge determination to tear this city apart to find him. All the while, she couldn't take her eyes from the grotesque display the killer had laid out for her.

There was no doubt in her mind this was a message, direct to her. The killer knew who she was, that she was trying to find him, and he was telling her she didn't stand a chance. She could almost hear his cruel laugh taunting her.

Chapter Forty-Five

The HMCU was bathed in silence. Matilda was in her office, elbows on her desk, holding her head up, a blank expression on her face. She'd been on the phone to Ridley, told him what had happened. He was on his way in. In the main suite, Scott and Zofia were awaiting instructions. Neither of them could get over what had been uncovered this morning.

Matilda stood up and went out to join them. 'Do we know who she is yet?' Her voice was quiet.

Scott nodded. 'I'm afraid so. We took her fingerprints, and she has a record for a few minor offences, shoplifting mostly. We've been through her backpack and there's a driving licence which confirms it. She's Tracey Ann Ward. Date of birth is the first of February 2001, making her nineteen.'

'Jesus Christ,' Matilda hissed.

'The address on the licence is a house in Jordanthorpe. Do you want me to send uniform round, or shall I go?' Scott asked. The look on his face suggested he'd rather someone else break this kind of news.

'Send uniform. Just tell them to inform them of the basics

for now. Send an FLO with them, too. When we know more, we'll go and give them chapter and verse.' Scott picked up the phone.

Matilda turned to Zofia. 'How do we tell the parents that their daughter has been turned into some sick diorama?'

'I've really no idea,' she said. 'Do we need to tell them everything?'

'They have a right to know. She's their daughter, after all.'

'Would you want to know?'

Matilda thought for a moment. 'I think I would, yes.'

The door to the suite opened and Chief Constable Ridley walked in, looking grave. It took Matilda a few moments to realise it was him. It was the first time she'd seen him out of uniform. He looked younger in casual clothing.

'Matilda, can I have a word in private?' he asked, heading straight for her office.

She followed and closed the door behind her. Ridley stood by the window, looking out at the bins.

'You were right,' he said, his back to her.

'Under any other circumstances I would have said I told you so.'

'This was always going to be the case, though, wasn't it? There's such a fast turnaround between victims,' he said, looking at her.

'Just a week since Tilly Hall.'

'What do we know of this new one?'

'Not much so far. We've got her address. Uniform are going there now to speak to her family. She's only nineteen.'

He sighed and shook his head. 'I've been onto my contact at BBC News. They're going to send a crew round this afternoon for you to give a recorded interview. It'll go out during this evening's programme and be shown at regular intervals on the news channel. You need to be clear and concise as to who we're looking for here, Matilda.'

'I will.'

'Go home, have a shower, change into something more professional, and we'll have a word in my office at lunchtime.' He headed for the door. He paused and turned back. 'Did you have a good Christmas?'

She really should mention the noose on the door. 'Lovely. Thank you. You?'

'Just me and the wife' was all he said. He left the room, leaving the door ajar.

Matilda sat down at her desk. Today was where it all changed. The whole country would know of this sick, despicable bastard in Sheffield, and everyone would be looking out for him. Hopefully, someone will know who he is. If not, she hoped the killer himself would be watching her interview and decide to make her his next victim. If he did, she'd be more than ready for him, and she'd tear his throat out with her bare hands if she had the chance.

Chapter Forty-Six

Matilda arrived back at the station after going home to shower and change into something the BBC would see as respectable. She'd gone for black trousers and a cream jumper. She'd styled her hair, taking time to make sure no scars could be visible, sprayed herself with an expensive perfume and added the littlest amount of make-up to hide her imperfections but not look like she was about to walk onto the dance floor on *Strictly*.

As she headed for Ridley's office, she saw DI Christian Brady up ahead. Suddenly, she knew why he'd taken the law into his own hands earlier this year, if he had been the one to pull the trigger. The complete disregard for human life this killer had – she would certainly enjoy killing him in revenge.

'Are you all right?' he asked.

'I'm fine.' She gave a nervous smile.

'I've heard you're giving an interview to the BBC. You don't usually like talking to the media directly.'

'I hate it.' She half-laughed.

'Have you spoken to Scott yet?'

'No. Why?'

'Uniform went round to Tracey's parents' house. Her mother was in tears, asking for all the details of what had happened to her daughter. The FLO thought it best to tell her what had happened. When she did, the stepdad laughed.'

'What?' She stopped in her tracks and turned to face Christian. 'He laughed? Why would he do that?'

'I don't know.'

'Bring him in. Question him. I want to know his entire movements for the whole of yesterday.' She reached Ridley's office and knocked.

'Matilda, can we talk?' Christian asked.

She was halfway through the door. She stopped and looked back at him. She nodded. 'Yes. Give me a couple of days, but yes. I'd like that.' She smiled.

He smiled back and walked away. Matilda closed the door behind her and went over to Ridley's desk. He told her to take a seat.

'Better not. These trousers wrinkle easily,' she said and gave a nervous smile.

'I've got some bad news,' Ridley said. His face was grave.

'I don't think I can cope with any more bad news.'

'The crew from the BBC are here. They're setting up in the media room.'

'Okay,' she said, wondering where this was going.

'They've sent Danny Hanson.'

'*Oh, for fuck's sake!*' Matilda screamed.

Danny Hanson was a permanent thorn in Matilda's side, though her feelings had waned slightly over the last few months.

While he was a junior reporter on the *Sheffield Star*, he saw Matilda as a chance to give his stalled career a boost.

He managed to get a few front-page leads out of her cases and it wasn't long before his confidence grew. He went freelance and somehow landed a job as the North of England Correspondent for BBC News. At the time of the shooting in January 2019, Danny was the roving reporter on duty and made sure the camera was always rolling. He'd won awards for his coverage, and he'd even posed as a doctor to gain access to Matilda's private room, taking photos of her while she was in a coma and slapping them all over the internet. Matilda loathed him with a passion, but used his services when she needed them, and during the historical sex abuse case earlier this year, when everyone was trying to silence her, he gave her a voice, and the case was blown wide open. She had a new-found respect for him for putting his own career on the line at her behest. She still couldn't stand the annoying little shit, though.

The media room was set up with two chairs (socially distanced) and a skeleton camera crew. One camera would be permanently on Matilda while a second would be pointing at Danny. Behind the chair Matilda would be sitting on was a board with five photos depicting the killer's victims so far.

Before she entered, she took a deep breath, and wished Sian was with her to give her a confidence-boosting pep talk. She tried to tell herself she was hot, as Adele suggested, but it didn't work.

'Matilda Darke, lovely to see you. Merry Christmas,' Danny Hanson said. He wore his trademark blue check shirt, and his dark wavy hair was perfectly styled in an unkempt way. He spoke cheerfully, as if they were simply meeting for a post-Christmas coffee in Costa.

She gave a pained smile and tried to hide wanting to slap the smug smile from his annoying face. 'Good morning, Danny,' she said. 'Am I sitting here?' She pointed to a chair.

'We just need to check the sound and lighting then we're ready to roll.'

One of the cameramen, masked to protect himself against Covid, told Matilda where to sit. He positioned a microphone towards her and asked her to say something random to check the equipment was working correctly.

'My name is Detective Chief Inspector Matilda Darke and Danny Hanson is wearing far too much make-up.'

There were giggles from the camera crew. It was a cheap shot, but it helped settle Matilda's nerves.

'Purely for the camera, Matilda,' Danny said. 'The last thing we want is glare from a shiny forehead.'

'I can understand that. It doesn't explain the mascara, though, does it?'

'Are we ready, Phil?' Danny, blushing, quickly asked the man behind him.

'Give me a minute,' he replied, stifling a laugh.

'Right, Matilda, I'm going to ask you about the case, and I want you to tell me about the victims and the dates,' Danny said, leaning forward. 'Be clear and talk slowly and calmly. When I ask you a question, answer it with facts. Don't do what politicians do and waffle. If you make a mistake, let me know, we can stop and pick up again. Any questions before we begin?'

'No.'

'Try not to look too nervous.'

She nodded. She really needed a wee.

'Okay, Danny. Ready when you are.'

He cleared his throat and looked directly into the camera just beyond Matilda.

'Over the past two months, five women have been brutally attacked in Sheffield, four of whom were killed. Despite the best efforts of South Yorkshire Police, they have been unable to identify the murderer. Now, they are turning to the public to help them find who is responsible before he strikes again. With me is Detective Chief Inspector Matilda Darke of the Homicide and Major Crime Unit who is leading the investigation. DCI Darke, if we could begin with a summary of the case. What's actually been happening?'

'As you can see on the wall behind me, five young women have been attacked and four of them have been murdered. The youngest, Tilly Hall, is just fourteen years old and recovering with life-changing injuries. The first was Daisy Clough, a twenty-three-year-old A&E nurse who was raped and murdered on her way home from working at the Northern General Hospital on Tuesday the twenty-ninth of October. She was found the following morning. All of the victims were raped and murdered. The second was Joanna Fielding on Wednesday the eighteenth of November. The third was Dawn Richardson on Saturday the fifth of December, Tilly Hall was attacked on December the fifteenth and the most recent was Tracey Ward on Christmas Day.' Matilda pointed at each of the photos in turn.

'How are the women murdered?' Danny asked.

'Their throats are cut. And not just once. The killer is savagely attacking them with something we believe is a hunter's knife. He then throws the bodies away when he's finished with them. This is a disturbed and depraved individual.'

'South Yorkshire Police have advised women not to go out alone while this man is on the loose. How are you protecting them?'

'We have extra patrols, both uniform and plain-clothed officers, on the streets, but we are advising women not to go out at all, unless they really need to. This man is very dangerous.'

'Is it true you have no forensic evidence from five crime scenes?' Danny asked, his inflection hinting at incredulity.

'The fifth scene is still being processed. However, from the previous four, it is true that we've found nothing to identify the killer. He's an intelligent man and knows exactly what he needs to do to evade capture.'

'Is it possible the killer could be someone who works within forensics, or possibly a police officer?'

'We are considering everyone who appears on our radar. Everyone is a suspect right now.'

'And now you're appealing for the public to help. What should they be looking for?'

Matilda took a deep and shaky breath. 'We're seeking a male in his late twenties to late forties. He's what we call a process-focused killer, who is addicted to the power and control he gets from committing the murders. He's organised and highly intelligent. While he's getting great enjoyment out of luring and capturing his victims, the driving force for him is the power and control he has over them.

'We're asking the public to look at all the men in their lives and see if they have noticed a change in their behaviour over the past two months. A man who has attacked five women, killing four of them, will have changed. Is he distant, quiet, more secretive than usual? Where was he on Thursday the twenty-ninth of October, Wednesday the eighteenth of November, Saturday the fifth of December, Tuesday the fifteenth of December, and especially on Christmas Day? It's this last date that may give him away as being someone without a family, but we believe he has close friends, neighbours, acquaintances. Do you know someone who was planning to spend Christmas Day on their own? If so, did they? Do you have any suspicions about the people in your life, who you believe have questionable alibis for any of those dates? If so, contact us. It is important you do not question these men yourself as he is very dangerous.'

'How much danger are the public in? Women in particular.'

'I believe we can catch this man very soon, with the public's help. For now, I'm appealing for all women of all ages to not go out alone, and especially at night. I'm also asking the public to call us if they suspect anyone, even if it's just the smallest hint of suspicion. I'd rather you call us and have us look into something than simply not call at all.'

'Do you have anything you'd like to say to the killer if he's watching?'

I know he's watching. I'm coming for you, you sick fucking bastard.

Matilda looked straight into the eye of the camera. This was her one and only chance. 'I'm aware of your issues with women. I know something happened to you that led to you having a problem with women, and you need help. But you're going about this the wrong way. I am prepared to talk to you, to listen to you. *You* just need to come to *me*.'

Danny's eyes widened. A silence descended between the two. Behind Matilda, the cameraman waved to get Danny's attention.

'One last question, Detective Chief Inspector,' he said, his voice more subdued. 'Given the fact South Yorkshire Police is in special measures, are you equipped for hunting a serial killer?'

Matilda looked directly to Danny. 'I have been a detective for a very long time. The force being in special measures has no impact on how I go about my work. I will catch this killer. Of that I have absolutely no doubt.'

'Detective Chief Inspector Matilda Darke, thank you.'

'Are you out of your mind?' Chief Constable Ridley was waiting for Matilda in the corridor outside the media room.

'I'm sweating through this jumper,' Matilda said, heading down the corridor.

'You practically looked into that camera and told the killer to come and get you.'

'I did not.'

'That's how he'll see it. You might as well have given him your address and the code for your alarm.'

'With all due respect, I need to lure him out. Our phone lines are going to be ringing off the hook with people reporting every bloke who's ever looked at them cock-eyed. We don't have the time to sift through all the crank calls to find the one that's going to lead us to him, so I need to get him to come to us.'

'I can't believe how reckless you've just been.'

'It wasn't live. If you want that interview edited then by all means do so, but don't expect to see me come into work tomorrow morning. You want my help with this, let me do it my way. Now, are you going to follow me into the toilets?'

He sighed. 'You'll be the death of me, Matilda.'

'Just … trust me. Please.'

She left him in the corridor and entered the toilets. She went over to the sink, ran the cold water and splashed some on her face. She looked up at her reflection and didn't like what was looking back at her.

Ridley was right. She had been reckless. And she was absolutely terrified of what was to come next.

Chapter Forty-Seven

Matilda entered the HMCU suite and found the lone figure of DC Zofia Nowak sitting at her desk, leaning in to her computer screen. She almost exploded and demanded to know where everyone else was until she remembered it was Boxing Day and nobody was scheduled to work today. The fact Zofia had come in on her day off was testament to her dedication to the investigation. Or maybe she simply needed an excuse to escape the suffocation of her mother's worries. Matilda preferred to think it was the first option.

'How did it go?' Zofia asked, wheeling herself over to the drinks station and flicking on the kettle.

'Fine. I think,' Matilda said. She pulled out the chair at Tom Simpson's desk and flopped into it. 'Part of me wishes it had gone out live. I'm worried the BBC are going to edit my words and it will lose impact. Although,' she began with a frown, 'I'm pretty sure I looked straight into the camera and challenged the killer to come for me.'

'Really?'

'I think so. It's all a bit of a blur, to be honest. I hate

speaking to the media. Especially when it involves Danny-cocking-Hanson.'

'You're really setting yourself up for the killer to come for you then?'

'I don't have any other choice. Thanks,' she said, taking the mug of tea from her and wrapping her hands around it. 'Literally the only thing we know about the killer is that he hates women. The fact that, after tonight, he'll know there's a woman leading the investigation into finding him will seriously piss him off. Deep down, he knows he's going to get arrested eventually and the last thing he'll want is to be led to a police car in handcuffs by a female detective. He'll want to take me out, so a man is in charge.'

'You're very brave.'

'You think so? Everyone else seems to think I'm being stupid.'

'No. I think you're being incredibly brave. Last year, when I put myself in front of that Land Rover, thinking I could stop the killer from driving away, that was stupid. A tiny little woman against a huge car like that. I didn't stand a chance. But you're actually telling the killer to come to you. And you're doing it because you know you'll win. I can see the determination in your eyes. That takes guts.'

A small smile appeared on Matilda's lips. 'Thank you, Zofia. That means a lot.'

'Now, I don't know if this will mean anything, but I've been scrolling through CCTV footage from Christmas Day around the amphitheatre and beyond. Fortunately, there's very little traffic about and I've picked up a silver Vauxhall Vivaro just off Norfolk Street with the same registration number as Laurence Dodds.' She brought up the feed on her computer, turned the screen around, and played the grainy footage for

Matilda. 'A few minutes later, he reverses out. Obviously, I don't know what he was doing, but there were no shops, banks or pubs open up there.'

'Do you find him anywhere else?'

'I'm afraid not. He travels out of the city centre, and I lose him after the ring road.'

'We need to interview Laurence Dodds again. Just so we can eliminate him. Where's Scott?'

'Ah. He's in Christian's old office,' Zofia said, almost reluctantly.

'Really?' Matilda leaned back on her chair and looked towards the office. It was in darkness.

'I think you need to go and talk to him.'

Matilda's frown deepened. She walked slowly to the office, pushed the door open and stepped inside. She flicked the light on and both she and Scott winced at the brightness.

'What are you doing in here on your own in the dark?'

Scott's face was pale. His eyes were red, evidence that he had recently been crying.

'I can't get that girl's body out of my head,' he said, tears running down his face.

Matilda closed the door to give them some privacy and went around to Scott. She put her arms around him and held him tight. He was so cold.

'He cut off her head and put it in her lap. He posed her like she was a piece of artwork or something. She was nineteen years old, for fuck's sake,' he sobbed. His hands were clenched into tight fists, his knuckles white. 'What is going on in his diseased mind where he even thought of doing something so … evil?' he said with his teeth clenched.

'I really don't know, Scott,' Matilda said, her voice barely above a whisper.

'When we catch him, he'll plead insanity. He'll have doctors saying he's not of sound mind and he'll spend the rest of his life in a cushy hospital somewhere. Meanwhile, four women have been slaughtered and poor Tilly Hall will never talk again. What kind of justice is that?'

Matilda held Scott even tighter, resting his head against her shoulder. 'I'm not going to allow that to happen, Scott. I promise you. He knows exactly what he's doing.'

'Precisely. He's playing a game, and he's a fucking master of it.'

'No he's not. Scott, look at me.' She waited until Scott wiped his eyes and looked up. 'I've been a detective for more than twenty years and I have a very high success rate. I'm the fucking master. Not him.'

His eyes widened. 'What are you going to do?'

'Whatever it takes,' she said, looking him straight in the eye.

Their eyes remained locked on each other, and a dark silence enveloped them both. The temperature suddenly dropped in the room and Scott shivered.

'Now,' Matilda said, turning away. 'Laurence Dodds's registration number has been picked up again around Norfolk Street. I want you to get the information from Zofia, then go and get Finn and pay him a visit.'

'Why? It's not him. He's gay.'

'We need to do this by the book, Scott. This is all about getting the force out of special measures. We can take no short cuts.'

Scott nodded. He slowly got up from the desk and headed for the door. He stopped and turned back. 'What you're planning, there's no coming back from it, is there?' he asked.

'Not for me, no.'

Chapter Forty-Eight

Matilda found Christian in his office, tucked away in the corner of the CID suite. There was a skeleton staff working today and only three were in the office. One detective was on the phone and two were holding mugs of tea and rifling through a tub of Celebrations. Matilda lightly tapped on Christian's door. He jumped and looked up. His face was worried and he faked a smile when he saw who his visitor was.

'Am I interrupting?' she asked.

'You are and you're very welcome,' he said. 'I can understand why DCI French is reluctant to return. All I seem to do is fill in forms.'

'I thought she was ill with long Covid.'

'So she says.'

'You're a cynical man, Christian.' Smiling, she pulled out a chair and sat down. 'How was your Christmas?'

'It was good. Quiet. Just me and Jennifer and the kids. It was a good day,' he said, with a genuine smile this time.

'And everyone's all right, with the pandemic and everything?'

'Yes. The kids were scared at the beginning, as you know. But we've turned hand washing and social distancing into a kind of game for them. Hopefully it won't be for much longer once we're all vaccinated.'

She nodded. 'Christian, tell me everything that happened at Magnolia House right after I took the gun from Jamie Cobb and handed it to you.'

The smile disappeared from Christian's face. 'Really? Now?'

'Now's a good a time as any.'

'I could do with a few drinks first.'

'Valerie always kept an emergency bottle of whisky in her filing cabinet.'

He turned to look at his filing cabinet. 'I don't have any room for a bottle of whisky among all the pointless forms and reports.'

'I really need to know.'

He took a slow, deep breath. 'You handed me the gun and went over to Kenneth Burr with Sian, and you began to untie him. You went down on your knees and untied his ankles, while Sian went around to untie his hands that were behind him. I'm afraid I sort of lost myself for a moment. I'm looking at Kenneth Burr, our Police and Crime Commissioner, and trying to make sense out of it all. I honestly didn't see Jamie grab the gun from me. The next thing, I heard a shot. Kenneth goes flying, you and Sian dive for cover and I've got ringing in my ears. When everything dies down, I see Jamie with the gun. He starts to turn it on himself, but Guy Grayston grabs it from him. The first thing that comes into my head is fingerprints. Stupid, I know. But I snatch the gun from Guy, and I make sure it's my fingerprints that are all over it. Not theirs. They both suffered so much at the hands of that man, the last thing they needed was a drawn-out investigation into who pulled the trigger. I should have known Jamie would take his own life at the earliest opportunity, but I didn't do anything to stop it. I didn't put any measures in place.'

Matilda watched Christian. She knew she was hearing the truth. 'Why didn't you tell me all this before?'

'I'm a victim of child abuse, just as Guy and Jamie and all the others were. I was protecting them. I had no idea you'd ever think it was me who shot Kenneth. I thought you'd know me well enough by now.'

She proffered a weak smile. 'I do. But when you see a man holding a smoking gun over a dead body and his are the only prints on it, you start to think the obvious.'

'I know. I guess we're both at fault for not talking sooner.'

She nodded. 'I'm sorry I ever doubted you.'

'I'm sorry I didn't come to you sooner and tell you everything.'

'After the shooting, Sian mentioned that you had regular appointments with a therapist after the few measly sessions the force gave you all. Was it so you could talk through the abuse?'

'No. I used the shooting as a reason to talk about going to therapy. The truth is, I've been seeing a therapist for years. It helps to talk.'

She smiled. 'So everyone keeps telling me. Listen, I'm going to be making a few recommendations to the Chief Constable once this case is solved. Would you be interested in going back to the Homicide and Major Crime Unit?'

'Of course,' he answered immediately.

'I don't want you there as a DI, though. I want you to head up the entire unit. I want you to be the DCI.'

He frowned. 'What about you?'

'I'm not coming back.'

'Why not?'

'You'll see.' She stood up. At the door, she stopped and looked back. 'Can I give you your first task as the new DCI?'

'Go on.'

'Make sure you get Sian back on your team.'

'I'll try. But wait, Matilda …'

'Thank you,' she said, leaving the office and closing the door behind her.

Matilda left the CID suite with her head down and didn't look back once. She had tears in her eyes and a lump in her throat. She walked down the empty corridors, her clacking shoes bouncing off the walls, and headed for the car park. She knew the killer would be coming for her after tonight, and she needed to prepare herself for him. The first thing she had to do was to send Adele and Pat away.

Chapter Forty-Nine

Zofia was talking Scott through the CCTV footage of the silver Vivaro. She zoomed in on the registration number for him to confirm himself it was the one belonging to Laurence Dodds.

'Aren't there any other cameras where we can see the front of the van so we can get a good description of who's driving?' He asked.

'I've tried. This is the best I've managed to get.'

The image that filled the screen was a wide shot showing the van turning into Norfolk Street. Unfortunately, light from the streetlights was bouncing off the windscreen. There was very little to make out of the driver, apart from gloved hands on the steering wheel.

'If you zoom in as close as possible, apart from giving yourself a headache from how pixelated the image is, you can just about make out that his arms are rigid and high.'

'What does that prove?'

'I think he's purposely sitting back in his seat so he's as far away from the camera as possible and he's hoping shadows will block his identity. I mean, if he's going to wear a mask, he'll stand out from other road users, won't he?'

'There are no other road users.'

'Not this time, but on other occasions.'

'True.'

'It's a shame that jogger refused to get involved. If he could have given us anything like a description, DCI Darke could have mentioned it in her interview and that could have narrowed things down for us other than saying he's a man in his twenties to forties,' Zofia said, sitting back and yawning.

'Zofia, why don't you go home? You've done more than enough today. It's supposed to be your day off and it's starting to go dark.'

'I think I might,' she said, stretching her hands above her head.

'Do you want me to give you a lift?'

'No. I'll call my dad. I'm going round there anyway for tea. Do you need me to look up Laurence Dodds's address, or do you still have it?'

'I've still got it.'

'Shall I call Finn and tell him to get ready for you?'

'No. I'll do that. Turn off your computers and go home.'

Scott made a play out of scrolling through his notes until Zofia had left the suite. He was alone and waited for the sound of the door slamming closed down the corridor before picking up his coat and car keys. He had no intention of phoning Finn and dragging him away from his family Christmas. Laurence Dodds could wait until tomorrow.

By the time Scott pulled up on Chelsea Road, darkness had fallen. He parked a few doors up from Malcolm Barker's house and watched with rapt attention to see if he could make out who was inside. All the curtains were closed, but there seemed to be a light on in every room. More than one silhouette could be seen moving around in what Scott guessed was the living room. If Malcolm was at home with his family, hopefully he would feel obliged to help.

Scott walked carefully along the icy pavement, his heavy shoes crunching the frost. It was another cold night. The sky was clear, an infinite number of stars twinkled and a bright full moon lit up the scene like a brilliant lunar torch. He knew he shouldn't be here on his own. He knew he shouldn't be here at all. Malcolm had said he didn't want to get involved and the police should accept that, but Scott couldn't get the image of Tracey Ward out of his mind. Her head had been removed and placed in her lap. It was the stuff of nightmares. This sick bastard needed stopping and Malcolm could help.

Scott knocked on the door with a clenched fist. He stood back and looked up at the expensive detached house with double garage. The bloke was an illustrator, living in an affluent part of Sheffield in a house worth upwards of a million pounds with a minimalist designer kitchen. His life existed within these four walls and he obviously didn't give a toss about anything that didn't affect him. Selfish bast—

The door opened. Scott was bathed in the warm light from within. Malcolm Barker recognised his visitor straightaway as his smile dropped.

'Good evening Mr Barker. I'm—'

'I know who you are,' he interrupted. 'I told you before, I'm not getting involved,' he hissed.

'Who is it?' A call came from somewhere within the house.

'Mr Barker,' Scott began. 'I can understand your reluctance to get involved. In your position, I'd probably feel the same. However, things have escalated since we last spoke. We have another victim.'

'I don't want to hear this,' he said, shaking his head.

'She's nineteen years old. She was decapitated, Mr Barker. The killer posed her. He put her head on her lap.'

'No. You've got no right coming to my house like this, disrupting my family and trying to make me feel guilty.'

'How would you feel if it was your wife or one of your children who was killed, and you knew there was a witness who refused to help?'

'I saw … nothing,' he said, unconvincingly.

'I don't believe you. You saw something. I know you did. You had to have, to have turned around so quickly and run away. Or is that what you've been doing all your life, running away? Are you a coward, Mr Barker?' Scott said, seething.

'Malcolm, you're letting all the warmth out.' Another call from inside the house.

'I am not a coward,' Malcolm said, his voice quiet but stern.

'Really? You've giving a very good impression of one.' Scott dug into his pocket, pulled out his mobile phone and selected an image. He showed it to Malcolm who immediately baulked. 'Tracey Ward. Nineteen years old. Her whole life ahead of her. She was raped and murdered on Christmas Day. She was decapitated. This is what the killer did with her body.'

'What the fuck?' Malcolm gasped. 'Why are you showing me this?'

'You need to help us.'

'The fuck I do. If you don't leave right now, I'm reporting

you.'

'What did you see?'

'I'm not talking to you.' Malcolm held up a hand, blocking his view of the phone in Scott's hand. He edged back into the house.

'You saw a man next to a van with a knife to a girl's throat, didn't you?'

'Leave. Right now.'

'What did he look like? Was he tall or short, fat or thin, black or white?' Scott edged closer, refusing to allow Malcolm Barker to go back to the safety and warmth of his happy middle-class family.

'I'm calling your boss. I'll have you sacked for this,' Malcolm said, slamming the door in Scott's face.

Scott banged hard on the door. 'Talk to me, Malcolm. What did you see?' He heard the sound of muffled conversation from behind the door and saw two shadows through the frosted glass. 'Mrs Barker, I'm with South Yorkshire Police,' Scott shouted. 'Ask your husband what he saw when he went for a jog along Brincliffe Edge Road last week. He witnessed a severe attack. We need him to give a statement. Four women have been murdered. Your husband can help but he's refusing to get involved.'

'Go away,' Malcolm shouted.

'Watch the BBC News tonight, Mrs Barker. Please. We need your help.'

Nothing else was said to him. Eventually, he began to back away. There was nothing more he could do here, and he was getting cold in the freezing night air.

As he went back to the car, he knew he was going to get into a shitload of trouble for what he'd just done, but he didn't care.

Chapter Fifty

'What did you think?' Matilda asked as she turned off the television.

Adele and Pat remained silence. She looked at each of them in turn.

'I spoke clearly and calmly, you can't deny that. And I mentioned everything you said about the killer, Pat.'

'You did.'

'Look, I know I'm no Judi Dench in front of the camera, but it wasn't that bad. I'm better than the wooden people they get to appear on *Gogglebox*.'

'It's not how you appeared, it's what you said,' Adele said. 'The way you stressed the words at the end. You literally told the killer to come and get you.'

'You've set him a challenge,' Pat said. 'He's going to hate that.'

'That was kind of my point. Adele, you've done the post mortems. You know we have nothing to go on to catch this bloke. The only way I can get him is for him to come to me.'

'What did Ridley have to say?'

'Well, he wasn't thrilled. He said he'll increase patrols in the area.'

'Is that all? Shouldn't he put an armed officer outside or something?' Adele asked, concern on her face.

'This isn't *Line of Duty*, Adele. It's real life. We don't do things like that. He suggested I put cameras up around the house and consider moving out, but that sort of defeats the purpose.'

'This is a very dangerous game you're playing. I don't like it.'

Matilda adjusted herself on the sofa. 'Look, I was thinking that maybe it might be better if you two sort of moved out, temporarily. Maybe, Pat, Adele could come and stay at your place for a while.'

'What?' Adele asked. 'This is my home.'

'I know. But like you've said, I've invited a killer to come for me. The last thing I want is you in the crossfire.'

'So, you want to be here all by yourself, with no neighbours close by to hear your screams?'

'Of course not, but I want you both to be safe. I'll get Scott to move in and sleep in the spare room for a while. I'll have my baton in bed with me. I just don't want either of you getting hurt.'

'I think Matilda's right, Adele,' Pat said. 'The killer will have watched that interview and he'll be fuming at a female detective seeking him out. He'll come for her. And soon. You're more than welcome to come to mine. I've plenty of room.'

Adele stood up. 'You've made my home unsafe. And I don't like it.'

'I had no choice.'

'You should have consulted me first.'

'Look, I'm going to call a security firm up once Christmas is out of the way. I'll get cameras put up all round the perimeter. We'll be completely safe.'

'I'm going to bed,' Adele said.

'It's not even seven o'clock yet.'

'I'm really angry right now with you, Matilda.' She looked over at Pat. 'Thanks, Pat, I'd love to stay at yours for a few days. I'll take tomorrow morning off work, and we'll move out then if that's okay with you?'

'Fine,' Pat said.

Adele left the room, closing the door firmly behind her.

'She's overreacting, isn't she?' Matilda asked.

'Two things. Firstly, she's worried about you putting yourself in front of the killer. She doesn't want to come back here to find you dead in a pool of your own blood.'

'That won't happen.'

'You don't know that. You haven't a clue who the killer is. All you know is what he's capable of, and after this latest victim, we know that's absolutely anything.'

'What's the other thing?'

'You asked her to move in with you after her son died. This is her home, too. Yet you're treating it like it's still yours and she's just a lodger. You're not being fair to her at all.'

'Ah. I didn't think of that.'

'I gathered. I think I'll have an early night with a good book.'

'You're going to bed, too?'

'You've a lot to think about, Matilda. It's fine to challenge a killer to come into the open, but it's not only your own life you're putting at risk. Adele lives here. Scott lives just across the driveway, and I've been staying here, too. You need to think of others. Goodnight,' she said, kissing her on the top of her head and leaving the room.

Matilda remained on the sofa, a heavy frown on her face. She had done everything wrong. She hadn't thought through who else would be involved in her decision-making. She hoped she'd thought of every possibility when it came to luring the killer out.

Former DS Sian Robinson had the living room to herself. Belinda was staying at a friend's house for the night, Gregory was staying with her mother and father for a couple of days, Danny was upstairs playing whatever game it was he'd badgered Sian to get him for Christmas, and Anthony had asked to borrow her van so he could visit his mates in Rotherham. He seemed to be using her van more than her lately. The dog walking business had hit a hiatus.

Her plan was to curl up on the sofa with a bottle of wine and a slushy movie on Netflix and when she turned the television on and Sheffield was mentioned, Sian's ears pricked up and she wondered if the killer had been caught. When she saw Matilda being interviewed by Danny Hanson, her interest was more than piqued. At the end of the interview when Matilda looked directly into the camera and challenge the killer to come after her, Sian almost exploded.

She scrambled around on the coffee table for her mobile, found it and fired off a text to Matilda.

Are you free tomorrow, at all? We need to talk.

Malcolm and Suzanne Barker watched the news in stony silence. Malcolm had been reluctant to sit down and watch it, but Suzanne was adamant. She wanted to know why a detective was so keen to talk to her husband and if he wouldn't tell her, she'd find out for herself. She sent the kids to play in their room and forced Malcolm to sit beside her and watch the whole news programme with her.

The main story was the killings in Sheffield. As soon as the newsreader changed stories and Covid was mentioned, Suzanne reached for the remote and muted the television.

'Is this what the detective was talking about?' she asked, turning to her husband. She was wearing slim jeans and a black sweater with a wide neck. She was fully made up and her hair perfectly styled, despite having not left the house all day.

'Yes,' he said, looking down.

'Four women have been murdered, Malcolm, and you don't want to get involved?'

'I was thinking about you and the kids.'

'And what if I cross paths with this killer and I'm his next victim? What will you tell the kids then?'

'That's not going to happen.'

'I'm guessing all those women thought it wouldn't happen to them either. The girl, the fourteen-year-old who can no longer talk, is she the one who was attacked around the corner from us?'

'Yes,' he said, still looking down.

'And did you see something?'

He nodded. 'But not enough to tell the police anything.'

'You don't know that. They might have caught him on CCTV or something. They may have a vague description from someone else and you might have the missing piece of information they're looking for.'

'I didn't see anything,' he said, quietly.

'You're lying. You saw more than you're letting on and tomorrow, we're going to the police station.'

'We bloody are not. You heard what that detective said on the news. He's a dangerous man. If he finds out someone has gone to the police about him, he'll come after us.'

Suzanne frowned. 'Did you recognise him?'

'No. Of course not.'

Her eyes widened. The penny dropped. 'He saw you. The killer, he saw you when you saw him, didn't he?' Malcolm didn't say anything. 'You made eye contact. That's why you don't want to get involved.'

'Yes!' he shouted.

'Jesus Christ, Malcolm. You cannot keep this to yourself.'

Tilly Hall couldn't sleep. She'd spent another day with her mother by her bed trying to think of something to say and struggling to make conversation. She tried to be sympathetic with her. It can't be easy trying to talk when you're not going to get anything back in return apart from a few words on an iPad. She just wished her mum would be more light-hearted, tell her a funny story or something quirky from school, something that would lighten the atmosphere. Every time Tilly looked across at her mum, she looked on the verge of tears. She probably was. Tilly imagined she went home every night, fed and walked the dogs, then went to bed, crying herself to sleep. She looked as if she'd lost weight.

Amy left around four o'clock. The nurses came in at five and changed her dressings and replaced her drip bag. She was left alone then. There was nothing she wanted to watch on television so she finished her *Planet Earth II* book. Amy promised to bring in her *Frozen Planet* book tomorrow. Tilly hoped, if Matilda came to visit her, they could look through it together. Matilda said she liked things to do with the Arctic. She'd love to see the photos of polar bears.

Tilly nodded off around nine o'clock and woke up just after midnight. Something woke her up, but she didn't know what. For a moment, she was scared, thinking someone was outside her room wanting to come in. She made sure the alert button was within reach. She rationalised it by telling herself the hospital was a twenty-four-hour working environment. There were bound to be noises at every hour of the day and night. Maybe someone slammed a door or dropped something.

She couldn't get back to sleep, so struggled to sit up and turned on the iPad. She'd downloaded a few games as Matilda said she could but decided to look on Twitter to see if any of her mates had posted anything about how their Christmases were going. She saw Sheffield was trending and followed the link to the BBC News website and read the story about the killings. She was named as a survivor. There had been four other murders, one of which was on Christmas Day. She watched the interview Matilda gave with that cute reporter, Danny Hanson. Anyone who had any information was to come forward and tell the police, help them to find the killer. Matilda looked almost frightened when she spoke to the camera.

She grabbed her phone and sent Matilda a text, hoping she'd act on it first thing in the morning.

Hello Matilda. It's Tilly. I'm sorry I didn't tell you this before, but the killer came into my room the other night. He threatened me and my mum not to tell you anything about him. I was so scared.

Chapter Fifty-One

Suzanne Barker was struggling to sleep. Her mind kept going over what she'd seen on the news earlier and the fact there had been a violent attack less than a ten-minute walk from the safety of her home. In bed next to her, Malcolm's snores were growing in volume. As tempted as she was to elbow him in the back, she decided to let him sleep. She swung back the duvet, got out of bed and left the room, putting on her dressing gown and giving Malcolm one last glance before heading downstairs.

Suzanne turned on the mood lighting in the extended kitchen and a soft glow came from above and below the fitted cabinets. The large bi-fold doors leading to the private back garden didn't have any blinds up at them, and it was the first time Suzanne regretted the decision to go for the stark, minimalist look. She'd measure the windows up at first light and arrange to have someone come round with fabric swatches. She wanted her family to be safe and hidden away from potential murderers.

While the kettle was boiling, Suzanne sat at the central

island, opened her iPad and went to the BBC News app. The murders in Sheffield were the leading story and Suzanne played the interview with DCI Matilda Darke again. She didn't know why, but there was something niggling away at the back of her mind that wanted to check something.

'…*The first was Daisy Clough, a twenty-three-year-old A&E nurse who was raped and murdered on her way home from working at the Northern General Hospital on Tuesday the twenty-ninth of October. She was found the following morning. All of the victims were raped and murdered. The second was Joanna Fielding on Wednesday the eighteenth of November. The third was Dawn Richardson on Saturday the fifth of December, Tilly Hall was attacked on December the fifteenth, and the most recent was Tracey Ward on Christmas Day.*'

Suzanne opened a drawer and took out a pad and pen she used for writing shopping lists. She noted down the dates of all the attacks and went to the diary she kept on her iPad where she put all the important events happening within the family. She started with the easiest one, Christmas Day. Everyone knew where they were on Christmas Day. Malcolm had gone to her mother's house at noon to bring her over for Christmas lunch. As much as Suzanne wanted her mum to spend the night, she was adamant she wanted to return home to the comfort of her own bed. Malcolm had driven her home at six o'clock in the evening. He didn't return until nine. He'd said he'd made sure she was settled and had a cup of tea and a chat with her before leaving and Suzanne hadn't questioned it. She'd give her mum a ring in the morning to confirm and put a question mark next to the date.

On December the fifteenth when Tilly Hall was attacked, police have him within metres of the crime scene. Another question mark.

On Saturday the fifth of December, Suzanne and the kids were at her mother's house all day as she was feeling unwell. They hadn't returned home until late. Malcolm had been alone for the majority of the day. A third question mark.

On Wednesday the eighteenth of November, according to her diary, Suzanne had worked late and picked up Juliet from her violin lesson on her way home, leaving Malcolm on his own with Alexander to cope with. Had he left Alexander alone while he'd gone out? Had he asked Mrs McCluskey from next door to look after Alexander for an hour or two? That would be tricky to find out without raising suspicion. Another question mark.

Finally, on Thursday October the twenty-ninth, Suzanne noted in her diary that she needed to finish work early because Malcolm had a job interview for more illustrating work. He later told her he didn't get the job, despite the fact Malcolm was an extremely talented artist and had never lost a commission yet. A final question mark.

Five dates. Five question marks. Her husband could not be accounted for on any of those days.

In the interview, DCI Darke said to look out for a change in behaviour. Malcolm had been quieter lately. She had questioned him in early December if everything was all right and he said he'd lost some work due to Covid and was slightly worried about their finances. They had savings, and she had a very good job. They were a long way from having their home repossessed and had simply shrugged off his worries, but was it more than that? Had he changed because he was affected by what he was doing to those women?

For the first time in her eleven-year marriage, Suzanne was afraid of her husband, and in fear of her children's lives.

Chapter Fifty-Two

Sunday 27th December 2020

Matilda was up early, not that she'd slept much. She looked out of the landing window, which overlooked the front of the house, and noticed Scott's car had already gone. She padded downstairs into the kitchen. It was quiet. Even Pat was still in bed. Matilda was sitting at the table, nursing a coffee, when Adele came into the room. She didn't wish her a good morning and she wasn't her usual bright and breezy self.

'Morning, Adele,' Matilda said.

'Morning,' she replied. There was an edge to her tone.

'Are you still angry with me?'

'Yes. I am,' she said, turning to her. 'I thought this was my home, too.'

'It is.'

'Then why didn't you tell me what you were planning?'

'Because I knew you'd try to talk me out of it.'

'Yes!' she stated. 'Because it's dangerous. If you were living on your own I could sort of get my head around why you're doing it, but you're putting other people's lives at risk, too. Mine. Pat's and Scott's.'

'I didn't think,' Matilda said, looking down into her coffee mug.

'And that's precisely my point. You didn't think. You need to realise who you're putting at risk with your decisions.' She pulled out a chair opposite Matilda and sat down. 'You said, not two weeks ago, that if you returned to work, it wouldn't be the number one priority in your life like it used to be, yet here we are.'

'I know. But if you'd seen Tilly—'

'No buts,' Adele interrupted. 'You're heading an elite unit. The cases you've worked on in the past should give you some kind of idea of the cases you'll get in the future. You knew something like this would come up eventually. You've allowed it to consume you to the point where you're pushing everyone around you away again. Do you enjoy being isolated and on your own?'

'No.'

'I'm beginning to wonder. Now, I will move out for a few days simply because I don't fancy being killed. I've got a book coming out in March and I've worked too bloody hard on it not to see it on a shelf in Waterstones. But this has to be the last time you do something so reckless. From now on, you need to realise there are people around you who could get hurt by your decisions.'

Matilda nodded. 'I really am sorry.'

'I know you are. Right then, I'm going to pack a few things. I want to pop into work later, so I'd better get started. What are your plans for the day?'

'I'm heading into work, too. I was hoping Scott would give me a lift, but he's already left.'

'Maybe he spent the night at Donal's.'

'Maybe.'

Adele stood up and made to leave the room. In the doorway, she stopped and turned back. 'Promise me one thing.'

'Go on.'

'When the killer does come round and you beat him to death, you'll put some plastic sheeting down first.' She smiled.

'That reminds me, I need to put bleach on the shopping list.'

Adele laughed, but it quickly faded. 'I don't think I've ever been more worried about you than I am right now.'

'Why?'

'Because I honestly don't know what's going on in your head. I don't know what you're planning, but I know it's something, and I am physically scared for you.'

Matilda swallowed hard and looked away.

Adele waited in the doorway for a long moment before leaving and heading upstairs.

'You're not the only one,' Matilda said to herself.

Chapter Fifty-Three

'This had better be good,' DC Finn Cotton said as he climbed into Scott's car. 'I'd booked today off as a holiday, you know. I'm owed so many days.'

'I fucked up. And I need you to help me cover it up.'

'I'm going back to bed,' Finn said, one hand on the door handle.

'Finn, wait, hear me out,' Scott said, pulling him back. 'I haven't committed a crime or anything. Well, I don't think I have. And if it turns out that I have then it's all me and nothing to do with you.'

'You're making no sense whatsoever.'

'Matilda asked me to go and chat with Laurence Dodds again last night and I didn't. I need you to come with me today, have a quick chat, get his alibi, then tell Matilda we really did it last night.'

'Why didn't you do it last night?'

'You don't want to know,' Scott said, turning on the ignition and setting off.

Finn sat back in his seat and wrapped his arms around him.

He was cold, but now he was nervous, too. He looked out of the window as a freezing cold Sheffield passed by in a blur. He had so many questions for Scott, but he didn't want to know the answers. He was applying for promotion to sergeant. He didn't want to jeopardise that.

Scott pulled up outside Laurence Dodds's home on Ballifield Road in Handsworth. The silver Vivaro was parked on the driveway and was covered in a thick layer of frost. They both leaned forward and looked at the innocuous house.

'It's not very Christmassy,' Finn said.

'No. I doubt he's even got a tree up.'

'What's he like?'

'Creepy.' Scott shuddered.

'In what way?'

'I think he took a bit of a shine to me. He was standing very close. I could feel his breath on my neck. He made my skin crawl.' He looked at Finn in his padded anorak and glasses. 'Maybe I should have brought Tom in his biker leathers. He might have left me alone then.'

'You like Tom, don't you?' Finn asked, studying Scott.

'Don't you start.' Scott opened the door and stepped out, almost slipping on black ice.

They walked up the short garden path and knocked on the door. It didn't take long for it to be opened. Laurence was wearing paint-splattered jeans and an old red sweater with holes in the shoulder. As soon as he saw his visitors, he smiled.

'Ah, Detective Sergeant Scott Andrews. It's lovely to see you again.'

Scott gave a nervous smile. 'Thank you. This is DC Finn Cotton. Could we have a word?'

Laurence turned to Finn, nodded in greeting, then turned back to Scott. 'Of course. Come on in. It's another freezing morning, isn't it? Eight days in a row the temperature hasn't risen above zero, according to the radio this morning. Again, if I can ask you to keep your voices down, my mum is sleeping in the living room. Go on through to the kitchen.'

Scott led the way while Laurence closed the front door. The kitchen was still a scene of chaos from Scott's last visit. The dishes had been done and the sink was empty, but work surfaces were cluttered, and the table was covered with Laurence's artwork again. Scott and Finn sat down at the table.

'Let me move this for you.' Laurence leaned close over Scott's shoulder and removed his easel. Finn struggled to stifle a smile. 'What do you think?' He showed the painting to Scott. 'It's almost finished.'

Scott was looking at a painting of the Park Hill flats. 'I'm afraid I don't know much about art.'

'You can tell what it is though, surely.'

'Oh. Yes. It's very good. You're very talented.'

'Thank you,' he said, his grin increasing. 'I rarely get visitors so it's nice to have praise heaped on me, even if I have to seek it out myself,' he said with a laugh to Finn. 'Now, let me make you both a cup of tea.'

He headed for the other side of the kitchen and began to fill the kettle.

'Told you, creepy,' Scott said quietly to Finn.

'So, what was it you wanted to talk to me about? Have you found out who cloned my registration plate? I hope I don't know him,' Laurence said, stopping what he was doing and looking to Scott with a hand on his chest. 'It would be awful if

I actually knew him. Mind you, I don't know that many people these days.'

'No, Mr Dodds.'

'Laurence, please.'

'Laurence. Did you happen to see the news last night?'

'No. I put Mother to bed around eight and I had an early night myself with John Grisham. I've heard the news on the radio this morning, though. Another woman was killed on Christmas Day of all days. They're talking about a serial killer. That and a pandemic, it makes you wonder what's happening to the world, doesn't it? Now, I remember you're milk and no sugar, how about your friend?' he asked Finn.

'Milk with one. Thanks.'

'Coming right up,' he said with a smile.

'Laurence, we've been looking through CCTV of the area where the latest victim was found and we've spotted your van, or a van with your registration number, on Norfolk Street around five o'clock on Christmas Day.'

'Good Lord.'

'Can you tell us where you were on Christmas Day?'

Laurence returned to the table with two mugs of tea. He went back to the cupboard, brought out a tub of Family Circle biscuits and placed it on the table.

'Help yourselves. There's only really me who eats them.' He pulled out a third chair and sat down next to Scott. Their legs were almost touching. 'I'm afraid, like last time, I don't have an alibi. I didn't leave the house at all on Christmas Day.'

'Can anyone verify that?' Finn asked, dunking a jammy dodger into his tea.

'No. We didn't have any visitors. I didn't even take the chain off the front door. It was just me and Mother.'

'Could we have a word with your mum?' Scott asked.

Laurence turned quickly to Scott. 'You want to talk to my mother?' he asked, incredulously.

'Yes. Just to confirm your story.'

'You don't believe me?'

'It's not a question of not believing you. We need to talk to everyone connected with the case.'

'But we're not connected to the case. I don't know any of the victims and haven't a clue who the killer could be.'

'But someone is using your registration number to hide their identity.'

'That's hardly my fault, though, is it?'

'No, it's not. But the killer has drawn you into this,' Scott said. 'Mr Dodds, I know you said your mother isn't in good health. I promise, we won't cause her any distress.'

'I know you wouldn't intentionally,' he said, leaning forward and placing a hand, briefly, on Scott's thigh. 'It's just, well, I'm not sure how much help she'd be. She's had several strokes; she can hardly talk, and she spends most of her days sleeping.'

Laurence seemed to think for a while, a long-drawn-out moment when he refused to take his eyes off Scott.

'Okay,' he relented. 'However, and no offence to you, DC Cotton, but I'd rather just DS Andrews chat to her on his own. I don't want her panicking unnecessarily.'

'Of course not,' Finn said. 'I'll stay here with the biscuits.'

Scott shot a daggered look at Finn.

'I'll go and make sure she's awake and decent,' Laurence said, getting up and leaving the kitchen.

'You'll pay for this,' Scott hissed at Finn as he followed Laurence out of the room.

Laurence tapped lightly on the living room door and

opened it a crack. Scott could feel the immense heat from within and unbuttoned his coat.

The room was softly lit by a single standard lamp over the back of an armchair. The curtains were drawn, and a small elderly woman was dozing in a recliner, her feet up. She wore a long navy skirt and a cream coloured cardigan, buttoned up to the neck. Both appeared to be in need of washing as they were splattered with food stains.

'Mother. Are you awake?' Laurence asked gently. He asked the question again, louder, when there was no response.

The woman struggled to raise her head. She made some kind of garbled noise.

'Mother, this is a friend of mine from the police, Detective Sergeant Andrews. It seems someone is using a replica of my van to commit a crime and he wants to know where I was on Christmas Day.' He spoke loud and clear. Scott guessed Finn heard every word in the kitchen.

'Christmas Day,' the woman said. Her words sounded like she was speaking with a mouthful of food, but they could just about be identified.

'Yes, mother. It was two days ago. I was here, wasn't I? We didn't leave the house all day, did we?'

'I haven't left the house for years,' she struggled to say.

'No,' Laurence looked to Scott and smiled. 'I look after you, don't I? I don't go out much.'

'If you can call it looking after me. I'm sitting here in my own piss.'

'No, you're not, Mother. We'd smell it if you were.' He turned back to Scott. 'She had a shower yesterday afternoon. A carer comes around to help me lift her. She's got this thing of smelling urine. No idea why.'

'That's okay. I don't think there's any need for me to ask her anything,' Scott said, edging out of the room.

'Where's my tea?' Laurence's mother shouted. 'I want my tea.'

'You've had two cups already this morning. I can make you another if you want.'

'Of course I want. That's why I asked. I want my tea,' she was almost screaming.

'I'm sorry,' Scott said.

'I'll get you a cup of tea, Mother. I won't be long.'

She continued to shout, but Laurence ignored her and closed the living room door.

'I'm afraid it doesn't take much for her to become distressed.'

'I'm sorry,' Scott said again.

'That's quite all right. You weren't to know.'

'Finn, we're going,' Scott called out.

'Is there anything else I can help you with?'

'No. No. It's fine. You've been very helpful. Again, I'm sorry,' Scott said, edging towards the front door.

Once out in the cold light of day, Scott breathed a sigh of relief. He headed for the car, taking large strides.

'Are you all right?' Finn asked.

'No,' Scott said, climbing in and slamming the door behind him. 'I feel bad for thinking he was a creepy pervert. I know his mother can't help being like she is after having several strokes, but he has a lot to put up with, caring for her twenty-four hours a day, hardly leaving the house. Poor bloke.'

'You could always offer to take him out for a meal. I'm sure he can get a sitter for his mum,' Finn said with a grin.

'I'm going to slap you so hard in a minute.'

Chapter Fifty-Four

Matilda stepped out of the hot shower, put on a dressing gown and wrapped a towel around her head. She went into her bedroom and sat down on the bed. Normally she jumped in and out of the shower, but this morning she needed a longer and hotter one to try to marshal her thoughts and stop the miasma of darkness intruding on what she needed to do in order to catch this killer.

Sitting on the edge of her bed she realised her head was still full and heavy. Steve Harrison and the noose on her door on Christmas Day took up a large amount of space. He had to be behind it. Who else would know to put a noose on her door? And why couldn't they have just let her have one day where she didn't think about work and killers? Did they really hate her so much?

She reached for her phone on her bedside table. There were a few text messages and emails from Ridley that she ignored, one from Sian asking if she was free to meet later. She wasn't, but she needed some time away from work so fired off a quick reply saying she'd meet her in Millhouses Park. And a final text from Tilly Hall. Matilda's eyes widened when she read that the killer had visited her in hospital and warned her against talking.

She quickly dressed, summoned an Uber and headed straight for the Children's Hospital. The team briefing could wait.

'I only just received your text, I'm so sorry,' Matilda said, charging into Tilly's room, rubbing her hands from where she'd squirted hand sanitiser on them.

'Text? What's going on?' Amy asked. She'd almost jumped out of her skin when Matilda barged in.

'Have you told your mum?' Matilda asked.

Tilly shook her head.

Matilda handed Tilly the iPad and told her to type everything that happened. Meanwhile she filled her mum in on what Tilly had said in her text last night.

'What? The killer came here. Oh my God!' Amy sat on the edge of the bed and wrapped her arms around her daughter. 'Why didn't you tell us, sweetheart? We could have moved you or something.' She looked to Matilda for an answer.

'I've spoken to one of the nurses. She's going to arrange to have you moved,' Matilda said. 'I've also been onto my boss and he's sending out two officers to sit outside your room. You'll be perfectly safe.'

'But I don't understand,' Amy said, wiping her eyes. 'Why would he come here? Hasn't he caused her enough pain?'

Matilda sat down on the edge of the bed. 'This man is incredibly clever, Amy. He knows exactly what to do to evade capture. He's left nothing at the crime scenes. I don't mean to sound harsh, but he made a mistake by keeping Tilly alive. She can identify him or give us information that could lead to him being identified. That's the last thing he wants to happen. Someone like him, he knows, eventually, that he'll be caught, but he'll want his fame to live on for a very long time.'

'Fame?' Amy said, disgust etched on her face.

'Serial killers are hot property, it saddens me to say. Journalists will be clambering over each other to get the official story from him. Once he's captured, the fear element has gone. The only thing left for him is to tell his story. He'll have books written about him, documentaries made, and he'll keep his fingers crossed for a film or TV drama to be made. He needs to keep this part going for as long as he can. That's why he came back.'

'How much danger is Tilly in?' Amy asked, squeezing her daughter tighter.

'We will do everything in our power to keep her safe. We'll move her to another part of the hospital. If there is any sign of him coming back, we'll move her completely to a different hospital. She will be guarded and everyone entering or leaving this room will be vetted.'

'What about me? Am I in danger at home?'

'I don't know. I'm guessing there's no chance of you being able to move out.'

'Not with the dogs, no.'

'Then I'll have patrols increased on your house. Maybe consider changing your locks and adding extra security … and, I shouldn't be saying this, but keeping a baseball bat or something by your bed might be useful.'

Amy looked horrified for a moment, before nodding. 'I've got a cricket bat in the shed.'

'That'll do.'

'How close are you to catching him?'

Matilda looked to Tilly then back to Amy. She couldn't lie to them. She released a heavy sigh. 'We're not. I'm hoping my interview on the news will lead to someone contacting us with information. I haven't been into the station yet, so I don't know what's come through overnight.'

'I saw the interview. You came across very well.'

'Thank you.'

Tilly handed Matilda the iPad and she read through everything that happened when the killer came into her room. She emailed it to her phone so she could share it with the team when she went in.

'Tilly, is there anything you haven't told me about the man who attacked you?' She handed her back the iPad so she could reply.

No. I told you everything before he came.

'Has his visit led you to remember anything else about him?'

No.

'Was it definitely the same man who attacked you who came to you here?'

Yes.

'Can you give me a clear and concise description of him?'

He's not very tall, but taller than both of you. He's slim as well, but really strong. He's not muscular at all, but his grip is really powerful. I haven't seen his face, only his eyes, but they're very starry, like he's looking through me. I think they might be blue. He's got a Sheffield accent, but I think he was trying to disguise his voice. It was deep and rough, but it sounded put on. He just seems really ordinary to look at.

Matilda read the description and nodded. 'This is very helpful, Tilly, thank you.' It hadn't given her much more to work on, but Tilly needed to know she was being useful. It might encourage her to think harder and maybe something else would come to mind.

'Do you think, if I brought in a police sketch artist, you might be able to come up with something that looked like him?'

Tilly thought for a moment before she began typing.

Not really. When he came in here he was masked up. Like I said, I only really saw his eyes. When he attacked me I had my eyes closed. I'm sorry.

'You have no need to apologise at all. You're doing incredibly well. Look, I need to get to the station. If I hear anything, or have any news, I'll let you know. Amy, you have my mobile number, call me any time if you're scared or think someone is hanging around your house.'

'I will. Thank you so much for being open with us about everything. I know you sometimes have to keep a lot back.'

Matilda smiled and promised she'd look in on them again tomorrow. When she left the room, she found two uniformed officers already sitting outside, keeping guard. She left the hospital feeling better about things, but only when it came to Tilly's safety. She was still no nearer to identifying the killer. She only hoped someone had called in overnight in response to her interview. If not, the only option left was for the killer to come to her.

Chapter Fifty-Five

M atilda entered the HMCU suite to find her full team assembled. They were hardly the Avengers, but Scott was writing something on one of the white boards, Finn was on the phone, and Zofia and Tom were laughing by the drinks station. If the public could see how a serial killer case was being investigated compared with how crime fiction dramas portrayed them, they'd be shocked.

'Andrew Lee Hawkesley has been found,' Scott said, turning from the white board.

Matilda frowned. 'Remind me.'

'The missing sex offender.'

'Oh, yes. Has he given a full confession and we can all go home?'

'Unfortunately not. He came in on Boxing Day evening with his sister. He's been in Norfolk for the past three months working on a poultry farm, cash in hand. He came back north late on Christmas Eve, saw his flat had been entered and went to his sister's in Rotherham in a panic. She urged him to come forward. Do you want us to charge him with anything?'

'God, no,' she said, taking the proffered mug of tea from Zofia. 'Do you blame him for working cash in hand? I certainly don't. When you see how the government waste our tax money, I'm thinking of asking the Chief Constable to give me my wages in a brown envelope under the table. Tell him to keep in touch with his parole officer more regularly or he'll end up back inside. Who interviewed Tracey Ward's stepdad?'

'I did,' Finn said. He'd ended his phone conversation and was updating one of the murder boards. 'My God, he's a prick. Tracey wasn't his daughter so he didn't see why he should have anything to do with her. According to her mother's statement, he made home life very difficult for Tracey. She'd been spending more time at home because of Covid. Her college course had finished, and she couldn't get a job. The atmosphere was heavy, and there was a blazing row. Tracey's mother sided with Liam, so Tracey left.'

'Poor girl. Where was she living?'

'She was couch-surfing but was homeless just before Christmas. She was sleeping on the streets.'

'Did her mum know this?'

'She tried to deny it, but her face gave her away.'

'Why didn't she have her back home?'

'Liam said no way. She'd left, she wasn't coming back.'

'What a charming man,' Matilda said. She turned to look at a photo of Tracey while she was still alive, happy and smiling, her arm around a friend. 'Has the post mortem been done yet?'

Scott looked at his watch. 'Any time now.'

'Ooh, that's new,' Matilda said, spying the watch.

'Christmas present from Donal,' he grinned. 'I can get texts and emails on it, make calls, and it will record all my fitness training.'

'I got a watch for Christmas, too.' Matilda rolled up her

sleeve. 'All it does is tell the time. So primitive.' She smiled. 'Right, everyone, can we all take our seats and begin the briefing.'

'Already seated,' Zofia said with a laugh in her voice.

'So I'm guessing you all saw my television appearance on the news last night,' Matilda began.

'I didn't, but I saw it on iPlayer this morning,' Tom said.

'Wow. As the newest member of the team, I expected serious sucking up from you, Tom. I thought you'd have been glued to the TV.'

His face paled. 'I'm so sorry.'

'I'm joking. Don't worry about it. Anyway, one person who did watch it was Tilly Hall. She sent me a message last night, though I didn't get it until this morning, telling me that the killer visited her in her hospital room and warned her against talking to me. She's been moved and we now have a police presence outside her room.'

'Could she give you a better description of the killer?' Zofia asked, pen poised over her pad as usual.

'No. He was masked up. She could only see his eyes.'

'How long was he in her room for?' Finn asked.

'I don't know,' Matilda answered. 'Long enough to threaten her. Why?'

'If he'd gone to all the trouble of sneaking into her room, why didn't he just kill her? She's incapacitated. She can't scream for help. She's severely injured so she can't struggle. It wouldn't have taken much to, I don't know, put a pillow over her face or make her throat injuries worse. Why just threaten her?'

Matilda frowned. She hadn't thought of that.

'He's enjoying taunting her,' Tom said. 'His previous victims, he'd killed. This one has survived, and he's seen the state she's in, the life-changing injuries. That's giving him more pleasure than simply killing them. And that's probably why he posed his latest victim. He's taking things up a notch.'

'He's realising how much fun there can be had after the killings,' Finn continued. 'With his first three, he killed them, threw them away, then went onto the next one. He's worked out that the fun doesn't need to stop with the death of his victims. He can either continue to haunt them, like he's doing with Tilly, or he can play with their bodies, pose them, like he did with Tracey. His confidence has gone through the roof and he's letting us know that we're nowhere close to catching him and he can do anything he wants.'

The room fell silent. A shiver ran down Matilda's spine. She took a lingering sip of her tea, giving her time to think.

'Scott, did you go to see Laurence Dodds last night?' She asked.

'Er, yes, I did. He says he spent all Christmas Day with his mother. I tried to talk to her to confirm his story, but she's useless as a witness. I don't think she knew I was there.'

'It was a long shot. The killer just needed a van like his to clone the number plate from. Give that vicar a call as well. I'm guessing Christmas Day is his busiest day of the year, but you never know. What's his name again?'

Scott looked down at his notes. 'Jeremy Keats.'

'That's it. Have any calls come through from my interview last night?'

'Loads,' Tom said.

'CID are going through them,' Zofia added as she tapped on her computer. 'Anything of importance, they'll pass onto us.'

Matilda looked crestfallen. 'I will not allow this bastard to claim another victim. We need to closely analyse every call that's come in and follow up every lead, no matter how tenuous it appears.'

'We don't have the womanpower for that,' Zofia said.

'We join forces with CID and uniform and use them. I'll have a word with Ridley. Screw breaking up parties, this is much more important. Did forensics find anything from where Tracey was found?'

'No. Nothing,' Tom said.

'Shit,' she uttered under her breath. 'Let's see if the post mortem delivers something. Who wants to come with me?'

Nobody raised their hands.

'Thanks for volunteering, Scott. Get your coat. Finn, if anything comes up, anything at all, call me,' she said, a serious and panicked determination to her voice.

'Hopefully, the women of Sheffield will realise how serious this is and keep indoors,' Finn said. 'Finding his next victim might be harder than he thinks.'

Unless I'm his next victim.

'Hold onto that thought, Finn.'

'Matilda!' Zofia called out, not taking her eyes from her computer screen.

'Yes.'

'I don't know why I do this, but whenever I hear a new name, I run it through the system. I typed in Jeremy Keats, and he's got a record.'

'The vicar?'

'In 2013, a woman named Rebecca Henderson took out a restraining order against him.'

Matilda frowned. 'A restraining order against a vicar. Why?'

'He asked her out a few times and wouldn't take no for an

answer,' Zofia read from the screen. 'He started pestering her, phoning her day and night, turning up on her doorstep.'

'Did he mention if he was married or not?' Matilda asked Scott.

'No.'

'Bring him in for questioning, Finn. We'll do a formal interview. A bloody vicar!' Matilda said incredulously as she left the room.

Chapter Fifty-Six

Suzanne Barker was sitting at the island in the kitchen. She had a full mug of coffee in front of her that had long since gone cold. Somewhere in the house, the sound of her young kids laughing and shouting could be heard. She had a pensive look on her face and wondered whether she should give the police a ring. She'd watched the interview with DCI Darke three times and as much as she tried to work out where her husband had been on the dates the women were killed, she couldn't place him for a single one.

'Everything all right?'

She jumped at the sound of Malcolm's voice. She looked up and saw him by the sink, getting a glass of water. She hadn't heard him come in the room.

'Fine,' she said, her voice barely a whisper.

'You looked deep in thought.'

'Did I?'

'Yes. Anything wrong?'

'No. Well, just a headache. I think I've overdone the wine this Christmas.' She gave a painful smile.

'Well, we're not as young as we used to be,' he said with a laugh.

She almost balked at his laugh. The sound she loved to hear now cut through her like a dentist's drill. She watched him drinking from the glass, looking at his hands, his artistic, creative hands. Why was she thinking of him as a multiple murderer, all of a sudden? He was her husband, the father of her children. He wouldn't. Would he?

'I think I might go and have a long soak in the bath,' she said, getting up from the stool and heading for the door. 'Will you watch the kids?' She didn't wait for a reply. She left the kitchen and ran up the stairs two at a time.

In the bedroom, she grabbed her mobile from the bedside cabinet and went into the en suite, closing and locking the door behind her. She put the plug in the bath and turned on the taps. She put the toilet lid down and sat on it, scrolling through her mobile for her mother's number.

'Hi, Mum, it's me.' She kept her voice low and tried to sound light so her mother wouldn't think there was anything amiss.

'Hello, love. Everything all right?'

'Yes. Fine. Erm … on Christmas Day when Malcolm drove you home, did he see you into the house?'

Her mother seemed to be thrown by the question. It was a long moment before she answered. 'Of course he did, dear. He always does. He went round and closed all the curtains for me.'

'Did he stay long?'

'Long enough to have a cup of tea. Oh, and he tightened the flush on the upstairs toilet for me as well.'

'What time did he leave?'

'What time? I don't know. I didn't look at the clock. What's the matter, Suze, you sound strange.'

A tear fell down Suzanne's face. She hadn't even known she was crying. She wiped it away. 'I just wondered where he was, that's all.'

'Surely, he's come home by now,' her mother laughed.

'Yes. He came back while I was watching *Call the Midwife*.'

'Oh, wasn't that a lovely episode? I did enjoy it.'

'Yes. It was good. Mum, have you seen the news lately, about those women being killed?'

'Yes, I have. Horrible, isn't it? I hope you're being safe when you go out on your own.'

She smiled. It felt warm to have a mother still worry about her. 'I am. I was just thinking, the dates of when those women were killed—' She stopped herself.

'Are you still there, Suze?'

'Yes. Mum, do you think …?'

'What is it?'

Suzanne wiped her tears away again. 'I'm going to have to go, Mum.'

'Is there something wrong?'

'No. Honestly, I'm fine. I'll call you later. Bye.' She quickly ended the call.

Sitting on the toilet seat, water rushing into the bath, steam filling the room, Suzanne thought about her life. She and Malcolm had good jobs and money in the bank. They hadn't been affected by the pandemic, apart from having to juggle home schooling with work. They didn't know anyone who had caught Covid. It hadn't touched their lives at all. In fact, life was good. A car each, holidays abroad every year. Money in the savings account. A beautiful extension on the house. Two adorable children. They had everything. Didn't they? Would Malcolm really risk all that by murdering women? She thought she knew everything about him. They'd been married for eleven years. They were happy. Was he leading a double life? Was he harbouring a dark secret? Was she sharing a bed with a man who could put a knife to a young girl's throat and …?

She quickly got up off the toilet, lifted the lid and vomited.

Suzanne leaned over the bath and turned off the taps. It was almost full. She dipped her hand into the hot water and pulled out the plug. She went to the sink, splashed some cold water on her face and looked at herself in the mirror. She didn't recognise the woman looking back at her. If she had suspicions about her husband, which she did, she needed to contact the police. They'd look into it and, hopefully, put her mind at ease. She took a deep breath and felt herself relax. She'd find some excuse to leave the house and make the call.

She opened the door and stepped into the bedroom. She stopped when she saw Malcolm sitting on the end of the bed.

'I thought you were having a bath,' he said.

'I … I changed my mind.'

'Who were you talking to?'

'When?'

'In the bathroom.'

'No one.'

'I heard voices.'

'Oh. I was … I was singing. To myself. You know, how you do when you're running a bath,' she said, trying to sound light-hearted. She went over to her dressing table and picked up her wallet. 'I think I might pop out to the shops. We're running low on milk, and I could do with some—'

'Suzanne, who were you talking to on the phone?'

She turned and looked at Malcolm. He was blocking her exit to the bedroom. His look was grave, and she felt her blood run cold.

Chapter Fifty-Seven

'Adele texted me this morning,' Scott began as he pulled up in the parking space next to the Medico Legal Centre on Watery Street. 'She told me you've asked her to move out.'

Matilda climbed out of the car. If it was possible, it seemed even colder than when she'd left the house this morning. The sky was grey and heavy. A few flakes of snow were slowly falling. She plunged her hands deep into her pockets for warmth.

'It's only temporary,' she said, not looking at her DS.

'She's worried about you.'

'There's no need.'

'You're setting yourself up as bait for the killer. There's every need. So, what, you're going to spend all night in your living room in the dark, waiting for him to turn up like the goat in *Jurassic Park*?'

Matilda half-smiled. 'Actually, I was going to ask if you'd stay up with me.'

'Oh, great, two goats.' He turned and headed for the entrance to the building.

Matilda followed. 'Does that mean you won't?'

'You know I will. But that's not the point. And that's why Adele is pissed off with you. You need to realise other people are affected by the decisions you make.'

Matilda nodded. 'I know. I've had this conversation with Adele. I'm sorry. I promise, from now on, I'll consult Adele and you and Pat and my mum before I do anything reckless again.'

'You could just not do anything reckless.' He held the door open for her and they went into the warmth.

'Where's the fun in that?' She looked at him and winked.

They washed their hands with hand sanitiser, put on a mask and worked their way through the warren of corridors to the mortuary suite. It was strange not to see Adele in her office. Simon Browes seemed to be making himself at home. He'd tidied up, too. Matilda wasn't sure what Adele would make of her new clean-lined office when she returned.

'Good morning, DCI Darke,' Simon said with a smile as he came out of the office. 'You've missed the fun. Tracey Ward is all stitched up and back in the fridge.'

There was something odd about Simon in that it was difficult to read his mood. Matilda never knew whether he was making light of the darkness of his work or whether he simply had a warped, ghoulish sense of humour. Had thirty years of working with the dead in a basement made him awkward around the living, or had he always been this way? Adele wasn't like that. She was a very personable woman. If Simon and Adele were on the cusp of becoming more than friends, maybe she should try to get to know him better, see the man beneath the scrubs.

'Please tell me you found something useful for our investigation.'

'I'm not sure about useful, but I certainly found something to brighten up an otherwise dull working day.'

He picked up a file and walked past her, towards the bank of fridges. She felt a chill.

Scott was looking around him, trying to spot Donal.

'If you're looking for Mr Youngblood, the last I saw of him he was in the staffroom with his head between his knees.'

'Is he all right?' Scott asked, a concerned expression on his face.

'I'm afraid he found Tracey Ward's post mortem a little difficult to contend with. I suppose it's not every day you get a body delivered with the head in a cardboard box like the final scene in *Seven*.'

Simon opened a fridge door and pulled out a trolley with ease. He flicked back the white sheet and revealed Tracey Ward like the finale of a magic trick. Her head was back in place, though not stitched back on.

'Can I go and see him?' Scott asked.

'He's in the staffroom. You're not staff,' Simon said, icily. 'Now, can we get on? I have a dozen Covid victims coming in within the hour and nowhere to put them.'

Matilda gave Scott a look and raised her eyebrows.

'Go on, Simon.'

'I know very little of your previous victims, apart from the brief glance I gave the reports from Dr Kean. However, this one is different in many ways. The first, obviously, is the fact she's been decapitated,' he said, his tone almost conversational. 'I'm afraid I can't tell you how long it took the killer, or how many slashes with the knife were needed to remove the head, but as you can see from the ragged tearing of skin, it was not a quick and painless death.'

'She was still alive when the head was removed?' Scott asked.

Simon looked at him quizzically. 'I hardly think so. Do you have any idea of the veins, muscles and arteries he would have had to cut through to severe the neck? She would have died from either blood loss or her heart giving out before the head was removed.'

'She would have suffered, though,' Matilda said, more to herself.

'Of course.' Simon looked at Scott, then opened his file. 'Judging by the paleness of your Detective Sergeant, I won't show the wounds, but will show you a photograph of Ms Ward's vagina.' He took out a photo and handed it to Matilda. 'She was vaginally raped, but not in the conventional sense, and not like your previous victims. A broken glass bottle was used to tear at the victim's vagina and cut away at her insides.'

'Oh my God!' Scott clamped a hand over his mouth and moved away.

'The younger generation are a very delicate group of people, don't you find, DCI Darke?'

'I'm feeling delicate myself, Simon. It's called empathy.'

He thought for a moment. 'I suppose it is. I'm guessing you need empathy to be a detective so you can feel something for the victim in order to catch their killer. Fortunately, that's not a requirement for my job.'

'Fortunately for you.' Matilda handed him back the photograph. 'Is there any evidence of him physically raping her himself before using a bottle?'

'No semen or pubic hairs were found. But then, I've noticed from the previous victims, no hairs have been found on them either. Your killer is certainly forensically aware. The glass bottle, by the way, was found a few feet away from the victim and has been sent off for testing. I believe it was a Lucozade bottle with the neck broken off.'

'This man is sick.' Matilda turned away.

Simon pushed the shelf back into the fridges and closed the door with a loud slam.

'A sick mind in a sick world, some would say.'

'Would you say that?'

'You're aware of the book I'm currently writing with Dr Kean?' Matilda nodded. 'In my research I've been looking back on my own career, at the cases I've had to work on. The number of people being murdered and brought into my labs has increased over the years. The inventiveness of their murders is getting ever more deplorable.' He went into Adele's office and sat down. 'I'm aware people think of me as aloof; some have even said to my face that my compassion died many years ago. It's not difficult to see why that is, is it?'

Matilda suddenly felt sorry for Simon. She'd often thought of him as an emotionless robot, but maybe he had forced himself to become like this so that he wasn't wrecked by the depravities he daily saw inflicted on others.

'No. It's not. I sometimes worry I'm too hardened to this job. Maybe I should be sitting in a room with my head between my knees.'

'You're a seasoned detective. Surely, you're past all that.'

'I don't want to get used to seeing victims with their heads hacked off or having been raped by a broken glass bottle.'

'No,' he said, almost wistfully. 'I'm afraid I'm too hardened to it. There's no going back for me. That was one of the reasons Rach—' He stopped himself.

'The necklace you gave Adele for Christmas is beautiful,' Matilda said, trying to lighten the mood.

'Yes.' He smiled. 'I bought it from an antique market in

London in the summer.' His face lit up. 'I think a lot of Adele. She's very special to me.'

'We need people in our lives, Simon, in order to stop us from shutting off our emotions to what's going on around us.'

He nodded. 'Like I said, it might be too late for me.'

'The bloke is a fucking cyborg,' Scott fumed as he made his way back to the car.

The snow was still falling slowly, in minute flakes, but it was starting to settle. Scott climbed in behind the steering wheel, slammed the door behind him and took out his mobile. He fired off a text to Donal, asking if he was all right.

'I used to think that,' Matilda said, getting in the car beside him. 'I just think he's taken his dedication to his career too far. Adele was telling me a few weeks ago about his upbringing. He had a very difficult childhood. His mother was an alcoholic. She used to beat him. A teacher took him under his wing and encouraged him. He qualified almost a year ahead of everyone else. He's a very intelligent man. A lot of highly intelligent people often find it difficult to talk to others. The mundanity of real life isn't mundane to them. It's actually very hard.'

'Adele isn't like that,' Scott said.

'She has people around her. She had Chris and there was always me and James. That's why Simon's marriage broke down. He had someone and let his career take over.'

'That's still no excuse to treat people the way he does. I wouldn't be surprised if he didn't shout at Donal for needing a break.'

'Look, Scott, just …' She stopped.

'What is it?' he asked.

Matilda was looking out of the passenger window. 'Did you see that van turn out of the street?'

'No.'

'I'm sure it was a …'

'What?'

'I thought it was a silver Vivaro.'

'I would love it if you shouted, "Follow that car" right now,' Scott said with a smile.

'Sorry to disappoint you.'

'Another time. Back to the station?'

'Actually, no. Could you drop me off somewhere?'

'Sure. Where?'

'I need to speak to Sian. I want to stop myself becoming a cyborg.'

Chapter Fifty-Eight

S cott pulled up at the entrance to Millhouses Park car park. Sian's van was the only vehicle in there.

'Go back to the station. Fill the others in on Tracey Ward's post mortem and check the calls from the interview. Someone must know who this killer is. I'll be back later,' Matilda said as she climbed out of the car.

'Do you want me to come and pick you up again?'

'No. I'll get an Uber.'

She closed the door, buttoned up her coat, raised the collar around her neck and headed into the park. It had stopped snowing, but the sky was still heavy. Snow was forecast for later in the week. An icy wind was blowing and as Matilda made her way into the park, she dug in her pockets for her gloves.

She spotted Sian almost straightaway. It was too cold for people to come for a walk in the park, apart from the hardy joggers and fellow dog walkers, but Sian stood out in her bright red winter coat and pink bobble hat. She only had one dog with her today, a miniature Dachshund, who seemed to be enjoying the fallen leaves being blown about by the wind.

'Tilly Hall has a Dachshund. She's called Sausage,' Matilda said.

Sian laughed. 'This one's called Wilfred.'

'Poor thing. I thought about getting a dog in the summer while I was off work.'

'Why didn't you?'

'I always thought I'd go back to work at some point. It wouldn't be fair to leave a dog at home all day.'

'You could have employed me as a dog walker.'

'Are you busy today?'

'I wish. Little Wilfred here is my only client for today. With Covid cases back on the rise and people working from home again, my services aren't required. I've only got Wilf because his owner's a paramedic.'

'What are you going to do?' Matilda asked.

Sian shrugged. 'I'm not sure. Keep my fingers crossed business picks up … or I was thinking of diversifying. I read a story in *Take A Break* last week about a woman who's a nude cleaner. She makes almost a thousand a week.'

'There are many things wrong with that sentence. First of all, why are you reading *Take A Break*?'

Sian laughed.

'You could always come back to the police force,' Matilda said.

'I don't think so.'

'You miss it. Don't you?'

'Speaking of the police,' Sian said, changing the subject, 'I need to have a serious word with you about your interview last night.'

'What about it?'

'I saw that look you gave to the camera at the end. You were speaking directly to the killer. You were practically telling him to come for you. What the hell were you thinking?'

'Sian, there's nothing else I can do. I'm out of options. He killed again on Christmas Day. He posed her. He decapitated her and he raped her with a broken glass bottle. He's escalating. I will not let him kill again.'

'So you're putting yourself at the front of the queue to be his next victim?'

'I'll not let that happen. I'll get him before he gets me.'

'You're sure of that, are you? We've been walking for ten minutes and not once have you looked around you. He could he here, in this park, right now. He could have followed you here and be waiting for the perfect time to pounce.'

'I'm sure Wilfred would leap to my defence.' Matilda smiled.

'You're playing an incredibly dangerous game,' Sian said.

A sudden gust of wind blew around them. They both shivered.

'I'm out of options, Sian. I know he hates women. I know he'll hate the fact a woman is looking for him. I need him to come and get me.'

'Is Ridley putting an armed guard outside your house?'

'I'm afraid not. Could I borrow Wilfred?'

Wilfred stopped and squatted. Sian took a poop sack from her coat pocket and picked it up.

'I spoke to Christian last night. He told me about your chat on Boxing Day.'

'Oh, yes.'

'Yes. He mentioned that you're not planning on returning to work full-time.'

Matilda didn't say anything.

'Yet you've just said to me that I could come back to the force. Why would you ask me to return if you're asking Christian to take over your job?'

'I'm in two minds. I don't know what I'm doing yet. One day I'd love to go back permanently and take over the old unit. Another I just want to spend my days at home.' *Liar*.

'Christian thinks you're going to do something ruthless during this case that will prevent you from returning to work.'

'Such as?' Matilda asked. She didn't look at Sian. They'd turned around and were heading, slowly, back to the car park. Matilda had her head down, kicking a stone, her hands plunged deep into her pockets.

'He doesn't know. He said you were giving off a strange vibe.'

'That was probably my deodorant. I'm trying a new brand.'

'Why do you always make a joke of everything?'

'Diana Cooper-bloody-sodding-smith calls it avoidance.'

'Does she let you get away with it in her sessions?'

'No. But then she doesn't have a sense of humour. I've only seen her smile once and I'm pretty sure that was wind.'

'Matilda, will you tell me what you're planning? I might be able to help you.'

Matilda stopped. She turned to Sian. 'I haven't a clue what I'm planning, Sian, and that really is the truth. Until I know who the killer is, or how our paths meet, I don't know what I'm going to do.'

'Are you scared?'

It was a while before Matilda answered. 'I'm petrified.'

'You think he's going to kill you?'

'No. I'm petrified that I'm going to kill him.'

'Jesus Christ, Matilda!'

'Even if he does come to my house and tries to attack me,

the only crime we'll be able to charge him with is the attack on me, none of the others, unless he confesses. And he won't do that. There's no evidence whatsoever to put him at the scene of those murders.'

'Could you kill him? If you had to.'

'I'd be preventing more murders. Yes, I could kill him. How I live with myself afterwards is anyone's guess.'

'I'm so glad I'm not in your shoes right now.'

'I wish I wasn't in them either.'

They'd reached the car park. Sian tossed the poop sack into a bin, and they headed for her van. She opened the back doors and lifted Wilfred inside, securing him in a small crate.

'I never realised before your van is a silver Vivaro.'

'It's grey, actually.'

'Is it?'

'Yes.'

'Oh. It looks silver to me.'

'Would you like a lift home?'

'I'm going back to the station.'

'I'll take you. It's not like I've much on for the rest of the day.'

They went to the front of the van and Matilda climbed in.

'Excuse the mess. Anthony's been using it to visit his mates in Rotherham. I've told him to clean up after himself until I'm blue in the face.'

'Anthony uses your van?'

'Yes. He's saving up for a car.'

'When did he last use it?'

'He's out in it every night. Lean back, I can't see in your wing mirror.'

As Sian drove along Abbeydale Road South, Matilda sat with a heavy expression on her face. She hadn't seen Sian's kids for a long time, not since they'd moved into their temporary home on Woodseats Road. She knew they'd all been affected by their father turning out to be a serial killer of sex workers. Gregory and Danny had become quieter. Belinda was trying to forget her father ever existed and Anthony ... Matilda had no idea how Anthony was coping. Surely, he wouldn't ... no. Matilda threw that suggestion out of her head straightaway. She leaned back in her seat and watched as Sheffield passed her by in a blur.

Three cars back, a silver Vauxhall Vivaro was following the dog walking van with Donnie Barko emblazoned on the sides.

The van pulled up opposite the main entrance of South Yorkshire Police Headquarters. From the passenger side, out stepped DCI Matilda Darke. He recognised her from the news last night. He knew what she was attempting to do with the interview. The way she looked right into the camera at the end and told him to come to her so they could sit down and have a chat. As if that was going to happen. He was pleased he knew who was in charge of the investigation to hunt him down, now. It gave him a sense of attachment to what he was doing. He didn't care about the victims but knowing that he was getting under the skin of a detective chief inspector, and her team, gave him a rush he only felt when he was slicing open one of his victims.

Matilda Darke. It was a good strong name. He liked her. She would be his best victim yet, but that would be too easy. Surely, a woman of her calibre knew that.

He watched as she got out of the van. She leaned inside and spoke more to the driver. She was smiling and then laughing. Why would Matilda be getting a lift to work from a dog walker, unless she knew this dog walker? Was she a relative or a close friend?

He'd parked a few car lengths back from the Donnie Barko van so as not to be seen. He waited until it performed a three-point turn in the road and headed back the way it came. He caught a glimpse of the driver, a slim, red-haired woman with a hint of sadness on her face. Who was she? More importantly, who was she to Matilda?

He performed a U-turn and followed the dog walking van. How would Matilda like it if his next victim was someone she knew very well?

He smiled to himself. He wished he could see her face when she stepped into that white forensic tent and saw a close acquaintance with her throat cut wide open, stark naked, blood covering her breasts, legs stretched wide open and all kinds of implements sticking out of her. Maybe he could rig up a camera somewhere to record a live feed of the unveiling.

He continued to follow the matching silver Vivaro. He'd found his next victim.

Chapter Fifty-Nine

Jeremy Keats had agreed to come into the station to be interviewed. When he arrived, he looked pale and nervous, though he might just have been cold from the bitter wind outside. He waited in reception, long overcoat unbuttoned, revealing his dog collar, and almost jumped out of his skin when DC Tom Simpson called for him.

'Can you tell me what this is about?' Keats asked as he followed Tom down a corridor towards an interview room.

'We need to ask you a few more questions about your connection to the investigation,' Tom said with a winning smile.

'I don't have a connection to the case.'

'Then it won't take long at all, then.' Tom opened the door and allowed the vicar to enter first. 'Can I get you a tea or coffee? I don't recommend them, I'm afraid.'

'Oh. Could I possibly have a drink of water?'

'Of course.'

Tom closed the door with a slam. The vicar jumped and

looked around him. His face was sour as he took in the cold, bare room.

'He can smell the fear and guilt of everyone who's been in there before him,' Matilda said to Zofia.

There were both crammed into the observation room next to interview room 1. It was a tiny, windowless room and they were in front of a one-way mirror. Zofia, as always, had a pad on her lap, pen poised, ready to write down something of importance. Matilda, meanwhile, was sitting back in her chair, arms folded against her chest.

'What do you think?' Matilda asked. 'Does he look scared or guilty?'

'He's definitely out of his comfort zone.'

Jeremy pulled out a chair and took a cotton handkerchief out of his pocket. He wiped imaginary dust off the seat before he sat. He knitted his hands together on the table in front of him and looked around the room. He looked over to the mirror on the far wall. He was intelligent enough to know there was someone sitting behind it and he couldn't take his eyes from it.

'Shall I wave?' Zofia asked.

Matilda laughed. 'He's really staring at us, isn't he?'

'I wonder what he's thinking.'

'Maybe that his luck has finally run out.'

The door to the interview room opened. Once again, Jeremy Keats jumped. Tom handed him a plastic cup of water and pulled out a chair to sit down. DC Finn Cotton followed him in. He held a cardboard file and sat down next to Tom, smoothing down his tie and clearing his throat.

'Mr Keats, thank you for coming in. We'll try and not take up too much of your time,' Finn said.

Matilda had told Finn to keep the interview casual. They had no proof Jeremy Keats was the killer and they wanted him to be at ease. If he thought this was simply a routine chat, then he'd relax, his confidence would grow and, hopefully, he'd trip himself up somewhere.

'It's my pleasure. Anything I can do to help.' He gave a nervous smile and took a large sip of water.

'When I came to see you at the church,' Finn began. 'I told you about a van belonging to an acquaintance of yours, Laurence Dodds. We're assuming the number plate of Mr Dodds's van has been cloned and possibly used in the murders of four women over the past two months.'

'That's awful,' Jeremy said. His voice was accentless and high-pitched. He couldn't stop playing with his fingers and his left leg was jiggling beneath the table.

'It is. We've spoken to Mr Dodds on a couple of occasions, and we believe him to be in the clear.'

'I should hope so, too,' Jeremy interrupted. 'Laurence is one of my most helpful volunteers. He hasn't a bad bone in his body. He does sterling work for the community.'

Finn maintained eye contact with Jeremy until he'd finished. 'He has told us that he's let only one person borrow his van, and that's you.'

'Yes. Yes. You said. And I've given you my whereabouts of the dates and times the murders were committed.'

'You have. Since we spoke, there has been a further murder. Can you tell us where you were on the evening of December the twenty-fifth? Christmas Day.'

'I did two services on Christmas Day. One at half past ten and the other at six o'clock.'

'What did you do between the services?' Tom asked.

Matilda had asked Finn to begin the interview and lead up to the questioning, then, once they were there, for them to take it in turns with the questions, try to wrong foot the vicar wherever possible.

'I went back to my flat and had a snack. I showered and watched the Queen's Christmas Message, and then I prepared for my evening sermon.'

'Were you with anyone?' Finn asked.

'No. I live alone.'

'You didn't call on any friends or family?' Tom asked.

'No.'

'You didn't pop round to someone's house with gifts?'

'No. I'd already handed out my cards and presents.'

'After the evening sermon, what did you do then?' Finn asked.

'I went back to my flat.'

'Alone?'

'Yes.'

'What time would that have been?'

'I'm not sure. About eight o'clock.'

'What did you do for the rest of the night?' Tom asked, leaning forward in his seat.

'I watched a film.'

'Which one?'

'*A Star Is Born*.'

'Original or remake?' Tom again.

'Oh. Does that matter?'

'It might.'

'Remake.'

'Did you enjoy it?'

'Not really. It passed a couple of hours.'

'Did you get any phone calls, emails or text messages?' Finn asked.

'No.'

'So you've no alibi?'

'Well, no, but then I don't need one. I haven't done anything wrong.' He fingered his collar. 'I'm innocent.'

'Then why is your leg jiggling and your brow sweating?'

'It's hot in here.'

'It's snowing outside and the radiator in here hasn't worked since Sheffield Wednesday were last in the Premier League,' Finn said. 'Is there something you'd like to tell us?'

'No. I … I'm not used to this kind of questioning. I'm … I suppose I'm nervous.'

'Do you have something to be nervous about?'

'No,' he almost shouted.

Finn opened his file. 'Tell us about Rebecca Henderson.'

'Oh, dear Lord,' Jeremy said, bowing his head. 'I knew you'd bring that up.' He picked up the plastic cup and drained it. He took a deep breath and looked up. 'Look, I liked Rebecca, I really did. She was a lovely woman. I thought she liked me, too. I read the situation wrong. That's all.'

'She took an injunction out against you,' Finn said.

'Lo-looking back,' Jeremy stuttered, 'my actions were a tad extreme …'

'You parked outside her house all night. You were waiting for her on her doorstep in the mornings. You followed her to work, to the gym, to the supermarket, to a family wedding in Whitby.' Finn read from the file. 'You sent her flowers and cards. You left notes for her under her windscreen wipers. On one occasion you phoned her twenty-three times in one night. You scared her, Mr Keats.'

Jeremy closed his eyes. He was on the verge of tears. 'I …

I've never had any success with women.' His voice was much quieter. 'They see the dog collar and it's an instant turn-off. Rebecca … She … she was nice. She liked me. I latched onto that. I'm sorry. I apologised to her. I'll be sorry until the day I die. I'm not your killer. I know it looks bad, but it's not me. It's not. I couldn't … I just … I …' He broke down.

'Is it my imagination or are men getting more pathetic these days,' Matilda said.

'It's not your imagination. I had to give my last boyfriend the elbow because he cried every time we had sex.'

'Bloody hell. Really?'

'Yes. He said he was just so happy, it was the only way to release the emotions.'

'Wow.'

'I know. We only lasted three weeks. I couldn't take any more. It was a shame, really, as he was so good in bed.'

'Okay, too much information there, Zofia.' Matilda pressed a button on the microphone in front of her. 'Let him go, Finn, but tell him we may need to speak to him again in the future. I very much doubt he's our guy.'

'Me, Scott and Finn were talking about the killer. Scott mentioned him being someone we see all the time but don't really take any notice of,' Zofia said. 'Who notices vicars? I certainly don't. Also, if Daisy Clough was lured into a van, like we assume, who better to do so than a kindly vicar?'

Matilda studied Jeremy Keats as he slowly stood up and was shown out of the interview room. He looked so twee and unassuming, so passive and fragile, that he was a world away from a man who had the capability to hack off a woman's head and pose her. But maybe that was the point.

Chapter Sixty

It seemed strange for Matilda to arrive home and not see a Porsche parked out front, or a light on inside. She felt guilty about Adele having to move out of her own home, even if it was for her own safety, and she'd sent many texts to her throughout the day, pleading for her forgiveness. It was almost teatime before she received a reply.

You're forgiven. Just don't let it happen again. I'm safely moved in with Pat. My room isn't as big as the one at home, but the bed is much comfier. I may have to go shopping when I'm allowed back home. I'm making Pat my world famous lasagne for tea. If you hear sirens, don't worry, it's just me blowing up Pat's kitchen. Stay safe. Don't do anything stupid. Ring me if you need me.

To combat being alone, and on the principle that there's safety in numbers, Scott and Donal had decided to move in for the foreseeable. They picked Donal up on the way home from work. He was already standing outside his flat with a bulging rucksack on his shoulders and a holdall at his feet.

'How long are you planning on staying?' Matilda asked as he packed everything into the boot.

'If the upstairs is as gorgeous as your downstairs, I'm claiming squatter's rights,' he said.

Matilda smiled. As they made their way home, Matilda realised what everyone had been saying to her for years was correct. She did need people around her. She couldn't face life's dangers and troubles alone. Adele, Pat, Sian, Christian, her mum and sister, Scott and now Donal. They were all people who could be buffers against the horrors of the world and make her small part of it a better, happier place. Why had it taken her so long to realise that?

———————

While Scott and Donal were making their new bedroom more like home, Matilda set about making their tea. There were plenty of leftovers from Christmas Day and the fridge and cupboards were bulging with food. She knew Scott was careful about what he ate, avoiding red meat and processed foods as much as possible, but she didn't know much about Donal and his tastes.

When they came downstairs, Donal told them both to stand back and allow him to take control of the kitchen. His mum had taught him everything he knew about rustling up a meal from scratch. He checked all the cupboards for what he needed and told them he was going to make caramelised garlic and spinach gnocchi with ricotta. Matilda's mouth watered just hearing about it.

Donal selected a playlist on his phone and began preparing the meal with 1980s rock music blaring while Matilda and

Scott went into the living room. Scott was on the water while Matilda had a large glass of white wine.

'Is everything all right with you two?' Matilda asked. She lit the fire and sat down, curling up in the corner of one of the Chesterfields.

Scott nodded. 'We had a good talk on Christmas Day. Despite everything, I still feel like I'm cheating on Chris. It's silly but, hand on heart, I know that we'd have grown old together and still been a couple when we were celebrating our hundredth birthday.' He gave a contemplative smile.

'That's how I feel about James.' Matilda looked at her wedding photo on the sleeper above the wood burner. 'People always say there's no such thing as the perfect man. James was far from perfect. But he was perfect for me.'

'Chris was perfect for me, too.'

'And Donal?'

Scott thought for a moment. 'He's the new normal. It's like this pandemic. When it's over with, life is going to be dramatically changed, isn't it? And we need to adapt, learn to live with what's left. I knew the world wasn't perfect before Chris was killed but I think I had blinkers on. Now, I know that horror can visit my home, and it's left me scarred. Inside, I feel darker, but Donal helps me see that there is good in the world.'

Matilda smiled. 'That's good. I'm so happy for you, Scott.'

'It's not too late for you to find someone else.'

'I know. The thing is, I never thought of myself as settling down, even when I was younger. Not long after I left university, three of my friends got engaged within a matter of weeks. I never thought that I was missing out. I just wanted to be a detective. Meeting James really was like being hit by a thunderbolt. Now he's gone, I'm back to being on my own, and I'm fine with that. I miss James so much that it hurts, but I've got good people around me. There's Adele, Sian, Pat, you, Christian, my mum, and Harriet. I can be happy being single.'

'Are you happy?'

She took a long slug of wine. 'Right now, no, I'm not. But I know why. Once this case is over with, I'll make things right with Adele and Pat. I'll try to get Sian back to work and the old unit reinstated. And do you know what else I'm going to do? I'm going to have a holiday. Pandemic permitting, obviously. But I want to go away. I want to swim in the sea. I want to eat outdoors with the sun blazing down on me. I want to get a tan and flirt with a waiter.'

Scott laughed.

'What?' she asked.

'You looked so happy then. I mean, genuinely happy.'

'Losing James, Carl Meagan going missing, the whole nightmare with Ben Hales and then being shot – I've had so much thrown at me over the last five years that I'm surprised I'm not in a padded cell. But I've learned to appreciate what I've got. I can be happy again. I will be happy again.' She gave a full, beaming smile.

'So we catch this killer, your life begins again and work isn't your main focus.'

'That's correct.'

Scott fell silent but his gaze remained fixed on Matilda.

'What?' she asked.

He took a breath. 'You're not coming back to work full-time. Are you?'

'I'm still thinking about it,' she lied. She doubted the Chief Constable would allow a killer to lead a prestigious unit. And if whoever was doing this entered her home, she'd make sure he left it feet first.

Donal had missed his vocation and could have been a chef in a top restaurant. The meal was delicious, and the presentation was beautiful.

'I did think of becoming a chef when I was in my teens, but I sat down and had a good long think and wondered what jobs were expendable should a pandemic strike,' he said with a wink. 'Obviously, restaurants would close, but mortuaries would stay open. So, trainee pathologist won.' He smiled.

'There's no way I could do what you and Adele do,' Matilda said. 'It's bad enough trying to get inside the head of a killer without getting inside the body of a victim.'

'Fortunately, they're not all as bad as what we had in today. If we had decapitation on a daily basis, I'd definitely give catering a second thought.'

'I don't know how Simon Browes can be so sanguine about it all,' Scott said.

'He's been doing it for thirty years,' Matilda said. 'I doubt there's little he hasn't seen.'

'But he needs to realise there are people around him who haven't seen it all. Donal's only been doing the job for two years. Of course he's going to be upset. It's natural. Simon should be more cognisant of people's feelings.'

'That's another reason to have second thoughts about this job. Do you mind if I have another glass of wine?' Donal asked Matilda.

'Help yourself.'

He refilled his glass. Matilda held out her half-empty glass and he topped her up. Scott was still on the water.

Donal continued. 'I don't want to become so hardened that when we get a victim brought in that's been blown to pieces and scooped up and I'm presented with severed limbs and burned organs I simply shrug and roll my sleeves up.'

'First of all,' Matilda began. 'Thanks for that imagery just after I've eaten. Secondly, I think Simon's a special case. He has seen a great deal. I don't think he's ever spoken about it. He's locked all his emotions and feelings up inside and built a massive wall around him. He shut his wife out and that's why his marriage ended. Adele's seen a lot, too. She's attended the aftermath of terrorist attacks, for crying out loud. They don't come much worse than that. Once a month, she talks to the therapist, unburdens herself. She's also got me, who she can spend an evening in front of the TV with and watch a Marvel film and ogle Sebastian Stan. You need to switch off. Simon never has. You have to make sure you do.'

'Do I switch off?' Donal asked Scott.

'Yes. You go fossil hunting. You go to museums. You watch David Attenborough documentaries on a loop. You've got me.' They smiled at each other. 'And, bizarrely, you've got *Iron Man*.'

'Really? You prefer Robert Downey Junior?' Matilda asked.

Donal blushed.

'He doesn't even fancy Chris Evans,' Scott said.

'What? And I've allowed you into my home?' Matilda said playfully. 'What about Jeremy Renner?'

'God, no,'

'Oh, my goodness!' Matilda exclaimed. She turned to Scott. 'I think you need to find someone else. This man is not for you. He's not normal.'

'I think I'll make a start on the dishes,' Donal said, standing up and gathering the empty plates.

'We'll do those,' Matilda said.

'While we're stacking the dishwasher,' Scott began, 'remind me to tell you who Donal's teenage crush was on.'

'Don't you dare,' Donal warned.

Matilda smiled and watched the banter between the two. It was fun to have the house filled with mirth and laughter again, and she was joining in, too. She felt light, a warmth from within, happy for the first time in as long as she could remember. Everything going on outside of that front door, the pandemic, the hunt for a disturbed serial killer, was momentarily forgotten.

Every window of the house was lit up. The owner of Donnie Barko either didn't care about her electricity bill or she didn't live alone.

The driver of the silver Vivaro was behind the wheel of his van, shrouded in darkness. He hadn't moved in hours and as the temperature had plummeted, he'd grown colder, too, but it didn't matter. He didn't care. His next victim was inside that house. He'd looked at the Facebook page advertised on the side of the van and saw that Sian Robinson was a former detective. He wondered why she no longer worked for the police force. He Googled her name, but nothing came up. Maybe it was too much for her. Maybe she couldn't stand the evils of human nature on a daily basis. She kept in touch with DCI Darke. They were obviously good friends. She really was the perfect victim for him.

He was tempted to knock on the door, charm his way in somehow, but there was a risk of being seen by a nosey neighbour. Or maybe she had a sensor light or a hidden camera. He'd taken a massive risk with Tilly Hall and almost lost. He wasn't ready to hand in his hunter's knife yet. He wanted more victims attached to his name. He wanted to spill more blood. He wanted DCI Matilda Darke to scream and cry and go mad with the horrors she witnessed, and there was no better horror than seeing someone she cared about, admired, maybe even loved, cut open, her blood and organs strewn about the cold, frosty, winter landscape. Sian Robinson's death was going to be his best one yet. But not tonight.

He was just about to turn the key in the ignition when the front door opened, and Sian stepped out followed by a young woman who was taller and younger. He opened his window a crack and strained to listen to their conversation.

'Mum, you really don't need to drive me everywhere. It's literally a ten-minute walk.'

'I don't care if she lives next door, Belinda. Until this killer is caught, I'm not allowing you to walk the streets alone.'

'God, it's like being a child again. I am over eighteen, or have you forgotten?'

'How can I forget when you keep reminding me every fifteen minutes? Legally being an adult does not make you immortal.'

Belinda climbed into the van and slammed the front passenger door hard behind it. It echoed around the silent neighbourhood.

'Make sure that door's closed, Belinda,' Sian said, sarcastically.

The van pulled away from the kerb and drove up the road. The man turned on his engine and decided to follow.

The one thing he wasn't looking forward to in killing one of Matilda's friends was the fact she was going to be older than his previous victims. He liked the younger girls. Their flesh was smoother and firmer. There was something beautiful about seeing warm blood running down perfect, unblemished skin. He smiled to himself as he followed Donnie Barko. Killing the daughter of Matilda's friend would be even more harrowing for the detective. This Belinda had her whole life ahead of her. It would be tragic to see it cut so brutally short.

The daughter first. Then the mother.

Chapter Sixty-One

Matilda was wide awake.

She'd spent a pleasant evening with Scott and Donal. They'd watched trash on television and ribbed Donal about him having a serious crush on Ross from *Friends* when he was growing up. At eleven o'clock, Matilda decided to go to bed and left the two of them to finish the Christmas film on some obscure channel. Just after midnight, she heard them quietly come upstairs and the door to the spare room close behind them.

The house began to settle and the odd noise and the howl of the strong wind caused Matilda to sit up a few times, wondering if this was the night the killer would make himself known to her. Had that really been a silver Vivaro she'd seen turning the corner at the bottom of Watery Street this morning? Maybe she should have told Scott to follow it. Was the killer following her? Had he worked out where she lived? She felt safer having Scott and Donal in the house with her, but this was a type of murderer she'd never faced before. He was sneaky, clever, dangerous, and took great pleasure in making his victims suffer. She hoped Scott and Donal didn't get in his way when he finally did come to her home.

She picked up her phone and looked at the time. It was three minutes past one. She'd been in bed for more than two hours and hadn't slept a wink yet. She sat up, turned on the light and picked up the new Val McDermid novel she'd started on Christmas Eve. She read a page and had to read it again as she hadn't taken in a single word.

'Sorry, Val,' she said, putting her bookmark between the pages and returning the book to the bedside cabinet.

Matilda turned the light off and snuggled back down under the duvet, hoping pure exhaustion would make her eyelids heavy and she'd nod off. But that didn't work either. Her mind was too active, too alert to every sound from outside. Living, as she did, on the edge of the countryside, she was often visited by various wildlife. It wasn't unusual for her to wake up in the morning to find foxes had been in her bins during the hours of darkness. With the gravel driveway now replaced with smooth, vulgar tarmac, she couldn't hear the foxes' stealthy approach. And she wouldn't hear her killer arrive either. Bloody Adele and her precious Porsche.

She flicked on the light again and pushed back the duvet. If she wasn't going to sleep, she might as well get up and do something constructive. She put her slippers and dressing gown on and went downstairs. Mug of tea made, and packet of biscuits in hand, she went into the living room. The fire was slowly dying but the room was still warm. She unplugged her iPad from where she'd left it charging and made herself comfortable on the sofa.

Chief Constable Ridley had advised her to beef up her security. She had a sensor light above the front and back doors and a burglar alarm, but that was all. The house was off the beaten track, and should she ever need to dial 999 in case of her being attacked it would take the police at least half an hour to get here. It wouldn't hurt to have extra security even after this killer was caught and languishing in a prison cell.

She opened the Google home page and typed in 'Sheffield security companies'. Within the next hour she'd asked for quotes on motion cameras around the perimeter of her land and covering every angle of the building. She wanted sensors on every window and every door. Was a panic button linked to South Yorkshire Police HQ too much? she wondered.

Once this killer was caught, he was bound to be sent to Wakefield Prison, also known as Monster Mansion, where all the evil and most deprived men were sent. Steve Harrison was there. They could end up having a cell next to each other. When they knew they had Matilda Darke in common, who knew what they could come up with to target her? No, a panic button was not too much to ask for.

Chapter Sixty-Two

Monday 28th December 2020

Matilda hadn't slept much and yawned all the way through Scott and Donal's conversation on the way to work. She didn't join in, simply sat in the front passenger seat, heavy head resting on her hand, and watched as a snowy Sheffield passed by.

They dropped Donal off at Watery Street then headed for HQ where Matilda dragged herself into her office and installed herself at her desk. She was waiting for the inevitable call from the Chief Constable, which came barely minutes after she'd sat down. She'd been summoned.

She knocked on Ridley's door and waited for the bark telling her to come in. She found Ridley by his window, looking out at the city. It had started to snow once again. Huge flakes were falling now. For once, the steel city almost looked beautiful.

'Have you seen the front pages?' Ridley asked, his back still to Matilda.

'No,' she said. Her eyes fell to his desk and saw the neat mound of all the dailies piled on top of each other.

The first one was the *Daily Mail*: BUTCHER SERIAL KILLER STALKS SHEFFIELD screamed the headline.

It makes a change from rising house prices.

Matilda bit the inside of her cheek. She could guess the rest without looking. The red-tops would love a serial killer to get their teeth into.

'I had a very unpleasant Zoom call with the Home Secretary this morning,' he said, pulling out his chair and sitting down.

'She does seem like an unpleasant woman,' Matilda said.

'This is not the time for flippancy, Matilda. Sit down.' She did as she was told. 'The last thing this force needs right now is more scrutiny from the media and the Home Office. And that's exactly what we've got, in bloody spades. Every single front page has got us as its lead story. *The Sun* has an exclusive with the woman who found Tracey Ward. It's all there in glorious Technicolor – the decapitation, the fact the body is posed, the victim holding her own head. You promised me you'd find this killer.'

'I did nothing of the sort. Look, me and my team are doing everything right. We're following the guidelines. We're doing everything we usually do when hunting for a killer. We follow the evidence. Unfortunately, in this case, there is no evidence.'

'I find that hard to believe.'

'Phone forensics. Phone Adele Kean and Simon Browes at Watery Street. Ask them to tell you what they've gleaned from the crime scenes and the bodies. Nothing. We have nothing,' she spat.

'The Home Secretary wants to bring in a special unit.'

'We are a special unit.'

'Unofficially.'

'Then make it official. Bring back the HMCU officially and give me the officers I need.'

'And what would be the point of that? You've just said you don't have the evidence to follow up on, so what do you need more officers for?'

'So what is the point in bringing in a special unit? You're contradicting yourself.'

'The Home Secretary—'

'Fuck the Home Secretary,' Matilda interrupted, standing up. 'You brought me back here. I was perfectly happy at home doing nothing. But you camped out on my doorstep. You practically begged me to come back. Just because I haven't found the killer straightaway, you can't turn this around and put all the blame on me. I went on television and practically challenged the killer to come for me, for crying out loud.'

'Matilda, calm down. This is out of my hands now. I managed to hold the Home Secretary off for forty-eight hours. You have until Wednesday to have made clear headway in this case and then she's handing it over to an outside unit.'

'Policing should not be about politics,' she said. Her voice was quiet and calm, but her tone was seething.

'It shouldn't. But it is. Everything is about politics these days. Sit back down.' Reluctantly, she did so. 'Look, I want you and the HMCU working full time in this force. You did stellar work and got good results. I know this killer is proving to be elusive, and even an outside unit would be able to see you've done nothing wrong, but we're under the microscope here. Everything, every decision, every delay, is magnified.'

Matilda inhaled. She looked past Ridley, through the window and into the outside world. She let out a deep breath and stood up.

'Forty-eight hours. It's long enough.'

'Sorry?'

'I'll get you your killer by Wednesday.'

'How?'

'I'll keep that to myself for now. Better not put anything else under that microscope of yours.' Matilda headed for the door. Before leaving, she turned back. 'The next time you have a call with the Home Secretary, will you give her a message from me? Tell her to go fuck herself.'

In the corridor outside Ridley's office, Matilda took out her mobile and scrolled through her contacts. She didn't even hesitate before she pressed the number.

'Danny Hanson,' the call was answered.

'Danny, it's Matilda Darke.'

'Oh. So it is. I didn't look at the display. How are you? Is it true the killer decapitated the last victim and posed her so it looked like …?'

'Danny, I don't have time for this right now. Remember how I sat down with you and gave you an in-depth interview after the Magnolia House case?'

'I do. The book is coming along nicely, too,' he said, an irritating smile in his voice.

Matilda could feel her flesh crawling. 'I want to offer you another deal. I'll give you an exclusive on this killer if you do me another favour.'

'Go on.'

She could almost hear him salivating. 'Do you still have that blog of yours?'

'I certainly do. I'm close to one hundred thousand subscribers.'

'Good. I'm going to send you something about the killer I want you to put on your blog. No editing. No adding your own brand of millennial bollocks. Just put it on word for word.'

'I'm not sure I like the sound of this.' Worry was creeping into his voice.

'Grow a pair, Danny. If this doesn't win you blogger of the year, nothing will.'

'Oh my God, is that a thing?' he asked, suddenly excited.

Matilda ended the call. 'Jesus Christ,' she muttered to herself, rolling her eyes.

Chapter Sixty-Three

The suite was hardly a hive of activity. Finn was staring intently at his computer screen with a heavy frown on his face. Scott was making a round of drinks and, as was the norm of late, Tom and Zofia were cosy together at the same desk. Judging by the smiles and giggles, they were doing very little work. This makeshift team wasn't working. This office needed Sian to put them back in order. Or Scott needed to channel his inner Sian, at least.

Matilda headed for her office. She waved away the offer of a coffee, closed the door behind her and pulled the blind shut. She needed peace and privacy.

An hour later, she'd cobbled together what she wanted Danny Hanson to reveal to the world, or to his one hundred thousand readers at least, and hoped it would go viral. It was a mock interview, written in the third person, as if Matilda had been speaking exclusively to Danny. She simply asked and answered the questions for him. In it, she revealed what kind of a man was doing these killings, but she used more derogatory language than she would be allowed to get away with on prime-time BBC1.

'...*We were under the illusion at the beginning that the killer hates women. But as he reveals more about himself through his method of murder, we can see the reason behind his hatred. He's not successful with women. He's tried, and he's failed. And that's been the story of his life. He's a failure in everything he's turned his hand to.*

'...*There's a rule of thumb that states a clever killer is highly intelligent, that he must have a technical job. While that may be true in some cases, in this one, I don't believe it is. With the internet and true-crime documentaries becoming ever more popular, it doesn't take a genius to know how to avoid leaving traces of yourself at a crime scene.*

'...*Sex is the killer's motivation. It's that basic. This is the only way the killer can have a sex life and that is by taking it for himself without consent. There's a reason for that. Not one single woman will give him a second glance.*

'...*His last victim was indeed posed. He was sending a message to the police, almost laughing at us. What he doesn't realise is that he revealed much more of himself than he ever thought possible. He's tried to be confident and clever, but he doesn't have the intellect for that. He's told us exactly who he is.*'

Matilda hit send on the email before she could change her mind. She needed to make the killer angry. Time was running out. She needed him to come to her. And it needed to be now.

Matilda was looking out of her window at the uninspiring view of the rear car park, the industrial bins and the memorial to the shooting. She watched the snow fall. It was almost hypnotic. The vibration from an incoming text made her jump. It was Danny Hanson asking if she was sure he wanted her to post what she'd written. He said he knew what she was trying to do and was putting herself in grave danger. He had more brain cells than she'd given him credit for. She sent him a quick reply telling him to blog it, or whatever the term was, and went back to watching the snow.

Background chatter from the suite outside her small office was becoming more raucous. It didn't sound like much work was being done. She sat back in her seat and listened.

'Listen to this one,' Tom said, laughter in his voice. 'The man opposite me at number nineteen used to say good morning to me on his way to work. He hasn't done for a number of weeks now and he didn't send me a Christmas card. Can you believe that? She's actually called the police and said she thinks her neighbour is a serial killer because he didn't send her a Christmas card.'

'I like this one here,' Zofia began. 'I haven't seen Sophia Burrows at number fifty-four for at least a month, but her husband is still there because I saw him put his bins out, and he never puts his bins out. It's always Sophia who does it. I was going to go over and see if she was all right, but I've got a grandchild in Adelaide I'm hoping to see when we can start travelling again.'

They both laughed.

'This is priceless,' Tom said. 'We could release a book. *Confessions of a Secret Detective.*'

Matilda yanked opened her door. Her face was like thunder.

'Do you think this is funny?' she shouted. 'Is that what this is to you, a joke?'

Tom immediately reddened. Zofia looked down at her desk.

'Four women have been raped and murdered,' she said, pointing to the murder board. 'A fourteen-year-old girl was raped and had her throat torn open. She will never speak again and go through life tormented by what's she gone through. Every single woman and girl in this city is at risk from being murdered and you two sit there and make fun at people showing their concern.'

'I'm really sorry, Matilda,' Zofia began, her voice quiet. 'It's been a difficult morning. We were just ... I don't know ... letting off a bit of steam.'

'By taking the piss? By making light of these murders?'

'No. I really am sorry,' she said softly.

'This is supposed to be an elite unit. You two need to think long and hard about what that means if you value your place on it.'

'I will,' Zofia said.

'Did you find all this funny, too?' she asked Finn.

'No. I was on the phone,' he said, a scared look on his face. 'A Vivaro was found burned out last night on Gleadless Valley. It's white not silver, but I'm having forensics impound it anyway.'

'See, this is what we do,' she said, turning back to Tom and Zofia. 'Same make of van, but different colour. However, we rule nothing out until the evidence tells us we can. And we certainly don't make fun of people who could possibly give us vital information.' She went over to the murder board and ripped off a few photos. She slammed them down on Tom's desk in front of him. 'Do you think this is funny?' She asked, pointing to the photo of Tracey Ward sitting on The Steel Steps, her head in her lap, dried blood pooling around her feet. 'Is this the kind of thing that makes you laugh?'

He shook his head.

'Matilda.' Scott said firmly.

She looked up at his grave face. She was going too far. She went back into her office, grabbed her coat and mobile phone and headed for the exit.

'Where are you going?' Scott asked.

She didn't reply.

Chapter Sixty-Four

Matilda knocked on the door of Tilly Hall's private room in the Children's Hospital and entered. Tilly was sitting up in bed watching the television on the opposite wall. She turned and smiled at Matilda.

'Hello. Is your mum not here?' Matilda asked as she looked around.

The private room, with two police officers guarding outside, was a marked improvement on the previous one. This was much larger, had a widescreen TV and a better view of Weston Park, and there was even an en suite. Tilly tapped on the iPad and handed it to Matilda.

Mum isn't feeling too well today. The doctors have told her to stay at home. She's been ringing practically every hour to see how I am.

Matilda looked up at Tilly who proffered a smile and shrugged her shoulders.

'I hope she's feeling better soon. Do you mind if I sit with you for a while?' Tilly shook her head. Matilda pulled out a chair and sat beside her. 'How are you feeling today?' Tilly held up seven fingers. 'That's great.'

Tilly's mobile buzzed on the locker beside her bed.

'You've had a text from Ryan,' Matilda said, looking at the phone. 'Do you want to read it?'

She shook her head.

'Has he been to see you?'

Tilly picked up the iPad and typed.

He's isolating. His mum's still testing positive for covid. He's been texting me a lot, but I haven't replied. I don't want him to feel like he has to stay with me when I'm like this.

'He obviously likes you. Your mum told me that you both had strong feelings for each other.'

We do. I like him a lot. About a week before this happened, we went to Starbucks, sat in the corner and had a long chat. A friend of mine, Jas, she had sex for the first time in the summer holidays. She's been going on about how amazing it is. I mentioned it to Ryan, but I'm nervous. After this has happened, I don't want to have sex at all. It was so painful.

When Matilda finished reading, she looked up and saw Tilly in tears. 'What's happened to you is the most violent thing that a woman can go through. For you to experience that when you've never been intimate in that way before is so horrific. I can completely understand you not wanting to have another man close to you. But the thing is, Tilly, when you find someone you truly love, sex is the most wonderful, natural, pleasurable thing in the world. Maybe Ryan isn't the right boy for you, maybe he is, but you won't know that until you see him again, see what the future holds for you both. Don't let anyone pressure you into having sex until you are ready.'

Tilly smiled through the tears.

Matilda wiped her eyes before her own tears had a chance to fall. 'I was seeing a man when I was shot. I pushed him away. He wanted to stay with me but I told him to go. The thing is, a small part of me regrets it. I wish I'd seen where life had taken us. I can't go back and change that. If you make a rash decision over Ryan, you won't be able to change that either, but you can always change your mind at a later date.'

Couldn't you get back in touch with your bf and ask if he wants to try again?

'Too much time has passed, now,' Matilda said. 'Besides, the last I heard, he's with someone else and she's pregnant.' She reached forward and took Tilly's hands in hers. 'What you need to concentrate on right now is yourself. Do what is important for you. The first step is getting well enough to leave here and go back home to your dogs.'

I miss my dogs. I think I prefer dogs to people. That's bad, isn't it?

Matilda smiled. 'Not at all. I can certainly understand that. In my job I see the worst of what people do to each other. A friend of mine has left the force recently and started a professional dog walking business. She's called it Donnie Barko. Sometimes I think I should join her.'

Donnie Barko is a great name. Don't you enjoy being a detective any more?

Matilda thought for a moment before answering. 'The world of policing has changed over the years, and not for the better, in my opinion. It's all about pleasing politicians. They're the decision-makers. The problem is, they haven't got a clue what's going on in the real world. I think I'm just feeling the winter blues. I'm sure I'll pick up in the spring,' she said with a fake smile, lying to herself. 'Actually, I was wondering if I could ask you a favour.' Matilda took her phone out of her pocket. 'I want to show you a photograph of someone. I want you to tell me if he's the man who attacked you.'

Tilly visibly paled and leaned further back into the bed.

'Don't worry,' Matilda soothed her. 'It's just a photo. It can't hurt you. And I'm right here.'

On her way over in the taxi, Matilda couldn't get the thought out of her mind that Sian drove a silver Vivaro, that her eldest son, Anthony, borrowed it on a regular basis and he'd last used it on Christmas Day. As much as she was ninety-nine percent sure Anthony wasn't the killer, the missing one percent needed finding.

Like everyone else in the country, Matilda had hundreds of photos on her phone that she never looked at, and she had spent most of the taxi journey scrolling through them trying to see if she had a picture of Sian's children. Eventually, she found one. A group shot of Sian with her now ex-husband and all four kids. She'd taken a screenshot of it, cropped it and zoomed in on Anthony so he was the main focus.

Tilly reached out and took Matilda's hand in hers. She squeezed tightly as Matilda slowly showed her the screen. Straightaway, Tilly relaxed and released her grip on Matilda. She shook her head.

'Are you sure?'

Tilly picked up the iPad.

100% sure. It's not him.

Matilda breathed a sigh of relief. 'Good. That's good. Thank you.' She hated herself almost straightaway for doubting him.

Can I ask you a favour now?

'Of course.'

Will you take me to the bathroom to see my scars. Mum says I'm not ready yet, but I am. I need to see them.

'Ah. Are you absolutely sure you want to?'

She nodded.

Matilda thought for a while. This really should be Amy

helping her daughter through this, not her. But she could understand Tilly needing to see what she looked like. She'd felt the same once she was conscious, lucid and able to get out of bed on her own. The first thing she'd done was go to the bathroom, look at herself in the mirror, at her shaven, misshapen head. She didn't recognise herself. It was weeks later before she dared look in the mirror again.

'Okay.'

Tilly pushed back the blankets and Matilda helped her out of bed. She held onto her as she led her into the small en suite bathroom. There were no windows in the room. Matilda turned on the light and both of them squinted under the brightness of the light from above.

They stood in front of the mirror above the sink. In this lighting, they both looked tired and drained. Tilly's eyes were full of tears.

'You don't have to do this now,' Matilda said.

Tilly nodded. Carefully, she undid the tape around her neck holding the padding in place. Slowly, she pulled it away from her skin, wincing at the discomfort. She closed her eyes. Matilda could feel her body stiffen and held onto her tighter.

Matilda looked at her own facial expression in the mirror. She could see what was lying beneath the padding. It was red and looked angry, but it was healing, which was the main thing. She knew Tilly wouldn't see it that way. She needed to be positive for her. She quickly softened her face.

'Whenever you're ready.'

Tilly took several, sharp, deep breaths and opened her eyes. Her face drained of colour when she saw what was staring back at her in the mirror. She opened her mouth wide and let out a silent scream.

Matilda practically carried her back to bed. She was so slight. She handed her a drink of water and told her to calm down, take slow, deep breaths and try to relax.

'It will heal. I promise you,' Matilda said. 'When I first looked in the mirror and saw my hair had been shaved off and the back of my head was all bumpy and out of shape, I cried for hours. But it grew back. You can't see the scar at all. When you've had all your procedures and the stitches removed there are all kinds of creams and lotions you can use that will help the scars to fade. It looks scary now, but it's not going to be like that forever. I promise you.'

I'm ugly.

'No, you're not. You're a very beautiful young woman. You've got lovely eyes and a stunning smile. The scars are still new so they're going to be a little frightening, but they fade.' Matilda sat on the edge of the bed and put her arm around Tilly's shoulders, pulling her close. 'You're at a very vulnerable stage in your life, even without being attacked. I can't even begin to understand how you're feeling. All I can tell you is that it will improve. You will feel better about things.'

Tilly reached for the iPad.

I wish I hadn't survived. Why couldn't he have killed me?

Matilda watched as she typed with one hand. Tears ran down her face. She held onto her tighter and didn't want to let go.

Chapter Sixty-Five

Scott's desk phone rang. He was reading through the myriad calls following Matilda's interview. The majority were a complete waste of time, but they all had to be read and a decision taken on whether further action was required. It was a laborious task. Every time the phone rang, he dreaded another member of the public thinking their neighbour was the serial killer just because his eyes seemed too close together.

'DS Andrews,' he answered, tiredly. It was starting to go dark, not that there had been much brightness today. Snow had started to fall, and he worried his shitty pool car wasn't going to get him home.

'I've got a Mr and Mrs Barker in reception wanting to speak to you,' the desk sergeant said.

'Me?' He frowned, trying to place the name.

'They asked for you specifically. They've got information on the killer for you.'

'Thanks. I'll come through.' He ended the call and then the penny dropped. Mr Barker. Malcolm Barker. The jogger who had turned on his heel and run home when he saw the killer. Scott had been to his house and threatened him on Christmas Day after Tracey Ward had been found. He hoped to God Malcolm wasn't here to make a complaint. Matilda would roast him alive.

He took a deep breath, rolled down his sleeves, ran his fingers through his hair and put his jacket on. He walked along the corridor to reception, straightening his tie, his heavy footsteps resounding off the walls. He felt like he was heading for the gallows.

Malcolm Barker was sitting in reception next to a woman Scott presumed was his wife. They were both in thick winter coats and had melting flakes of snow on their shoulders. They looked shattered, with dark semi-circles beneath their eyes. Their faces gave nothing away. They were blank and Scott feared this was the beginning of the end of his career.

'Mr and Mrs Barker?' Scott asked. His mouth was suddenly very dry.

Malcolm stood up slowly. His wife with him. Their arms were linked.

'I need to make a statement,' Malcolm said.

'Right. Okay.'

'Room one's free,' the desk sergeant said.

'Thanks. Follow me, please.'

Scott led the way to interview room 1. He pushed open the door and flicked on the light. It was cold in here and had a throat-scratching smell of strong disinfectant.

'Please, take a seat. I'd keep your coats on if I were you.' He bent down to fiddle with the control on the radiator. It was already set to maximum, but it was stone cold.

Scott pulled out a chair and sat down. He looked at

Malcolm and his wife in turn. They looked scared. He was dreading where this was going.

'So, what can I do for you?' he asked, interlocking his fingers on the desk. He gave him what he hoped was a comforting smile.

Malcolm licked his lips and swallowed hard a few times. He cleared his throat. 'When I was jogging on the fifteenth of December. When I was picked up on that doorbell camera. I did see something. I was running away. I've felt bad about it ever since, but I just kept thinking of my wife and kids. I wanted to keep them safe. You can understand that, surely.'

'Of course I can.'

'I've been quiet and distant. Suzanne actually thought I was the killer.' He smiled nervously. 'I was scaring her. And the children.'

Beneath the table, Suzanne and Malcolm's hands were tightly clasped together. Neither was planning on letting go of the other.

'We spent all of yesterday, last night and most of today talking,' Suzanne said. 'He told me everything he saw that day. I can perfectly understand why he hasn't said anything. But he needs to. Not just for Tilly Hall and to help the investigation, but for himself, too. For us.'

Scott nodded. 'Okay. And you're wanting to make a full statement now?'

'Yes.'

Scott was relieved. He wasn't going to get into trouble for intimidation. Maybe he actually helped matters by going round. Suzanne had obviously heard the commotion on the doorstep and managed to convince her husband to come forward. This could be the break they needed.

'Okay. We'll go through the basics now, and then I'll get you to give a full, detailed statement which you'll need to sign afterwards. Is that all right?'

'Sure.'

'Right then. In your own time, tell me exactly what you saw.'

Malcolm turned to his wife. She nodded encouragingly, and, if it was possible, she hitched her chair even closer. He took a deep breath.

'I go jogging most nights. I work from home all day so don't go out much. It helps to stop me going mad seeing the same four walls day in, day out. I go at the same time and always take the same route. I turned into Brincliffe Edge Road, and I just stopped dead. There was a van close to the entrance to the woods that I go through. It was under a streetlight. I saw a man and he had his arm around who I now know was Tilly Hall. I could see he had a knife in his hand as the light caught the blade. I didn't know what to do. I froze. I …'

'It's all right. Take your time,' Scott said. He could see how distressing this was for Malcolm.

'We made eye contact. I was far away, but our eyes met. I looked right at him, and I could feel him looking straight into me. I looked away. I looked at Tilly. She was so … she was so frightened … so small. I … I couldn't do anything.'

Suzanne fished in her coat pocket and pulled out a small packet of tissues. She took one out and handed it to Malcolm, who wiped his eyes.

'I looked back at the man. He smiled at me. He … he cut … there was so much blood.'

'Would you like a drink?'

'I'd love a whisky right now.'

Scott smiled. 'I can only offer tea, coffee or water.'

'Coffee. Please. The strongest you have.'

———————

Scott went into the HMCU suite and asked Finn if he'd make coffees for Malcolm and Suzanne and bring them through. He then asked Tom to get onto Matilda and tell her of the potential breakthrough.

'Scott, I think you should see this,' Zofia said, waving him over to her desk.

'What is it?'

'I'm checking the internet and social media and I'm getting flagged with certain key words to do with this case. I've found a blog written by Danny Hanson. He's written a piece about the killer we're hunting. He's describing him as pathetic, a loser, basically. The thing is, it reads like he's sat down, and Matilda has told him all of this stuff.'

Scott leaned over Zofia's shoulder and looked at the screen. His skim-read it. 'But she gave him an interview. It went out on the BBC. None of this was mentioned.'

'Precisely.'

'She wouldn't have met up with him again. She can't stand him.'

'He's made all this up then, hasn't he?' Zofia asked. 'This is just his opinion piece, but he's written it like this to get himself more followers, make it look like he's in with the police.'

'The bastard,' Scott said, slamming his fist down on the desk. 'Matilda's going to kick right off when she sees this. Look, Zofia, I haven't got time for this right now, I need to get back in with the Barkers—'

'Coffee's up,' Finn interrupted.

'I'll be right there. Keep an eye on this,' he said to Zofia. 'Look at the comments people post, see if anything stands out. Maybe the killer will see it and post something.'

'If the killer does see it, he may think Matilda has said all these things. He could go after her.'

'Well, hopefully Malcolm can give us a good description and we can arrest him before it goes that far.'

'And if he doesn't?'

'Then I hope Matilda knows Krav Maga because she's going to bloody well need it.'

' Erm …' Tom began, 'does anyone know where Matilda is right now?'

The room fell silent.

'Shit. Find her. Tell her wherever she is to stay there and get uniform to pick her up and bring her in here for her own safety.'

Scott headed for the door with Finn following carrying a tray of coffee.

'Why do I get the feeling this is going to end with more bloodshed?' Scott asked.

———

Back in the interview room, Scott introduced DC Finn Cotton to the Barkers and asked if they minded him sitting in and making notes. They didn't.

Malcolm took the coffee and wrapped his hands around the mug. He inhaled and took a sip.

'Wow. This is strong,' he said with a weak smile.

'On TV dramas they always joke about the tea and coffee in police stations being horrible,' Suzanne said with a laugh.

'A detective and bad coffee don't go together. We need the good stuff,' Scott said.

'If I'd got it for you from one of the machines, you would have been spitting it out all over the floor,'

Finn said. 'This is from our own supply.'

'Malcolm, did you get a good look at the man who attacked Tilly and his vehicle?'

He took another lingering sip of his coffee and nodded. 'It was a silver Vauxhall. I don't know what make, but I know the badge of a Vauxhall. It was my first car years ago.'

'Okay. Did you get the registration number?'

'YY67 MTC.'

'You're sure?'

'Positive. My own car is YY67 and I just remember MTC. It stuck in my head.'

'That's brilliant, Malcolm. Thank you so much. Now, about the man who attacked Tilly. What did he look like?'

He took another drink of his coffee. 'Are you sure you can't put any whisky in this?' He asked, giving an exaggerated laugh.

'We'll have one when we get home,' Suzanne said, rubbing his arm.

'He wasn't very tall. I'd say about five seven, maybe five eight. He was slim, too. He was wearing dark jeans and big footwear. Maybe walking shoes. He had a coat on, but it was open, and he was wearing a light-coloured sweater. His hair was short and receding. He had a high forehead. I don't think he was old, though. Maybe middle forties. He was standing right under the streetlamp, so the light was shining down on him. I couldn't see what colour his hair was, maybe light. He didn't have deep wrinkles on his face or anything, but he looked … I don't know … sort of, tired, perhaps.'

'Would you recognise him again if you saw him?' Scott asked.

'Without a doubt,' Malcolm answered straightaway and with confidence.

Scott smiled.

'You know who he is, don't you?' Suzanne asked.

'I'm afraid I do.'

Chapter Sixty-Six

Matilda was sitting on the bed beside Tilly. They were on their third episode of *The Big Bang Theory*. Amy had brought in the first season on DVD for Tilly to watch to make the achingly slow time in hospital go just that little bit faster.

Matilda kept stealing glances at Tilly. She looked brighter since they'd had their chat. Tilly had tapped out on the iPad that she was grateful to Matilda for coming to see her, talking to her, sharing her own experience. It was helping. She was feeling stronger with each passing day. Tilly smiled. She actually smiled. Now, she looked content, silently laughing during the American comedy.

Matilda's phone vibrated in her pocket. She took it out, saw it was Scott calling and climbed off the bed, moving away, to answer it.

'Where are you?' Scott asked. He sounded agitated.

'I'm at the hospital with Tilly. I needed to—'

'I know who he is,' he interrupted.

'Sorry?'

'The killer. I know who he is. To cut a long story short, Malcolm Barker and his wife have been in and he's given us a full statement. He saw the man who attacked Tilly. He's given us a good description. I … Jesus Christ, Matilda, it's Laurence Dodds.'

'What?' She frowned. 'Are you sure?'

'The description fits.'

'But … I … his van was on his drive during the attacks. He's gay, for crying out loud.'

'I know. I don't know what's going on, but Malcolm Barker described Laurence Dodds to a tee.'

'Okay.' She ran her fingers through her hair. 'Come to the hospital and pick me up. Get Finn and Tom to go to Dodds's house and have a team on standby. Nobody is to do anything until I get there.' She suddenly remembered where she was, looked over her shoulder and saw Tilly watching her, her face grave. 'Scott, do we have a photo of Laurence Dodds.'

'No.'

'Shame. Never mind.' She ended the call. 'I need to go. Something's come up. Look, you have police outside, everything will be fine. I promise.

Tilly held up the iPad.

Please stay safe.

Matilda gave a nervous smile. 'I will.'

Matilda was waiting for Scott in the entrance to the hospital. Thick flakes of snow were falling heavily now, and traffic was light. Despite the urgency, Scott's driving was cautious, and he tapped the brakes lightly when he pulled up outside. She ran to the car, climbed in and slammed the door behind her. She was freezing cold and had forgotten her gloves.

'Tell me everything,' she said as Scott pulled away from the hospital and headed for Ballifield Road in Handsworth.

'There's nothing else to tell. Malcolm Barker just came in and said he wanted to give a statement.'

'Why the sudden change of heart?'

'I don't know,' Scott said, not looking at Matilda and making a play out of keeping his eyes firmly on the road ahead.

'This doesn't make sense,' Matilda said, chewing her fingernails as she thought. 'Laurence seems so … I don't know … meek.'

'I know. And I've seen his mother. There's no way he'd leave her without someone to take care of her while he's out killing. But then that would be obvious he's the killer.'

'Unless …' She suddenly stopped.

'What?' Scott asked.

'Unless there's two of them.'

'Two killers?' he asked, incredulously.

'It's possible.'

'Laurence and who else?'

'The vicar?' Matilda shrugged.

They pulled up on Ballifield Road, a few doors away from Laurence's house. Several cars Matilda recognised were already haphazardly parked and Tom's motorbike was next to a pool car, a covering of snow on it.

Matilda looked at Laurence's house. Whereas all the others in the street were lit up, this one was in total darkness. The van was in the driveway, but it was far too early for him to have gone to bed. It was only seven o'clock. She got out of the car and shivered in the freezing temperature. Scott followed and Finn and Tom got out of the pool car.

'YY67 MTC,' Scott said. 'Malcolm Barker said that was the number he saw.'

'How could he remember it? He must have only seen it for a few seconds.'

'His own car begins YY67, and he said he just remembered the rest.'

Matilda nodded to a uniformed officer, held up two fingers and pointed for them to go around the back of the house.

'Is that the new uniform now?' she asked Tom as she made her way to Laurence's house.

Tom was in full biker leathers. 'I was on my way home when the call came in.'

She smiled and knocked on Laurence's front door. The bang echoed around the quiet neighbourhood.

'No lights on upstairs,' Scott said, standing back and looking up.

'The curtains are closed in the living room,' Finn said. He was by the large window, leaning in, cupping his hands around his eyes.

'His mum might be asleep,' Scott said. 'She does sleep a lot, according to Laurence.'

Matilda rang the bell and knocked louder.

'Is anything wrong?'

Matilda jumped, turned around and saw an elderly woman in a dressing gown and wellington boots standing on the pavement.

'Has anything happened to Laurence and his mum?'

'No. I'm DCI Matilda Darke. South Yorkshire Police. We

need to speak to Laurence urgently about a matter he's helping us with. You don't know if he's in, do you?'

'I'd have thought so. His van's there. He never goes out without asking me to sit in with his mum. She's very ill, you know.'

'Yes. We're aware. Do you have a spare key?'

'I do actually. Would you like me to fetch it?'

'Please. Finn, could you go with her?'

Matilda watched as the elderly lady took her time walking across the snow-laden road. Finn held her by the elbow so she wouldn't slip.

'This would be funny if people's lives weren't in danger,' Matilda said.

'I could throw her over my shoulder and run her into her house,' Scott said.

Matilda laughed. 'I would love to see that.'

It was a good couple of minutes until Finn and the old woman came back out of the house. Tom ran across the road, took the key from her and came running back to Matilda.

She knocked one last time and unlocked the door. She pushed it open and was hit by the central heating straightaway. It seemed to be turned up to full blast.

'Mr Dodds. It's DCI Matilda Darke from South Yorkshire Police. We need to have a word with you.'

The inside of the house was still and in darkness. There was no movement. The whole place seemed empty.

Cautiously, Matilda stepped inside. She walked down the hallway. Her hand brushed the radiator and she immediately pulled it away. It was practically nuclear.

The door to the kitchen was open. She leaned closer but couldn't see anything in the darkness. She knocked lightly on the living room door.

'Mrs Dodds. It's the police. Are you all right in there?'

'She's very hard of hearing,' Scott said from behind.

Matilda pushed the door open. If it was possible, it was even hotter in here and the room was shrouded in darkness. She fumbled along the side of the wall for a light switch, flicking it on, and a warm but dull light from the single bulb in the centre of the ceiling began to glow.

'Oh my God,' Matilda said.

'What is it?' Scott asked, pushing by to enter.

Mrs Dodds was sitting in her usual armchair, her head back, her eyes closed, and her throat slit wide open.

Chapter Sixty-Seven

A full forensic team was searching through the Dodds home. Arc lights had been placed in every room and white-suited officers wandered around like alien invaders. In the living room, Simon Browes and Donal Youngblood were helping to process the scene with Laurence's mother.

In the kitchen, Matilda and Scott were sitting at the table. Fortunately, the heating had been turned down. Matilda was flicking through Laurence's sketch book.

'Why didn't we see this?' she asked.

'What was there to see? A little bloke who looks after his disabled mother, has a van that hardly ever moves, and rarely leaves the house.'

'We should have looked further into his life.'

'We did. We went to see the vicar. We talked to his neighbours. They all said the same thing.'

'Has anyone checked to see where the vicar is?'

'Finn's on the phone now.'

'Why kill his mother? She was housebound. She was deaf and could hardly talk. There was no reason to kill her.'

'It's like we've said all along – he hates women,' Scott said.

'If she's the source of his hate, why not kill her first? Why wait until now? Why care for her round the clock for as long as he has and then kill her? I can't get my head around any of this. What aren't we seeing?'

'Okay.' Finn entered the kitchen, wiping snow off his shoulders. 'I've just been speaking to Father Jeremy, and he hasn't seen Laurence since well before Christmas. Laurence was down to help out with the food bank donations on Christmas Eve but didn't turn up. Jeremy said he wasn't worried as he sometimes doesn't if his mum needs him and he can't arrange a sitter.'

'So, if Laurence is the killer, and he's been acting alone, he's got two identical vans, with identical registration numbers, and he's been ten steps ahead of us all along,' Scott said.

'If there is a second van, then he'll need to have kept it hidden somewhere, a garage, most likely,' Matilda said. 'If so, he'll have keys or paperwork lying around here somewhere.'

'There's a fingertip search going on in every room,' Scott said. 'But the guy's a hoarder. Every drawer and cupboard is choc-full of paperwork. It could take time.'

'We don't have time. He's killed his mother. He knows we're onto him, or he knows the end is coming. He'll be planning something big.'

'Like what?'

'I don't know,' Matilda answered, almost shouting.

Everyone fell silent.

'I'll go and see if they need a hand upstairs,' Finn said, making an excuse to leave the tense kitchen.

Scott went over to the door and closed it, leaving him and Matilda in private. 'Matilda, the blog Danny Hanson wrote, did you put him up to it?'

Matilda had moved over to the sink. She was staring at her reflection in the black mirror of the window. She looked at Scott and nodded.

'Why?'

'I needed to draw him out. I needed him to come for me. I didn't think he'd kill his own mother.' She looked at Scott again, saw the disappointment on his face. 'Don't look at me like that, Scott. I had no choice. I've had Ridley on my back every hour asking for a progress report. We had no evidence, no witnesses, nothing. I had to do something.'

'He's going to kill again, tonight, isn't he?'

'I thought he'd come for me,' she said, quietly. 'I thought he'd hate me enough after the interview and the blog, and he'd come for me.'

'So why hasn't he?'

She shook her head. 'I don't know. I've read this whole case completely wrong. I had him down as someone who hates women, especially those who are in a position of power. What if he's just a sick bastard who enjoys killing people? What if it's simply about destroying people? What if they were all meant to survive, like Tilly, and live a life remembering their attacker?'

Scott didn't answer. He couldn't.

Matilda's phone started ringing. They both jumped at the sound coming from inside her jacket pocket. She looked at the screen and saw it was Sian calling. She swiped to answer.

'I'm a bit busy right now, Sian. Can I call you back in—'

'Belinda's been kidnapped,' Sian said, her voice full of tears.

'What?'

'Belinda. She went to a friend's house. I dropped her off. I said I'd pick her back up. I was worried about her with this killer on the loose, but she didn't call and when I called her friend up, she said she'd left over an hour ago. It's a five-minute walk away.' She was speaking so quickly her words were practically falling over each other.

'Wait. Sian. How do you know she's been kidnapped? Maybe she's gone to see—'

'He's sent me a *fucking photo*!' she screamed.

'Oh my God.' Matilda put the call on speaker so Scott could hear.

'She's tied up. She in the back of a van or something. It's all dark. I can't make it out. She's gagged and she looks so scared. Matilda, you need to find her.'

Matilda visibly balked. She had to hold onto the side of the sink to stop herself from collapsing.

'Sian, it's Scott. Send the photo to Matilda's phone. And mine. We'll find her. I promise.'

'I can't lose her, Scott,' Sian was crying. 'After everything that's happened to us. I can't lose my daughter as well.'

'You won't. I promise you, Sian. I will find her for you.'

Sian tried to talk, but she was crying so much that her words were lost.

'It's Anthony. Is there anything I can do?' Sian's oldest child asked. He sounded almost as frightened as his mother.

'Stay with your mum,' Scott said, firmly. 'None of you should leave the house. Keep the phone on and if there are any other calls or photos, let me know. We'll find her, Anthony.'

Scott ended the call. He was about to hand it back to Matilda when the phone beeped an incoming text. He opened it and showed the photo to Matilda.

'Oh, God, no,' Matilda said, tears running down her face.

Belinda was in the back of a van; tape covered her mouth.

Her wrists and ankles were tied. She was crying and her left eye was bruised. She looked petrified.

'He's been following me. This is no coincidence,' Matilda said. 'I was right. He is a woman hater. I wanted him to hate me and that's what he's doing. He's going to hurt me by hurting those closest to me. He knows I'll take Belinda's death personally. He knows it will break my friendship with Sian. This has been his plan all along. He's not intending to kill women at all, he wants them to live in agony for the rest of their lives. He succeeded with Tilly and he'll succeed with me.'

'But what about Tracey Ward? He posed her, for crying out loud. There was no way she could survive that.'

'That was a message. He won't think of her as being one of his victims. She was just a message.'

'Sick bastard.'

'Precisely.'

'So, where is he?'

Matilda took a deep breath. 'I've no idea.'

'Zofia's running Laurence's number plates through CCTV and ANPR,' Tom said, coming into the kitchen and ending his call. 'Nothing yet, but she'll let me know the second something comes up.'

Finn had been searching through the kitchen dresser but hadn't found anything. He was currently going through the folder of sketches on the table.

'Thanks, Tom. Have the neighbours said anything useful?' Matilda asked.

'No. The old lady across the road who has a key to here, I sat her down and told her that Laurence's mother was dead and that we think Laurence killed her. I thought it might unlock something in her mind that Laurence isn't the perfect son he's painted himself out to be.'

'Did it?'

'No. All she said was that it's always the quiet ones and she thought he was too good to be true.'

'Isn't hindsight a wonderful thing,' Finn said. He went back to flicking through the sketchbook and stopped dead as he turned a page. 'I think you'd better come and look at this.'

They all gathered around and saw a pencil drawing of Matilda. It was incredibly detailed, and Laurence had evidently taken a great deal of time and attention over it.

'Wow,' Tom said. 'That's brilliant.'

'It looks like he really does have a fixation on you, Matilda,' Scott said.

'And we can clearly state that his lusting after Scott was a ruse all along. If he really did fancy you as much as he led us to believe, this would be a picture of you, not Matilda,' Finn said.

'He's not attracted to Matilda, though, is he?' Scott asked.

'No. But the level of detail, the time and effort he's put into this drawing, shows how much she's occupying his mind.'

'And that's why he's taken Belinda,' Matilda said. 'He's thought long and hard about what will hurt me the most. He's seen me with Sian, followed her and seen Belinda, and decided she will be his next victim. I'm going to rip his balls off with my bare hands if he's laid so much as a finger on her,' she seethed.

'Hang on a minute,' Finn said, racing through the pages of the sketchbook. 'I think I might have something here. Look at these drawings: Park Hill flats, the clock tower at the Northern, Weston Park Museum, the Cholera Monument, another one here of the amphitheatre. These are all places where his victims were found.'

'What?' Matilda asked, taking the book from him and flicking through the pages. 'My God, he's right. Jesus, I actually sat at this table and looked through this book. It didn't occur to me these were close to where all the victims were found.'

'Is there anything in there where we haven't found a victim?'

'No. I don't think so,' Finn said. He tipped out the large folder and began scrutinising every loose sheet of paper and every drawing.

'He killed twice close to Park Hill flats. Could he have gone back there?' Tom suggested.

'I doubt it,' Matilda said. 'It's too obvious.'

Matilda's phone started ringing. She looked and saw it was Sian again. She handed the phone to Scott. 'I can't talk to her until I know where Belinda is. I need some air.' She barged past him and headed out to the hallway, past a white-suited forensic officer who was taking a swab from the fleck of blood on the frame of the living room door. She reached the front door and stopped dead in her tracks. She turned back and looked at the framed painting of the Arts Tower. She ripped it off the wall and ran into the kitchen.

'I know where she is. I know where Belinda is.'

Chapter Sixty-Eight

Matilda and Scott jumped into one pool car, Finn into another, and Tom dusted off the snow on his bike. With Finn leading, they all headed for the Arts Tower on Bolsover Street.

'Remember when I said how much I liked the painting?' Matilda asked. 'Laurence said he used to work there. It's obviously a place that's special to him. He painted it and framed it, after all.'

They were driving slowly as the weather was treacherous. Matilda's Range Rover would have come in very handy right now. Unfortunately, a Peugeot without snow tyres was the best they could do.

Matilda scrolled through her phone and selected Zofia's number. It was answered in less than two rings.

'Zofia, find out who's in charge at the Arts Tower. Ask them if they know Laurence Dodds and find out why he left his employment there.'

'Will do.'

'Also, get an armed response team on standby to meet me there.'

'Give me a couple of seconds,' she said. Matilda could hear her fingers hammering the keyboard. 'We've got an ANPR camera round there. Okay, nothing there. There's a CCTV camera just around the corner. Don't ask how I can get into the footage, you don't want to know. Yes, I've got it,' she said, excitement in her voice. 'A silver Vauxhall Vivaro with the registration number Yankee Yankee six seven Michael Tango Charlie is parked to the rear of the building.'

'Zofia, you're a star.' Matilda ended the call. 'He's at the Arts Tower,' she said, turning to Scott. 'How long before we get there?'

'In this weather, who knows.'

'Jesus Christ, I hope he hasn't hurt her. She's been through so much with her father, the last thing she—'

Matilda stopped dead.

It all happened so quickly.

As if from nowhere, a car shot out of a side road and ploughed straight into the Astra Finn was driving. Scott slammed on the brakes, but the snow hampered his stopping time and they hit the back of Finn's car. They both shot forward in their seats. Scott's airbag deployed, throwing him back in his seat, but Matilda's didn't.

'Are you all right?' she asked.

'Yes. Fine,' he said, fighting with the deflating airbag.

'Shit. Finn.'

Matilda opened the door and stepped out. She ran to the car in front, pulled open the front passenger door and found Finn slumped over the steering wheel, his head resting on the air bag. He was unconscious and blood was running down the side of his face. She reached in and felt for a pulse. She found one and, luckily, it was strong.

'Call an ambulance,' she screamed.

'Already on it,' Scott called out.

'Are you all right, madam?' Matilda heard Tom talking to someone. She turned and saw the driver of the Punto still sitting behind the wheel of the car. She was talking so she wasn't injured. Matilda frowned; she looked familiar.

She went back to the car she and Scott had been driving in. There was no way she'd be able to get to the Arts Tower now.

'Tom, have you got a spare helmet?'

'Always.'

'Take me to the Arts Tower.'

'You're not serious?' Scott asked.

'Stay here with Finn. Go with him to the hospital and call his wife. Tell her what's happened.'

Tom handed her the helmet. As she put it on and fastened the strap beneath her chin, her eyes fell on the driver of the Punto with her dark hair severely cut in a shoulder-length bob. *Where do I know you from?*

She shook the thought from her head and swung her leg over Tom's all black Yamaha R1. She wrapped her arms around his waist and held on for dear life.

Chapter Sixty-Nine

Matilda Darke kept her eyes closed for most of the ride to the Arts Tower. She'd been in speeding cars before on many occasions, but never on a bike, never exposed to the elements. She could feel the wind and the snow lashing against her helmet and she leaned into Tom, squeezing him tight around his waist. Whichever direction he leaned, she copied. He felt relaxed, composed, but she was rigid with fear and when they finally came to a stop, it was a long while before she felt she could unlock her fingers and release the young DC from her hold.

Eventually, she opened her eyes, and the first thing she saw was the silver Vauxhall Vivaro belonging to Laurence Dodds. Seeing the second van confirmed what she feared. It was a simple ruse, having two identical vans with a cloned number plate, but an effective one. Her thoughts now went to Belinda. She had to save her. She had to take her home to her mother.

Carefully, she swung her leg off the bike.

'I've never been more scared in my life,' she said, slowly removing the helmet.

'First time on a bike?'

'And the last.'

'You wanted to get here quickly.'

'I know. I'd have preferred a TARDIS. Listen, Tom, I need you to stay here. Call Christian, tell him what's happened and get him to come—'

'Don't you want me to come up there with you?' he interrupted.

'No.'

'Why not? You've seen the knife he uses. You don't know what he could do with it.'

'Tom, please, just do as I say.'

They made eye contact. Matilda's were wide and staring. She was full of determination and fire.

'Okay. Sure.'

'Thanks, Tom.' She handed him back the helmet, then headed for the building.

The Arts Tower was the second tallest building in Sheffield, after St Paul's Tower on Arundel Gate. It was part of the University of Sheffield and was home to the archaeology department, though there were rumours that was to close in the near future. Matilda looked up at the seventy-eight-metre-tall building. There were twenty floors, and she had no idea where Laurence might be hiding with Belinda. She reached the glass doors and expected them to be locked. It was night, it was dark, and the university was closed for the Christmas holidays. However, she pulled the handle and it opened. Another of Laurence's games. He wanted her to find him. He wanted there to be an endgame.

Standing in the vast foyer, the only sound came from the paternoster lift, one of only a few surviving in the whole of the country, and the largest, containing thirty-eight cars. She'd only used one once and hated it. Surely, it contravened all twenty-first-century health-and-safety laws.

She had no idea where to go and took out her mobile phone. She'd missed several texts and phone calls from Sian. They must have arrived while she was clinging onto Tom for dear life on the back of his bike.

She listened to the voicemail and was surprised to hear Anthony's voice. *'Matilda, it's Anthony. We've had another photo of Belinda. I'm sending it to you. Is there any news? I don't know what to do. Mum is hysterical. Please call me as soon as you can.'*

'Shit,' Matilda said to herself. She could feel the tears building up inside her.

Over the past eighteen months, Sian had been through a great deal. Her husband of more than twenty-five years being exposed as a serial killer of sex workers, being sent to prison and placed on the never-never list by the Home Secretary; having to sell her beautiful four-bedroom home and live in a cramped terraced on Woodseats; giving up the job she loved … She was struggling to cope with it all, for the sake of her four kids. Now, one of them was missing and in the hands of a clever, violent and sadistic killer. Losing Belinda would be the end for Sian. Matilda could not allow that to happen.

She opened the text and looked at the photo. It showed Belinda outside somewhere. There was snow falling around her. She was still tied up, still had her mouth taped, a nasty-looking bruise surrounding her left eye. Her hair was being blown by a fierce wind. She was high up. It was evident she was on the roof of the Arts Tower.

Laurence knew this photo would end up being sent to

Matilda. He was talking to her. He was sending her messages to challenge him.

Matilda pressed the button for the lift, but nothing happened. The button didn't light up and there was no sound from behind the closed steel doors. She'd have to use the paternoster.

Matilda stood in front of it and watched the cars, each one just big enough to house two people, slowly pass her. She stepped onto the next one and stood firmly against the back. It took thirteen seconds to move between two floors and Matilda had to go all the way up to the roof. She watched each floor pass her by. They were all the same, plunged into darkness and silent. She wondered how long it would take Christian to get here.

Her mobile pinged an incoming text. It was from Zofia.

Ruby Marks is a kind of supervisor for the Arts Tower. Laurence Dodds was a general caretaker and handyman. He'd been working there for more than twenty years. However, he and Ruby clashed when she was promoted, and she started watching him closely. There were things going missing. Then, students started reporting personal items going missing. Then, a female student said she felt uncomfortable around Laurence. He always seemed to go into the girls' toilets with a mop and bucket while she was in there. Ruby told him that if he resigned, there would be no further repercussions. He refused and she threatened him with the police. One day he didn't turn up, and she left it at that.

Matilda read the message with interest. Another woman who stopped him doing what he obviously enjoyed doing for twenty years. His mother needing round-the-clock care stopped him living his own life and his boss lost him his job.

Ruby Marks should have taken things further. She should have contacted the police and sent them round to Laurence's house, even if it was simply to get the keys to the Arts Tower from him.

She reached the top floor and threw herself out, glad to be out of the paternoster.

Who the bloody hell thought they were a good idea?

She had no idea where to go next and wandered aimlessly, looking for a door to lead her to the roof. She turned to the left and stopped. Taped to the door was a sheet of A4 paper with 'I'M UP HERE' written on it.

'Bastard,' Matilda said to herself.

She suddenly realised she wasn't armed. She didn't have her telescopic baton on her or a canister of CS spray. If she went up there, on the roof, it would just be her and a madman with a very sharp knife.

She had no choice. Belinda was up there. She looked around her for something she could use as a weapon, but there was nothing. She took a deep breath, steeled herself for a battle and opened the door.

Chapter Seventy

There was a flight of stone stairs in front of Matilda. She felt the icy cold wind blowing down them and shivered. Snow was falling, too. A door from the building had been left open, obviously for her to access the roof. She held onto the banister and slowly walked up the stairs, hoping she wasn't making any noise and could surprise Laurence. He'd planned this so well, she doubted he'd be surprised.

When she reached the top, she squinted as the snowflakes hit her face. The wind was strong and tore through her. She turned around and that's when she saw Laurence Dodds standing with his back to the city, his left arm around Belinda's neck, a hunter's knife to her throat.

Matilda wanted to cry. It wasn't only Sian who was suffering the effects of what her husband had done, Belinda had been going through hell, too. Her father was a serial killer. There was never a good time to hear news like that, but Belinda was struggling with exams and her sexuality. She didn't need more drama in her life. However, she'd stepped up to the task of being a young adult, concentrated on her exams, achieved the grades she needed and planned for a future away from Sheffield, away from being the daughter of a multiple murderer. And now here she was, in the evil clutches of another killer. She looked so much younger. Tears were rolling down her face, the wind blowing them away. Her mouth was taped. She was pale, cold, frightened, fearing for her life. Matilda didn't have a clue how either of them was going to walk away from this.

'Good evening, Detective Chief Inspector. Or can I call you Matilda?' Laurence shouted above the wind.

'Why here, Laurence?' Matilda shouted back. The snow was hitting her face hard, pinching at her skin.

'I was at my happiest here. It was a shit job, but I was good at it, and I actually enjoyed being in charge of this beautiful building.'

'You weren't in charge of it, though, were you? You were a handyman and caretaker. You made sure the toilets weren't blocked, that there was always a fresh supply of loo rolls, and that the floors were clean. This was never your building. You just thought it was. You gave yourself an elevated sense of entitlement. You took it too far. That's why you had to leave.'

'My, my, someone's been reading *Psychology for Dummies*. What are you going to come up with next? Are you going to ask me how old I was when I stopped wetting the bed?'

'Why have you been doing all this?'

'Why? Does there have to be a reason? Isn't it much scarier when there's no motive?'

Matilda sniggered. 'You're not in a horror film, Laurence. There's always a motive. Trust me, you're not clever enough to be one of the great serial killers.'

'I fooled you. You didn't know about my second van, did you?'

'True. I didn't. But you don't need a great mind to come up with that one. I'll bet you had an end story worked out, didn't you? Let me see, you were going to set up Jeremy Keats as the killer.' She saw Laurence's face drop slightly. She knew she was right. 'You didn't give a toss about helping out with the food bank and the elderly having their shopping delivered, you just wanted to draw Jeremy into your confidence. You came across as this meek, mild-mannered, confused man who spent his days caring for his elderly mother. You said you were religious but wrestling with your sexuality as you didn't think the church would accept you as a gay man. You even invented having a casual partner. You wanted to appear the complete opposite of how the killer would be viewed, in order to escape detection. Did Jeremy tell you things about his life, too, during your little chats? Did he talk about his family and past? Did you store it all up here?' she asked, tapping the side of her head. 'So you could use it against him when the police came calling?'

Laurence gave a lop-sided smile. 'Jeremy thought he could save me. He wanted me to be one of his flock. I'll give him his due, he does good things for the community, but he can't see past the surface, what's going on with people beneath. I could have told him anything and he'd believe it.'

Matilda made eye contact with Belinda. She raised her left eyebrow and indicated her left elbow, moving it slightly, communicating what Belinda should do.

'So, you kill women because you hate them.' Matilda exaggerated a yawn. 'Hardly original. Oh, but, no, I'm wrong. Your plan wasn't to kill them at all, was it? You thought you were being a master criminal by keeping them alive. You wanted your victims to live with the damage you inflicted for the rest of their lives, so they'd always remember you.

Unfortunately, like everything else in your life, you fucked it up, and the first three died. So, you simply threw them away.'

Laurence nodded. 'That was the original plan. But do you know something, Matilda, when you've got a woman at your mercy –' he tightened the hold on Belinda's neck and she gave a muffled cry '– when she's crying, pleading, begging you to stop, it gives you such a rush, that you genuinely can't stop. I wanted to keep them alive, but once I started hacking away at their throats with the knife, it was the best feeling in the world and I couldn't stop. I was a god.'

'*NOW!*' Matilda screamed.

Belinda swiftly used her elbow to hit Laurence right in the crotch. He yelled and doubled over in pain, releasing his grip on her. She flung back her head, hitting Laurence in the mouth, incapacitating him just enough for her to stumble away from him and run into Matilda's arms. Matilda quickly pulled the tape from her mouth and untied the rope behind her back.

'Are you all right?' she asked, holding her face, looking at her bruised eye.

'Yes.'

'Are you sure?'

'Yes.'

'Did you touch you?'

'No.'

'Okay. Go down these stairs and use the paternoster to go to the ground floor. Go out the main doors and you'll see a man on a motorbike in full leathers. He's a detective. Tell him who you are and what's happened. Stay with him.'

'What are you going to do?'

'Just go.' She practically pushed Belinda to the stairs and turned back to Laurence.

Laurence Dodds was on the floor, holding his crotch, tears running down his face, blood leaking from his lip.

'So you think you're a god, do you? You don't look like one from where I'm standing. You look more like a pathetic piece of shit. Do you want me to tell you what the problem with men is? You think you're superior to women. You think you're better than us. You're not. I'm not saying women are better. I'm saying that we're all the same. We're all equal. We're all trying to do the best we can in this fucker of a world, but there are some men, like you, who really do believe you're superior.'

She leaned down, grabbed him by the collar of his jacket and pulled him up. She slammed him against the edge of the roof, the concrete slabs hitting him in the lower back. He cried out in pain.

'Let me guess, your mother has dominated you for your entire life. You've never been married and I'm guessing your longest relationship has been less than a week. Your bosses have always been female, and you've hated that. Is that why you started all this, because Ruby Marks was going to call the police and tell them what a thieving pervert you are?'

Laurence started to laugh. It obviously caused him some pain, but he still laughed.

'You've got it wrong. You've got it so wrong.'

'Then tell me,' she said through gritted teeth, maintaining her hold on his collar.

'Let go of me and I will.'

Matilda looked around her. The knife was close by, so she kicked it further away. She pushed Laurence down onto the floor and stood back but remained close enough to pounce on him if he tried anything.

Laurence sat himself up. He wiped his bloody lip on his sleeve and looked at the smear it left behind.

'I never knew who my dad was,' he began. 'Well, I had a couple of photos of him, and Mum told me stories, but that was all. She never said what happened to him. It was years before I realised the photos she'd been showing me were what she got from magazines and just put in an album. The pictures were of some American bit-part actor. When she moved into my house after her first stroke, I was going through all of her things, and I found a photo of a man. It was just this one photo. I showed it to her, asked who he was, and she told me. I think the stroke might have damaged some part of her brain that made her forget who she was talking to, I don't know, but she didn't try to hide any of it. The man in the picture raped her. She didn't report it. She didn't tell anyone. She should have aborted me, but she didn't. She was weak.'

'You can hardly call her weak because she was raped. It wasn't your mother's fault.'

'Of course it was.'

'How can you say that? It was your father's fault. Nobody has the right to demand sex from a woman.'

'She was weak,' he spat. 'She should have taken control of her life and aborted me. She didn't. She gave birth to me and spent the whole of my life telling me how useless men are, how hateful they are, how they're a scourge of society.'

'And you're using that as an excuse for rape and murder?'

'I'm my father's son.' He smiled at her.

'Another excuse. You're just pathetic. There was a time I actually thought I was up against a highly intelligent, dangerous criminal. You're not. Not at all.'

'I got inside your head, Matilda. You're going to be seeing that homeless bitch on those steps, holding her head in her hands, for the rest of your life.'

'Of course I will. Because I have empathy. But I won't

remember you. I won't be scared of you. I'll think of her and the life she had. You are nothing.'

'I'm a serial killer. There'll be books about me.'

'You'll be in prison for the rest of your life, and it will be hell for a wanky mummy's boy like you. They'll eat you alive.'

'Do you honestly think I'll see inside a prison cell? I haven't been doing these killings, your honour, I was told to do them. God was speaking to me.' He smiled at Matilda.

Matilda paled. A man who could pose a woman after decapitating her was obviously someone with serial mental health issues. He'd use that as his defence. He'd never set foot in a courtroom, let alone a prison. He'll pretend he's mad. He'll convince all the doctors, the psychologists, the solicitors, the judge, that he's completely insane. Those four dead women, and Tilly Hall, would never get the justice they deserved.

'I decapitated a woman, for fuck's sake. I posed her. I even killed my own mother. Is that really the mindset of a sane man?' He gave Matilda a cruel smile.

Slowly, Matilda walked towards him. She bent down, gripped the collar of his jacket and pulled him up his feet.

'Tell me that again,' she said softly.

Laurence's smile dropped.

Outside the main entrance to the Arts Tower, DI Christian Brady had arrived along with an armed response team who were getting ready to enter the building. Belinda had run out, terrified, into the arms of DC Tom Simpson. Brady had grabbed a blanket from the boot of his car, wrapped it around her shoulders and sat her down in the front passenger seat.

'Are you all right?' he asked her.

'I'm fine.'

'Tom, call for an ambulance.'

'I'm fine, honestly. He didn't touch me.'

'We need to get you checked over. It's routine. Now, what's going on in there?'

'Matilda,' she said, swallowed hard. 'She was telling me what to do with her eyes, signalling to her elbow, telling me to hit him in the balls. She was amazing.'

Christian smiled. 'Where is she now? Is she following you down?'

'I don't know.'

A piercing scream filled the air, and everyone turned to look at the top of the Arts Tower. Something was falling.

Before anyone had time to react, it landed. A body hit the concrete walkway with a heavy thud. Bones shattered, limbs detached and organs were obliterated.

———————

On the roof, Matilda looked down over the edge and saw the broken body of Laurence Dodds through the falling flakes of snow. She stepped back. Her face was impassive. She was soaked and freezing cold, but she didn't make for the stairs. She remained where she was, standing on the top of the Arts Tower, more than two hundred and fifty feet in the air. Her mind was full, dark thoughts racing around her head.

It was a good five minutes before she saw movement out of the corner of her eye. Christian stepped out onto the roof.

'Matilda.'

She turned to look at him and gave a weak smile.

'Are you all right?'

'I'm fine,' she said, barely audibly, visibly shaking. 'The knife's on the ground over there.' She pointed.

He shook off his coat and wrapped it around Matilda. 'Come inside. You're freezing.'

Matilda was crying. 'I'm so sorry.'

'What for?'

'For the way I've been treating you over the last few months, after everything that happened at Magnolia House.'

'Don't worry about it.'

'I do worry, though.'

'It's forgotten as far as I'm concerned.'

'I see what Jamie Carr meant now.'

Christian frowned. 'What are you talking about?'

'What he said in Magnolia House about the best kind of justice is one delivered by your own hand. I didn't believe him before. I do now.'

Christian didn't say anything. They remained in the cold for a few minutes, the wind and the snow whipping around them.

'Matilda, come on, let's go inside where it's warm.'

'Did you hear what I said?'

'Matilda, in this wind, I can't hear a bloody thing. Now, come on, before we both freeze to death.'

Chapter Seventy-One

Thursday 31st December 2020

Matilda knocked on the door of Tilly Hall's private room and walked in. Amy was back in her usual position by the bed. They both turned to look at her.

'Am I all right to come in?' Matilda asked.

'Of course you are,' Amy said. She stood up and held out a hand for Matilda to shake. 'We heard all about what happened on the roof of the Arts Tower. You're a very brave woman, Matilda Darke.'

Matilda shook her hand. 'I don't know about that. I was scared out of my wits. I've never been a huge fan of heights. How are you?' she asked Tilly.

Tilly smiled and held up eight fingers.

'Wow. That's a massive improvement. How did the second operation go?' She asked, sitting down at the end of the bed.

'Really well,' Amy said. 'The doctors are very impressed by how quickly she's healing. It probably has a lot to do with how young she is. They've done everything they can to repair the damage to her throat. As soon as this has healed, it'll be skin grafts.'

The difference between mother and daughter in just a few days was immense. The atmosphere in the room seemed much lighter and the smile on Tilly's face warmed Matilda's heart.

Matilda sat on the edge of Tilly's bed. 'Then after that it won't be long before you're back home in your own bed.'

'Matilda,' Amy began. 'We've both seen the news and read about it in the papers, about Laurence Dodds. Did he give you any clue to why he did what he was doing?'

Matilda took a deep breath. 'He did. What you have to remember is that the motive of a serial killer often sounds banal and pathetic to us. To the killer, it's the most important thing in the world. We assumed he had a deep-seated hatred of women, and I really think he did, but a lot of men have domineering mothers, or female bosses who sack them, or problems with forming relationships, and they don't all turn into murderers. In fact, very few do. Laurence Dodds was a severely disturbed individual.'

'So, Tilly was just in the wrong place at the wrong time?'

'You see, I don't believe in things like that. We live in a democratic country. Unless you're trespassing on private land, which Tilly wasn't, you're free to do whatever you like, wherever you like, and nobody has the right to stop you. She wasn't in the wrong place at the wrong time.' She turned to Tilly. 'And don't ever think twice about doing whatever it is you want to do. Just go and do it.' She smiled and Tilly smiled back.

'Tilly said she wants self-defence classes when she's well enough.'

'I don't blame her. Personally, I think self-defence classes should be taught in schools. Here's a tip from me, Tilly. If ever you find yourself in a situation you can't get out of with a man, aim for the balls, or the nose. That will certainly incapacitate him for long enough for you to get away.'

Tilly touched her mother's arm and pointed towards the drawer in her bedside locker. Amy opened it and took out an envelope, handing it to Matilda.

'Tilly's written a letter to you. She wouldn't let me read it. She says it's private between the two of you.'

Matilda took the envelope. 'Thank you. Well, I'd better be heading home.'

'Can I give you a lift?' Amy asked.

'I've got a friend waiting for me outside. I just wanted to call in and see how Tilly's doing. How you're both doing.'

'You can come and see us any time you want.'

'I will.'

Amy stood up and hugged Matilda tight. 'Thank you so much. For everything,' she whispered into her ear. 'Happy New Year,' she said when she pulled out of the embrace.

Matilda swallowed her tears. 'Happy New Year.' She looked over Amy's shoulder to Tilly. 'It's going to be a big year for you, Tilly. Embrace it. Do whatever you want with it, but remember, it's your life, and your main priority is whatever makes you happy.'

A tear rolled down Tilly's cheek.

Matilda went into the nearest toilets, into the furthest cubicle, closed the door behind her and sat down. She opened the envelope and took out the letter. Despite Tilly's right arm being out of plaster, the handwriting was still shaky.

Dear Matilda,

Thank you so much for coming to see me over the past few weeks. I've really enjoyed your company. You've talked more sense about recovering and what it means to be a survivor than my mum and all the doctors and nurses put together.

I've watched the news and read online a lot about what happened with Laurence on the roof of the Arts Tower. I almost cried when I saw his photo. It was definitely him who tried to kill me. Part of me is pleased he's dead. I don't think I could have gone through having to give evidence at a trial and looking at him again. Obviously, I don't know what happened on that rooftop, nobody does apart from you and Laurence and he's dead. However, I'm glad it ended the way it did. Thank you.

I've been texting Ryan quite a bit lately. He says he still wants to go out with me, but I'm stalling him coming to see me in hospital until the redness has gone from the latest operation. I'm not building my hopes up. I'll know by his face when he sees me for the first time if he can live with me looking like this, and not being able to talk. I really like Ryan. A lot. He's lovely and very good looking, but if he can't cope with me how I now am, well, that's life, isn't it? It's his problem, not mine. I can do perfectly well without a man in my life. Mum hasn't had one for years and she's doing all right.

I've decided I'm going to take a leaf out of your book. I've read a lot of stories online about you and everything you've been through over the years. You're a survivor. You've suffered so much loss but you're able to function, to get up in the morning and go to work. I don't know what you're like in bed at night when you're on your own, but from the outside, to the untrained eye, you seem to be doing just fine.

I really hope the police reinstate your unit and you go back to work. The police force needs more women like you. The world needs more women like you. Like us.

We're survivors. We're alive. And we can do anything.

Lots of love, Tilly, xxx

Matilda realised she was crying. She looked down at the letter and carefully folded it in half, placing it in her inside pocket.

'I'm a survivor,' she said to herself. Her voice was shaking and there was no strength to it at all. She took a deep breath. 'I'm a survivor,' she said, much louder.

From the next cubicle, a woman began singing *Survivor* by Destiny's Child and Matilda burst into laughter.

Epilogue

Scott pulled up outside Matilda's house and turned off the engine. It had been another bitterly cold day, but the sky was bright and a cool sun shone down on Sheffield. Now, it was pitch-dark, and the temperature was well below freezing. It had been a long, harsh winter already and it was far from over.

'A good start to the new year,' Scott said.

'Sorry?' Matilda asked.

'The Chief Constable reinstating the unit, Finn getting the all-clear to return, and Sian back at work.'

'Yes.'

'She told me this afternoon that if she'd remained a detective, the killer might not have seen you two in the park and gone after Belinda. Personally, I think she's using that as an excuse to come back. She's really missed it. Only two days back and it's like she's never been away. Have you seen the snack drawer? I bet Cadbury's share price is going to go through the roof,' he said with a laugh.

Matilda didn't say anything.

'Are you listening to me?'

'Sorry? I'm sorry, Scott. I'm a bit distracted. It's been a long day. And the, er … the meeting with Ridley took longer than I expected.'

'Is everything okay?'

Matilda didn't answer and a dark silence filled the car.

'No lights on,' Scott said, simply for something to say. 'Isn't Adele home today?'

'I got a message from her earlier. Human remains have been found. She and Simon are going to be out there for a while yet.'

'Whereabouts?'

'I … I'm not sure. She did say.'

'Is everything all right?' he asked again.

'Yes. Fine. Why?'

'You seem distracted. In fact, you've been quiet since your meeting with the Chief Constable. Everything went okay, didn't it?'

Matilda nodded.

'The enquiry into Laurence Dodds's death is all over with now, isn't it?'

'Yes,' she said, quietly. 'Actually, Scott, are you in a rush to get anywhere? Could I have a word?'

'Erm … sure,' he said, slightly worried.

'This needs to be between you and me. You can't tell anyone. Not Adele. Not Donal.'

'Okay, now I'm scared.'

'Come inside, I'll pour us both a drink.'

'Do I need a drink?' he asked, taking his seatbelt off.

'I do.'

Matilda opened the front passenger door and was hit by a blast of cold air. She shivered, and not just from the cold.

She unlocked her front door and stepped inside. The heating had come on as timed and it was homely and warm. She flicked on the light as Scott was closing the front door behind him. The house remained in darkness.

'Huh,' she said. She flicked the light switch on and off a few times. 'Bloody hell, the power's gone out. There's no light on the router.'

'I've got a torch in the glove box. Shall I go and fetch it?'

'Please. The fuse box is in the utility room, I'll be in there.'

Matilda headed for the kitchen. She patted the fridge as she passed. 'Don't go melting on me, ice cream. Mummy loves you.'

She fumbled along in the dark, banging into the table. She pulled her phone out of her pocket and turned on its torch. 'If you can't find a torch, Scott, I'll use my phone,' she called out.

She heard a cry come from the hallway, followed by a thud.

'Scott? Is everything all right?'

There was no reply. She turned and slowly walked out into the hallway. Scott was on the floor, bleeding heavily from what appeared to be his stomach. He had his hand over a large slash wound, and blood was seeping out between his fingers.

'*Jesus Christ! Scott!*' Matilda screamed.

'Stay right where you are.'

Matilda couldn't see who had entered the house. The shadowy figure stepped forward. As they came closer, Matilda could make out it was a woman. She was tall and slim, dressed in layers against the cold, her shoulder-length hair cut into a severe bob.

'You just won't die, will you, Matilda? Who do you think you are, Sidney fucking Prescott?'

'I recognise you.'

'I tried twice to run you off the road but failed both times. My own fault. I should have listened, but thought I knew best. I won't make that mistake again.'

'Who are you?'

From her deep coat pockets, the woman pulled out a Taser, stepped towards Matilda and fired. The barbs made contact with Matilda's chest and hit her with fifty thousand volts. She fell to the ground, screaming in agony.

The woman leaned down next to her. She shook off her backpack and took out a roll of duct tape, tore off a strip and placed it across Matilda's mouth. From the bag, she also took out a syringe, removed the protective cap and flicked the chamber a couple of times to remove any air bubbles.

'Oh, before I forget, Steve Harrison says hello.'

Matilda was injected and slipped into unconsciousness.

Matilda Darke will return...

Acknowledgments

There are many people who work hard on the creation of a novel, and I'd like to use this space to say a massive thank you to everyone who helped me write *Silent Victim*, the tenth in the DCI Matilda Darke series.

Firstly, my editor, Bethan Morgan, and everyone at One More Chapter and HarperCollins, for giving me the freedom to write the stories I want to write, and my agent, Jamie Cowen, at The Ampersand Agency, for all his behind-the-scenes work.

Secondly, a novel couldn't be written without the experts who supply me with the technical information I need to make my books as authentic as possible. There are times when I take liberties with certain areas, but they're not mistakes, they're inventions for the purposes of fictional storytelling.

Philip Lumb for his expert pathology knowledge and for sharing it all with me.

Simon Browes for his detailed information in all things medical.

'Mr Tidd' for sharing his experience of the police force and procedural matters.

Andrew Barrett for answering my many forensic questions.

Donna Ricketts (my sister) for talking me through the aftermath of suffering a traumatic experience at a young age.

Finally, I'd like to thank the people who support me during everyday life. My Mum (for supplying cakes and championing my books). Chris Schofield (who 'helped' so much in writing this book that I almost missed my deadline). Kevin Embleton (who has never read my books and doesn't have a clue what's going on in the series, but I can't really leave out). Jonas Alexander (who will one day direct an adaptation of one of my novels). And last, but not least, Maxwell Dog (who genuinely did help in the writing of this book).

YOUR NUMBER ONE STOP

ONE MORE CHAPTER

FOR PAGETURNING BOOKS

One More Chapter is an
award-winning global
division of HarperCollins.

Sign up to our newsletter to get our
latest eBook deals and stay up to date
with our weekly Book Club!
<u>Subscribe here.</u>

Meet the team at
<u>www.onemorechapter.com</u>

Follow us!
 <u>@OneMoreChapter_</u>
 <u>@OneMoreChapter</u>
 <u>@onemorechapterhc</u>

Do you write unputdownable fiction?
We love to hear from new voices.
Find out how to submit your novel at
<u>www.onemorechapter.com/submissions</u>